C

MASK OF THE ANDES

As a novelist who combines action and excitement with vividness and authenticity of background and character Jon Cleary has few rivals.

In a remote village of the Andes, McKenna, an American priest, is trying to win the confidence of his bitterly poor, Indian parishioners who for centuries have known nothing but cruelty and exploitation. His enlightened liberalism makes him as suspect to his flock as to his superiors. And his friendship with the Englishman Taber, a free-speaking, free-thinking FAO agronomist who has come to teach the peasants how to improve their pathetic agriculture, aggravates a situation already tense enough. For the long fuse that leads to the revolutionary powder keg of Castro and Guevara is already alight; and the descendants of the Conquistadores who own everything and control both Church and State are shifting uncomfortably in the freezing winds that are blowing from the snow-capped sierras. Such people will not easily be dislodged; and the pent-up hatreds of 400 years cannot be denied an outlet for ever. The explosion when it comes is not unworthy of its magnificent and terrible setting.

Jon Cleary's narrative skill, his understanding of the situations he creates, his power of evoking wild and romantic scenery, above all his grasp of action make this book a real *tour de force* in a field that he has made particularly his own.

MASK OF THE ANDES

Jon Cleary

COLLINS

St James's Place, London 1971

William Collins Sons & Co Ltd
London · Glasgow · Sydney · Auckland
Toronto · Johannesburg

To be published in America under the title
THE LIBERATORS

First published 1971
© Sundowner Productions Pty.
ISBN 0 00 221730 9
Set in Monotype Imprint
Made and Printed in Great Britain by
William Collins Sons & Co Ltd Glasgow

Chapter 1

1

McKenna straightened up from laying out the catch of fish and looked out across the lake. On the far side of the bright blue pan of water the mountains rose like crumpled iron, cold to the eye and the soul: gods as well as men had died in these ranges. Through a gap he could see the glacier, a white cataract frozen forever, coming down from the highest snow-capped peaks that stood against the stark sky. At this height in the Andes McKenna could never think of the sky as being gentle. That was for less harsh climes, for other times, the sky of boyhood memory.

"Padre – " Agostino Mamani was fifteen, but no longer a boy. Here on the Bolivian altiplano, the Indian peasant, the campesino, was fortunate if he lived beyond forty: one could not waste too many years in childhood. "I have to go down to San Sebastian to-day."

"Why do you have to go, Agostino?" San Sebastian was ten miles by road and 2,000 feet in altitude below the lake; it was not just a city but another world to the campesinos of Altea, the village half a mile down from the lake. "When did you last go to the city?"

Agostino shrugged: time was a dimension he did not understand. "A long time, padre. I was – " He held out his hand opposite his hip; short and squat, no more than an American child's height even now, he said, "I was just a small boy."

"Why do you have to go to-day?"

"My mother has to see the doctor at the hospital."

"Has she been ill?" McKenna remembered that he had not seen Agostino's mother for almost a month. She was one of the more cheerful, intelligent and approachable of the village women, a plump bundle made even plumper by her voluminous skirts, a woman whose one sin, until recently, had been her

5

vanity about her hats. Vance Packard's status-seeking society had its pockets of competition even up here on the altiplano; poverty was no bar to conceit. Any campesino woman who had a different hat for each day of the week, as Maria Mamani had, had a top rating in Altea. The Joneses, McKenna had wryly noted, were a widespread family: everyone everywhere was trying to keep up with them. "Maybe I could drive you and your mother down in the Jeep? It would be no trouble."

Agostino scratched a bare toe in the rocky earth. His flat, dark face lost all expression, became the mask that McKenna knew so well and hated so much. Sometimes, in his wilder moments of depressed fantasy, he imagined he was surrounded only by masks, that behind the dark faces of the Indians there were no skulls, no brains, nothing. "My mother and I will catch the bus, padre."

McKenna recognised he was being shut out, but he persisted. Back home in California, though never shy, he had always been careful of other people's reticences; Americans, though the most confessional of people, could be violently jealous about those things they did not want to expose. But a missionary could not afford such courtesies. He had come to know, a little too late perhaps, that a missionary, if he was to be a successful one, had to be something of a busybody. Besides, he always had the feeling he was doing too little for the campesinos, that if he could not help them more than they had so far allowed him to, he might as well pack up and go home. So he forced his help on them, grabbing at straws: even the offer of a lift in the Jeep would be a plus mark in the day's good works.

"That's crazy, Agostino. The bus is always full and it's so – so dangerous." He knew that was no argument at all; the campesinos boarded the ancient rickety buses with a stoic disregard of the fact that they might never complete their journey. He tried another tack: "If your mother is ill, she would be more comfortable in the Jeep."

"No, padre." His face still closed, Agostino stared out across the lake.

McKenna was about to give up, but tried once more. He had had a sudden thought and he could hear the disappointment in his voice as he asked, "Is she going to have a baby, Agostino? Is that why she is going to the doctor?"

"I don't know, padre." Agostino was not embarrassed by the question; in the two-room adobe hut that was home the facts of life had never been a secret to him. "How should I know that?"

McKenna gazed at the young Indian, but the mask was shut against him: Agostino was going to tell him nothing. He turned and looked out at the lake again, wondering, as he had so many times since coming here nine months ago, if and when he would ever be fully accepted by the Indians. Dear God, he prayed, why did you make the bastards so sullen? For Christ's sake, as the saying goes, inject them with a little of the grace of co-operation.

He continued to stare out across the lake, trapped, as he always was, by his inability to walk away from an unresolved situation. Maybe, he thought, only the successful can make exits. His father had been a successful man and had made successful exits, from Bolivia, from his family, from life. He had got out of Bolivia when the price for silver was high and foreigners had still been tolerated. He had walked out on his wife and children while he was still virile enough to attract other women. And he had exited from life with a panache that his son could never hope to equal: he had plunged into San Diego harbour in his private plane on a day when the stock market had hit an all-time peak. Only failures, McKenna thought, stumble around looking for ways out.

So he stared at the landscape, seeking distraction in it while he hoped Agostino would move off up to the mission. He heard the dull boom as the fishermen out on the lake dynamited for fish; then he saw the cauldron of water bubble up between the three boats. He never dynamited for fish himself and he wished the local Indians had never discovered the method; there were two men in the village who had stumps for arms and he was always expecting a major tragedy, two, three or half a dozen deaths. The water settled and the boats moved in to collect the stunned and dead fish as they floated to the surface.

A flight of coots planed down towards the water, a black arrowhead that was suddenly studded with bright coral as the

birds turned and the still-rising sun caught their vivid feet.
An Andean gull, an intruder in the totora rushes where the
coots built their nests, rose up and winged away in the gust of
wind that abruptly slapped at the lake's surface. McKenna saw
the three small fishing boats, all of them made from totoras,
rock violently.

He turned to Agostino, who had not moved. "You better tell
your father and others to come in," he said, his voice sharper
than he had intended. Damn the kid, why did he have to make
things so difficult?

Agostino looked out at the three men, each of them alone in
his frail craft. "A son does not tell his father what to do, padre."

McKenna sighed, gave up: his Irish father had had exactly
the same philosophy. "Okay, Agostino, you win."

For a moment the boy's mask broke; he looked puzzled.
McKenna, trying to struggle out of the web of talk, mutely
waved to him to pick up the fish and take it up to the mission.
The Quechua language, which McKenna had taken such pains
to re-learn, had its own wry notes, but he still found conversation with the Indians had its limitations. At times he felt it was
like walking on loose snowshoes across a field of chilled custard.
Or like talking to his own mother.

He shook his head, half-angrily, as he thought of her. She
would have gone to bed last night with her usual prayers for
himself and his sister Carmel: the prayers for him thanking God
that he was a priest, those for Carmel asking Him to drive the
devil out of her. Nell McKenna broadcast her prayers as if
they were gossip; the Lord, if He didn't hear them direct, must
always pick them up somewhere along the grapevine. Nell
would be rising in a few hours, her lips pursed with piety even
before she had put in her expensive dentures, the first thing she
did every morning. It was her belief that no *lady* was ever seen
without her teeth, not even by her husband or her children;
with the slackening of standards hats and gloves were no longer
de rigueur for ladies, but teeth were another matter. She would
dress as carefully as for a Papal audience and go to the church
in Beverly Hills where she took daily communion. Later in the
day she might drive downtown to Los Angeles and have coffee
with the cardinal, the two of them sitting there discussing a

Church from which McKenna, the adored son, the one the Lord had blessed her with, felt he was fast slipping away.

Agostino had already gone up to the mission with as many fish as he could carry. They had gone out just before dawn, when the lake had still been silver under the last light of the moon, and the catch this morning had been bigger than usual. The lake abounded in fish and the villagers of Altea saw that no strangers came to fish it dry; even the citizens of San Sebastian had been warned off. During the revolution of 1952 the campesinos had all been given rifles and they had never returned them; some of the old revolutionaries from San Sebastian, grown fat and bourgeois now, did not appreciate the irony of looking down the barrels of guns they had handed out in the cause of freedom. But that was what they had met when they had come up here to try some fishing, and finally the message had been recognised: the lake fishing was only for the villagers of Altea. It had been McKenna's first sign of acceptance, limited though it was, when he had been allowed to join Agostino's father, Jesu Mamani, in one of the totora boats and throw out a line. When he had had a boat of his own shipped up from Antofagasta, a fibreglass skiff to which he had fitted a small outboard motor, one or two rifles had been brought out again; but Jesu Mamani, after some deliberation, had ordered them put away. McKenna was allowed to fish so long as he kept the catch only for himself. Fish and potatoes were the villagers' only cash crops and they wanted no competition from outsiders.

As McKenna straightened up with the last of the fish catch, four large salmon, he felt another gust of wind, much stronger than the first. At the same time there was another dull boom, as a second stick of dynamite was exploded. Instinctively he looked out towards the lake, squinting against the wind's force. He saw Jesu Mamani, standing up in his boat, sway, then bend over to clutch at the boat's side. The tiny craft rocked, then tilted as the water seemed to rise under it. Mamani went over the side without a cry, almost as if his plunge were intentional; the boat took in water, tilted further, then turned over and sank. The two fishermen in the other two boats swung round and McKenna waited for them to row towards the

9

drowning Mamani; but each of them sat stockstill, staring across the choppy water at the floundering man, but making no attempt to save him. In another minute or so McKenna knew Jesu Mamani would be beyond saving.

He dropped the fish, leapt at the skiff's rope and wrenched it from the mooring post. He caught a glimpse of Agostino, now half-way back down the slope from the mission, and he yelled at him to run. But the boy had stopped, stood absolutely motionless, staring with the same frozen look as that of the two fishermen at his drowning father. As McKenna scrambled into the skiff he yelled again at Agostino, but already he knew there would be no help from that quarter. Or from anywhere.

The motor barked into life at once. On full throttle McKenna bounced the skiff over the uneven water; he had no more than fifty yards to travel but it seemed ten times that distance. Mamani had disappeared beneath the surface, but his head and flailing arms suddenly broke into view again as McKenna skidded the skiff to a halt among the dead fish that had floated up from the sunken boat. McKenna cut the motor, jumped to the front of the skiff and reached out to the hand that clutched desperately at his. As he felt the frenzied fingers tear at his hand, McKenna also felt the cold that was already killing the man: the hand that clutched his was like a jagged piece of ice. Mamani's eyes were wild and white in a face that was now almost black; his mouth was wide open, but there was no air left in him for any sound. Frantically McKenna pulled the man towards him; the skiff tilted and for one awful moment he thought he was going to join the Indian in the freezing water. He flung himself backwards, still hauling on Mamani's arm; he could feel his chest heave and tighten as both the thin air and fear caught at him. Oh God, help me! His eyes seemed to be bursting from their sockets as he struggled to pull Mamani from the water; then through his fractured stare he saw the Indian's other hand take hold of the side of the skiff. McKenna lay back praying for strength that he knew wouldn't be his own, that he would have to borrow from faith. He reached behind him, wrapped his arm round the cross-seat, gave one last agonising tug that seemed to burst his chest, and fell back into the bottom of the skiff as the cold sodden bundle of Mamani tumbled in on him.

McKenna lay gasping, every breath like a gulped mouthful of powdered glass. He could feel something warm on his upper lip and knew his nose was bleeding, something that hadn't happened to him for months, not since he had become accustomed to the 13,000 feet altitude here on the altiplano. His head was splitting apart and his eyes were almost blind. But, though only half-conscious, he still knew whose was the desperate plight. Somehow or other he managed to roll out from under the unconscious Mamani. He struggled up on to his knees, feeling the iron vice that wrapped his chest, and crawled to the back of the skiff. Still unable to see properly, he fumbled for the starter of the motor. He made three grabs at it before he found it; beyond praying, cursing now, he jerked it savagely, half-expecting the motor just to cough and die on him. The motor did cough, then it sent the skiff shooting towards the shore. It went past the two Indians in their totora boats, its wash rocking them dangerously. They stared at McKenna, but he did not look at them. He drove the skiff straight on into the shore, cutting the motor a fraction too late so that they hit the rocky beach with a thump hard enough to send him sprawling forward on to the still inert Mamani.

He picked himself up, dimly aware that he had scraped his knees and knuckles. He was still having difficulty getting his breath and his head felt as if it had been cleft by an axe, but he had got back some of his strength and he could once more see clearly. He stumbled over the side of the skiff, feeling the icy water bite at his ankles as he stepped into it, and hitched the rope round the mooring post. As he turned back, wondering if he would have the strength to lift Mamani out of the boat, a voice said in English, "I'll give you a hand."

He looked up at the stranger who had appeared out of nowhere. He had an impression of a tall thin man in a checked tweed cap and a bright red quilted jacket, but there was no time to take further stock of the newcomer. McKenna clambered back into the skiff, grabbed at Mamani's wet clothes that felt as if they were already turning to ice under the now constant wind, and heaved the Indian into a sitting position. As he pushed Mamani towards the outstretched arms of the stranger he said, "I'm glad you're here."

"I'll bet you are. Where do we take him? If he's worth taking anywhere – "

"What d'you mean by that?" McKenna straightened up.

"Don't waste time." The stranger spoke as if he were used to authority, to not having people argue with him. "I mean if he's still alive. The poor bugger should be dead."

They carried Mamani up the slope to the mission. McKenna was a stocky man of medium height and the stranger, bony rather than thin, as McKenna had first thought, was three or four inches over six feet; they made a poor team as they struggled up the slope with the unconscious Indian between them. They stopped once for McKenna to wipe his nose, but the bleeding had already begun to dry up. As they came to the still motionless Agostino, McKenna gasped at him to run up and put buckets of water on the fire. The boy stared at the limp heap that was his father, and McKenna, wheezing for words to curse at him, thought he wasn't going to move. Then abruptly Agostino spun round and went running up the slope.

By the time McKenna and the stranger, with their burden, had reached the mission, a dozen or more Indians had materialised out of the bare rocky landscape. They stood in a silent expressionless group at the gate as McKenna and the stranger carried Mamani in through the rough rock wall of the compound and into the larger of the two adobe huts that made up the mission. Passing them, McKenna thought, was like walking past a jury.

Mamani, his face a dark blue death mask with a dribble of water running from a corner of the almost black lips, was laid on the single bed in the small inner room of the hut. McKenna was about to strip the Indian of his clothing, but the stranger gently pushed him aside. "Let me do it. You've done enough."

McKenna moved back, all at once glad to have someone else take over. It was not just that he wanted to be relieved of any further physical effort, though God knew he welcomed that: he was on the point of collapse and he knew he was going to be sick if his headache did not ease soon. But more than anything else he suddenly wanted to be relieved of responsibility; or at least have someone share it with him. None of the Indians was going to do that. He sank down on to a chair and looked at the faces, still as stone, that filled the doorway. The Indians, including the two fishermen from the lake, had crowded into the outer room and stood staring in at the stranger as he quickly peeled off Mamani's clothing, covered the seemingly dead man with a blanket, then bent down and began to give the kiss-of-life. A small child, only its eyes showing among the undergrowth of legs in the doorway, giggled, but was abruptly cuffed into silence. The tall man had taken off his cap, showing a mop of thick dark red hair. He was working his mouth against Mamani's, occasionally pulling his head back to look at the Indian. After a few minutes he glanced across at McKenna.

"He's still with us. Get that kid in here with the hot water. And get that cheering crowd of spectators out of here before I murder the bloody lot of them!"

He glowered at the Indians, then went back to working on Mamani. McKenna, already feeling better, as if the stranger were breathing new life into *him*, stood up and ushered the campesinos ahead of him out into the yard. Then he went back inside and helped Agostino carry the old tin tub and several buckets of hot water into the bedroom. Mamani, covered by all four of McKenna's blankets but still shivering, was conscious now, gazing unblinking at the roof but with the mask of his face scarred by a deep frown. He was alive, but it was difficult to tell whether he was puzzled, pleased or angry. Even he thinks we did the wrong thing, McKenna thought.

Mamani protested, shaking his head vigorously, as the stranger pulled the blankets from him and jerked a thumb at the steaming water in the tub. But the stranger was taking no argument. He grabbed Mamani by the shoulder and raised a large bony fist.

"Get in there, you dirty bugger! This isn't just to get you clean – we want the blood moving in you again. Get in!"

He had spoken in English, but Mamani, one eye on the fist close to his face, got the message. Abruptly he slid out of bed, still shivering, both hands cupped modestly over his genitals, and stepped into the water, flinching at the heat of it. The stranger put both hands on Mamani's shoulders and pushed him down into it. The Indian let out a cry, struggled a moment, then suddenly relaxed. He lay back in the tub, his hands still in the September Morn position. McKenna held back his smile, knowing the extremes of modesty and immodesty, according to their moods, that the Indians could go to. Now was no time to offend Mamani.

"I wonder when he last had a bath." The stranger, McKenna now realised, was English. His voice was flatter and more matter-of-fact than those of the few Englishmen, mostly junior diplomats, whom McKenna had met here in Bolivia. "One whiff of him is enough."

"Some of them never have a bath from the day they are born," McKenna said. The hot water had begun to open up Mamani's pores and a slightly sickening odour came out of him. "Smell the coca weed coming out of him."

"I could taste it when I was working on him," said the stranger, and looked around for a place to spit as he curled his lips. He went outside, then came back and looked down at Mamani. "He's going to live."

Mamani lay in the water and looked up at his son, the priest and the stranger. "I am alive again," he said in Quechua.

McKenna leaned forward, desperate to know. "Does that please you, Jesu?"

Mamani stared up at him. God, McKenna thought, who would know that once, as kids, we had shared secrets? But now Mamani was as secretive as the rest of them, locked in against the world. The Indian said nothing for almost a minute, then at last he nodded. "Yes, padre."

"So it bloody well should," said the stranger in English; then in rough Quechua he added, "Gods are not always right."

Mamani stiffened in the tub, glanced quickly at McKenna. The latter stood up, aware that the stranger was eyeing him expectantly. I'm in no mood for argument this morning, he thought. "It depends who judges them."

The stranger grinned with good humour. "A good ecclesiastical answer." Then he looked back at Mamani and said in Quechua, "Rub, man, rub. The water will not hurt you."

Mamani still lay stiffly in the tub. He flicked a glance at Agostino, but his gaze was concentrated on the tall man standing over him. I'm watching a man make an enemy, McKenna thought; and decided it was time to break up the scene. He moved towards the door, motioning the stranger to follow him. "Let's have some coffee. You can get rid of the coca weed taste."

The tall man hesitated, then picked up his cap from the bed and followed McKenna into the larger room. He sat down at the table in the middle of the room and looked about him while the priest went outside. He saw a dirt-floored room that appeared to be used partly for living, partly for worship, partly for schooling. A small wooden altar stood against one adobe wall; it could have been mistaken for an ordinary sideboard but for the small tabernacle and brass crucifix that rested on its top; a rough home-made prie-dieu stood in front of it. The centre of the room was taken up by the table and half a dozen uncomfortable wooden chairs. In one corner was a small upright piano, its castors resting in rusted cans full of water to keep it free from termites. On top of it were piled sheets of religious music and a stack of popular music: Bach and "Get Me To The Church On Time" lay side by side; all the popular music looked old and tattered. In another corner was a blackboard with some simple Spanish words chalked on it; beside it stood a table on which were stacked some dog-eared exercise books. The stranger looked about him once more, shook his head, then sat back as McKenna came in with a pot of coffee and two tin mugs.

"The kitchen's next door. Some day I'm going to knock a hole in the wall, save myself going out in the wind and the rain."

"The whole place will crumble to pieces if you do."

"I know. That's why I keep putting it off. Everything's likely to crumble," he said, and looked across at the altar as if that, too, might turn to dust. Then he looked back at the stranger and put out his hand. "My name's McKenna. Terence McKenna."

"Harry Taber. I'm from FAO."

"The Food and Agriculture Organisation? You here to stay?" McKenna pushed a cup of coffee across the table. He was trying to make up his mind about the newcomer. He welcomed anyone who spoke his own language; he doubted if he would ever be fluent enough in Spanish or Quechua to catch the nuances of conversation in those languages. Yet Taber had already suggested that he had nuances of his own, that he might be a hard man to know.

"Depends." Taber sipped his coffee, scratched his red head with a large hand on which McKenna could see small sun cancers; this man had spent a good many years away from the gentle sun of his native England. He was not a handsome man, his face was too bony and his hooked nose too large for that, but he suggested a strength that might prove comforting to a lot of women; and maybe to a lot of men, too, McKenna thought. He did not move gracefully, but he had a sort of angular ease that conserved his energy. He was a man in his mid-thirties and the total impression of him was of someone who knew his own competence and had confidence in it. "I'm here to see if the locals really want some assistance or are just after another hand-out from the World Bank."

"They could do with some help. Real help, I mean."

"Who? The campesinos or the criollos?"

This man knows the situation, McKenna thought. It was the campesinos, the Indians, who needed the help, but they could only ask for it through the criollos, the Spanish-bloods. "How long have you been in Bolivia?"

"Two weeks. I've just come down from La Paz. But I've had six years in South America. Brazil, Paraguay, Peru. I know the score." He sipped his coffee. "Whose side are you on? The campesinos' or the criollos'?"

McKenna had never been asked that before, but he had had the answer for months. "The campesinos'."

"The Church is on the other side."

"Not entirely." His headache was gradually going, but it would come back if this argument kept on. "Whose side is FAO on?"

Taber smiled, raising his mug in acknowledgement. "A good question. Are you a Jesuit?"

It was McKenna's turn to smile. "Do you think a Jesuit would live like this?" He gestured at his surroundings.

"Tell you the truth, I'm still trying to make up my mind whose side FAO is on."

McKenna knew the Food and Agriculture Organisation had a lot of dedicated men working for it and it did a tremendous amount of good; but like all divisions of the United Nations it suffered from the demands and prejudices of the member governments of the world body. Here in South America, where most of the governments were made up of criollos, the F A O, like the Church, had its problems.

"What do you do here?" Taber asked.

"I'm trying to get a school started. About eighty per cent, maybe more, of the Indians up here on the altiplano are illiterate."

"How are you making out?"

McKenna shook his head. "It's tough. I'm a foreign gringo – they naturally think I'm here to exploit them. These Indians have long memories – I think they still remember, as if they were alive then, what Pizarro did to them."

Then Jesu Mamani and Agostino came into the room. Mamani had wrung out his wet clothes and put them back on. He was slightly taller than the average campesino and held himself very erect, as if determined not to be towered over by the two white men. Though his face was not expressive, there was a look of intelligence in his eyes that hinted that his mind had not become dulled by coca weed and misery.

McKenna went past him into the bedroom, came back with a blanket and threw it round the Indian's shoulders. "Agostino can bring it back to-morrow. He says he is going down to the hospital in San Sebastian with his mother. Is she ill, Jesu?"

Mamani's face closed up, just as his son's had. "We do not know, padre. Thank you for what you did this morning."

He included both men in his look. Then, followed by Agostino, he went out of the hut, across the yard and down the road towards Altea. McKenna stood at the door watching father and son going down the slope with the shuffling Indian run that never seemed to tire them, that could carry them thirty or forty miles a day without effort. It had been tireless runners like these who had been the messengers in the Inca days, who had kept the communications system going that had kept the empire together until the day of the Spaniards.

When McKenna turned back into the room Taber was

gazing steadily at him. "Is that lake out there sacred to the Indians?"

"Yes. Inti Huara, the daughter of the Sun, is supposed to have drunk from it."

"You did the wrong thing, then, dragging that bloke out of it."

"Don't you think I know that?" McKenna said angrily; he was not angry at Taber but at the superstitions he had to fight. "The lake is entitled to its victims – that's why those other two fishermen wouldn't help me. But what would F A O have done?"

Taber smiled. "Don't tell me it was the Catholic Church went out in that outboard this morning. It could never respond that fast, not on this continent. It was McKenna went out there. Man, not priest."

"Would you have come with me if I'd seen you in time?"

"Mate, I'm like you. I kid myself I'm civilised. I don't like to see people die, especially because of superstition. Though you have plenty of that in the Church."

"We're slowly getting rid of it," said McKenna, wondering why he felt so much on the defensive. But it was the old story: you could criticise as much as you liked from the inside, but you felt outsiders should mind their own business. God, he thought, I'm starting to sound like my mother.

"Too slowly," said Taber, and stood up, putting on his cap. "Do they complain about that in the confessional?"

"That's one of the secrets of the confessional."

Taber threw back his head and laughed, a much more full-bodied laugh than McKenna expected; he had come to think that Taber was capable of no more than a wry smile. "I think you and I might make this place interesting for each other. It seems to me it could be pretty bloody awful otherwise."

"That might describe it," said McKenna. "It can only get better, nothing else."

2

Harry Taber had never been in a confessional in his life. He had never been in a church except to attend the weddings and funerals of friends and relatives, and then only reluctantly. His father and mother had been passionate humanists as well as passionate socialists; Bill Taber, in his drunken moments, had been known to insist that God was a Tory invention. When Harry Taber had first fallen in love, almost overnight, he had been dismayed to find that his girl was a Catholic who believed in all the claptrap of religion and particularly in the necessity of being married by a priest. They had argued about the matter for a whole year, then Beth, the girl, had discovered she was pregnant; suddenly depressed, she had capitulated and they had been married in a registry office. Two months later she had lost the baby and twelve months later they had separated. Taber had blamed the break-up on religion but as time had gone on he had come to the conviction that there had been nothing and no one to blame but himself. But the judgment of himself had made him no more tolerant of religion, only more careful when he had chosen his second wife.

However, he confided none of this to McKenna immediately. Once he had left university his life had been so peripatetic that friendships had come to have the impermanent qualities of those photographs one took in those do-it-yourself kiosks on seaside promenades: instant development and already fading before you were out of sight of the kiosk. Over the last five years he had come to appreciate the poor value of such friendships and he had become increasingly stingy in paying out himself to chance acquaintances. But he still valued companionship, even if he now looked for it with a cautious eye. The man with no friends is the one who appreciates most that no man is an island; he is the one who never asks for whom the bell tolls, for he knows. Taber was doing his best to turn a deaf ear to bells of any sort.

When McKenna said he had to get ready to go down to San Sebastian, Taber said, "May I ride back with you?"

McKenna looked surprised. "How did you get up here?"

"I have a Land-Rover, brought it down from La Paz with me. My driver went back down to Altea to buy some fish. I was going to walk down there and pick him up. But – "

"I'll be glad of your company," said McKenna eagerly, and

disappeared into the bedroom. "And I'll give you some fish. I've got far too much."

Taber walked out into the yard. The wind was still blowing, bringing with it the chill of the distant snow. The mission had a beautiful view of the lake and the jagged wall of mountains rising beyond it, but it was completely exposed to the wind up here at the top of the slope. In one corner of the stone-walled compound some chickens huddled mournfully together in a small tin-roofed coop; in another corner a thin sad cow looked as if she might yield only iced yoghurt. A small vegetable garden had been attempted on the sheltered side of the kitchen hut, but it looked more like a gesture than a productive enterprise. The huts themselves, of adobe walls and corrugated-iron roofs, suggested an isolated slum, a tiny section that had somehow drifted apart from the rest of the world's poverty. What a miserable bloody existence he must lead, Taber thought; and wondered why Christ had always made a virtue of poverty. Still maybe this went over better with the Indians than would the affluence of the Vatican he had seen when last in Rome. The world even now wasn't ready for missionaries in Mercedes-Benz.

McKenna came out in a well-cut black suit and wearing a clerical collar; he was hardly recognisable as the man who ten minutes before had been in a torn turtleneck sweater and faded jeans. "I may run into the Bishop – he has some idea that God is fashion-conscious. Here's your fish."

Taber took the three salmon strung on a piece of wire. "Are you having tea or sacramental wine or whatever it is you have at the cathedral?"

"I'm on my way to see some people named Ruiz. You know them?"

"I know *of* them. I'm supposed to call on Alejandro Ruiz. I gather he's the big-wig around here."

"That describes him. He's the one I'm going to see. I got a message last night he wanted to see me. Not even us foreigners ignore an invitation from a Ruiz." He shot a careful glance at Taber. "You might remember that."

He led the way round to the back of the larger hut. There, under a lean-to, stood a late-model Jeep fitted out elaborately for camping; as Taber climbed into the front seat he glanced back and saw the bunk, the folding table and the built-in cupboards. The contrast to what surrounded it was too much for Taber and he could not hide his surprise.

"A present from my mother," said McKenna, who was watching him closely. He reached back and unhooked something from the roof; a large crucifix swung down. "For when I'm supposed to be saying Mass from the back of the Jeep. She thinks I'm doing a Billy Graham down here in Bolivia – I'm waiting for her to send down one of Ringling Brothers's old tents."

"Not an old one, surely. Wouldn't she buy a new one?" Then he pulled off his cap and scratched his head, a habit he had when embarrassed. "Sorry. I shouldn't talk about your mother like that. She obviously means well."

"Too well," said McKenna, but his voice was flat of any emphasis. He started up the Jeep and they drove out of the yard and down the road. "Why don't you come to the Ruiz' with me now? I can introduce you."

Taber hesitated, then shook his head. "You know how formal these criollos are. You don't just drop in on them."

"I'll explain the circumstances, that you helped me save Jesu Mamani from the lake. It will give them something to talk about. All they have to live on is gossip." He looked directly at Taber and again there was the eagerness: "Come with me! I can face them better with someone to back me up."

"What are they – holdovers from the Inquisition or something?"

McKenna grinned, embarrassed in his turn. "They're medieval – or damned near it. The original Ruiz came over here from Spain about ten years after Pizarro – and *these* Ruiz think that time was the high spot of world history. They live in the past, every one of them thinking he's the ghost of some conquistador. At one time they owned all the silver mines around, but that was over a hundred, maybe a hundred and fifty years ago. They lost them some time after Bolivar liberated the country. After that they owned only land, but they had enough of that, something like five thousand square miles of it. They lost most of that in the 1952 revolution – they still own some up beyond the lake that the government, somehow, never got around to parcelling up amongst the campesinos – but they're still the wealthiest family in this part of the country and they've got fortunes salted away in Switzerland. Whoever happens to be in power up in La Paz still listens to them. I think maybe what makes me uncomfortable when I'm with them is that they should be finished, that they're an anachronism to-day, yet they still have power."

"I thought you'd be used to that."

"What d'you mean?"

"You've just described your Church."

"Put your needle away," said McKenna. "I'll bet there are some F A O guys who should be defrocked for saying the same thing about your organisation. You might make a good heretic yourself."

"It's funny, both of us having our headquarters in Rome. I wonder if the Pope and my boss ever ring each other for advice?"

McKenna laughed. "It's a thought. But watch your heresy where we're going. One of the Ruiz, Alejandro's second brother, is my immediate boss. He's the Bishop of San Sebastian."

They came into Altea. At a distance it looked like a landslide of huge boulders in the shallow ravine in which it lay; the thatched roofs could have been dead scrub that had been carried down in the same slide, except that none of the surrounding slopes grew any scrub. Only the whitewashed tower of the adobe church, rising above the jumble of huts like a pinnacle of dirty ice, was a landmark; the rest of the village was part of the landscape, washed by the rain and scoured by the wind into the dun-coloured slopes of the ravine. In a vague way it reminded Taber of the hovels in the villages on the Anatolian plateau of Turkey; in his imagination poverty itself had become dun-coloured. In the landscape of his memory Altea would eventually run into a hundred other places.

McKenna brought the Jeep to a halt beside a Land-Rover. Taber got out, found his driver, gave him the three salmon, then came back and climbed into the Jeep again. As he did so, a short, fat priest in a shabby black soutane went by. McKenna spoke to him, but the priest ignored him and hurried on to disappear into the shabby hovel of a church. They match each other, Taber thought, the priest and the church.

"He didn't look too friendly," he said as McKenna drove down the rutted street. Half a dozen llamas, herded by a small boy playing on a quena pipe, came out of a side alley and McKenna had to brake sharply. The llamas passed in front of them, turning inquisitive heads on their long elegant necks, their soft eyes reproachful; then the small boy went past, his music as melancholy as the day which had now turned grey. McKenna drove on out of the village.

"I've trodden on that priest's toes a few times. He's a mestizo – they're the ones, I find, who can never make up their minds about foreigners."

"Half-bloods are the same anywhere. What's his grudge against you?"

"I made the mistake of baptising some of the children for free. He believes in resale price maintenance, I think you British call it. That's how he makes his living, charging for baptisms and weddings and funerals. He'd starve to death on what the Church pays him up here. It's damned difficult for me. Most of these campesinos can't afford to pay for the graces of the Church, but what do I do? Put that guy out of business?"

"Are the Indians willing to pay?"

"That's the irony of it – yes. They're like the snobs back home in the States – if it's for free, it can't be any good."

A squall of rain came on the wind, shutting out the country-side for a few minutes; then abruptly they drove out into bright sunshine. Taber was learning that this was how the weather was in these high sierras; he would learn, too, that men's tempers were the same. The altiplano stretched ahead of them, brown and bleak, drawing their gaze till their eyes ached with the stretching. In the far distance herds of llamas and alpaca moved slowly like cloud-shadow in the clear glare, their very insubstantiality adding to the emptiness of the landscape. The rutted road ran straight as a rod for five or six miles, encountering neither fence nor house that would have caused it to bend.

"This was all Ruiz land at one time," said McKenna. "You think you could get anything to grow on it?"

"I'm no miracle worker," said Taber, staring unhopefully out at the barren land. "But down in Australia they turned a desert into a wheat-field. There's always the chance – "

"No point in growing wheat up here. Isn't there a world surplus? They want a cash crop they can export."

"Who doesn't?" said Taber, who had heard the same suggestion everywhere he had worked.

The Jeep bumped along the road, seeming to make no headway in the landscape that offered no perspective. Once, some distance off to their left, they saw an Indian woman sitting in the middle of nowhere: no llamas, no alpaca, not even a dog, only she sitting there, a human cairn marking the loneliness.

"You wonder what they think about," said McKenna.

"Perhaps nothing. If you don't know anything, what's to fire your imagination?"

"You're mistaken if you think their intelligence isn't much above the animal level."

"I didn't say that." Taber slumped in the corner of the seat, took off his cap and scratched his head. But he did not look embarrassed this time, only sad. "But sometimes I think the poor buggers would be better off if that *was* their level."

Then the road curved and began to dip and soon they were riding on tarmac. A wide bowl opened up in the altiplano and there at the bottom of it was San Sebastian. The road went down in a series of bends, starting where the airport had been built on the very edge of the bowl. As they passed the airport an old DC-3 took off, already airborne 2,000 feet as it left the end of the runway and flew out over the city. The Jeep went down round the bends, came to a level where a thin forest of Australian red gums grew on each side of the road.

"They were planted by the British, when they owned the railroad," McKenna said. "The early locos were wood-burners."

"Those gums look pretty good. Why don't they try planting some up on the altiplano as windbreaks?"

McKenna shrugged. "The people down here don't care what happens up there. The Indians have been wind-blown for centuries – why change it? Even the Indians themselves seem to have the same idea. I'm trying to get a few saplings going in back of my place, but the Indians just look at them and shake their heads. I'm the nutty one, not them."

A ramshackle truck, loaded high with a mixed freight of crates, tyres and half a dozen Indian women perched high on top like a covey of coots, went rattling by, its brakes shrieking as it came to a bend but doing nothing to decrease its speed. Somehow or other the driver negotiated the curve, going within a foot of the edge of the road and a thousand-foot drop, then tearing on towards the next bend. Taber and McKenna looked at each other and shook their heads. There was nothing to say: each of them had seen the results of such decrepit trucks and such drivers.

The road straightened out, became the main street of the city, running through to the main plaza. The traffic thickened: a few modern cars, but most of it cars ten, twenty, thirty years old and trucks that looked even more ancient: to Taber it was like travelling through a big moving junk yard. They swung round the plaza, past the eucalyptuses, the occasional pine and the tall column with the golden condor perched atop it and the boy bootblacks clustered round its base like starlings. They passed the cathedral, baroque as a religious nightmare; gold-leafed saints looked out in agony from niches in the walls; between the two tall domed towers was a minaret, as if the sixteenth century builder, brought here from Spain, had not been able to deny his Moorish blood. They went past a mansion half-hidden behind tall railing gates ("The Bishop's palace," said McKenna. "Whose else?" said Taber), turned down a side street and came to a smaller plaza. There were no shops or public buildings here; Taber recognised at once that this was a residential plaza and a very restricted one. A fountain dribbled lethargically in the centre of the square and a few Indians sat round it, their backs to it, their blank, indifferent faces staring across at the high walls surrounding the plaza. In each wall was a pair of tall wooden gates, the barriers between two worlds.

McKenna pulled the Jeep up outside the biggest of the gates. They got out and crossed to a small door let into the gates. There were two iron knockers, each in the shape of a mailed fist, one at face level for the caller on foot, one at a level for a caller on horseback: this was a house that had known visitors

25

for centuries. McKenna clanged the lower knocker and almost immediately the door was opened by an unsmiling Indian houseboy. Taber followed the priest in under the massive gates to a courtyard in which stood four Cadillacs, none of them less than twenty years old.

"Since the revolution," said McKenna in a low voice, "they don't advertise their wealth so much here at home. They go to Europe every year – they keep a Rolls-Royce there."

"*Four* Cadillacs?" Taber had taken off his cap and was trying to comb his hair with his fingers. Alongside the now spruce McKenna he looked a trifle unkempt. He had a natural contempt for people who concerned themselves with clothes, but he had learned to make concessions to the criollos' sense of formality. He always carried a tie with him, but to-day he had left it in the Land-Rover.

"One of them is the Bishop's. I don't know why the Ruiz have all three of theirs out of the garages. Maybe they're going up to La Paz. They usually take their servants with them – they have a house up there, too."

"I think I'd better back out now. Go back to the hotel, come another day when my socialist hackles are lying down flat."

"Too late. Start smiling and acting feudal."

The iron-studded front door, adorned with another mailed fist knocker, had swung open. An Indian butler in white jacket and white gloves stood waiting for them. Taber had only time to notice that the house was a large two-storied Spanish colonial building before he was ushered with McKenna into a hall that rose to the full height of the house. The walls were panelled and hung with tapestries; Pizarro, ugly and vicious, galloped round the hall in pursuit of Atahualpa; Christ, Taber thought, can't these people recognise the real hero? Two suits of conquistador armour, helmets and breastplates, hung on rods, stood like steel scarecrows at the foot of a wide curving staircase. A balcony ran round three walls and above it the thick beams of the roof were lost in a gloom that Taber imagined had been gathering for centuries. The hall set the period for the house and the family: as McKenna had said, the Ruiz lived in the past.

The butler, silent as the empty suits of armour, led the two men down a long passage, their footsteps echoing on the tiled floor, and into a room that at once struck Taber as a museum. He guessed there was nothing in the long, high ceilinged room that did not have its historical value; the New World had long since become the old. But there was no time to take note of any details. Five people were gathered in front of the huge stone fireplace. McKenna pulled up sharply, staring incredulously at the girl who was smiling at him. Taber, following on, bumped awkwardly into him. I knew it, he thought, we've come at the right time.

"Padre McKenna, welcome." Alejandro Ruiz Cordobes came forward. He was a big man, not so tall as thick; he filled his stiff-collared white shirt and his dark expensive suit so that there seemed no room for creases. He had a heavy shock of grey hair and a thick grey moustache that was like a small bar of iron laid across his upper lip. He moved with almost comical deliberateness, as if no matter where he went, he went in dignified procession. But the smile for McKenna was genuine, not the grimace of formal politeness. He had spoken first in Spanish, but now he broke into fluent but accentuated English. "We have a surprise for you, as you can see – that was why I asked you to come this morning. But first we must meet your friend."

McKenna, flustered, introduced Taber with no reference to what had happened up at the lake. Ruiz took the Englishman's arm and led him towards the group, none of whom had moved.

"My wife. My brother, the Bishop. My nephew – but not the son of the Bishop." A beautiful set of dentures flashed beneath the iron bar. "My son Francisco, who has just to-day come home from the Sorbonne. And the surprise for Padre McKenna – Miss Carmel McKenna, his sister."

Taber would need second looks to remember the others, but he had taken in Carmel McKenna at first glance. It could have been her beauty, which was striking; it could have been the modernity of her, which, in the room and against the conservative dress of the others, was also striking. Whatever it was, she had filled Taber's eye, made her impression on him at once. Dark-haired and finely-boned, full-breasted in her grey cashmere sweater, long thighs showing beneath her tweed miniskirt, brown suède boots reaching to just below her knees, she looked to Taber like one of those mythical creatures he saw in

27

Vogue, a magazine he sometimes read because he found it funnier than *Punch.* Perhaps she was too full-breasted, too sexual, for that unconsciously sexless magazine; she was certainly too sexual for her present surroundings. Taber, irrationally, suddenly prudish, felt embarrassed for the Ruiz, embarrassed particularly for McKenna.

Carmel McKenna gave him a quick smile and a nod, pushed past him towards her brother. "Terry darling! God, it's good to see you!" Her voice was deep, but too loud, one that had been trained at cocktail parties. She grabbed her brother by the elbows. "Do you kiss a priest hello, when he's your brother?" Still holding McKenna by the elbows, she looked over her shoulder at the others. "I was in Rome in June – you know what the joke there was? Priests and nuns can kiss each other hello so long as they don't get into the habit."

She's trying too hard, Taber thought: this room was no place for swingers. What the hell was she trying to prove? That San Sebastian was out of touch with the real world? But the Ruiz family was unconvinced or shocked: it was impossible to tell: their faces were as stiff as those of their Indian servants. McKenna did his best to cover up his sister's gaffe. He leant forward, kissed her on the cheek and said, "I heard that one my first year in the seminary."

Bishop Ruiz, as thick-bodied as his brother but bald, suddenly smiled, taking the tension out of the room. "We joked a lot when I was a young priest. Now – " He spread a regretful hand, the ring on his finger glistening like a large drop of dark blood. There's dark blood in all of them, Taber thought, remarking the high flat cheekbones in all four of the Ruiz men; they might dream of Spain long ago and of the conquistadores, but somewhere in the family's history a Ruiz had been conquered by an Inca. The Bishop looked at Taber. "Do the bishops joke in England, Senor Taber?"

Taber was about to say that the bishops in England *were* a joke, but he checked himself. "I couldn't say, sir. It's quite a while since I swapped jokes with a bishop."

Taber saw McKenna's quick, amused glance. And for the first time Carmel looked at him with interest. She raised an eyebrow and half-smiled, as if by some intuition she had understood that he was not a lover of bishops nor what they stood for. Then she put her arm in her brother's and drew him towards Francisco Ruiz.

"Pancho and I met at a party in Paris. When he said he came from Bolivia I at once thought of you. How long is it since we saw each other – four, five years? I called Mother and when she said you were near San Sebastian, I just *had* to come down here with Pancho – "

"We are very happy to have Francisco home with us," said Romola Ruiz, with just enough emphasis on her son's name to hint that she preferred it to the diminutive. She was a slim woman who had so far won out over the creeping erosion of middle age; there was no grey in her brownish-blonde hair and her handsome, rather than beautiful face showed no trace of lines nor any vagueness along her jawline. She looked a woman who would have her own opinions and Taber guessed there might often be a clash of wills between her and her husband. "Where do you live, Senor Taber?"

"Where F A O sends me, senora."

"You do not have a home in England?" The Ruiz family and Carmel had been drinking coffee and now the butler brought cups for Taber and McKenna. Romola Ruiz poured from the big silver pot that looked as old as the rest of the room's furniture.

"My parents are dead, so their house is gone. And I'm unmarried." Or twice divorced, if you like; but he did not say that. He did not think the Ruiz would have a high opinion of divorce, especially with a bishop in the family. He tried for some graciousness, lying like a diplomat, which he was in effect but which he often forgot: "You have a beautiful home."

Romola Ruiz surprised him: "It could be modernised. Museums are not for living in."

"This house is the continuum in our family," said her husband. He sat in an upright, leather-backed monk's chair, one that had for three centuries supported Ruiz men in the same uncomfortable way. Taber guessed that few Ruiz women would have sat in it and certainly not Romola Ruiz. "It was built in 1580. The history of our country has passed through this room."

"My family came to San Sebastian only in 1825," Romola Ruiz told Taber. "Our house fell down in 1925. They don't build them like they used to."

Her husband smiled, but it was an effort. "It is my wife's joke that her family are Johnny-come-latelies. But her ancestor who settled here was one of Bolivar's principal lieutenants. He is honoured in our history." He looked with pride about the room. "This house is necessary. One needs something unchanging in this changing world."

"Perhaps Senor Taber would not agree with you," said the Bishop, who had chosen a comfortable couch on which to sit. He looked across at Taber, the non-religious non-ascetic who had found himself perched awkwardly in another monk's chair. "You are here to change things, are you not, Senor Taber? Otherwise the F A O would not have sent you."

"Let's say I'm here to try and help improve things."

"Improvement *is* change." Francisco Ruiz still stood in front of the big stone fireplace with the McKennas. He was a darkly handsome young man with his mother's slim build and his father's intensity that he had not yet learned how to control as the older man had. "Don't you agree, Padre McKenna? The Church is trying to improve things by changing them."

McKenna looked warily at the Bishop, who waved a permissive hand. "Go ahead, my son. We are always interested in what the younger generation has to say."

"Change must come," said McKenna, still wary. "It's inevitable."

"You can't hold progress back. Look at the emancipation of women," said Carmel, as emancipated as a woman was likely to be, short of taking over the dominant role in the sex act. And I shouldn't put that past her, thought Taber.

"What does Hernando think?" said Romola Ruiz.

The nephew had been sitting on a third uncomfortable chair, his short legs dangling a few inches above the thick rugs that lay strewn about the tiled floor. He was a muscular young man, already destined to be bald like his uncle the Bishop, with a quietness about him that could have been shyness or that sort of arrogance that did not need to be displayed because it was so sure of itself.

"Everything must be seen in its context," he said in a deep voice that only just escaped being pompous. "We were supposed to have had progress here after the revolution. Have we had it?"

He sounds like a politician, thought Taber. He's just said something and said nothing.

"What exactly are you going to do here, Mr Taber?" said Alejandro Ruiz, ignoring his nephew's rhetorical question: he was one man who was not interested in what the younger generation had to say.

"Well, I'm basically a soil scientist, so that's my first job – to see what deficiences there are in the soil around here and if something can be done to improve crops. But I'm also supposed to report on things in general – livestock, for instance. To answer the Bishop's question, and if Senor Francisco is right about improvement being change – yes, I suppose I am here to change things."

"The Indians resent change," said Alejandro Ruiz, sitting upright in his chair like a judge delivering sentence. "We are called reactionaries by outsiders, but it is not that we are against change just for our own sakes. We are realists, we see things, as my nephew puts it, in their context. The Indians are far more reactionary than we are, Senor Taber. I think Padre McKenna will have discovered that in the short time he has been here. We Ruiz have learned it over four hundred years."

Taber had heard this argument all over South America; it was an argument that had its echoes from history all over the world. It had a degree of truth in it, but then men in general hated change: necessity, and not the desire for a better neighbourhood, had driven Early Man out of his cave and into villages. But it was too early yet to set up antagonisms; they would come soon enough. He did not want to have to depart before he had unpacked his bags.

"What were you studying at the Sorbonne?" asked McKenna, changing the subject and looking at Francisco. Everyone was still throwing smiles into his conversation, like sugar into bitter coffee, but a certain tension hung in the room.

"History," said Francisco, and looked at his cousin. "You should go there, Hernando. If only to meet girls like Carmel."

"I wasn't studying history, darling," said Carmel.

"What were you studying?" asked Romola Ruiz.

"Life," said Carmel. "And men."

Don't try so bloody hard, said Taber silently. There's no one with-it in this room, not even me; you'll get no converts among this lot.

"There is no better place to study men than South America," said Romola Ruiz; Taber was not surprised, coming now to expect the unexpected from her. "It is one of the last male strongholds, except of course in the animal world."

Alejandro Ruiz smiled a snarl at his wife; it reminded Taber of lions he had seen in East Africa when they were hungry. "My wife likes her little joke. But ask Jorge, my dear – he will tell you that men everywhere are the same in the confessional."

But the Bishop was too shrewd to be drawn into a domestic argument. "I have only sat in the confessional in South America."

"And am I not right, Jorge?" Romola Ruiz would never surrender without a fight.

Jorge Ruiz rubbed the ruby of his ring. "Ah, that is one of the secrets of the confessional, Romola."

Taber looked up at McKenna and the two men winked at each other; Carmel caught the wink and once again looked with interest at Taber. He stared back at her, then abruptly winked at her, too. She looked puzzled for a moment, tilting her head to one side, then she smiled and winked back. Neither of them had communicated anything to each other, the winks were meaningless, but a door had been unlocked, if not opened between them. Then Taber looked away and saw that both Francisco and Hernando had been watching them. Hernando's face was expressionless, but Francisco's was fierce with jealousy. I've just trodden on his balls, Taber thought, bruised his machismo.

Taber stood up. "I must be going, Senor Ruiz. I have intruded long enough. I only came because Padre McKenna insisted – "

"He helped me save an Indian from the lake," said McKenna.

"Actually dragged him out of the water?" said Alejandro Ruiz. "They'll never forgive you for that."

Taber was going to deny that he had had anything to do with

the actual rescue of Jesu Mamani, but he let it go. If you did not believe in superstition, you should not make an issue of it.

"They've spent the last 400 years not forgiving people for what has been done to them. One more won't matter."

Then he realised what he had said, where he was. He scratched his head and determined to get out of here before he trod on more toes, balls or whatever else got in his way. The Food and Agriculture Organisation had never chosen their field workers for their diplomacy alone, but in him it had landed itself with a man whose tongue was fluent in everything but diplomacy. He could speak English, Turkish, Arabic, Swahili, Portuguese, Spanish and some rough Quechua, but he had an awkward, treacherous tongue in the soft-soap language of social goodwill. He retreated towards the door, somehow managing not to look as embarrassed as he felt. These Ruiz were wrong in their outlook, but he did not have to tell them that in their own home, the last fortress they had.

"I hope we may meet again, Senor Ruiz."

"We shall," said Alejandro Ruiz flatly; he had not missed Taber's gaffe. "If you are trying to bring change to this part of the world, it is inevitable we shall meet again. Adios."

Taber nodded to the other men, bowed his head to Romola Ruiz and Carmel McKenna, and escaped. As he went down the long passage away from the room he heard Bishop Ruiz say, "He will learn, like everyone else who comes here. Bolivia has lessons for everyone."

"We shall teach him," said Alejandro Ruiz.

The voices faded, voices from the past.

3

"You better get yourself some longer skirts."

"Oh God, Terry, don't start talking like a priest!"

"I'm not talking as a priest. But this isn't Paris or Rome or wherever you've been these past five years. Women here are expected to be modest, at least in public – "

Carmel put a hand on McKenna's arm. "I'm sorry, darling. All right, you win. I'll buy some nice modest skirts to-day. I

B   33 don't want to spoil your image in front of the Bishop and your flock."

McKenna grinned wryly. "It's not *my* image I'm worried about – I don't even know that I've got one."

They were sitting out in a small patio behind the Ruiz house. A walnut tree leaned against its own sharp-edged shadow in one corner and ancient vines, just beginning to leaf, climbed like snakes to the rusted spikes that topped the high stone wall. The McKennas sat on a wooden bench in the brilliant sunlight in the centre of the patio. Carmel, though she wore dark glasses, kept glancing towards the shadow beneath the walnut tree.

"We'll sit over there if you like," said McKenna. "But you'll freeze. At this altitude there's a difference of twenty, twenty-five degrees between sunlight and shade."

"Pancho warned me to take it easy for a few days. I already have a headache. Is that usual?"

"Pretty usual. You probably won't sleep well, either, for the first few nights. You should've lain down for a couple of hours as soon as you got here – that helps your body adjust. But if you go tearing around – Do you still tear around like you used to?"

She nodded. "I guess so."

"Why run so fast, Carmel?" McKenna searched in his pockets, found his own dark glasses, put them on: as much a protection against her as against the glare. He and Carmel had never been particularly close even as children; the six years' difference in their ages had been too big a handicap. He had gone away to prep school at twelve, then on to college; she had gone to a day school in Westwood, then persuaded her mother to send her to a finishing school in Switzerland. They had written each other spasmodically, but they had been the non-committal letters of acquaintances rather than of blood relatives. They were strangers with the same name; but he knew that committal had at last presented itself. She had not come all this way on a whim, he was sure of that. Nor because she had a yen for Francisco Ruiz, he was equally sure of that. Something was troubling her and for some reason she had reached out to him. And he, the missionary, the helper, suddenly was wary.

34

"Would you rather I hadn't come?" It was as if she had read his thoughts: she had her own wariness.

He was glad of the dark glasses, the one great advance in deception since man had first learned to lie; he knew his eyes were often too candid for his own good. "No. No, I'm glad to see you. But it's a long way – I – "

"You don't understand why I bothered?" She sat back, put an arm along the back of the bench, slowly drummed her fingers. "It's crazy, isn't it? We should be able to talk to each other more easily than this. I'm twenty-four and you're – what? – thirty? – and I don't suppose we've ever had more than an hour's serious conversation together in all that time."

"Whose fault do you think it was?" He didn't mean it as an aggressive question, but he couldn't think of anything else to say.

"I don't know. I sometimes wonder if it was Mother's." She raised her head and even behind her dark glasses he was aware of her careful gaze.

"How was she when you called her?" He avoided the silent question she had put to him.

"Hysterical, when I said I was coming down to see you. Hysterically glad, I mean. Jealous, too, I think," she added, and looked away from him, not even trusting to the dark glasses.

He stared down at the ground at their shadows, razor-edged and dead as paper silhouettes. Shadows at this altitude were always much more clear-cut than at less rarified heights; the mental processes were also said to be sharper: but only keener in being aware of problems, not in solving them. He had solved nothing in the nine months he had been here and he knew he could not solve this new problem of himself and Carmel. But he was now acutely conscious of it as he had never been before. He realised for the first time that she was jealous of him.

"There's nothing to stop her coming down here," he said, dodging the real issue for the moment.

"Do you want her to?"

"No-o." It was the first time he had ever admitted it, even to himself.

Was he mistaken or did something like delight flick across

her face? "She said you'd never asked her down here. When I told her I was coming down to surprise you, she said it was only correct for a lady to wait till she was asked. God, she's like something out of Henry James!"

He nodded, smiling, and impulsively she put her hand on his. He had not liked her when they had been in the house with the Ruiz family, had been annoyed by her brashness and a quality of hardness that had looked as if it could never be cracked. But now she was softer, even vulnerable, and suddenly he felt a warmth of feeling that he recognised as love, something he had not felt for any of the family in years. He squeezed her fingers.

"We should feel sorry for her – "

"I do, Terry. Really. I don't hate her, though God knows – " She took off her dark glasses as if she wanted him to see the truth of what she was about to say. "She made me hate you. I was so damned jealous of you – "

"I never knew," he said. "Not till just now."

She squeezed his hand again, as if making up for lost time in a display of affection. "I think you have some of Dad's sensitivity in you. He was a selfish, randy old fool, running after those girls the way he did – in a way, I suppose, he was a real sonofabitch, leaving us like that – but he had his moments, sometimes he knew exactly what I was trying to say even though I couldn't open my mouth – " She put her glasses back on, stared at the darkness of the past. "It was a pity he wasn't always like that. He might have saved Mother from herself. And saved us from her."

A tall hedge lined one side of the patio, separating it from a large garden. Through the hedge he could see an Indian gardener lazily turning over the yellow soil among some shrubs; some buds on rose bushes promised the coming of summer. The gardener wore a tribal headband that strapped something to his ear; it was a moment or two before McKenna recognised that the small package was a transistor radio. The gardener moved zombie-like through the motions of his work, his face stiff and blank; whatever he was listening to on the radio, talk or music or a description of a football game, seemed to have no effect on him; the radio could have been no more than an uncomfortable earmuff. To McKenna it seemed to typify the Indians: they were of the world but they were deaf to it. Just as the McKennas had been deaf to each other for years.

"Why *did* you come?" he asked, sure enough of her now to put the question.

She, too, was looking through the hedge at the gardener; but he was just part of the scenery to her, someone to be captured on film by a tourist's camera. "I wanted to see what you had done with your life."

"Not much," he confessed; then added defensively, "At least not yet."

"At least you're doing *something*. I've done nothing, absolutely goddam nothing. I'm what you preach against – a parasite."

"If I preached against parasites around here, I'd be branded a Communist." He had automatically lowered his voice, glanced over his shoulder towards the house. When he looked back at her she was smiling. "What's so funny?"

"You. The one thing I remember about you was that you were never scared. Cautious, yes, but never frightened of anything. That time you were home from school on vacation and the burglars broke into the house. You locked Mother and me in her bedroom and went downstairs on your own. The guys, whoever they were, heard you coming and ran. But you went down there, that was the thing – you were my hero for a day or two."

"I was scared stiff," he said, not asking why he had remained her hero only for a day or two.

She nodded towards the house. "What were you then – cautious or scared?"

"Cautious, I guess. It's the only way to get by up here. Nobody here, neither the criollos nor the campesinos, accept you on your own terms. It's their terms all the time or nothing."

"Is that why you haven't made much of your life here so far?" He nodded and she put her hand sympathetically on his again. Then she said, "That was my mistake, I think. I tried living on my own terms. I've only just discovered I was never really sure what they were."

"Then we're alike," he said, and she looked pleased. "I'm never quite sure about people who say they'll only live on their own terms, whether they're conceited or selfish or just insecure. I've never been convinced it's an entirely noble attitude."

"To thine own self be true – You think Polonius was wrong?"

"In the Church, anyway, I've never found him proved right." He stood up, smiling now to divert her from what he had just let slip; it was too soon, he did not know her well enough yet, to confess his doubts. "I better go see what the Bishop wants."

She stood up beside him. "You're not annoyed because I came, Terry?"

"No. I'm glad," he said, and meant it. He had reached a depth of loneliness where reunion even with someone half a stranger had its comfort. "Will you be staying long?"

"A week or two. Until we get to know each other again."

"Will you stay here?" He nodded at the house.

"Depends. Not if Pancho becomes too possessive."

"Is it serious with him?"

"On my part, you mean?" She shook her head. "He's the latest in a long line. I haven't been a very good girl – the nuns at Marymount must be wearing out their rosaries praying for me. I'm not exactly the right sort of sister for a priest. I think I have too much of Dad in me." She smiled wryly, nothing at all like the brash girl he had met an hour earlier. "Father, forgive me, for I have sinned – "

"Who hasn't?" he said, unembarrassed.

He left the Ruiz house and drove back to the main plaza. The benches in the square were now occupied by old men dressed in old-fashioned dark suits, their wary faces hidden in the shade of broad-brimmed felt hats; they looked like retired gangsters from movies of the thirties, men who had stepped out of frame but not out of costume. But McKenna knew that they were not as interesting as old-time gangsters. They were just middle-class criollos living on dreams that were as dim as their eyesight, selling off their possessions piece by piece, hoping that at the end they would have enough left to pay for a funeral befitting their blood. A flock of young children, criollos and mestizos, wafted up the broad steps of the cathedral, two nuns fluttering behind them like Black Orpington hens. An army truck went round the plaza and pulled up outside the prison on the other side of the square. Half a dozen prisoners,

all Indians, chained together, got down from the back of the
truck and were pushed through the small door in the tall wooden
gates. The truck drove off and that side of the square was once
more quiet and deserted. No one in the square had done more
than glance casually across at the prisoners. Too much interest,
McKenna knew, might have brought an inquiry from the
security police on the third floor of the government palace on
the northern side of the plaza. He looked across and saw the
man at the third floor window: the sun flashed on his binoculars
as he turned them from the prison gates on to McKenna himself
as the latter got out of the Jeep outside the Bishop's palace. For
one mad moment the priest wanted to turn and jerk his thumb
at the watcher, but reason prevailed. You did not make rude
gestures in front of the Bishop's palace, certainly not at the
security police.

As McKenna crossed the tessellated pavement a small boy
flung himself at his feet; but he was not a juvenile sinner seeking
absolution, just a bootblack claiming the Americano padre could
not visit the Bishop with dirty shoes. McKenna submitted to
the blackmail, gave the boy a lavish tip, then went into the
palace spotless at least up to the ankles. Behind him the bootblack, clutching half a day's income in his hand, told him he
was a saint.

If it were only so easy, McKenna told himself.

Bishop Ruiz was in his study reading *The Wall Street
Journal*; he nodded at it as he put it down. "There are so many
Bibles to get through these days. Do you read it, Padre
McKenna?"

"No, your grace. I am stupid when it comes to understanding
high finance."

"Your father never taught you anything about it? He was a
rich man."

"My father used to say that a fool and his father's money
are soon parted, so he never gave me any. Not till he died."

"I knew him when he owned the San Cristobal mine. I was
a young priest then – I baptised you, did you know that?"

"No," said McKenna, and wondered if he was expected to
feel honoured. He also wondered how much the Bishop, a
wealthy man even as a priest, had charged for the service.

"I used to go out and say Mass for the miners. Your father would count the heads at Mass and then give me an American dollar for each one – he always seemed to have a bank of dollars. He would joke that he was buying his way into Heaven on the bended knees of the Indians."

"What did the Indians think of him?" McKenna had never known the Bishop to talk of his father before and he wondered if this was the reason he had been brought here. The Bishop had chosen to speak in Spanish and that meant this was more than just a social call. McKenna was puzzled, seeking a connection between himself and his father that would concern the Bishop, but he could think of none. Even the older Indians up on the altiplano, ones such as Jesu Mamani, had never asked McKenna about his father.

Bishop Ruiz hesitated, then said, "I do not know, to be truthful. I have never known the miners to love any of the mine owners."

They didn't love my father, McKenna thought. You know the truth about him but you can't condemn him because that would mean condemning your own kind.

"When your father sold out to that other company, they worked the mine out in five years, drove the miners like dogs, then closed it down and went home. They left a caretaker-manager and his wife there, Americans. When the revolution came in 1952, the miners went back there and killed them – horribly. I saw the bodies – " He shook his head, worked his mouth at an old vile taste, shuddered because he knew the future might one day taste the same. "The miners all went to communion the next morning and the priest up in Altea, poor Padre Luis, was too frightened to turn them away from the altar rail. He was afraid they would have killed him, too, if he had refused them." He looked across his wide, leather-topped desk at McKenna. "Those are the sort of people you are dealing with, my son."

Now he's getting to the reason for my being here, McKenna thought. But he was still puzzled: "I don't think they connect me with the mine. What that other company did, I mean. As for what my father did – " He tailed off, not wanting to condemn his father to this man who would give absolution too easily, because his own money came from the same sort of exploitation.

"I did not say they did," said Bishop Ruiz patiently. In the cathedral next door the bells tolled for the midday Angelus. One of the bells was cracked and it sounded what could have been a blasphemous note; but the bells had been rung for 400 years and tradition won out over music. The Bishop listened to it, flinching a little, then put it out of his mind; he would leave the question of a new bell to his successor, just as his predecessor had left it to him. He looked across at the young priest who was a more immediate problem. "Padre McKenna, did you read the Pope's encyclical on birth control, *Humanae Vitae?*"

"Of course," said McKenna, and knew now why he had been sent for.

"It has come to our ears – " Bishop Ruiz sat up straight. That's it, thought McKenna, never lounge when using the royal or episcopal plural; the day, only half over, had been full of shock and now he was beginning to feel hysterically facetious. "It has come to our ears that you have been giving the Pill to some of the women up in Altea."

"Where did you hear that, your grace?"

"We have our sources," said the Bishop; and McKenna had a vision of the fat little priest Padre Luis sitting exactly where he himself was sitting now. Padre Luis didn't have the courage to condemn murder but he could condemn a priest who went against the Holy Father's orders. "We are assured they are reliable. Are the reports true?"

McKenna sighed inwardly, then nodded. "Yes, your grace."

"Does the Superior of your order condone this?"

"He doesn't know. I bought the supply of the Pill out of my own funds, had them mailed down to me from the States."

"Addressed to you as a *priest?*" The Bishop's voice, which had become formal once he had got down to business, suddenly broke. The bells next door abruptly subsided, the cracked bell clanging out the last note sardonically.

"No. They were addressed to Senor T. J. McKenna, care of general delivery at the post office here in San Sebastian. I did my best to be discreet, your grace."

41

Bishop Ruiz had a sense of humour; he permitted himself a smile at the young rebel. "That seems to be where your discretion stopped, at the post office. Padre, do you realise the magnitude of what you have done? It is one thing to sit in the confessional and condone what married couples tell you they have done. But you have – " He threw up his elegant hands. "You are doing far worse than question the Holy Father's dictum, you are actually sinning against it actively. As much – as much as if you were bedding with these women yourself!"

McKenna had expected a more sophisticated reprimand than that. "The thought couldn't have been farther from my mind. I mean about going to bed with these women."

"Don't joke," said the Bishop sharply, realising he was not dealing with a stupid village priest like Padre Luis. I keep forgetting, he thought, this young man comes from the same class as myself. Well, almost: the blood may be coarser, but he has as much education and money.

"I'm sorry. I didn't mean to sound facetious – "

"Did the women come to you and ask your help in this way?"

"Well, not exactly – " McKenna hesitated, knowing even now that nothing he might say was going to win justification for what he had done.

"What does that mean?"

"One woman talked to me in the confessional. She has had twelve children in sixteen years – only four of them have survived."

"That was God's will," said the Bishop, tasting the brass of an old platitude.

"Forgive me for saying so, your grace, but I was the woman's confessor. As far as I could tell, she had done nothing to warrant God's punishment like that."

"Are you questioning God's will?"

McKenna took a deep breath. "I guess I'm questioning the Church's interpretation of God's will. I can't bring myself to believe that He meant these people to live like they have to, that poverty and the annual grief at the loss of a child are necessary for a state of grace. Forgive me again, but the Church in this country has done little, if anything, to alleviate the poverty of the Indians. I don't know what the full answer to the problem is, but after listening to that woman I knew I had to do *something*. And cutting down the number of mouths to feed seemed to me at least a start towards defeating poverty. I didn't hand out the Pill indiscriminately – I warned the women about possible side effects, but they were willing to take the risk. Women, even simple peasant women, get tired of being continually pregnant. Men, especially priests, too often forget that. The Church isn't just Rome, your grace – I'm part of it, too. I didn't do this hurriedly or without a great deal of soul-searching – "

"Do you think the Holy Father did not search *his* soul before he made his decision? You should not question his wisdom. A son does not tell his father what to do."

McKenna heard the echo of Agostino's remark earlier this morning. Oh God, he thought admiringly, how You weave Your web up there in Heaven. It had been Agostino's mother, Maria Mamani, who had told him in the confessional that she wanted no more children.

"Do you still have a supply of the contraceptive?"

"Yes." He had ordered enough to supply every woman in Altea for a year; so far only Maria and three other women had come to him. He could imagine the snickering that had gone on in the mail order warehouse in Chicago when his order had arrived; some randy guy down there in Bolivia, Senor T. J. McKenna, was having a ball with a tribe of Indians or something. Storing the pills had become a problem in itself; one box of them had already been eaten by rats. At least he might have achieved something there, cut down on the rodent birth rate. "Quite a lot of it."

"You will dispose of it – *immediately*. I shall write your Superior and inform him of what you have done. I shall leave him to punish you or order your penance. In the meantime I shall put you on probation for six months. If you are intransigent again, Padre McKenna, I shall order your removal from my diocese."

He called me intransigent, not sinful, McKenna noted. Did that mean the Bishop had his own doubts? "Yes, your grace."

"My son," Bishop Ruiz's tone softened again, shed formality as he might shed a chasuble, "you cannot change things overnight. Not on this continent. You and Senor Taber come down here, full of good intentions, no one doubts your sincerity, but – but you look at us from the *outside*. We are another world. We shall come into your world in time, it is inevitable, but you must *give* us time. We understand the campesinos better than you. Do you not think that I, as a man of God, want their lives improved? But you have to be patient, my son. Che Guevara came here with good intentions, though misguided ones, but even he did not understand the campesinos. And he was a *South* American, an Argentinian, not a North American like you. Reform will come, but you must allow us to make our own pace."

McKenna wanted to ask who had put the brakes on since the reforms of 1952, but he knew the interview was over. "Yes, your grace."

Bishop Ruiz rose, came round his desk and held out his hand. McKenna hesitated. The ring glinted on the finger, an invitation to bow to authority: should I ignore it? Then discretion overcame bravado: I'm on probation *right now*. He bent and kissed the ring.

"God be with you, my son." Then the Bishop looked him up and down. "You look very smart to-day. You wouldn't be out of place in some rich parish in the United States."

"I think I would be," said McKenna, and after a moment the Bishop smiled and nodded in agreement.

McKenna went out of the room and Bishop Ruiz returned to his chair. He picked up *The Wall Street Journal*, but he was reading a foreign language, one that suddenly, if only temporarily, he did not feel comfortable with. He dropped the newspaper back on the desk and sat staring across the room. He reached across, took a cigar from a tooled leather box, lit it and sat back again. His purple biretta rested on one corner of the desk and he picked it up and examined it as a mining engineer might examine a piece of quartz. Is this what I have spent my life working for?

Or had he worked for it? The second son of the Ruiz had always been meant for the Church. It had been that way for generations; one or two second sons had rebelled, but the family had fixed that: they had been banished and the third sons had taken their places. The succession had been as ordained as that in a royal family: the eldest son to run the estates, the second son to enter the Church, the other sons to stand by in case of replacement: just like a royal family or a football team, the Bishop mused. It had not been a difficult life in the priesthood; no Ruiz could be expected to take vows of poverty so none was ever expected to join an ascetic order unless he wished to. Sometimes the Bishop, a naturally sensual man, had regretted the absence of women in his life; but then he consoled himself that, had he been permitted a wife, he might have made a bad choice. All the prayers in the world could not guarantee a good wife; woman was God's best joke on man. He saw that every time he went to his brother's house. Alejandro, who thought of himself as a king, was mocked by his queen; Romola was her husband's purgatory here on earth and she enjoyed every minute of her punishment of him. The Lord had at least protected the Bishop from someone like her.

He swung his chair round, looked out the window. The young American priest was just getting into his Jeep; a young bootblack rushed at him, but McKenna brusquely waved him away. The young man was angry. And I am responsible, thought the Bishop. But what else could I do? The world, *our* world, does need changing; who knows that better than I? Some day the campesinos will rise up and cut all our throats, even mine or anyway that of one of my successors; the purple biretta won't be a protection, only a target. We shall be killed because we are Ruiz; if not Alejandro and I, then Francisco and his brother Jorge now in the seminary up at La Paz. Time is running out for us.

Cigar ash fell on his soutane and he fastidiously brushed it off. He swung his chair round and looked back into the room. It was a room that suggested luxury, one that would not have been out of place in the Ruiz family mansion; he never made the mistake of receiving any of the campesinos or any of the Leftist government officials here. But it typified him, he knew: he was a lover of the good life, of privilege and the past: he was a Ruiz. And that is why, even though I think he may have the right approach, I cannot condone what McKenna has done. It is too late: I am too soft, corrupt, if you like, to join the protestors;

old men do not make good revolutionaries. I am not old in years, it is true; but like Alejandro I am old in my ways, trapped by history. All I can do is pray that God forgives the reactionaries of the world.

There was a knock on his door and his secretary, a small, thin mestizo priest, older than himself, came in. "Senor Obermaier is here to see you, your grace."

The ex-Nazi: now there was a real reactionary, one through conviction, not through laziness. The Bishop sat up, feeling a little less condemned. He put out his cigar, straightened his soutane. Though he did not like Karl Obermaier, he was easy to talk to: he was another man who lived in the past.

"Show Senor Obermaier in. And bring us some wine. The Niersteiner would be appropriate, I think."

Chapter 2

I

The driver pulled up the Land-Rover outside the railway station and Taber and Pereira got out. A blind Indian woman, led by a small girl, came shuffling towards them; the child guided the claw of a hand up to the coin that Pereira dropped into it. A policeman, dark eyes blank under the stiff vertical peak of his cap that seemed to be an extension of the planes of his face, stood by the kerb but made no attempt to move the beggar woman on. He was an Indian, too: criollos and gringos were fair game.

"Begging is against the law," said Pereira as he and Taber went on into the big deserted hall of the station. "But no one ever takes any notice of it, least of all the minions of the law."

Miguel Pereira was a chubby little man in his mid-thirties with a handlebar moustache, bad breath that he constantly sweetened with mints, and a vocabulary derived from a library of Victorian English novels. He had graduated as an agronomist from the University of San Marcos in Lima, then had had an extra year at Texas A & M on an American grant. He had come back to San Sebastian, married a local girl and now had four children and two jobs. He was the government agricultural adviser and, under a pseudonym that everyone knew of, he also managed the largest cinema in town.

"It is the only way one can survive," he had told Taber when the latter had arrived a week ago. "The government does not reward its devoted minions. I grew up as a child expecting a life of comfort – my family were of wealthy means. But we lost all that in the revolution – we were not as fortunate as some people. I was suddenly thrown on the world – " He had spread dramatic hands; Taber listened for violins, but heard none. "When one is born with a silver spoon in one's mouth, one

47

finds it difficult to adapt to a life of penury. Luxury is in the blood, don't you think?"

"I couldn't say," said Taber mildly. "It's quite a while since I've had a blood test."

"A sense of humour!" Pereira clapped his hands together as if Taber had just announced a World Bank grant for penurious agronomists. "The sign of an educated man. We are going to be very amicable colleagues, Senor Taber. You will be my guest any night you wish at the cinema. To-night, perhaps? We are showing *Rosemary's Baby*, a jolly comedy about witchcraft in New York. The campesinos will love it, though they may find it a little unsophisticated."

"Some other time. I like Westerns."

"Who doesn't?" Pereira put his hands on his plump hips as if he were about to draw six-guns. "John Wayne. The campesinos flock to see his movies. They are waiting for the one where he is shot in the back by an Indian or a Mexican bandit. I await with dread the night it happens. They will burn down the cinema in celebration."

Now, in the station, he said, "This way to the Customs chief. His name is Suarez – he is a very difficult man."

"They always are," said Taber, with memories of other Customs chiefs in a dozen other countries. "It's in their blood."

"A sense of humour!" Pereira burbled admiringly. "How it makes life bearable!"

Their footsteps echoing hollowly on the stone floor, they walked across the wide main hall. Only four trains a week now arrived at and departed from San Sebastian; the station was a monument from and to the past; it had been superseded by the still half-constructed airport terminal up on the altiplano. Birds flew in and out through the upper reaches of the high domed roof, the only arrivals and departures for to-day. From the hall Taber could see the empty platforms stretching away down toiwards the marshalling yards, currents of rust showing clearly n the river of rails. In the yards two ancient engines, British made at the turn of the century, shunted some equally ancient wagons back and forth as if the drivers were intent only on keeping the stock rolling, otherwise they would be out of a job. I'm in another museum, Taber thought.

Suarez's office was like that of the director of a museum. Yellowed sheets of regulations hung on the wall like ancient scrolls; a Wanted smuggler stared out from a poster like a cave dweller. Suarez himself was a dapper mestizo with one eye that was walled and the other suspicious. He nodded without smiling and waited for Taber to make the opening remark. All right, you bastard, Taber thought, no pleasantries.

"An F A O officer was here on a short visit three months ago. He recommended that sulphur, fertiliser and some other soil additives should be used around here. He ordered it and it was dispatched at once. Senor Pereira understands the shipment has now arrived."

Suarez nodded, a barely imperceptible movement. "Yes."

"Then we'd like to take delivery of it."

"That is impossible. The necessary papers have not arrived." He spoke Spanish with the correctness of someone who had had to learn it; Quechua had been his childhood language. These are the worst, Taber thought. The converts to a way of life were as dedicated as the converts to a religion.

"I have the papers here with me. Duplicates."

"I must have the originals. They have not arrived."

"Where are they?"

Suarez shrugged, his good eye as blank as the other.

"How long will they be arriving?"

Another shrug. Out in the yards the engines hooted: derisively, thought Taber, trying to hold on to his temper.

"The chemicals are urgently necessary. The farmers need them."

A third shrug. "The papers are also necessary."

Taber looked around the office, wondering if it was worthwhile wrecking. But the steel cabinet, the plain table and chairs, the old rusty typewriter, were government issue: Suarez would probably be glad to have them replaced. Taber looked down at the dapper little man and wondered what the penalty would be for wrecking a corrupt Customs chief. Death, probably: the system had to be protected.

"I shall write to La Paz at once and ask them to send the papers special delivery."

49

Suarez shrugged yet again. "It will be no use hurrying them. They are notoriously slow and inefficient up in La Paz."

"Shall I quote you?"

For a moment the good eye flickered; then there was a fifth shrug. "As you wish."

One more shrug, you little bastard, and I'll risk the firing squad. "I shall write to-day. Adios."

Outside in the main hall again Pereira, hurrying to keep up with Taber's long strides, said, "It's his way of surviving. Why didn't you pay him the bribe he wanted?"

"One more remark like that and I'll wreck *you*." Taber stopped, looked about him, blind with rage. "I'll bloody wreck someone!"

Pereira backed away, hands held up in front of him; all his gestures seemed borrowed from old silent movies. "A man of principle! So inspiring to see – "

Suddenly Taber's rage went, he took off his cap, scratched his head and laughed. "Miguel, you're a beaut. When did you last take out a principle and look at it?"

Pereira was offended. He said nothing till they were back at the Land-Rover. "It is not easy to be a man of principle all the time, not when one has to survive – "

Taber felt sorry for the chubby little man; after all, his own survival was guaranteed. "Miguel, I'm no paragon. I've bent my principles so often I could have strung them together and made a hippie necklace out of them. But I like to tell myself that when I've bent them, no one else has suffered – at least not as far as I know. But that bastard inside there – !" He looked back into the station, his temper rising again. "I'm here to help you people and I'm buggered if I'm going to pay through the nose for the privilege!"

"You would not have to pay, Harry, not personally. Suarez will not want much, a few dollars, that's all, a token payment – "

"It's just the principle of the thing with him, that what you mean?"

"Yes," said Pereira eagerly; then realised he had been trapped. Plaintively he said, "Harry, it has been the system for centuries. The Spanish officials started it as soon as they arrived here after Pizarro. It is a way of life. Do not the English treat the welfare state as a way of life?"

"Go on," said Taber, avoiding a touchy point.

"Suarez is not a rich man, he has a wife and five children to support. Is not FAO's annual budget ten to fifteen million dollars a year? A few dollars – will they be missed from petty cash?"

"They will be by me," said Taber emphatically, made even sorer by the reference to the welfare state; he was glad his father and mother had died before they had seen their ideal abused. "Look, Miguel, I've paid bribes before. But now I'm growing tired of it. If it were just to get something of my own, something personal, I might slip Suarez a few bob. But this is not for me, it's for the campesinos you and I are supposed to be helping – "

"Oh, I appreciate the horns of your dilemma, Harry! Oh, indeed I do. One side of me has nothing but disgust for my compatriot Suarez. But the other side – " He shrugged; and Taber almost hit him. "I am a practical man, Harry. It is the only way to survive."

"Then we're going to be impractical and take the risk of survival. At least as far as Suarez is concerned."

"The sulphur and the rest of it will stay in his sheds till he expires. Then we shall only have his successor to deal with. He will be exactly the same, Harry. A Customs man who did not take bribes would never be promoted, not in this province. It would destroy the system. So how do you propose to have the shipment cleared?"

"I'll think of something," said Taber doggedly, and succeeded in hiding his hopelessness. He had been battling graft for years, never winning even a skirmish with a corrupt official; there had been places, East Africa for instance, where there had been honest officials eager to help rather than to hinder; but he had heard with despair that the system had begun to creep in even there. He had once met an official in Brazil who boasted of his "honest corruption", who set a price according to the income of the man seeking the favour and never went above it. But now Taber had reached the end of his patience. Not just with corruption, but with bureaucracy, obstruction, betrayal, even with FAO itself. He had once been a dedicated team man, but he had become a loner because the team had let him down. Bribery was part of the subscription fee as a member of the team and he was no longer going to subscribe. "I'll think of something."

He left Pereira to return to the office in the Land-Rover with the driver. Though he did not dislike the little man, he had had enough of him for the moment; Pereira could not stop talking and he would only continue the argument throughout the day that one should compromise, should accept the realities of a way of life. Taber knew the Bolivian was right, that he should not attempt to bring in here the standards of an outsider. But that did not mean he had to suffer a lecture all day long. He excused himself, saying he had to buy some personal necessities, and quickly left Pereira before the latter could protest he would accompany him. He crossed the road, narrowly avoiding being hit by a truck whose driver, one of an international breed, held to the principle that pedestrians were an expendable nuisance. He made it safely to the opposite side and dived into the crowd of Indians drifting through the big market opposite the station.

Taber always enjoyed markets anywhere in the world. It was an exposure of people's lives; they revealed not only their wants but their character. Smithfield and Covent Garden and market day in any county town revealed more of the English character than any Gallup poll; and he believed it was the same all over the world. The bright fruits, the coloured rubble of vegetables, the rugs, the copper utensils, were only the surface kaleidoscope; the faces of the sellers and buyers were the real essence. Here even the Indians opened up their expressions, shucked off their masks and revealed the living people behind them.

He wandered through the alleys between the stalls, looking at the jumble of goods displayed. Battered pots and pans, brass ornaments that promised luck, bundles of candles, cane quena flutes, tiny guitar-like kirkinchos, sandals cut from old tyres, bowler hats, wood carvings of the Christ, the Virgin and the Sun God, take your pick, faded magazines from which Marilyn Monroe, Elvis Presley and Elizabeth Taylor smiled their empty international smiles: there was something for everyone, if everyone had money. A woman, small bowler hat sitting high on the pumpkin of her head, stopped by a stall and held out a string bag full of potatoes. The stall-owner shook his head, but the woman persisted. The man hesitated, then picked up two candles, gave them to the woman and took the potatoes. The woman went away, heading for the small church that stood on the other side of the plaza at the far end of the market. The candles would be lit and offered up for God knew what reason. The stall-owner looked at Taber, then held up the bag of potatoes. Taber smiled, shook his head and moved on. He had as little use for potatoes as he had for votive candles.

He stopped in front of a woman selling coca leaves. She sat huddled under a poncho; a baby hung in a shawl from her back like a growth. She looked up when Taber's shadow fell across her, then looked away at once: gringos did not buy the coca leaf. A boy of about twelve, barefooted and ragged, crept along the wall of the store outside which the woman sat; he stopped by her, then held out a grimy hand in which lay some coins. The woman looked at him, then scooped some of the pale green leaves into a horn of paper, dropped some grey lime into another horn and handed them to him. The boy at once dropped down on his haunches against the wall, took some of the leaves and began to chew them.

"What's he doing?"

Carmel McKenna had stepped out from between two stalls. She was dressed in slacks and a suède jacket and had a pair of sunglasses pushed back on her head like a glass tiara.

"Watch him."

The boy took the small wet ball of leaves from his mouth, added some of the powdered lime, then popped the ball back into his mouth. He sat back against the wall, turned his face up to the sun, closed his eyes and began to chew.

"It's cocaine, only here they chew it instead of sniffing it. He puts the lime in it as an alkaline, to bring out the taste." As they watched, the boy, still with his eyes closed, tilted his head to one side and spat. "He's an expert."

"What sort of expert?"

"The trick is to spit out the saliva without burning your lips from the lime. He's got it down to a fine art."

"But he only looks about ten or twelve!"

"They start up here at about seven. They don't do it for kicks. They do it as an escape from the bloody misery of their existence." He did not condone the habit of coca chewing, but he was abruptly angry with her. Damned outsiders . . . Then he remembered the outsider's standards he had tried to introduce over at the station. He smiled, his stern bony face suddenly made attractive. "I'm sorry."

"Why?"

"I was angry with you."

"I wouldn't have known. You look pretty sour all the time. You'd have a ghastly temper, wouldn't you?" He had noticed that she had all the adjectives they seemed to teach at expensive schools: *ghastly* was a class badge. But even as he thought it he smiled inwardly at himself: he still had a county grammar school mentality. They began to walk slowly up between the stalls, the Indians watching them with wary curiosity. "Why were you angry with me?"

"I don't know," he lied.

"You're a very difficult man, Mr Taber," she said, then let him off her hook. "Tell me more about why young kids like that boy take to cocaine so young."

"Well, for one thing, by chewing it they can go for days without food. That boy probably doesn't know what a square meal looks like."

"He had enough money to pay for the leaves and the lime."

"A few cents. That'll keep him going for two or three days. If he'd bought food with it, he'd have got enough for two or three mouthfuls."

"Do they become addicted to the drug?"

"What do you think?" he said, his voice irritable again. Christ, these outsiders lived in a cocoon; and this time he did not include himself with her as an outsider. "Look."

A youth of about twenty lay sprawled against a wall. Taber took Carmel's arm and moved her closer. The Indian's mouth gaped open, exposing green stumps of teeth against whitish gums. Black stains ran down from the corners of his mouth where the saliva had dribbled. His skin was yellow and there were deep purple rings round his eyes. Though he was unconscious, indeed looked dead, his pale lips occasionally quivered, like a silent appeal for help.

"He's a goner," said Taber. "He'll be dead in twelve months at the outside."

"You don't sound very upset," said Carmel, turning away, feeling suddenly cold: it was as if for the first time she had seen the skull of a living man, smelt the turned earth of his waiting grave.

"I've spent twelve years among people who die every day from malnutrition. I'm still upset by it, but I have to keep it to myself. That chap won't die from drug addiction, that'll only be the means. He'll die because he's never had enough to eat, because he was born to a miserable bloody existence that no human being, in to-day's world, should have to endure!"

"You're angry again," she said. "But this time I understand."

"I should hope to Christ you would," he said and did not apologise. "If you don't, after seeing that, there's no bloody hope for him and his people. Or for you."

They had come out of the market into a plaza. They walked beneath a colonnade above which hung farolas, the closed-in, carved wooden balconies from old Spain. Hidalgos of past centuries had walked here, secure in their own present, careless of the future; now their descendants, old men in stiff white collars and stiff black suits, walked with the same dignity but not the same confidence. The stores along the colonnade that had once only wooden shutters now had plate-glass windows; none of the stores had any customers, as if all stocks had been sold and the store owners had not thought it worth while re-ordering. Then Taber and Carmel passed a café crowded with criollo boys and girls of high school age; the place bulged with the high spirits that passed for optimism. Above the door was a carved profile of St Sebastian, chipped and smoothed by age: the patron saint of the town looked worn and dejected. Beneath the carving was an enamel sign advertising a soft drink.

"Inca Cola?" Carmel's eyebrows went up in amusement.

"The Incas never discovered the wheel, but they used clocks, guano fertiliser, they built aqueducts and bridges, they knew all about agricultural terracing and they knew how to make metal alloys. Why shouldn't they have invented Coca-Cola?"

"You're putting me on. *Inca* Cola." She shook her head and they walked on. "I'll bet there's some American influence there." He said nothing and she looked up at him. "Are you anti-American, Mr Taber?"

"I'm not anti-anyone till people make fools of themselves."

"Have we made fools of ourselves down here?"

"Sometimes. You still have to make your biggest mistake."

"What's that?"

"Turning your back on South America because it won't develop the way Washington thinks it should. Anti-Communist, capitalistic and with preference for only American investment."

"Do you think we will turn our back on it?"

"I hope not. There are some people in Washington who are at last beginning to realise that nationalism and Communism are not the same thing. There are a lot of nationalists on this continent, in this country, who have no more love for Communism than they have for your country. But unless they sing *God Bless America* and let American investment come in here with no strings attached, Washington wants nothing to do with them."

"Don't you think our State Department knows what to do?"

"Forgive the vulgarity, Miss McKenna, but your State Department, when it comes to South America, always reminds me of *The Perfumed Garden*. It has twenty-five positions on any given situation."

She laughed so heartily that two of the passing old men turned back to look at her. "I don't think that's vulgar."

"I didn't think you would. But I apologised, just in case."

She stopped laughing. "Why did you think I wouldn't think it was vulgar?"

"Listening to you the other day. You were flat out trying to prove how broad-minded you were."

"You're vulgarly rude, you know that?" She looked at him sideways, studying him hard for the first time; then she looked ahead again and nodded. "I *was* trying too hard. I always do that among strangers. You may not believe it, Mr Taber, but I'm basically a shy girl. The shy ones are always the ones who try too hard."

They passed out of the shade of the colonnade, feeling the warmth of the sun as soon as they stepped into it, crossed the road and were moving into the small garden square in the centre of the plaza when they heard the shots.

Taber at once put his arm about Carmel, pulling her to him and looking wildly around. The shots had been close, too close for comfort. The small pack of bootblacks at the intersection of the paths through the square suddenly scattered, diving into the shrubs like so many shrieking birds; a flock of birds exploded out of the bushes, whistling frantically, and swept away out of sight. Half a dozen women who had been sitting on the ground at the foot of the statue of Simon Bolivar in the centre of the square flung themselves flat, their faces pressed into the mosaic tiles of the path. A small child came running towards the group and its mother screamed at it to get down; the child fell down, skidding along on its face, and for one awful moment Taber thought it had been hit. Then as he pushed Carmel down on to the path he saw the child crawl forward and disappear into the spreadeagled cluster of women as into a pile of dark rocks. A bullet smacked into a seat right beside Taber and Carmel, hit the ironwork and went ricocheting off with that whine that was both frightening and fascinating. Another bullet chipped a piece off the Great Liberator; Taber, looking up, saw that the statue was pockmarked with bullet holes. There were more shots, several yells, then suddenly there was a dull boom.

Taber raised his head and looked across the square. People were lying flat everywhere, even the old men in their stiff black suits: dignity was no protection against indiscriminate bullets. Smoke was flowering out of the doors and windows of the bank on the corner of the plaza; a man staggered out of the front door, his hands to his face, and collapsed in a sitting position on the pavement. Two cars, engines roaring, were pulling away from in front of the bank. Suddenly one of them stalled, but the other, tyres screeching, swung round the square, heading for the main street that ran out of town. Three men fell out of the stalled car and came running across the square; the second car had shuddered to a stop and was waiting for them. One of the Indian women at the foot of the statue sat up, her back to the advancing bank robbers. One of the men ran right into her, plunging over her and falling headlong. His pistol shot out of his hand, slid across the tiled path towards Taber like a challenge. He moved his head up and the gun slid in under him, clunking against his breastbone.

The bank robber, a thickset man in a black hood, scrambled to his feet and hurled himself at Taber. The latter rolled aside, away from Carmel, automatically snatching at the gun as he did so. The man aimed a kick at Taber's head but missed as the Englishman continued rolling. Taber came up on one knee, the pistol raised; then he froze, the gun a heavy weight in the hand that could barely hold it. The other two bank robbers, both hooded, stood over him, their guns aimed directly at his head. He drew a deep breath, then tossed the gun at the feet of its owner. The man picked it up, growled something that was muffled by the hood; then the three men, in answer to the urgent hooting of the horn of the car waiting for them, went running across the square. As they ran one of the men snatched some leaflets from his pocket and hurled them into the air. A gust of wind caught the leaflets and some of them were still floating across the gardens as the running men jumped into the car and it went roaring off out of the plaza.

Taber stood up, crossed quickly to Carmel and helped her to her feet. She was struggling to get her breath, her pale face turning slightly blue. Taber pushed her down on to the nearby seat, took a tablet from a tin in his pocket and forced it between her lips. "Take this, it'll slow down your pulse. I'll try and get you some oxygen. There's a hotel over there – they'd have a cylinder – "

She clutched his arm, shook her head. "Don't – leave – me!"

He looked around. The old men were getting painfully and awkwardly to their feet, dusting themselves off and looking bewilderedly around as if searching for lost dignity; the Indian women were moving in a tight group across to join the growing crowd outside the bank. Three policemen, each blowing his whistle in a loud cheep of authority, came running from different directions; a truck, horn blowing, came lurching round the plaza, pulled up in front of the bank and disgorged a dozen soldiers. People were appearing from everywhere, but now, with the arrival of the soldiers, the small crowd outside the bank began to disintegrate. The group of Indian women suddenly about-turned and trotted back to sit once more at the foot of the statue of the Liberator. The old men stood in their own group across at the bank; an image sprang into Taber's mind of photos he had seen of delegates to international conferences in the thirties, formally dressed old men with tight worried faces who saw the coming of the end of their world. The high school students had come out of the café, chattering among themselves but, unlike teenagers Taber had seen elsewhere, minding their own business and making no attempt to move down towards the bank. People, criollos and Indians, lined the edges of the plaza or stayed stiffly where they were in the gardens; but no one made a move towards the bank now the soldiers had arrived. The clerk who had staggered out of the bank still sat on the pavement, swaying back and forth and holding his face; against the wall of the bank Taber saw for the first time the crumpled body of a policeman. A car, siren wailing, came into the plaza and juddered to a sharp stop behind the military truck. Three officers got out and hurried into the bank.

Taber helped Carmel to her feet, putting his arm round her. Something blew against his feet; it was one of the leaflets tossed away by the bank robbers. He picked it up, held it crushed in his hand as he began to help the still gasping Carmel across the square.

"My hotel's not far from here. They'll have an oxygen cylinder."

They walked slowly, she leaning on him like an old woman. People watched them curiously, but no one stepped forward to ask if they could help. Carmel was still fighting for her breath, but Taber, his arm round her, could feel the gasping slowly subsiding.

It was perhaps three hundred yards to Taber's hotel, but it took them almost ten minutes to reach it. It was a ten-year-old concrete building that looked uncomfortably out of place among its old stone, tile-roofed neighbours; even its name, the Dorchester, was a brash piece of bravado that had not quite come off: the two middle letters of the neon sign did not work. It was owned and run by a Bulgarian and his wife and was,

Pereira had assured Taber, absolutely the best hostelry in town.

Taber helped Carmel up the steps into the small lobby, sat her down on one of the bright yellow plastic-upholstered couches against the bright blue wall. The owner, a stout bald-headed man with gold-rimmed glasses and an air of being constantly harassed, came across from behind the desk with a small cylinder of oxygen.

"The altitude, senor? Or excitement – I heard the shots – ?"

"Both," said Taber, watching to see that Carmel did not gulp in too much of the oxygen. He took the face-piece away from her and handed the cylinder back to the owner. "That's enough. The senorita will be all right now. Will you get me a taxi?"

The hotel owner turned to call the Indian boy out from behind the desk, but stopped as the front door swung open and a police officer came in. The officer walked straight up to Taber and held out his hand.

"The leaflet, senor." He was a short, thin-faced mestizo in his late forties, a man drugged by addiction to authority; he quivered now as if he were high on it, his eyes wide as he glared at Taber. "Hand it over at once."

Taber looked down, saw that he still held crumpled in his hand the leaflet he had picked up in the plaza. He smoothed out the paper, held it up to read it. The officer made a grab at it, but Taber jerked it away. He was aware of the tension in the lobby, of the Indian boy half-crouched behind the desk and the owner holding the oxygen cylinder in front of him like a bomb he did not want; out of the corner of his eye he saw Carmel gasping no longer but now holding her breath, and beyond her he was aware of the owner's angular wife standing unmoving in the doorway to the office. But he was not going to allow him-self to be pushed around like some misbehaving tourist by this arrogant little policeman. He was here at the invitation of the government and the police had better get the message right at the start.

He read the leaflet: Death to the Jackboot! The People's Revolutionary Committee . . . There was more in the same strain; he had read it all before, in three or four other languages.

This one was in Spanish and Quechua; he wondered which language would get the greater response. He screwed up the leaflet and handed it to the officer.

"It is an offence against the law to have such literature."

"You flatter it calling it literature. I picked it up in the plaza. I was just helping to keep the city clean."

The police officer evidently did not appreciate irony. "You gave a gun to one of the terrorists."

"I gave him back his own gun. If I hadn't, his friends would have shot me."

Carmel had stood up, put her hand on Taber's arm. She did not understand the Spanish dialogue, but she had made her own position clear: she was backing up Taber. He felt grateful to her, suddenly warming to her, and he put his own hand on hers. They stood in front of the police officer like a couple about to be married.

"Who reported me?" Taber wondered which of the dozens of people in the plaza had tried to curry favour with the police; none of them would probably dare to inform on one of the locals, but there was no danger in putting the finger on an outsider.

"It is of no concern," said the officer; for the first time he looked unsure of himself. "Your name?"

Taber gave it. "I am already registered at your headquarters. I am an official guest of your government."

"The senorita?"

"Senorita McKenna. She is a guest of Senor Alejandro Ruiz Cordobes, staying in his house."

The officer's face twitched as if he had been stung; or as if the drug of authority had suddenly worn off. He stuffed the leaflet into a pocket of his tunic, saluted perfunctorily, then turned on his heel and without another word went out of the lobby. The hotel owner let out a loud sigh; it sounded as if he had pressed the valve on the cylinder he still held. He looked at Taber.

"The police chief himself, Captain Condoris. He has never been here before. Let us hope he does not come back."

"He won't," said Taber, wondering why the police chief

61

had not sent a junior officer after him. Or had Condoris thought he, Taber, had been an accomplice of the robbers and had had thoughts of making a spectacular arrest himself? He's made a fool of himself, Taber thought, and he's not going to like me from now on. "Get your boy to call a taxi, Senor Vazov."

When the taxi arrived Taber took Carmel out, put her in and closed the door. He leaned in the open window. "Go straight back to the Ruiz's. No sightseeing, at least not till to-morrow."

"Will things be all right again by to-morrow?"

"They'll be all right again in an hour or two. But it would be better if you didn't go out on your own again to-day, just in case there's some more shooting."

"Will there be more of that?"

"I don't know. Sometimes in these countries the soldiers or police shoot up a suspect's home just as a warning. They order everyone out of the house, then let fly. It's bad luck if someone gets in the way of a bullet."

She shuddered, lay back against the torn leatherette of the taxi's seat; stuffing stuck out beside her head like grey moss. "I think I'll be glad to leave here."

He felt a slight twinge of regret. "I'll be sorry to see you go."

She leant forward. "I haven't thanked you."

"What for?"

"For looking after me the way you did. You're not bad, Mr Taber." She looked at him and nodded approvingly, looking through the exterior of him as an intelligent woman would. "I've met much worse."

"That's the story of my life. Negative compliments." But he grinned, pleased by what she had said. In his turn he had met much worse than her, but he didn't tell her that. "I'll see you to-night. Ruiz has invited me to the welcome home reception for his son."

The taxi, an old fin-tailed Plymouth, drove off, its transmission grinding alarmingly. I hope she makes it, Taber thought; and chided himself for not thinking to call Pereira for the Land-Rover. He found himself wishing that no harm should come to Carmel McKenna.

As he turned to go back up into the hotel he saw the policeman, a young stupid-looking Indian, already taking up his watching post on the other side of the street. Christ Almighty, Taber thought, they're so afraid they have to suspect everyone.

2

Alejandro Ruiz moved through the slow surf of his guests like a dreadnought looking for a place to beach itself. He was accustomed to people coming to *him*, but this evening his wife had insisted that he must circulate.

"You make me sound like a red corpuscle," he had protested.

"Not red, my dear. You would have to be blue."

Their exchange of humour had the usual heaviness of domestic sarcasm, but this evening there had been no real sourness between them. Both of them were so pleased to have Francisco home again with them that their lack of patience with each other, and their occasional deep bitterness, had been put aside. Alejandro was happy to play host to his friends at this party in honour of Francisco, but he was not happy to be told to remain on his feet all evening like his own butler. Especially since there were some guests, not friends, for whom, in normal circumstances, he would never rise to his feet.

Carmel, looking about her as she stood in the big living-room, felt she could have been in Seville. She had spent a month there two years ago when she had thought she was falling in love with a film director who had proved to be in love with bull-fighters. It had been an unsatisfactory month and a further part of her education in men, but she had enjoyed the Seville social scene, though she would not have wanted to belong to it permanently. This was a smaller Seville and suggested a much older one. But that impression came only from the men; the women, rebelling in their own way, in fashion, looked as smart and modern as any she had seen in Europe. No see-through dresses or precipitously plunging necklines, but then aristocrats never went in for those attention-getters anyway. And these people, though they held no titles, looked upon themselves as aristocrats.

She had left off her own see-through blouses in favour of the only modest dress she owned, a black Givenchy that was her all-purpose model. She saw her brother looking approvingly at her and she moved to join him. "It's my papal audience dress."

"Did you get to see him?"

"No. Mother wanted me to go with her last year, but it seemed too hypocritical. I haven't been to Mass in, oh, I don't know how long."

"How about coming to-morrow morning? I'm saying early Mass at the cathedral."

"I'll see. What time?"

"Six o'clock."

"Oh my God, you're joking! If I'm ever up at six, it's only because I haven't been to bed the night before." Then she saw the disappointment, which he had tried to hide, in his face. She pressed his arm. "All right, darling. I'll try to be there. I've never heard you say Mass. I don't think Mother has forgiven me for that."

"I'm not the best of performers," he said, trying to get rid of the shadow of their mother. "Some fellers are real showmen. Don't expect a spectacular."

Then a woman, a year or two older than Carmel, came through the swirl of guests towards them. She was not strictly beautiful, except for her eyes which were dark and had extraordinarily long lashes, but there was something about her that held one's attention while more beautiful women in the room passed by. This one would never need a see-through blouse, thought Carmel. She was not sure what the other woman had: perhaps it was her air of serenity, but it was a serenity that suggested control rather than the passivity that some of the older women in the room had. Hidden in the woman was some passion, for love or truth or justice, for *something*. She would not take life for granted and that, too, set her apart from so many of the other women at the reception.

"Carmel, this is Dolores Schiller." McKenna's face had lit up as the woman had approached them. Carmel noticed it, but put it down to her brother's relief at being interrupted; she knew now that their mother was always going to be a difficult subject between them. "She is the mission's biggest supporter."

"What I give the mission is a pittance." Her voice was so soft that Carmel, in the hubbub of other voices, had to lean forward to hear her.

"I meant your moral support," said McKenna. "Everyone else here thinks I'm wasting my time or I'm just a nuisance."

"Are you a newcomer like me?" Carmel asked.

Dolores Schiller smiled. "One side of the family has been here as long as the Ruiz. But my grandfather interrupted the sequence – he was a German and a rather lowly one, I'm afraid. He was a socialist journalist, something the family did not discover till after he and my grandmother were married. They had eloped, which no one ever did in San Sebastian society, not in those days."

Then Taber, looking uncomfortable in a black tie and dinner jacket, loomed up beside them. His red hair had been slicked down with water when he arrived, but now it was once again beginning to rebel against its combing.

"You look absolutely elegant," said Carmel. "But where's your tweed cap?"

"If you think I look elegant, you're either astigmatic or you have no taste," said Taber with a grin. "When I approach Savile Row back home, they throw up the barricades. I'm on their black list."

McKenna introduced him to Dolores Schiller, who said, "I've heard about you, Senor Taber, from Hernando Ruiz. He admired your remark the other day, about the Indians' patient tolerance of us criollos."

"I'm surprised he did," said Taber. "It was an unintentional insult to all the Ruiz. Fact is, I'm surprised I was asked to come this evening."

"The Ruiz have a certain tolerance of their own. Mainly because of Senora Romola."

An elderly couple drifted by, the man tall and straight-backed, white-haired and with a military moustache, the woman with blue-rinsed grey hair and an expression of such superiority that Carmel wondered if she spoke even to her husband. They bowed to Dolores Schiller, who put out a hand to them.

c

"Doctor and Senora Partridge – " She introduced them to the McKennas and Taber.

"Howdyoudo." It was all one word the way Dr Partridge said it. "Absolutely splendid party, what? Lots of dashed pretty gels. Always make for a jolly show."

I'm hearing things, thought Carmel.

"My husband is always looking at the gels," said Senora Partridge. "Still thinks he is a medical student, you know. Silly old dear, aren't you, Bunty?"

They can't be real, Carmel thought. These were people right out of those old British movies of the nineteen thirties that one saw on the Late Late Late Show; the Partridges belonged with Clive Brook and Constance Collier and the country cottage in the Home Counties. "Have you been out here long?" she said.

The Partridges looked offended. "We belong here. Well, not *here*, actually. We came up here – when was it, old gel?"

"Never remember years," said Senora Partridge, and laughed a horse's laugh straight out of the pages of *The Tatler: Dr and Senora Partridge enjoy a gay joke at the Hunt Ball*. "Never pays at my age, you know."

They moved on, vice-regally, and Carmel, slightly stupefied, looked at her brother. "Are they for real?"

"They're Anglo-Brazilians. They've never seen England, except for a three weeks' honeymoon God knows how long ago. They still talk about the Royal garden party they went to and how King George the Fifth shook hands with the doc."

"They're more British than the British!"

"You find them all over South America," said Taber. "Still whistling *Land of Hope and Glory* in the bathroom, celebrating the Queen's Birthday, cursing Harold Wilson and the Socialists – you can't laugh at them, you have to feel sorry for them. They are born here, they live here all their lives, yet they can never bring themselves to call it home. Home is where their father or their grandfather came from."

"Oh, my God, how sad!"

McKenna said to Taber, "I want to thank you for getting Carmel out of that trouble this morning. You're making a habit of helping out the McKennas."

"What trouble was that?" said Dolores Schiller. "When the guerrillas blew up the bank?"

"We were just across the plaza," said Carmel; then glanced at Taber, looking at him with a new eye to-night. "Did your friend the police chief come back?"

"He's coming back now," said Taber. "Who's the bloke with him, Terry?"

McKenna had only time to say, "Karl Obermaier. He's an ex-Nazi. Or maybe not so ex."

Condoris, the police chief, and the short muscular man with him paused in front of Dolores Schiller, both bowing and clicking their heels. This is an unreal, three-o'clock-in-the-morning night, Carmel thought: where is Conrad Veidt?

"Senorita Schiller, how was the ski-ing?" Condoris asked in Spanish, ignoring the three foreigners.

"I go ski-ing in Chile every winter," Dolores explained to Carmel; then still speaking English she introduced Carmel and Taber to the German. Her snub of the police chief was as blunt as a blow to his long sharp nose. But he did not flush or blink an eye; he was obviously accustomed to being snubbed in company like this. But he must know how necessary he is, to put up with it, thought Taber; and looked with sharper interest at Condoris. The man knew where the bodies were buried; or, worse still, knew where they were *going* to be buried.

Obermaier, having bowed and clicked his heels, now stood with his hands behind his back. He had a strong emperor's face, the sort one saw on Roman coins; Taber wondered what empire he ran here. Obermaier was not the first ex-Nazi he had met in South America, but he was certainly the cockiest. He looked Taber up and down like a Storm Trooper colonel inspecting a new recruit.

"Captain Condoris tells me you were almost shot by the terrorists, Senor Taber."

Well, I'm glad he didn't call me Herr Taber. "I think it was a threat more than a real intention."

"Their intentions are real enough, Senor Taber. We have to stamp them out – ruthlessly."

Sieg Heil, Sieg Heil. Hold on, mate, this isn't Europe in the thirties. "*We*, Herr Obermaier?"

67

"It is the task of everyone who lives here in Bolivia. Or anywhere in South America."

"Does Herr Bormann believe that, too?"

There was just a faint stiffening of Obermaier's face. "Herr Bormann?"

"Martin Bormann. I understand he lives in Paraguay, on the Bolivian border."

"You should not believe the propaganda, Senor Taber. Martin Bormann died in Berlin at the end of the war."

Dolores Schiller broke up the tension. Her voice faintly mocking, she said, "Senor Obermaier escaped from Berlin just at that time. He came here and helped train our army up till the revolution occurred. You were a panzer commander, weren't you, Karl? He follows in an old tradition – Germans have always been popular here in Bolivia. Except Socialist ones, of course," she said with a tiny smile. "Captain Ernst Roehm trained our army before he went back to Germany and led the S S for Hitler."

"A panzer commander?" said Carmel, thinking the baiting of Obermaier had gone too far. After what she had seen this morning she had become afraid of violence, knowing she would no longer be surprised where it broke out.

Obermaier waved a deprecating hand, but even that gesture looked cocky. He's cocky, not arrogant, thought Taber. There's a difference; and saw the difference when he looked around the room at Alejandro Ruiz and some of the older criollos. "What do you do now, Herr Obermaier?"

"I run the brewery," said Obermaier. "I come from Munich. Naturally, I understand beer."

"Naturally," said Taber; but Obermaier was another man who did not understand irony.

"Will the terrorists blow up the brewery?" Carmel asked.

"That could be one of their prime targets," said Taber.

"Why should it be that, Senor Taber?" demanded Obermaier.

Taber shrugged, looking innocent. "I don't know. But one can never be sure what terrorists will blow up. I have had more experience of them than you, Herr Obermaier."

He knew he had said the wrong thing as soon as he saw Captain Condoris look hard at him; he had thought the police chief did not understand English. "What experience have you had, Senor Taber?"

"Only indirectly, Captain. I have worked in countries where some of my projects have been blown up."

"What countries were they?"

"I never speak ill of old clients," said Taber.

McKenna got him off the hook. "The raid on the bank this morning was pretty stupid. I understand they didn't even try to heist any of the money. Is that right, Captain?"

"Heist?" Condoris's English was limited.

"Did they attempt to steal any money?"

"No."

"So they killed a policeman and blinded the bank clerk. What good will that do their cause?"

"No good at all. We should have more such raids." Alejandro Ruiz, tired of circulating, had seated himself in one of the monk's chairs beside the group. "We should throw open the banks, let them overdraw on their account of what goodwill they have with the campesinos. The dead policeman's father is a campesino. The clerk was a mestizo, with a dozen cousins who are campesinos." He read the expression on Taber's face. "You are surprised at my knowledge, Senor Taber? I own the bank. To-day's raid was a demonstration against me personally."

Carmel, still unsettled by this casual talk of terrorism, said, "Aren't you afraid they might try to raid your house to-night? I mean – " She gestured at the guests, every one a possible target for the revolutionaries.

"Why do you think the chief of police is here? How many men do you have out in the plaza, Captain?"

"Fifty," said Condoris. "Another thirty in the field behind your house. You are safe, Senor Ruiz."

Ruiz nodded, taking his impregnability for granted. "We shall soon be rid of them. They will never succeed, because they are mostly outsiders and the campesinos will have nothing to do with them when it comes to full revolution."

"What if they raise a local leader, one of us?" Dolores Schiller's voice had risen a little: no one had to lean forward to hear her now.

"Where will they get him?"

Dolores shook her head. "You are the only one who is so confident. The rest of us – " The other guests drifted past, their small talk showing the smallness of their circle: they had no one to talk about but themselves. They had already exhausted the main topic of the evening, the bombing of the bank: it dignified one's enemies to discuss them too long and too openly. But they were uneasy, moving restlessly throughout the house, as if to stand too long in the one place would only invite attack. "Have you asked the young men what they think? Francisco and Hernando?"

On cue Francisco came up, nodded coolly to Taber, then put his hand possessively under Carmel's arm. "My friends want to meet you. Everyone on this side of the room looks so serious – "

Carmel went with Francisco, and Alejandro Ruiz laughed. "There is your answer, Dolores. The younger men want only to enjoy themselves."

"To-night, perhaps," said Dolores. "But to-morrow – ?"

No one was prepared to discuss to-morrow. Obermaier and Condoris moved off, bowing stiffly like twin automatons as they passed people; Taber wondered if Condoris had ever been a cadet under Obermaier. McKenna took Dolores's arm. "I think I better go and pay my respects to the Bishop. He's over there with his Jesuit buddy from the university. Maybe they can tell us about to-morrow."

"Not my brother," said Alejandro Ruiz. "He leaves to-morrow to God."

"And the Jesuit?"

"He will prefer to discuss the past. He's been fed on logic and logic is safer when discussing history. You'll never find a crystal ball in a Jesuit's cell."

Taber and Ruiz were left alone. They looked at each other, Taber warily, Ruiz with the confident stare of a man master in his own house. "Have you improved anything since we last met, Senor Taber?"

"Nothing," Taber admitted. "But I've only just learned you are chairman of the local Agrarian Reform Council. Perhaps you can help me improve things."

"How?"

"I have a shipment held up by the local Customs chief. I think he is waiting for some graft."

"Did he ask you for money?"

"You know he wouldn't do that. But I know the system as well as you, Senor Ruiz."

"I pay graft to no one."

I'm suffering from foot-in-mouth disease, Taber thought. "I did not mean to suggest that you did. But neither do I – pay graft, I mean. That's why I have several thousand dollars' worth of stuff stuck down at the railway yards and can't get at it."

Ruiz had seen his wife, across the room, nod peremptorily at him to begin recirculating. He got wearily to his feet, sourly aware that there were times when he was not master in his own house. "I shall see what can be done, Senor Taber. But I can promise nothing. There is room for improvement in our Customs."

Taber had a sudden intuition: Ruiz was putting him on trial. Everything he was going to do for FAO here in San Sebastian province would eventually have to go through the Agrarian Reform Council. Nothing would come out of Customs till he had proved himself. And proving himself meant proving that he was not a radical, that he would not advocate too much change.

"Excuse me," said Ruiz. "I have my other guests to attend to."

Taber was left alone. He looked across the room and saw Carmel surrounded by half a dozen young men and girls; she smiled at him, then she was blotted out by Francisco, who moved deliberately in front of her. Taber looked around, saw the Partridges bearing down on him, and escaped into a side room. Obermaier and Condoris were there, heads close together; they looked up as he came into the room, then turned away. He moved on, looking for a place to sit, to put up his feet and be alone. He might even try getting slightly drunk on Obermaier's beer, if he could find any.

He stopped one of the servants. "Could you get me two – no, four bottles of beer? Brewery beer, not chicha." He wanted none of the Indians' maize beer. "I'll be in this room here."

It was not so much a room as an alcove off the long hall. He sat down in another monk's chair, thinking, Christ, isn't there a comfortable chair anywhere in this house? Did the bloody Spaniards believe in making themselves uncomfortable when they sat, as a penance for all their other excesses? He felt he was being watched and he looked up into a pair of gimlet eyes on the wall: a Ruiz glared at him from the seventeenth century. Get stuffed, Alejandro or Francisco or Hernando or whatever-the-hell-your-name-was. None of you, neither past Ruiz nor present Ruiz, is going to stop me doing my job here. I may never feel at home in your house, I will never be part of history; but none of that is going to stop me from doing my job. I'm here to improve things, to *change* things, and I'm going to bloody well do my best to see that it happens. So put that in your arquebus and see if you can fire it.

He heard voices coming down the hall and he sat farther back in the chair, hoping he would not be seen. McKenna and Dolores Schiller went by, heads close together, talking in low voices. They had passed on out of sight before Taber realised how close together they had been. He could not remember ever having seen a priest and a young attractive woman walking hand in hand like lovers.

3

Carmel heard the door of her bedroom open quietly, then close again. She sat up in bed, at once feeling the cold air that came in through the open window. Francisco, in pyjamas and thick dressing-gown, crossed to the window and closed it. Then he came and stood by the side of the bed.

"I haven't come to your room before. I know how the altitude bothers one at first."

"It is still bothering me, Pancho. Too much for any of *that*."

"Lie down or you will catch cold." He looked around the room, dimly lit by the moonlight filtering through the curtained window. He found the large convector heater and plugged it in. "Father really should have the house centrally heated."

Carmel lay back in the wide canopied bed. Francisco came back, took off his dressing-gown and got into bed with her. He reached for her breast, but she stopped his hand, holding it against her rib cage. She was wearing wool pyjamas, something she had not worn since she had been a child; it was remarkable how virtuous and safe wool made you feel. She would have to recommend it to the Wool Secretariat or whatever it was, as another selling point. "I said no."

"You were gay enough to-night at the party. No sign of soroche."

She knew that was the name for altitude sickness; she had a bottle of soroche pills on the table beside the bed. "It was the party that brought it on. Maybe I was too gay."

He rolled away from her, lay flat on his back. "It is not because of Taber, is it?"

She laughed, genuinely amused. "You're crazy, Pancho. My God, I haven't even thought of him that way – "

"He's a man." He rolled back towards her, close to her, proving he was a man, too.

"So's your uncle the Bishop. So were fifty per cent of the guests to-night. I don't mentally fall into bed with every man I meet, Pancho. You better watch your manners or you're likely to get kicked where the stallion got the knife. Cojones, isn't that what they're called in Spanish?"

"I do not like vulgar women."

"Said he, trying to put his hand between her legs. Pancho, I'm not going to let you make love to me – "

"You have not stopped me before. Not even our first night."

"That was Paris. There was no soroche there." Nor love, either; only the making of love.

"Most people are over soroche in a day or two. You have been here four days."

"Maybe to-day set me back. Most people don't have bullets zipping close to them when they first arrive. I could have been killed, Pancho," she said with exaggeration, and felt a sick thrill at the thought: she would have died like her father, violently.

73

Then she added maliciously, "I might have been, if it hadn't been for Mr Taber."

"You were not in danger."

"How do you know?"

"The guerrillas do not kill innocent bystanders."

"They killed an innocent policeman."

"One expects that. It's the risk of being a policeman."

She sat up in bed, suddenly warm with indignation. "You don't care a damn about that poor man!"

"Carissima – "

"Don't Carissima me! My God, you don't put any value on a human life if it's that of an Indian – "

"I didn't come to your room to discuss moral issues," he said stiffly; and despite her indignation she almost laughed. He got out of bed and put on his dressing-gown, tying the cord with the deliberateness of a comic opera general putting on his military gun belt. "I do value human life, that of Indians as well as my own. But would even a social worker discuss such things in bed with the woman he loves?"

Don't be so pompous, Pancho. But she said gently, because she had never liked hurting her lovers, "You don't love me, darling."

"Do you know what love is?"

Men can be cruel at three o'clock in the morning, she thought: that is when they reveal their true selves. And she had met so many three-o'clock-in-the-morning men. "Maybe not. But I'm a student of it. And it's a much harder subject than history." She lay back in bed, pulling the old-fashioned quilted covers up to her chin. "Good night, Pancho. Some other time."

He stood rigid for a moment, then he turned abruptly and went out of the room, closing the door quietly behind him. She understood why he did not slam the door, as a North American man might have: he had to protect his machismo, he could not let the others in the house know that she had sent him packing. Poor Pancho, she thought; then cursed him for leaving the window shut and the heater on. She got out of bed, unplugged the heater and opened the window. She stood at the window for a moment looking up at the wall of the bowl in which the city lay. The moon was full and bright in a cloudless sky; it rested on the rim of the bowl like an open silver lid. Below it one side of the bowl glittered as if molten metal had been spilt into it; it was a moment or two before she realised that it was moonlight reflected from the corrugated-tin roofs of the shacks on the terraces round the bowl. The almost vertical slums, like a skyscraper of poverty laid against the steep slope, looked beautiful in this light; but she had seen them in daylight when she had been driven down through them from the airport. The Indians who lived in those shacks would never see their homes from this viewpoint.

She shivered and hurried back to bed. Curled in a ball, her hands between her knees, the way she had lain ever since she was a small child, she stared out the window, having pulled the curtains back so that she could see the silver flood creep slowly down the bowl. She felt the loneliness creeping back on her at the same steady rate, as if the loneliness and the moonlight were related. They were, of course; or anyway, loneliness and night. She rarely felt lonely in the daytime, except when she had been to bed with some man in the afternoon and he had got up and left her while there were still some hours of daylight left. Then dusk, the death of day, became even lonelier than the night. But generally the days had not been too bad, nor many of the nights. At least not till recently.

She had been lonely as a child, but she had been in her teens before she had properly recognised the symptoms. There had always been plenty of other children to ask her to their parties and to come to hers; she had been at a party the day her father had dived into San Diego harbour in his plane. That was the day she had at last recognised loneliness for what it was. Her mother had called for her and the two of them had ridden home in the big black limousine, she weeping, her mother praying silently, and Oscar, the chauffeur, sitting up front and watching them, his yellow eyeballs reflected in the driving mirror. She felt the loss of her father, but that had not in itself caused the sense of loneliness.

That had come when she had been alone in her room and had realised she had no one in whom she could confide the extent of her loss. Her mother would not listen to her, she knew; that afternoon in the car Nell McKenna had prayed for herself and her children, not for the departed soul of Patrick McKenna; so long as hell existed, it could have him. Carmel had not been able to talk to her brother; he had been away at his last year at school and had only come home for the funeral two days after she had needed him. She had lain there on the bed in exactly the same position as now, staring out the window at the Santa Monica hills vaporising into the grey-brown smog, and thought of all the girls she knew, none of whom had ever exchanged a locked door, cross-your-heart-you-won't-tell secret with her. She had exchanged presents and birthday and Christmas cards; but never confidences. And realised then that it had been all her own fault. She had never given anything of herself away to anyone. Not since her father had closed the door on her when she was four years old and gone off to live his own life.

That was all so long ago. She had lived her own life since then: on her own terms, though she would never confess that to Terry. But the loneliness had only grown bigger and more painful. And she had come to ask herself: had her father been full of unbearable loneliness when he had slammed his plane into the water? But Patrick McKenna had never been a man for writing notes, especially suicide ones. He had died incommunicado, as it were, leaving his wife and children four million dollars and not a word of farewell.

When I go, she had thought last month in Paris when the loneliness had become as agonising as cancer in its terminal stages, I want someone to say farewell to. One should not leave the world without saying good-bye; you should always leave an echo or what had been the point of living? She could not say farewell to her mother; she could barely bring herself to say hello; there would be no echo there. Then she had met Pancho and he had said, "I come from San Sebastian in Bolivia," and from out of the past had come an echo she had forgotten.

"I'm your brother, and brothers are supposed to help. That's the only reason *for* them, isn't it?"

She could not remember the occasion or the reason; all she could remember was that Terry, twelve or thirteen then, had said the words. And so she had come to San Sebastian in

Bolivia, not to have Pancho make love to her, but to find a brother whom she could say farewell to.

"Do you know what love is?" Pancho had asked her.

Yes, she said as she fell asleep, yes, yes, yes; but the definition escaped her in her dreams.

Chapter 3

I

McKenna woke with an erection. He lay in bed debating whether to douse it with prayer or cold water; but less than a minute after getting out of bed the freezing morning air had reduced him to flaccid modesty again. He dressed quickly, knelt down and hurriedly said his prayers; he was running late for Mass. "And, Father, keep me from such thoughts as I dreamed last night . . ."

When Alejandro Ruiz had learned that his brother had invited McKenna to say first Mass at the cathedral, he had sent a message that McKenna was to stay overnight at the Ruiz house instead of returning to the mission after the party. McKenna had been thankful for the suggestion; he had not relished the idea of the twelve-mile drive in from the lake at five o'clock in the morning. At that time the campesinos were bringing in their trucks to the market, hurtling along the narrow roads without brakes or lights; the drivers themselves would be half-asleep and each journey completed safely was a miracle. McKenna was not a cowardly man, but he believed in percentages; sooner or later one of those trucks would wipe his Jeep right off the road if he kept thumbing his nose at the odds. If he was going to be a martyr, die in the cause of the Faith, he wanted to go out with more style than that.

He went quietly downstairs, carrying his small suitcase. That had been another present from his mother, an expensive Mark Cross piece of leather goods that his mother had brought back from New York, where she had gone to attend the funeral of Cardinal Spellman, a prelate whom she had never met but who she thought should have been Pope: she believed it inevitable and right that an American must one day be Pope. McKenna had done his best to scuff up the suitcase before arriving in Bolivia, but he had been very conscious of the sardonic glances cast at the suitcase by the priests at the mission up in La Paz where he had stayed for his first week.

The butler, unrecognisable in a black cardigan, a cast-off of his master's that hung on his thin frame like a poncho, was already up. He let McKenna out the front door, then crossed the courtyard to open the big gates. McKenna drove the Jeep out, then pulled up sharply as he saw someone come out the front door and run across the courtyard after him. It was Carmel, dressed in slacks and a mink coat. Oh God, he thought, hasn't our family ever heard of sackcloth?

"I've decided to come to Mass. Okay?"

"Of course," he said, and felt a sudden warmth that threw off the chill of the morning. "It'll make it a personal Mass for me."

"I'm not being reconverted," she said defensively. "This is more a – a social call. I'm just visiting."

"Six o'clock in the morning – my favourite time for social visiting." He took the Jeep round the small plaza. Two police-men bestirred themselves from a seat in the middle of the plaza, stood up to show they were alert for the advent of any terrorists; but they were already back on the seat before McKenna had taken the Jeep up the side street that led out of the plaza. "Carmie, let's get one thing straight from the start. I'm not going to do any preaching. You know what the Church is all about. If you want to come back to it and you want some advice, I'll be glad to help. But I'm not going to be a missionary to my own family."

"Thanks. Carmie – you haven't called me that since we were kids."

"It slipped out."

"I didn't mind – I mean between ourselves." She snuggled down into the mink coat. "But I wouldn't want the others calling me Carmie. What do you call Dolores Schiller when you're alone with her?"

His foot jerked on the accelerator. "What do you mean?"

She laughed. "Don't be upset, darling. I'm not accusing you of breaking your celibacy vows or anything. But you are pretty friendly with her, aren't you?"

He was glad it was not a twelve-mile drive to the cathedral.

"I guess so. But only because we're interested in the same things." He drove into the alley beside the cathedral, got out and lifted out his suitcase. "She believes in a better deal for the campesinos. She would like to do social work amongst them. But society here – her crowd, the ones you met last night – they would never allow it."

"How could they stop her?" Carmel got out of the Jeep, came round to join him. She noticed he had not attempted to help her out of the vehicle and wondered if the lack of gallantry was because he was a priest or because he was her brother. Would he have helped Dolores out?

"They'd do it with the greatest of ease. The police could forbid her to visit those shacks up there on the slopes." Carmel looked up towards the rim of the bowl, saw the hovels now in their undisguised ugliness in the grey morning light. "They'd tell her it was for her own safety. She could also find all her money frozen in the bank – while they checked on some book-keeping errors, they'd say – "

"You're exaggerating!"

"Nothing in this country is exaggerated." He led her in through a side door of the cathedral, the cold gloom at once reducing them both in size and personality. Cathedrals had always had this effect on Carmel, as if the architects, from an omnipotence of their own, were determined to prove to her her insignificance. "It's what beats all of us when we first come in here from outside."

"How long does it take to get used to it?"

"Ask me in another twenty years. That's what one of our priests up in La Paz told me when I first arrived here."

"How long had he been here?"

"Thirty years."

He left her and went into the vestry to change. As he put on his vestments he found himself trembling; Carmel's mention of Dolores had unnerved him. *I'm not accusing you of breaking your celibacy vows* . . . Yet in his dream last night that was exactly what he had done. It had not been Dolores who had been in his bed, but a succubus who had had her form and face, a demon woman whom he had hated at the same time as he had loved her.

An Indian boy who was to serve as altar boy came in, sniffling against the cold. He mumbled good morning to McKenna, slipped into his own modest vestments and went out on to the main altar to switch on the lights. McKenna, dressed and ready, stood at the door of the vestry and looked out into the body of the cathedral.

It took him a minute or two to find Carmel. She was in a pew halfway back, sitting in the shadow of one of the big stone pillars; there were no criollos, there never were at this first Mass, but there were about a hundred Indians. Some of them were coming up the side aisles, bringing with them their family crucifixes to be blessed; to-day, he realised, was a feast day, another of those minor holy days that crowded the Latin-American calendar and which he could never remember. A family of six came up one of the aisles, a middle-aged couple, a girl of about sixteen, two younger children and a burly young man of about twenty who carried the largest family crucifix McKenna had ever seen. The young Indian held it in front of him, the foot of the cross socketed into a leather pouch at the end of a long strap slung round his neck: he reminded McKenna of flag-bearers he had seen in Legion marches back home. The family came up to the altar rail and the assistant priest on duty for the morning, a mestizo with a look of sour superiority, an ecclesiastical civil servant who knew there would be no more promotion, opened the altar gates and directed the young man to take the crucifix across and leave it with the dozen or more that stood against a side wall. The young man carefully set the wooden cross against the wall and modestly rearranged the red velvet cloth, edged with gold lace, that wrapped the Christ's loins. The wooden figure of Christ, mocking the red velvet, was disgustingly gruesome, covered from head to foot in carved and painted sores and lacerations. But the young man thought it beautiful; the worse the suffering, the more the sublimation. These are the ones who will always demand a market for hair-shirts, McKenna thought; but could not bring himself to condemn the young man and his family. Whatever you wore along the way, hair-shirts or mink, if you were going to make it at all, you would arrive naked.

The mother of the family knelt down at the altar rail and held up a small personal crucifix. The mestizo priest, making no attempt to hide his boredom, gestured a contemptuous blessing above it. You sonofabitch, McKenna thought, give them credit for *believing*. What they have may not be pure Christianity, the criollos' Christianity, but their faith is stronger. The mother continued to kneel, staring at the crucifix still held up in front of her, her face wide open but blank as if she were in some sort of trance; then suddenly a spasm gripped her, some tremendous agony shot through her, and a babble of prayer burst out of her in Quechua. She brought the crucifix down hard against her mouth, so hard that McKenna was sure she must have split her lips; she held it there, still babbling prayers, her face alight now with a passion that made McKenna ashamed for the lukewarmness of his own faith. He tried to remain indifferent to such sublimation, feeling that it verged on hysteria, but each time he saw such expressions on the faces of the Indians he was, despite himself, overcome with humility.

Then the father of the family led his wife away and it was time to begin Mass. McKenna went out on to the altar. He was not a perfunctory Mass sayer, he had never believed in throwing away lines, like a veteran repertory actor, as one moved through the various parts of the service; but as always when he said Mass in a strange church he was disturbed by his surroundings. He had said Mass twice before here at the cathedral and he had felt ill at ease each time.

The huge altar, vulgar with gold and its trimmings of small electric globes, towered above him, a monument to an amalgam religion that it had taken him some time to accept. This was a Catholic cathedral built of the stones from an Inca temple; ghosts of ancestors who had worshipped at the Temple of the Sun lingered in the round skulls of the campesinos crouched in the cold hard pews. Mysteries lurked in the shadows beyond the flickering candles set in iron stands round the statues of the saints in the side aisles; in a dimly lit alcove a stone figure lay behind bars, the Madonna or perhaps the Coya, the Inca Queen. The light from the candles trembled on treasure, gold statues, silver ornaments, crucifixes studded with gems: Catholicism and paganism had met in their one mutuality, a love of vulgar flamboyance. Does God Himself have taste?

McKenna wondered; and lifted high the golden, ruby-encrusted chalice that mocked the simple Host it contained. But this, he knew, was what the Indians wanted. Their own religion had been taken away from them, wrenched out of them in torture, but so long as the opulence of their heritage, the dazzle of gold and silver and gems, the exalting escapism, was not taken away from them they would accept this amalgam in its place.

Bells rang in the towers of the cathedral, the sound coming down to boom through the vaulted roof, the cracked bell rumbling like thunder. Birds were disturbed from their nests and flew like dark lost souls through the limbo gloom, but only Carmel, the stranger, looked up at them. The sound of the bells died away and was replaced by a muffled murmuring. Carmel, puzzled, looked at the Indians in front of her. She saw the women reach back, swing round the shawls on their shoulders, each take out a baby; blouses were opened, plump brown breasts were exposed and the babies, their whimpering ceasing, fastened their hungry mouths to the nipples. My God, Carmel thought, how I'd love to see this in the Church of the Good Shepherd in Beverly Hills! The mothers, still suckling their children, continued with their prayers.

Then Mass was over. McKenna gave the final blessing, the Indians picked up their bundles and their children, collected their crucifixes and hurried out with their shuffling run to grab their places in the market square. Carmel waited till they had all gone, then went out the side door and waited in the Jeep for her brother.

McKenna came out, got in beside her. "Well?"

"Well what? Was I impressed? Yes, I think so. I found those Indians more, I don't know, *convincing*, I guess, than Mother's pasteurised piety. But if you're asking me if I'm now back in the Church, the answer is no. Disappointed?"

"A bit." He started up the motor. "I'll drive you back to the Ruiz's."

"I'd like to come out and see your mission. But drive me back to the Ruiz's first, so's I can tell them."

"If you come up to my place, could you leave the mink behind? The campesinos wouldn't know what mink is, but they'd know it wasn't alpaca or llama wool."

"Don't they wear vicuna up here?"

"Not any longer. Not when they know they can get such a price for it from suckers like you."

She smiled. "All right, darling. I'll leave the mink behind and try and look like a missionary's sister should. I have a nice little number in sackcloth by Givenchy."

But when she came out of the Ruiz house to rejoin him she was wearing a turtleneck sweater and a suède jacket above her slacks. She still looked too smart, too expensive, he thought; but he said nothing, just glad to have her coming up to the mission with him. If she stayed in San Sebastian long enough, maybe Dolores would come up with her.

The sun was up as they climbed up out of the bowl of the city. There was no wind this morning and in the clear silver light the altiplano lost some of its bleakness. In the distance the snow-topped mountains sketched a jagged white horizon along the bottom of the brilliantly blue sky; they were peaks that would always deny man; no matter how many times they were climbed they would never show the marks of their conquerors. Not like the Indians, McKenna thought.

Carmel gasped at the vastness of it all and McKenna felt that warm, almost juvenile glow that comes to someone who feels he can accept the extraordinary with a familiar shrug. "You get used to it," he said, but it was a lie. He would never get used to it: the day he did, he might as well pack up and go home. For the country itself held him as much as the people.

Carmel had chattered all the way through the drive till they passed through Altea; the desolate look of the village suddenly sobered her and she sat in silence as they drove up past the lake to the mission. She got out of the Jeep, waited till he unlocked the door of the main hut and followed him into it.

Her tour of inspection took only a minute or two. Then she said, "God, Terry, how do you live in conditions like these?"

He led her across to the kitchen hut and started making coffee. "I live better than about eighty per cent of the people on this continent, maybe better than ninety per cent here in Bolivia. At least I have the luxury of knowing I can opt out. I saw the look on your face when we came through Altea. Those people

down there have no options at all. That is their life, from birth
to death."

He took the coffee pot off the fire, took down two tin mugs
from the rough kitchen dresser, shook them upside down.

"What did you do that for?"

"Make sure there were no insects in them. There's a nasty
little bug, about half an inch long, that comes out of the 'dobe.
Called a bloodsucker. If it bites you, it gives you a blood
infection that's just about incurable." He grinned. "But it's
harmless in hot coffee."

She made a face and followed him back to the main hut. He
crossed to the small altar in the living-room, pulled back the
embroidered draping that covered the base and exposed a
cupboard. He opened it: the cupboard was full of tinned food.
"You see? I'm not entirely on the breadline. I have to keep it in
here, otherwise my houseboy would swipe it. But he won't
touch anything that's on the altar – he's a good Catholic." He
winked, came back to the table with a tin of English biscuits.
"Mom sent them. Every month she has one of the food stores
in Beverly Hills send me down a food parcel. Sometimes they
disappear – I'm watching one of the Customs guys who seems
to be putting on weight – but mostly they get through. I have
a twinge of conscience each time they arrive, but when I console
myself that the Indians probably wouldn't like rollmops – "

"Mother doesn't send you *those!*"

"She does, or there's a Jewish clerk in the store who's putting
one over on Rome." He grinned, talking to her easily now; the
barriers were almost down. "There are four jars of maraschino
cherries there under the altar. I don't know what I'm supposed
to do with them, unless she thinks I should have them in a
sacramental cocktail. I tell you, we have a crazy mother."

"Crazy," she said. "And sad."

"Yes," he said, and stopped smiling. They looked at each
other, growing closer together in the realisation that they had
the same feeling towards their mother: a pitying love mixed
with angry irritation. A mother deserves more, he thought; and
wondered why he still felt love for his father, the man who had
broken up the family. Impulsively he said, "Next time I'm home,
be there in Los Angeles, will you?"

Just as impulsively she said, "Of course. When are you going home?"

He slumped back in his chair, grinned wryly. "Five years at least. This isn't like Vietnam, regular R and R for the troops. Some of the priests and nuns down here never go home."

"Don't let that happen to you. I mean, never go home."

"I won't," he said, and was grateful for her concern for him. But then he was disposed to say, "Still, I never really think of Beverly Hills as home. I was at prep school by the time we moved there. The memories that stick with me were when we lived at La Jolla. I never understood why Mom left there."

"It was too close to San Diego," Carmel said, and smiled at him, feeling so much older and more worldly than he. "How understanding are you of women in the confessional?"

"More than you'd believe," he defended himself, but did not give any reasons. Then he said cautiously, "What I really think of as home is where I was born."

She wrinkled her brows. "In San Sebastian? In a hospital?"

"I wasn't born in a hospital. Mom had me in the house up at our mine. She wouldn't trust the local hospital in those days and the idea was for her to go home to the States to have me. But she kept putting it off, not wanting to leave Dad – that was when she still loved him – and then there was an early winter that year and they were snowed in. I was delivered by a couple of Indian women. Evidently I didn't want to be born and Mom had a hard time with me. It was touch-and-go for a while. According to Dad, the Indian women saved Mom's and my life."

"Who told you all this?"

"Dad. Mom never mentioned it."

"Then that's why I've never heard of it." She finished her coffee and put down the tin mug. She had not liked drinking from the mug and she had found the coffee bitter, but she was careful not to be openly critical of her brother's hospitality. It was the first time that either of them had offered it to the other. "How far is it to the mine from here?"

"Would you like to see it?"

His eagerness was so apparent. God, Carmel thought, he must be so lonely. Even as little as I knew him, I can't remember him being like this. "Could we see it to-day?"

He packed a lunch from the canned goods his mother had sent him and they left almost immediately in the Jeep. They drove round the lake on a bumpy track, then began to climb into the mountains. Carmel, a city girl to her nerve ends, went through torture as she lurched from side to side in the bumping vehicle. But she said nothing and her brother, hearing no complaint, took it for granted that this sort of travelling was nothing new to her. He lives in a little world all his own, she thought; then realised sadly how perfectly true her casual thought had been.

"You feeling the altitude?" he asked.

"Not so far. But how high do we go?"

"Sixteen thousand feet. I was a very high-born baby." It was a feeble joke, but they both laughed, still warm in the company of each other.

"No wonder Mother had a ghastly time with you."

They were climbing up the side of a glacier, the track skirting the white frozen cataract. A herd of llamas stood on an outcrop of rock, looking down at the slowly moving vehicle with curious stares. "They have such beautiful soft eyes," said Carmel. "They remind me of inquisitive but frightened virgins."

"The resemblance had never struck me. These days you can never recognise a virgin by her looks."

We're on dangerous ground here, she thought.

"It gets a bit tricky here," he said.

He slowed the Jeep to a halt, took it round beneath an overhang of rock. The track itself was rock here, worn smooth by the hooves of mules; a patch of ice lay in shadow where the sun never reached it. McKenna edged the Jeep round; a moment ago his face had been relaxed in a smile, but now it was tense. He had driven over this track half a dozen times, always aware of the risks but never troubled for himself by them. But now he was suddenly conscious that he had put someone else in danger, someone he – loved?

There was no time to consider the last question. The rear wheels slipped, the back of the Jeep broke away. He felt a stab of fear, like a physical blow. Out of the corner of his eye he could see the glacier, now two or three hundred feet below them. He worked desperately on the steering wheel, trying to get some grip on the front tyres. Then abruptly they took hold, pulled the rear wheels forward off the ice; the Jeep crept forward, negotiated the bend. McKenna, feeling the sweat on him turn cold, kept the Jeep going up the track.

"Okay?" He glanced at Carmel, waiting for her to condemn him.

Face as white as the snow lying in shaded hollows beside the track, she nodded. When she spoke her voice was a faint croak. "How on earth did they get the trucks down with the silver ore?"

Relieved that she was not going to scold him for endangering her life, he exploded with explanation: "They didn't use trucks in those days, not even the people who bought out Dad. Mules, that was all, trains of them. Mom came up here on the back of a mule – it must have been rough on her, coming from Brooklyn Heights – "

"I've got new respect for her."

"Like I said, she loved Dad in those days. When you're in love, I guess you'll go anywhere."

I wouldn't know, she thought. But that, too, was dangerous ground.

Then she saw the skeleton buildings up ahead, a large single-storied house and thirty or forty huts, all of them without roofs or walls. "They were built of corrugated iron," said McKenna. "But when the mining company moved out, the Indians came up here and stripped the place."

The camp was built on a wide shelf of iron-hard earth; when the house and huts had been complete, they must have looked precariously anchored on the steep slope of the mountainside. Fierce ridges, like chipped and rusted axe blades, ran down the mountain on either side of the shelf; a thousand feet below it a narrow canyon, perpetually flooded in chilling dark blue shadow, cut down towards the glacier. Above the camp was the mine itself, two small caves that would have been unnoticed but for the broken winches outside them and the heaps of mullock now frozen into the slope of the mountain. Above it all towered the peaks, a jagged wall of ice and rock that held its own awesome threat.

"They lived here?" Carmel said incredulously.

"They not only lived here, they worked here. Or the Indians did. I don't think Dad when he was here, or the white engineers from the mining company, did much in the way of physical labour."

"But how could they? I mean, why didn't the Indians just collapse?"

"It has to do with their physical make-up. Their lung capacity is about a third more than yours or mine, they have four or five more pints of blood than you or I would have, and they have a much slower heart beat. If anyone lives up here long enough he eventually adapts – for instance, my own red corpuscle count has gone up, according to a check they did on me down at the hospital – but no outsider, no matter how long he lives here, would ever equal the Indians for endurance."

They got out of the Jeep and walked among the skeleton huts, came to the house, a stark grove of weathered posts. "And that's what you think of as home?"

"It doesn't look like much, does it? But I lived here with Dad till I was almost seven – Mom had gone back to the States to have you."

"I gave her no trouble. Not then, anyway."

"No," he said noncommittally; he had already made up his mind he was not going to act as father-confessor to her. He went on, moving through the bones of home, "I can remember what it was like in those days. There was a veranda here – you could only sit on it in the mornings when the sun was on it, it was too cold other times – and I'd stand out here and look down that glacier and imagine I was Atahualpa waiting for Pizarro to come. There was another kid, an Indian boy named Jesu Mamani, who used to play the game with me. He was Pizarro."

"An Indian playing Pizarro?"

"Kids don't draw the line at nationalities. That only comes later," he said, and thought sadly of Jesu, the stranger who would never play a Spaniard these days.

"Are they books?" She pointed to a dirt-covered heap that lay in one corner of the framework of the house.

He picked up a faded tattered book and brushed the dirt from it. "*The Grapes of Wrath.*" He picked up some others, squinted at the almost obliterated titles. "*King Solomon's*

Mines. Three Weeks. These were all the Indians left when they stripped the place."

They walked up a slippery slope, he holding her hand and pulling her after him. They passed a garden of crosses, the wooden markers weathered to the colour of the frozen earth in which they leaned drunkenly as if the men beneath them had clutched at the buried ends of the stakes and tried to wave them, a last cry for help when it was already too late. "Miners," said McKenna. "All Indians, all given a nice Christian burial. Pity they hadn't been given a Christian living."

"What do you mean?"

"You'll see in a minute." He had brought up two pairs of gumboots from the Jeep, slung over his shoulder from a strap run through their loops. "Put these on. And button up your jacket – it's going to be pretty cold inside."

Without a word she did as she was told, then followed him into the nearest mine shaft. McKenna had brought a large flashlight with him; she was beginning to remember that he had always been a boy who was well prepared; unlike herself he went to meet circumstances. The shaft ran straight into the side of the mountain so that walking was comparatively easy except for the uneven surface beneath their feet. She had gone no more than ten yards when she slipped and fell. McKenna turned the flashlight on her and only then did she see that almost the entire floor of the shaft was ice.

"When the mine was being worked, that would all have been water up to their ankles." McKenna helped her to her feet, turned the flashlight on the walls. Ice hung on the rock face, like frozen Spanish moss; when he raised the beam of the flash she saw that they stood under a ceiling of ice, one long chandelier of stalactites that reflected the light in a myriad multi-coloured gleams. "But the ice would always have been on the walls, except where the heat from the lamps would have melted it. The miners worked ten hours a day, six days a week in these conditions."

He led her farther into the mine, up and down side galleries, taking her into the heart of the mountain. The cold had gone through her now into the heart of herself and she was having difficulty in breathing; her nose was clogged with the dank smell that made her think this was how a grave must smell. But she allowed herself to be led on without complaint, knowing now that Terry was taking her through some kind of purgatory, though so far she could not guess at the reason for it. The mine was silent but for the scraping of their boots on the slippery floor; but she was now aware of the mountain moving around them, slight murmurings of rock against rock. She stopped once and McKenna, turning back, saw her listening.

"It's the mountain breathing," he said. "That's the way Dad used to describe it."

"Did they ever have any cave-ins?"

"Two while I lived here. That's what I wanted to show you." He led her on till they came to a jumble of rocks and timber beams blocking the shaft. He flashed the light over the impenetrable barrier. "There are forty-two men buried behind that. One of them was the father of the kid I used to play with, Jesu. Another was his elder brother, except that he wasn't a man. He was only thirteen years old."

She shivered and looked around apprehensively. She was not accustomed to the presence of death; the men behind the barricade had died twenty-five or more years ago, but the atmosphere of their death was as tangible as smoke from a recently doused fire. Her teeth chattered in a morse code of fear and at once McKenna was contrite. "I'm sorry. You're scared stiff, aren't you?"

She did not deny it. "What if there was another fall? Why did you bring me all the way in here?"

"Let's get outside first," he said, his own ears suddenly conscious of the shifting mountain. He took her arm and led her back through the cold dark tunnel and out on to the ledge where the rusted and broken winch stood like the fossilised remains of an ancient beast.

He leant on the winch and gestured back towards the mine shaft. "That's how our beloved father made his original money. Seventy-five cents a day he paid the miners, but he buried them free and gave their widows fifty dollars. He wasn't the only one who did such things – the Bolivian mine owners treated their workers just as badly, if not worse – but he was one of the reasons Americans are hated on this continent. He was just a

small looter compared to the big companies, but he was the
only one I ever knew personally."

"When did you learn all this?"

"When I came back here nine months ago. I didn't come back
here as a matter of conscience. I truly believed I had a vocation
as a missionary. But now – " He looked back into the black,
dead mouth of the mine; in his mind he heard the screams of
dying men. "Now I'm not sure that something wasn't working
on me all the time I was growing up. I never had any thought
of being a priest while I was at school, in spite of all the propaganda Mom fed me. You think she drove me to being a priest,
don't you?"

"She was always working on me to become a nun. It was one
way to be safe from men, she told me."

"I didn't get that line – I mean about women. No, it was in
my last year at college I knew what I wanted to be and where
I wanted to come to work." He looked about him. "I'd have set
up the mission here if there'd been any Indians still here.
Instead, I settled for where I am now, down by the lake. Most
of the miners and their families went back to Altea when the
company closed down the mine."

"Why did they close it down?"

"It's worked out. The company never got out of it what they
paid Dad for it – he played them for suckers, I think. Our
money, Carmie, is about as dirty as you could get. About the
only thing the Old Man didn't do was make money out of coca
weed."

"Does Mother know all this?"

"I don't know. Sometimes I think of telling her, then I
think, what the hell? Dad is enough of a sinner in her eyes.
Part of her revenge was seeing that none of his fancy dames ever
got a dime of the money he left. She'd hate him even more if
her conscience made her give up what she might call blood
money."

"Do you think she'd have that much conscience?"

He hesitated, then said, "No."

"Do you think I should have any conscience about my
share?"

He shook his head. "I told you, I'm not playing priest or

missionary to you. I have enough problems with the people I've got. All I can say is, if people had any conscience about their inheritances, three-quarters of the world's fortunes would be given away. The fact that they're not shows that either conscience is an adaptable thing or the world is tolerant of the children of bloodsuckers."

"You think Dad was a bloodsucker?"

"Don't you?"

"You mentioned that insect, the bloodsucker, the one that infects the blood. Do you think we're infected?"

"I don't know. But I wouldn't guarantee our immunity. My sense of charity has never really been tested."

She looked back at the entrance to the mine. All her life she had been protected from the misery of poverty and slow death; her paths had never run through the ghettos; the hotels Pierre, Dorchester, Crillon, Excelsior were not vantage points for watching people die of despair and malnutrition. She was not unintelligent, she knew such conditions existed; she had been intelligent enough to selfishly ignore them. But it had never been suggested to her nor had she ever thought that the money that protected her from such misery had itself come from such a source. She had had her own misery, but it had not grown out of the difficulties of surviving. Nor, she realised now, out of an awareness of one's responsibilities.

"What do we do for them now? The Indians, I mean."

He shook his head again, defeated. "I don't know. If we came in here throwing our money around, we'd soon find ourselves in trouble. Charity is suspect – unless the local officials can have a hand in it."

"You mean they'd want their share?" It was an easy way out, but that seemed to decide her: "I think I'll hang on to my share of the money. Oh, you can have as much as you want, whenever you want it – "

"I have enough of my own. More than enough. I just don't know how to use it, that's all. Not without having about fifty per cent milked off the top. It doesn't happen just here, it happens all over. I heard about aid that was sent out to Bengal when a typhoon wiped out hundreds of villages and killed thousands of people. Stuff arrived there, food, blankets, medical supplies, everything that was needed at once. But somehow or other, almost half of it disappeared. That doesn't excuse us Haves for being stingy with our charity, but at least you can understand why the man in Main Street back home, when told that Washington is giving away half a billion or whatever it is in world aid, asks, Who gets my buck? The peasant who needs it or the government man who is supposed to be handing it out?"

They went back down to the Jeep. As they reached it something moved in the skeleton of a hut at the end of the camp, a hunch-backed figure that sent a chill through Carmel. "There's someone there!"

Then suddenly the figure expanded, became a bird that took off on giant wings, something, an animal or another bird, clutched in its talons. "It's a condor," said McKenna, watching it catch a current of air and plane down towards a distant gap in the mountains. "There are stories that they carry off Indian babies, but I've never been able to track down anyone who's known of it actually happening. But I guess if they were hungry enough, they could do it. The thing about this country is never disbelieve anything just because it's incredible."

"I'm only just beginning to appreciate that," she said. "I'm glad you brought me up here."

"I hoped you might be," he said; then smiled. "It was a bit of missionary work, in a way."

2

They drove back down the track, negotiating the tricky bend without incident. At the bottom of the glacier McKenna pulled up and looked back up at the mountain. "On the other side of that range they are still working the silver mines, been working them for 400 years, though they're nearly worked out of silver now and they're mining tin. Farther south there's Potosi, a pretty dead city now. But over three hundred years ago 160,000 people lived in the city. Its coat of arms said something like, I am the rich Potosi, treasurer of the world, king of mountains, the envy of kings. For over a hundred years it financed all the wars of Europe. The mountain just outside it was almost literally a hill of silver, it had the richest deposits of silver the world has ever known. But whoever hears of it now? There's a city a couple of hundred miles from here, Sucre, that had a university twelve years before Harvard was founded. But who knows that in the States?"

"I didn't."

"You're not the only one, by something like a couple of hundred million. This country is the other side of the moon to most Americans – so is most of South America. But some day the people back home are going to have to look at this continent. You can't be neighbour to a volcano and keep your back turned to it all the time."

When they got back to the mission they found Taber sitting in his Land-Rover in the yard. His bony face creased stiffly as he smiled hello, as if the muscles of it had set while he had spent the last half-hour in deep thought. He had the facility to isolate himself mentally from his surroundings while he pondered problems and his face meanwhile, like a cramped and unused limb, would go to sleep. His awakening smile now, though it looked like a grimace, was nonetheless sincere. He was glad to see them both, especially Carmel. She no longer irritated him, though he was still unsure what he did exactly feel towards her. She attracted him sexually, but he was not going to join a queue. Hidden somewhere under her silver-plated personality, the product of expensive schools and even more expensive resorts, was a magnetism, of charity or sympathy or understanding – he wasn't sure which, because all three virtues did not necessarily coincide – that pulled him towards her while at the same time he was repelled by her public character. She was a complex girl and that, too, worried him. Both his wives had been simple girls and he had had great difficulty in understanding either of them.

He got out of the Land-Rover with the slow leg-finding motion of a giraffe getting to its feet; he seemed continually embarrassed by his long legs, as if they had only grown on him over the past year or two. "I've been down in Altea, talking with some of the campesinos, looking at what they grow up there behind the village."

"Where's the john?" Carmel asked.

"In the back," McKenna told her. "It's a Chic Sale special." When she had gone he looked back at Taber. "I've been showing her where I was born."

"You were born here?" Taber showed his surprise.

"Up there in the mountains. I'd claim to be a Bolivian, if it was worth anything."

"The Ruiz and their friends last night think it is worth something."

"Only if you've got Spanish blood. Mine's Irish-American. That puts me only one rung above the Indians." He changed the subject. Showing the mine to Carmel had been intended as a lesson for her; not a malicious, hurtful one but one which he had felt she needed if ever she was to have any perspective on their money. But the visit had upset him as much as her, because the truth had hurt her more than he had expected. He had not realised till to-day how much she had worshipped their father despite his desertion of them. "What do you think of the farming prospects down at Altea?"

"The soil is about as poor as I've seen. They'll never get any better crops than they're getting now. I'm going to try and talk them into moving."

"Where to?"

Taber nodded across towards the northern end of the lake. "Over there beyond the moraine at the bottom of the glacier. They'll have a fair way to get to it, but that soil, with some fertiliser added, could produce three times the amount of crops they're getting down where they are."

"That's Ruiz land," said McKenna. "You try to take that over – "

"I know," said Taber morosely. "I've had it happen before. You're invited in to help and you put in your report and invariably the first thing you have to recommend is land reform. And then, as you Yanks say, the shit hits the fan. You're accused of being a Communist, an undercover man for the revolution – " He looked across the lake, took off his cap and scratched his head, put his cap back on. His red hair stuck out in tufts from under it; he looked like a mournful clown. "But if the Ruiz own all the land up here and they have enough influence to be able to hang on to it, how else am I going to help the campesinos without stirring up trouble? I didn't bloody well come here to help people like the Ruiz get richer."

Then Carmel came back before McKenna got too involved with talk about riches. She went over to a barrel of water beside the kitchen door, dipped in the small bucket that hung on the wall, poured water over her hands, then came towards the two men wiping her hands on a handkerchief large enough to have dried a mouse. "If you two are talking improvements around here, I'll vote for a new john. I thought something like that went out when Calvin Coolidge left office."

McKenna grinned at Taber, mock-apologised for his sister. He had noticed how quiet she had been on the drive back from the mine, but now she seemed to have recovered her gaiety. "She's been brought up in indoor bathrooms, three or four to a house. She doesn't know how the other half lives." Then he realised what he had said and he had to smile hard at her to take the edge off it.

Taber offered to drive Carmel back to San Sebastian. Just before they drove off she reached out of the Land-Rover and took McKenna's hand. "You're worried you did the wrong thing by taking me up to the mine."

"Yes," he said reluctantly.

"Don't be, Terry. I'm getting used to having my eyes opened. Even Harry has helped." She looked at Taber, drawing him even closer into their circle; they were no longer foreigners but fellow citizens in the land of private doubt. "I think I'll take you to lunch if there's a decent restaurant in San Sebastian. You never did open those sandwiches you brought," she said to McKenna.

"Sorry. You just didn't look as if you wanted to eat."

"I do now. What about it, Harry?"

"There's no Maxim's or Mirabelle," said Taber, showing he knew a decent restaurant or two, even if he had never eaten there; his liking for rich food had been developed in the private homes of those who had later branded him a Communist. "But wherever we go, I'll pay. I'll write you off against expenses. I have my pride."

"Who said only the Latins know how to be gallant?"

They drove off laughing, glad to be in each other's company;

D

97

and McKenna was surprised at how much he envied them. There is nothing between them, he thought, but there could be if they wanted it. But not between Dolores and me: we can laugh all we want when we're together, but the laughter, and not much else, is all we can share. He went into the larger hut, suddenly unhappy and hopeless. Carmel's unexpected arrival in San Sebastian had, though welcome, only increased his awareness of his loneliness; her apparent affection for him, if only lately realised, had been the litmus to prove that he needed love and companionship. Isolation, he knew, was a hothouse in which self-pity could grow as luxuriantly as self-knowledge; he had learned that in the week-end retreats of silent meditation in the seminary, long before he had been sent out into the field and the real test of his self-reliance. He had failed in the test: God and himself were not enough. Which was why he had grasped at Dolores Schiller, if only metaphorically so far, when she had presented herself as being interested in the same cause as himself. The campesinos were their children, bastards who could be blessed and better cared for if he and Dolores were married. But the Church would not allow it; and neither, he guessed, would she, though he had never got as far as mentioning it to her. He was a sufficiently charitable priest not to burden someone else with a sense of sin.

He was standing in front of the mirror in his bedroom shaving, meanwhile looking at his broad-planed face with a layman's eye and wondering if a woman would think it attractive or just plain dull, when he heard a truck drive into the yard outside. It was an Indian's truck; the asthmatic engine, the grinding of an axle and the thin squeal of ineffective brakes told him he was not being visited by any criollo. Not that any criollos had ever visited him, not even Dolores. But he lived in hopes.

Half of his face still bearded with lather, he went out through the living-room to the door. The truck stood in the middle of the yard, a dozen campesinos lined up beside it like the employees of some transport company posing for a photograph for the home office magazine. *Loyal workers of our Bolivian branch* . . . all of whom, McKenna noticed, carried rifles or machetes.

"What is it, Jesu?"

Jesu Mamani stood slightly in front of the other men, his

rifle held loosely in the crook of his arm, a long knife stuck in his belt. "It is about our women, padre."

Even though he did not yet fully comprehend, McKenna felt a chill of fear. All his senses sharpened; he smelled the lather on his cheek, the expensive mockery concocted by Princess Zara or whoever name was on the elegant, mock-leather aerosol can: a ridiculous birthday present from his mother, along with talcum powder, hair lotion and something called a skin tightener. Though, God knew, his skin was tight enough now.

"What about them?"

He could see now that all the campesinos had been drinking; one or two of them blinked stupidly and leaned back against the truck. Mamani had been drinking, but he was far from being drunk or stupid. He was the voice of these men and every word was as sharp as the glistening knife in his belt. "You have taught them to sin, padre."

McKenna might have laughed in other circumstances; but the circumstances were too far away, back in his own country where sin had become a minor routine fashion. But these men were fundamentalists; they had been given a sense of sin as unquestioning as that of a child and they clung to it as more sophisticated men might cling to an ideal. They would also have, he knew, a fundamental approach to anyone who had interfered with their women.

"What do you mean?" he said, stalling for time even though he knew time meant nothing now: none of these men owned a watch, a day or an hour was all the same to them, they had the patience of animals. A tuft of lather, whipped by the wind, blew up on his cheek. White-bearded on one side of his face, he wondered how ridiculous he looked to these half-drunken men who had come to kill him.

"Four of our wives are not pregnant," said Mamani. "Yet we have been sleeping with them all the time, padre, doing the thing husbands and wives do together. Then my wife told me – you gave her and the other women a pill to stop them having babies."

He waited for confirmation and McKenna, conscious of the confirmation of the guns and machetes, said hoarsely, "Yes."

How will they kill me? he wondered. Quickly, or slowly after their own barbaric fashion? He had heard how the mine manager had died after the 1952 revolution: tied with barbed wire, nails driven into his eyes, then finally his throat cut: all that by the men before the women moved in to mutilate the body in a horrible way. When it came to killing, killing as punishment or revenge, an eye for an eye and a tooth for a tooth, they lost all sense of sin. But that was fundamentalist, too: their ancestors had got the seal of approval on their barbarism from the Inquisition. Oh God, he prayed, why have You let so many sins be committed in Your name?

"That is a sin, padre. God decides how many children a woman should have, not man."

"Don't you help decide by forcing your wife to accept you every time you want her? Your wife was tired of having a child every year, Jesu – "

"Did she tell you that?"

"No," he lied hurriedly; he did not want Maria Mamani and the other women punished for his sin. "But anyone could see she was exhausted – "

"The doctor at the hospital in San Sebastian said she could have many more children."

"My wife, too!" cried the man standing immediately behind Mamani; an ugly little man whose one good eye was bleary with drink; his wall eye, in contrast, looked cold with intelligence. "Padre Luis says the Holy Father says to use the pills is a great sin – "

"It's a matter of conscience," McKenna said bleakly; but he knew these men would never hone their consciences to such a refinement. He had taken the packets of pills down to the lake yesterday and thrown them out like bird seed; but even as he had scattered them to the wind he had had no feeling that he had done wrong; he had been obeying the Bishop, not his own conscience. "I wanted a better life for the children you already have – "

"My children are fine," said Mamani.

"What about the ones your wife lost?"

But the argument was also lost. The other campesinos, tired of words they did not fully understand, wanting vengeance before the effect of the chicha beer wore off, yelled at Mamani. The lather whipped off McKenna's cheek and across his eyes like a flurry of snow. He shivered, feeling the wind through the vest and shirt he wore; he had taken off his sweater while he shaved and had come to the door without it. But he shivered, too, with fear: he knew now that he was not going to die simply.

"We are men!" cried Mamani, his voice rising like a screeching bird on the wind; beyond him the lake turned dark as if shadows had come up from its depths. Dark clouds tumbled down the mountainsides like falling peaks; a flock of geese rose out of the totoras by the shore and at once were scattered as if by shrapnel. A storm, instantly born, would hit the mission any moment. "God judges a man by the children he has – the more children, the more souls for heaven – "

The voice of the village priest, Padre Luis; and of Nell McKenna, who had never been able to get her husband to bed again after the birth of Carmel. You win, Lord, said McKenna silently; and began to babble in his mind an act of contrition. This is the way we die, he thought, abject with contrition because we're afraid of what follows. Was God capable of sardonic laughter?

But he was not going to be abject in front of the campesinos. Paralysed with fear, he tried to give an appearance of rigid defiance. "You're not thinking of God – you're thinking of machismo! Proving the power of your cojones – "

But the wind was howling round the corner of the house now, blowing the Indians forward across the yard. They came at him, machetes upraised; he tried to back through the doorway, but they were too quick for him. They grabbed him, strong hands turned savage by drink and wounded male pride. They dragged him across the yard and round the corner of the house; against the back wall of the compound the trees he had planted threshed in the rampaging wind. He struggled with equal frenzy, but the campesinos were too strong for him. Mamani was somewhere at the back of him – avoiding him? he wondered. They had played this game as children; but it had been *only* a game. Pizarro had never really killed Atahualpa, not in their version. He was yelling a prayer, God, help me!; but he had no hope he would be heard. The rain, cold as bullets of ice, hit him in the face as the men slammed him against one of the trees.

They forced his arms behind him, wrapping them round the whipping, trembling trunk of the tree. They tied his wrists together with rope: thank God for small mercies: they hadn't used barbed wire. The tree at once seemed to steady itself, strengthened by the stake of his body. The rain pelted at him at a low angle, the wind tore at his face: all the lather was gone now. He was assaulted by men and the elements: take your pound of flesh, Lord, he thought; and was not resentful. He would be dead in a minute or two and would know if faith had all been worthwhile. Suddenly he was no longer afraid, only disappointed. He had done nothing: he was going to die without a credit to his name.

Then he felt the hands tearing at his belt. His trousers were jerked down; the wind and the rain lashed at his belly. Then he saw the knife in Mamani's hand, felt the other hand grab at his testicles. Oh Christ no! He screamed aloud, heard himself even above the shriek of the wind; and Taber, rifle in hand, came plunging round the corner of the house. There was a shot, smoke whipped away from the barrel of Taber's rifle, and the Indians spun round, letting go of McKenna.

Taber's fury was terrible to see. His face was contorted with a savagery that equalled that of the campesinos; but theirs now abruptly gave way to fear as the Englishman waved the gun barrel at them. "Get out of here! Get out of here before I kill the bloody lot of you!"

He shouted at them in English, but the gun translated for him. The Indians stared at him belligerently, but Taber raised the gun and fired another shot close above their heads. All at once they turned and ran on wobbly legs round the corner of the house, their faces idiotic with sudden sobriety as they realised that the next shot might kill any one of them. Mamani, knife still in hand, did not run at once; he looked at McKenna, his face impassive, then he turned and followed the other men. But he walked, he did not run. He passed within a foot of Taber, but did not look at him, then he had disappeared round the corner.

McKenna hung forward from the tree, unconscious of the

pain in his arms and shoulders. His trousers were still about his ankles, the wind and the rain still slashing at his loins; his genitals shrivelled by cold and fear and shame, he hung his head on his chest. Taber came forward, undid the priest's wrists, pulled up his trousers and tightened his belt.

"The bastards! I'd have shot the balls off the lot of them! Christ, why? Why do that to you?"

Then Carmel, her face blurred with tears and worry, came round the corner. "What were they going to do?"

Taber, careful even of a priest's male shame, said, "They looked as if they were going to shoot him."

He and Carmel helped McKenna into the house. He slumped on a chair while Taber looked for something to revive him. "Haven't you anything stronger than coffee or altar wine?"

"There's some Scotch – " McKenna's voice was thin and high, a castrato note, as if the knife had done its work even though it had not touched him.

Carmel found the whisky, knowing where to look; it was beneath the altar, with the Huntley and Palmer biscuits and the rollmops. She poured him a stiff drink while Taber explained why they had come back. "We passed the truck just as it left the village. It was obvious they were all drunk – they nearly drove us off the road. I stopped in the village to see Mamani again about that Ruiz land, tell him I'd changed my mind. His missus said he'd come up here to see you – him and the other men. I could see something was on – she was as frantic as a woman trying to give birth through a chastity belt – "

"The description fits her," said Carmel, smiling at her brother as she saw the whisky bringing some life back into him. She stroked his wet head as if he were ten years younger than she. "Darling, why were they going to – ?" She couldn't bring herself to say *kill you*. She was still inoculated against certain realities: murder happened to other people, not to one's own.

Strengthened by the whisky, McKenna conversely was too weak for lies: "I'd been giving the Pill to some of their wives."

"But most men would be glad to know it worked!"

"Not these jokers," said Taber, and looked at McKenna. "The old machismo thing, that was it, wasn't it? And who taught it to them – your bloody Christian Spaniards! Do you know what machismo means?" he asked Carmel.

"Of course," she said too emphatically, unfortunately suggesting a long queue of Latin lovers. And suddenly felt embarrassed, something that had not happened to her in a long time. To cover up, she offered McKenna another drink, but he shook his head. "Are you all right now?"

"I'll be okay." He had found his proper voice again. "They won't be back – not with their guns and machetes, anyway. I think it was the beer acting on them – "

He tried to reduce the drama to an everyday happening; he felt a need to protect her from nightmares of what might have happened. His own fear had gone now, but he could still feel his genitals chilled and shrivelled. The day had begun with an erection and almost ended with a castration: a warning could not be more obvious than that. But Dolores Schiller and the women of Altea were not connected by the same sin on his part; and though he had gabbled contrition, he was still not convinced he had been wrong in the way he had tried to help Maria Mamani and the other women. He believed in signs, the Church's history was illuminated with them, but signs were like proverbs: they tended to cancel each other out. He would stop giving the Pill to the women, but he would not stop trying to find some way of alleviating their poverty and their bearing of children who stood only one chance in three of reaching the age of ten. It might be that he would have to sin again, in some other way, but sin had been invented by men and was interpreted by men. He would just have to take the long view, wait for another, more hopeful sign.

"Would you like me to leave my gun?" Taber asked. He held it up, a Mannlicher that would have blown holes in any of the Indians if he had shot at them. "I don't know why I brought it here with me. It's too heavy for the game up here. I used to shoot lion with it in Kenya."

"I won't need it. I'll go down to-morrow and try and iron things out with them."

"Give them absolution? Don't be too bloody charitable with them, mate. Just because you and I are here trying to help them, we don't have to crawl to them."

"You sound like a couple of pretty aggressive Samaritans," said Carmel.

"To-day a Samaritan has got to be like a businessman – he has to have a streak of bastard in him if he wants to succeed." Taber passed by McKenna on his way to the door, squeezed the priest's shoulder in a gesture of affection that surprised McKenna; he hadn't expected the Englishman to go in for public demonstrations of sympathy. The hand on his shoulder warmed McKenna more than the whisky had. "Don't let 'em get you down, mate. They'll see the light some day."

McKenna pulled on a coat and followed his sister and Taber out to the Land-Rover. "Thanks, Harry. I hope – " He stopped and grinned. "I was going to say I hope I can do as much for you some day."

Taber also grinned. "I hope not. I value mine too much to want to risk them like that. Take care, Terry, when you go down to see them to-morrow."

"Please do that," said Carmel with real concern, and McKenna promised that he would.

The Land-Rover drove away, was soon reduced to a moving speck in the vastness. The rain had stopped and the wind had dropped; sunlight was a colonnade of golden pillars growing out of the lake. A boy went along the shore playing a quena pipe; the notes came up on the remnants of the wind, fell against the ear with the sadness of a child's dying sigh. Then far down the road, just passed by the Land-Rover, McKenna saw the figure trudging up from Altea. The Land-Rover stopped, backed up to the figure, paused a while, then drove on, dropped down into the ravine that hid Altea. Reassured, McKenna waited.

It was twenty minutes before the figure was close enough to be recognised. Then he walked down to the gate of the compound to welcome Agostino. "Hello, Agostino. Have you come back to stay?"

The boy nodded. "My mother thought you might need me, padre."

"I do indeed," said McKenna.

It was another sign, of forgiveness.

Chapter 4

I

. . . We must once again emphasise that only by co-operation with the local authorities can our purposes be achieved. And once again we must emphasise that it is not, repeat not, one of our purposes to reform wholesale those countries which seek FAO's help. Twice now, Mr Taber, this headquarters has received complaints about your misplaced zeal . . .

Ah, if only Verdoux, the regional director, would write the same sort of tart letters to those government authorities who had lodged the complaints. But Verdoux, the Swiss, believed in neutrality when it came to dealing with government bodies. All his aggressiveness was reserved for those whom he was supposed to support.

. . . This assignment in Bolivia is your last chance. One more complaint and we shall have to refer the question of your future employment to Rome . . .

And I can join the heretical priests and questioning nuns and rebellious laymen on the road to excommunication, thought Taber. Stand before the Curia of the FAO, Taber, and confess your sins: too little concern for the rich, too much concern for the poor, too little diplomacy, too much faith in an ideal. *Mea culpa, mea culpa.* Maybe when I'm back there in Rome I should cross the Tiber and see how I would get on if charged with the same sins before the real Curia.

The letter had been waiting for him yesterday evening when he had returned to the hotel. It had arrived with the rest of his mail: the two-weeks-old copy of *Newsweek*, the six-weeks-old copy of *The New Statesman*, the two letters from his brother and his sister.

He folded Verdoux's letter, put it in his pocket, crossed to the bedroom window and looked out into the street. The policeman had gone from his post opposite the hotel; after two days,

Condoris must have decided he was no longer worth watching. He turned back and looked at the bedroom. He felt at home in it; it was exactly like a hundred others he had known. The varnished floorboards, the rug beside the bed that always slipped when you stepped on it, the fly-speckled shade on the light, the faded and rippled print in the cheap frame on the wall: it was home, just as the hundred others had been. The identification, his mark, were the three battered suitcases standing in the corner: all that he owned.

Those suitcases had been the trouble, of course. They had been all he had offered both his wives, other than himself. Beth had never really had time to complain about them; their marriage was over before she had realised that, had it survived, her rival for him would have been his job. Sandra had been fascinated by his job at first; born and raised in a dull, hill-enclosed market town in Shropshire, she had been as much in love with distant horizons as with him. Disillusion had set in early when she had discovered that the towns in East Africa, where she sat at home and waited for him while he went off on long field trips, were just as dull and provincial as the town she had fled. She had come to hate his suitcases, swearing at him every time he took them down to pack them; then one day he had arrived back early from a trip, dumped the suitcases in the living-room and walked into the bedroom and found her in bed with the local postmaster, a man who never had to travel. He had broken the postmaster's nose and then thrown him naked out of the house, to the delight of the native garden boy who had at once spread the news faster than could have the post office's telegraph system. Taber had then sat in the kitchen and methodically got drunk while Sandra had railed at him that he had only himself and his job to blame for what had happened. He had sat there without answering her, knowing she was right but knowing, too, that the suitcases could never be thrown away, that he would go on packing them till F A O decided he was too old to be useful any more and would pension him off. Finally Sandra had packed her own suitcases and departed, going back to England and the divorce courts. That had been six years ago and now she was married to a delicatessen owner in Ealing, a man who was home all the time. It did not please Taber, an unvindictive man, to hear that she was desperately unhappy.

He threw the suitcases on the bed and began to pack. He was moving out of the hotel this morning. Pereira had found him a furnished house where he could live and also set up his office and laboratory. It was the home of an army officer who had been posted abroad as military attaché to one of the Bolivian embassies; the rent had been doubled when the officer had learned that a U N agency would be paying it. But that was par for the course, not only here but everywhere in the world; the United Nations and its agencies were supposed to operate without prejudice or favour for the benefit of all, privileged as well as unprivileged. The army officer could not be blamed for falling in with standard practice. After all the military mind was not trained to attempt innovation.

An hour later Taber was in the house. It was a relatively new house, five or six years old, a two-storey building that would not have looked out of place in the suburbs of a dozen cities in a dozen other lands; the blight of suburbia was spreading like the effects of D D T, gradually reducing the world to the one characterless landscape. Even Taber, a man not normally interested in houses as symbols of security and the personality of their owners, was disappointed in the anonymity of this particular one. Atahualpa, had he lived to see it, would have recognised the final conquest of his empire.

But Pereira was impressed. Expansive and envious at the same time, he went around opening and shutting doors and windows, turning taps on and off, tapping walls. "Very well constructed. You are most fortunate, Harry. This is the sort of house I crave. And the furniture! You are extremely fortunate to be ensconced in such luxury."

"I shouldn't call it luxury," said Taber, looking around at the furniture which might have been shipped out from some bargain store in Oxford Street or Tottenham Court Road; but at least there were no monk's chairs and no suits of armour. "Still, it'll be comfortable. And the kitchen is just right for the laboratory. We'll set the office up in the dining-room. You'd better get us an office girl."

"Already arranged," said Pereira with that smug look that

settles on the inefficient when they are surprised by their own occasional efficiency. "A delightful young damsel named Isabella. She is the cashier at my cinema."

"Can she take dictation?"

Pereira spread his hands. "Is it necessary? There is no need for urgency about our letters. The less letters one writes and the slower their delivery, the longer one survives. If you are patient with Isabella, she will be patient with you."

"I shall look forward to her tolerance," said Taber dryly, knowing he had already lost the battle for whatever efficiency he himself had had in mind. "Okay, get the Land-Rover out. We're going up to Altea."

"I understand there was a disturbance up at Padre McKenna's mission yesterday." Pereira cocked a wary eye, like a man tossing pebbles at a dog that might bite.

"Where did you hear that?" Taber snapped.

Pereira raised defensive hands. "Do not blame me for spreading the gossip any further, Harry. I am as averse to gossip as you are – "

"Who told you, then?"

"A man at the cinema last night, in the intermission. He had heard it from his brother, who got it from Padre Luis. I understand you were there?" The last was a tentative question.

He wants to hear it from the horse's mouth, Taber thought, but he's going to be disappointed. "It was nothing, just a misunderstanding. If you hear any more gossip about it, tell them that's all it was – a misunderstanding."

Pereira was becoming accustomed to the swift changes in Taber's moods. "Mum is the word, Harry. You can trust me. The gossip, no matter what it is, will die with me."

"There's no need to be a bloody martyr," said Taber, trying to pull rein on his anger; he might look up Padre Luis and tell the fat little trouble-maker to keep his mouth shut. Then he remembered the letter still in his pocket: *it is not, repeat not, one of our purposes to reform wholesale* . . . Padre Luis was McKenna's problem and he, Taber, had better learn how to stay out of it.

But his mood remained with him all the way up to Altea and Pereira, recognising the possibilities of a storm, managed somehow to remain silent without tying his tongue in a knot. The driver, an Indian who was indifferent to the moods of criollos and gringoes, brought the Land-Rover to a halt in front of Jesu Mamani's house. As Taber got out he noticed the long pole hung beside the door with the white square of cloth tacked to it. Mamani had been brewing chicha beer; the makeshift flag was the sign that he had some for sale. Taber wondered if it had been Mamani's beer that had brought on yesterday's mission expedition.

Maria Mamani came to the door when Taber knocked. The skirt and sweater she wore were patched and faded, the sort of dress a woman would wear about her house when she was working; but as soon as Maria had heard the Land-Rover draw up outside her house she had put on her bowler hat before she had opened the door. She reminded Taber of some of the old ladies of Kensington who would never venture out of doors without a hat, the mark of gentility. Maria wiped her nose with the back of her hand and stood looking cautiously at Taber.

"I want to see your husband. Where is he?"

Maria looked out past Taber at the Land-Rover, seemed satisfied that he had only Pereira and the driver with him. "Why do you want him?"

Taber had to go carefully with his Quechua, picking his way through the minefield of meanings: so many of the words, to a foreign ear, sounded so much alike. "I want to talk to him about the crops."

"You shot at him yesterday with your gun." There was no accusation in her voice, just a flat statement.

"That was only to frighten him. I meant him no harm." How would that remark go down with Verdoux?

A child poked its basin-cropped head round the big bulge of her hip. Without looking at it she put her hand in its face and pushed it back out of sight. "I do not think you should see Jesu, senor. He is very angry with you."

Taber sighed. "Where is he working? I *have* to see him."

Maria Mamani hesitated, then jerked her head in the direction of the top of the village street. "He and the men have gone up to the Ruiz land. I do not think you should go to see him to-day, senor."

"Does he have his gun with him?"

"Yes." Again there was just the flat note to her voice. These people carry violence in them like haemophilia, Taber thought: it's something they've inherited, something they live with.

When he got back into the Land-Rover Pereira said, "I think the woman is right, Harry. We should not go up to see the campesinos this morning."

"I'm the sort of pig-headed bloke who never takes a woman's advice. If you want to wait here – ?"

"I never shirk duty, Harry. If you say we go, then we go. Drive on!" Pereira flourished an imperious hand at the driver, Pizarro on his way to Cajamarca. The driver's only response was to ignore Pereira and continue to stare languidly at Taber.

Taber, reduced to good-humoured resignation, just nodded at the driver. "Let's go, Jose. You are not afraid of Mamani's gun, are you?"

"He will not shoot me, senor," said the driver with the impartial lack of interest of a man going to a boxing match where he had no bets.

"I am not afraid of Mamani's gun," said Pereira with offended pride, and Taber knew he had made a mistake with his casual remark to the driver: he was here to work with Pereira, not with the Indian. "But you Anglo-Saxons have never appreciated the advantages of *mañana*. It would be better to come and see Mamani to-morrow."

"To-morrow may be too late," said Taber, trying to keep the edge out of his voice, to placate Pereira. "If Mamani thinks I did wrong yesterday, I can't let him brood too long on it."

They drove up out of the village to the road that turned off to run round the northern end of the lake. As they reached the turn-off they saw McKenna's Jeep speeding down towards them from the mission. They waited for him and Taber got out of the Land-Rover and crossed to the Jeep as it skidded to a stop in the loose gravel.

"I'm on my way down to see Mamani," said McKenna. "I'm a one-man peace delegation."

"Let's make it a two-man job," said Taber, got in beside McKenna and waved to the Land-Rover to follow them. He saw the look of irritation on Pereira's face at being left alone in the Land-Rover with Jose, but he did not want the Bolivian along with him till he had found out if McKenna had recovered from yesterday's shock. "He and the other fellers are up on the Ruiz land. How do you feel this morning?"

McKenna kept his attention on the rough road ahead of them. "I'm not quite sure. Physiologically, maybe psychologically, I don't know, I'm in a bit of a mess. When I went to have a leak this morning it was like passing razor blades. I guess that's going to keep up till the shock wears off."

We'd all miss them if they cut them off, thought Taber. Even the priests, who weren't supposed to have need of them, wanted some symbol of their manhood.

"How do you feel about Mamani?"

"Do you mean have I forgiven him? No, I don't think so. I'm no saint – I've got no more charity than the next guy when it comes to forgiving a man who tried to mutilate me. But I've got to live with him, so I'll have to make a pretence that I'm going to let bygones be bygones."

"Do you think he'll have forgiven you? I mean, giving the Pill to his missus."

"Probably not till she's pregnant again." McKenna grinned. "To hell with the population explosion. Now I'll be praying for her to get pregnant as soon as she can."

The road dropped down below the level of the lake and as they drove along Taber looked up at the tumbled mass of rock that formed the wall holding back the water at this end. One or two rivulets gleamed like snail trails on the slope, but the wall of rock and earth looked solid enough.

"That was the original moraine," said McKenna. "I've done a little amateur geology while I've been here. The glacier came right down to that pile of rocks once. Then there must have been an earthquake, maybe two or three thousand years ago, maybe more, and the course of the glacier shifted."

"It makes a pretty effective dam. Maybe with some irrigation up here and some soil additives – " Then it was Taber's turn to grin. "I once had dreams of changing the face of Anatolia. The Turks patted me on the head and said how nice it was to have a man with big ideas. Then they wrote to Rome and asked

FAO to send someone a little more practical. It was my first job," he said in extenuation.

"I know the feeling. When I first arrived out here I thought I was expected to save a soul a day. Then one of the older guys came down from La Paz, gave me the word. Forget about souls, he said. Save the people and if you happen to save a soul – well, that's just a dividend."

"How does the Bishop feel about that attitude?"

"I'd hate to put it to him as bluntly as that. Any priest working amongst the poor comes up against this dilemma. If you go along with everything the hierarchy says, you find yourself ignoring the real needs of those you're supposed to be caring for. If you do your best to help the poor, satisfy their needs, you find the hierarchy threatening you with hell's fire. You become either a Pharisee or a rebel, when you really didn't want to be either."

"Do you think we stand much chance of saving these blokes?" Taber nodded up ahead to where the Altea men, a couple of dozen of them, stood grouped round their truck beside the road.

"We'll know in the next ten minutes," said McKenna. He brought the Jeep to a halt, switched off the motor and looked across at the silent group of Indians. "Who goes first? Or do we go together?"

"Together, I think."

They got out of the Jeep, feeling the chill of the wind at once. Here the road was above the level of the lake again and they could see the wind coming across the water in waves of dark shadow. A flight of yellow-shouldered marsh birds sent up a shower of silver splinters as they alighted on the lake; down among the totora reeds some cormorants moved in lazy sociability. The Indians were dressed as they had been yesterday, in worn sweaters, patched trousers and some with coloured ponchos thrown over their shoulders; they also carried machetes and guns, just as they had yesterday. It's just as if no time at all has passed, thought Taber, seeing the sullen, angry looks on the dark faces.

The Land-Rover arrived, pulled in behind the Jeep. But Pereira, a prudent man determined to survive, did not get out. Taber caught a glimpse of the apprehensive chubby face, but

for once Pereira was totally silent. The Indians on the other side
of the road did not even glance at the Land-Rover; they were
not interested in the criollo, only in the two gringoes. A criollo
could wait, there would always be time for him.

"You can put your gun away, Jesu," said McKenna. "We
have come to make peace with you."

Mamani held the gun at his side, the barrel pointing at the
feet of the two white men. A dog, a miserable black cur no more
substantial than its own shadow, moved towards Taber and
McKenna, its tail wagging nervously, but one of the Indians
snapped at it and, whimpering, it crept back beneath the truck.
Mamani had not taken his eyes off the Englishman and the
American; he shifted his grip on the gun and the barrel came up
higher. Taber could feel a chill grip him even through the
quilted jacket he wore. He had had no fear yesterday when he
had rescued McKenna, and anger had made him hot; but this
cold-blooded facing down of a gun, of trying to reason with men
whose thought processes he did not yet fully understand, was
another thing. Perhaps Pereira had been right: *mañana* would
have been better.

"I am here to work with you," he said. "Yesterday is forgotten."

For a moment it looked as if Mamani would make no reply,
then he said, "It is not forgotten. The padre taught our women
to sin!"

Taber glanced at McKenna, who spread his hands des-
pairingly. "Jesu, that was not my intention – to teach them to
sin, I mean. I did the wrong thing, but I was only trying to help.
That is my only reason for being here in Altea – to help you."

"Mine, too," said Taber, thinking, you dumb bloody clot,
why else would a man subject himself to the isolation, the dis-
comforts, the frustrating oppositions of this place?

There was no change of expression on the faces of the
Indians, but suspicion emanated from them like a smell. One of
them coughed and spat and the others looked at him as if he had
made some remark with which they did not agree. Why do we
bother with them? Taber thought; but knew it was a question
every humanist asked himself at some time or other when faced
with his fellow men; the religious were not the only ones who

occasionally suffered from a lack of faith. Faith in human nature required more determination than faith in a god; the reasons for your doubts were there all around you every day. Do you ever have doubts such as mine? Taber silently asked McKenna; but the priest, perversely, right then was placing his faith in the vagaries of human nature: "We were friends once, Jesu – we can be friends again. Let us make a new start – "

Mamani looked around at the other men, then back at Taber and McKenna. "Will you help us grow crops here on this land?"

That's torn it, Taber thought. "This is Ruiz land – "

"We know that. You said yesterday that it is better than our own land."

Verdoux's letter was burning a hole in Taber's pocket. "It would be a mistake to take the land without permission."

"Senor Ruiz would never give permission. We must take it for ourselves, plant our crops on it and show them we shall stay on it."

"How will you show them?"

Mamani held up his rifle and a moment afterwards the other men raised their guns and their machetes.

Taber shook his head. "It is not enough. They would send up the police or the soldiers."

"We would fight them."

"You could not win," said McKenna. "Jesu, can't you see? Some of you would be killed – "

"We would send a message to the government in La Paz. They are on the side of the campesinos."

"It would be too late. Bullets travel faster than messages." Taber looked across at Pereira still sitting in the Land-Rover, still waiting to see how the argument was going to go. He'll survive, Taber thought; and suddenly envied the Bolivian's talent for compromise. But then that's what I'm doing now. If I had any real guts, took the short humane view instead of the long pragmatic one, I'd take my stand on this land with the Indians and defy Ruiz and the police to throw us off. And we might win in the short term. But then in six months I'd find myself transferred, or out of a job altogether, and a month after that Mamani and his mates would be off the land, in prison or dead. Compromise is the thing, Harry. To coin another Taber maxim: ideals don't sprout on another man's land, not when he has the police as harvesters.

"Mamani," he said, "let us go back to your own land. We shall add fertiliser to it, increase your crops. In the meantime we shall send a petition to La Paz, ask the government to grant you some of this Ruiz land."

There was a murmur from one or two of the men, and Mamani looked at them. The group crowded together, their masks cracking with animation as they argued among themselves. It seemed to Taber and McKenna that it was Mamani against the majority; at last Mamani turned back to the two foreigners and said grudgingly, "We shall till our own land if you can get us the fertiliser. But if the crops do not grow better than now, we shall come up here and take this land, no matter what Senor Ruiz or the government will say."

McKenna looked at Taber. "So it's up to you, Harry. Where's the fertiliser?"

"That's the snag," said Taber in English. "It's down in Customs and I can't get it out unless I pay a bribe to the chief, Suarez."

"How much does he want?"

"I don't know. But whatever it is, I'm not going to pay it," Taber said stubbornly. "If I pay him once, he'll expect me to shell out for everything else I bring in in the future."

"What is the matter?" asked Mamani, not understanding the gringoes' language but catching the tone of their voices.

McKenna explained in Quechua: " – and Senor Taber refuses to pay the bribe."

"We could go and take the fertiliser," said Mamani, raising his gun again.

"That's an idea!" McKenna exclaimed. To Taber the priest seemed too eager to go along with the campesinos, anything as atonement for his sin: he saw the irony of the reversal, the priest seeking the layman's absolution, but he wondered if McKenna appreciated it. McKenna went on, "We could get the stuff out of Customs if we went in there at night – "

"There would be guards," said Taber, thinking, Christ, someone around here has to have some common sense. "And there's quite a bit of stuff in there. We'd need at least two trucks and a dozen men to load them. How are you going to get into the railway yards without causing a commotion? And where do we hide it when we get it?"

"We can hide it in our houses," said Mamani, and the other campesinos, suddenly promised action, nodded enthusiastically.

"The first places the police would search," said Taber.

"Can't we split it up?" said McKenna. "You could take some to that new house of yours – the police wouldn't dare to go there, you have some sort of diplomatic immunity, haven't you?"

"None at all," said Taber, feeling like the boy at the party who wouldn't let the others use his cricket bat. Christ, he thought, this is right against my character. But the letter in his pocket crackled a warning.

"Harry – " McKenna reverted to English. "Let's take a risk. We can get these guys back on our side. We're working for the same thing, aren't we? To get them out of their damned misery? Are you afraid of losing your job or something?"

"Yes."

That nonplussed McKenna for a moment. "Would they really fire you? I mean kick you right out of F A O?"

"Maybe not fire me altogether. They'd probably take me back to Rome, and that would be just as bad."

"I see your point," said McKenna sympathetically. Then he shrugged. "Well, it's up to you. If you say no, the scheme is off."

"A matter of my own conscience, is that what you mean?"

McKenna looked innocent. "I didn't say that."

"I don't know how Machiavelli never got to be Pope – he had the right sort of conniving mind for your crowd. You'll finish up a cardinal one day."

McKenna grinned. "I wouldn't want to influence you in any way."

"Not bloody much," said Taber. "All right, where do we hide the rest of the stuff? I'll take as much as I can in my house."

McKenna's grin broadened with delight. "I'll take some up at the mission – I'd complain to the Bishop if Suarez tried to search there and I think I'd win. I don't think I'd even have to go to the Bishop – just telling Suarez that's what I'd do would be enough."

"That would still leave quite a bit to be hidden."

McKenna was as enthusiastic as the Indians now; he was like a college student planning a sit-in in the president's study. Priests for a Democratic Society, Taber thought; revolution was breaking out all over. "We can take the rest of it up to our old mine. Will the cold affect it?"

"No-o," said Taber, resigned now. "Not so long as we can keep it dry."

"Then we'll have to steal some tarpaulins, too."

"Who hears your confession?"

McKenna grinned even more broadly. "I'll give myself absolution on this one. What d'you say, Harry? Let's give it a try."

"What are you looking for? To help these blokes or to get back in their good graces?"

"Both," McKenna conceded. "But I've been here longer than you. I know how hard it is to get them to even halfway co-operate with you. They're on your side now. If you could bring this off, most of your troubles with them will be over. They'll go along with you on anything you suggest from now on."

The letter in Taber's pocket had gone cold, was silent. After all Verdoux was down in Santiago in Chile, 1,200 miles away; if they managed to get away with the stuff from the Customs shed, Suarez might never report it; he might be operating according to the system, but he was not operating according to the law. Everything, then, might only depend on a successful heist, as McKenna, the bandit priest, would call it; the hiding of the stuff would not be a major problem. "We'd have to spread the fertiliser at night. The Altea land needs sulphur, mostly. If Mamani and his mates spread it during the day, we'd be in trouble if Suarez came up to the village and started sniffing around. He might then get the police to take it out on the campesinos, just out of sheer bloodymindedness."

"How long would it take to spread the stuff and turn it into the soil?"

"As I remember the size of the Altea land, about five or six hours. But that would mean everyone in the village working, women as well as men. There'll be some extra ploughing to do."

"Okay, so that means we've got to hit the Customs shed some time before midnight, maybe no later than ten o'clock."

It was Taber's turn to grin. "Were you ever in the Mafia? Or do they train you for this sort of caper in the seminary?"

"You should read the history of the Church, the unexpurgated version. Some of the best gangsters of all time were some of the cardinals of the Renaissance." If McKenna had any conscience about his intended plunge into banditry, it did not show; his face glowed with enthusiasm. "One of the things they teach you as a missionary is organisation. This thing has got to be properly organised."

"All right, how do we get into town at ten o'clock at night without being held? Two trucks loaded with campesinos driving *into* the city, not out of it, we're sure to pick up an inquisitive copper. Especially since that attack on the bank the other day."

"You're not going to believe this," said McKenna with a schoolboy's grin, "but I think I can black out the city."

"You're right," said Taber. "I don't believe it."

"The night supervisor at the power station owes me something. I'll have a word with him."

Taber hesitated, then shrugged. "All right. But if we're caught, you and I are both likely to be excommunicated."

"There's one consolation," said McKenna. "They've given up burning at the stake."

2

"You're asking too much, padre," the night supervisor said. "I can't cut off the power. Not for an hour. For ten minutes, perhaps, but not for an hour."

"Alfonso, when you came up to see me at the mission, asked me to recommend your son for an aid grant from our embassy in La Paz so he could go to an American college, did you not say you would be in my debt forever?"

"A figure of speech, padre –"

"Alfonso, I used my influence at our embassy – it was very difficult – " God, forgive me these lies, McKenna thought, they are all in a good cause. The embassy, eager to hand out aid, glad to be relieved of the chore of seeking out suitable candidates, had welcomed McKenna's recommendation of Alfonso Olavero's son as if it had been an edict from the White House itself. "I cannot tell you why I want the blackout, except to say your people will benefit."

Olavero was a mestizo. "Which people?"

McKenna was specific: "Your mother's people. But I promise you no criollos will be hurt." That, at least, was no lie: Suarez was a mestizo and the guards were sure to be Indians.

"Why must it be between ten and eleven o'clock? Why not three or four in the morning? People would notice it less then."

"It must be at ten. We need the rest of the night for other things."

"What things?"

"Trust me, Alfonso. After all, I am a priest, am I not?"

"Forgive me, padre, but if one trusted *all* the priests in South America, a man would never reach Heaven." Olavero sighed, ran a resigned hand over the black coxcomb that surmounted his parrot's face. "All right, ten o'clock to-morrow night for one hour. Pray for me, padre."

"I'll pray for both of us," said McKenna with sincerity; despite his enthusiasm he knew the risks of what they were about to attempt. He had prayed hard last night when he had got to bed and the horror of that morning had come flooding back in the darkness. He had suffered agonies of doubt as well as of memory; the threatened castration had reduced him not only as a man but as a priest. Am I a good priest? he had asked God again and again; but God last night had been no more than a silent darkness. And when he had got no answer from God, he had asked himself if he was a good priest. But there had been no answer there, though he knew that in the final analysis a man must judge himself a success or failure. Other men might judge you a saint, but he had never aspired to that.

Now, driving down the winding road to San Sebastian, he looked at his watch. "Nine-forty."

"Did you synchronise your watch with the night supervisor's?" Taber asked. "South American time is as unreliable as Irish time."

"Synchronised right to the second. I'm beginning to think I'd make a better general than a bishop."

"If ever you make it to bishop, I might consider joining the Church. Just for the raiding expeditions."

McKenna grinned broadly, flushed with the excitement of what lay ahead and pleased at Taber's oblique compliment. He was driving, Taber sat next to him and the owner of the truck, a squat buck-toothed Indian named Toribio, sat on the outside. Toribio had been reluctant to turn his truck over to McKenna, but both the priest and Taber had privately decided they were not going to risk their lives to the Indian's driving. There had been some argument, but McKenna, who had become more and more militant, the raid now grown in his mind into a crusade, had been emphatic that as leader of the expedition he should drive the lead truck. Mamani had settled the argument by saying that he would only bring his own truck if the padre led the way. Toribio, his moment of glory filched from him before it had even been sparked, had sullenly given up the driver's seat.

McKenna was driving without lights; an Indian truck with its headlamps blazing would have aroused curiosity. The brake pedal was useless and McKenna was continuously busy working the gear lever and the hand-brake; Taber, his feet buried in the floor-boards, watched with horrified fascination each time a corner came up ahead of them. When they reached the bottom of the winding descent both white men blew out loud sighs of relief.

The two-truck convoy did not follow the main avenue into town. The Indians in the back of each truck had been instructed to lie down, but McKenna knew that some inquisitive heads would be poked up above the trucks' sides; very few of Altea's campesinos came down here after dark and there would be some who would want to see what the city looked like at night. So McKenna turned off the main avenue at once and led the way down through side streets.

A traffic light glowed up ahead, a dragon's eye, and McKenna, less careful now that he was down in the flat streets of the city, thoughtlessly put his foot on the brake pedal. Nothing happened; the truck went through the red light at a brisk thirty miles an hour. McKenna saw the glare of headlamps on his right, heard the screech of brakes, then the crunch of metal and the tinkling of glass as the oncoming car mounted the pavement and hit a lamp-post. McKenna instinctively took his foot off the accelerator.

"Don't be bloody stupid!" Taber snapped. "This is no time for road courtesy. Step on it!"

McKenna speeded up, swung left at the next intersection, right at the next, driving with nervous desperation that had Taber and even Toribio on the verge of abandoning their seats beside him. At last the truck pulled into the deserted market square opposite the station; McKenna ran it in between two empty stalls and switched off the engine. Then he sat back, suddenly drained of confidence and enthusiasm.

"Oh God," he said in half-prayer, half-question, "how did I get into this?"

"I'll tell you how *I* got into it," said Taber. "You bloody talked me into it."

"Maybe I'm not such a crusader after all."

"It's a bit late to find that out. If we back out now, these fellers will castrate both of us."

"Do you think someone might have been hurt in that car back there?"

"I hope not. But to-night isn't the time to find out." Taber looked at his watch. "It's five to ten. We seem to have lost Mamani and the other truck."

But even as he spoke Toribio nudged him and pointed across the square. The second truck, lights out, was nosing down between the empty stalls. Taber was reminded of elephants he had seen seeking each other out on the banks of moonlit rivers in East Africa. Toribio swung open the rusty door of the driving cabin, jumped down and scuttled bandy-legged between the stalls and across the square. A minute later Mamani's truck came grunting its way between the stalls and pulled up behind the first truck. Toribio came back and climbed into the cabin.

"Okay," said McKenna, gathering his breath and his courage. "It's almost time."

He and Taber were dressed in dark sweaters and jeans and each of them wore a ragged straw hat. They were both too tall to be mistaken for Indians, but they had darkened their faces with dirt and hoped that if they were spotted at all they would be taken for mestizos. The night was cold and both of them were wearing gloves. McKenna raised a gloved hand now and blessed himself; Toribio did the same. Taber, sitting between them, embarrassed by the superstitious gestures, raised his wrist and made a pretence of looking at his watch.

"Now!"

Right on the second the lights in the square and in the railway station went out. McKenna pressed the starter and nothing happened; then there was a loud crash as Mamani's truck drove into them from behind. Toribio's truck lurched forward under the impact and, brakeless, began to roll out into the open street between the square and the station. Two cars came down the street, blew their horns, then swung desperately aside to miss the rolling truck.

"For Christ's sake, get it started!"

"What the hell do you think I'm trying to do?" McKenna was stabbing furiously at the starter. The truck was right out in the open now, rolling sedately towards the main entrance to the station. "Everybody off and push!"

But Toribio and the Indians in the back of the truck, old hands at this sort of emergency, had already dropped overboard. They crowded in behind the truck, began to push the still-rolling vehicle into a faster pace. McKenna threw it into gear, eased out the worn clutch; the engine coughed, died, coughed again, then suddenly roared into life. The truck shot forward; three Indians fell down on their faces and the others fell over them. Mamani's truck, following on, had to swing abruptly to the side to avoid running over them. Oh Christ, thought Taber, I'm in a Laurel and Hardy film.

McKenna turned the truck round, pulled up while the Indians, giggling happily, clambered back aboard. Taber looked at the priest and even in the darkness saw the flash of McKenna's teeth.

"What's so funny?"

"I'll bet none of the Renaissance cardinals ever went out on a raid like this one." The foolish mishap had acted like adrenalin on McKenna; in laughter he had found his confidence again.

"I'll have to keep the motor running once we get into the yards."

The two trucks swung down the side of the station building. The main hall had been lit when the trucks had first arrived, but now it was dark like everything else. McKenna and Mamani were still driving without lights; the moon was not yet up and the streets were as dark as ravines. McKenna leaned forward over the wheel, peering into the darkness for the gates into the railway yards. He almost drove by them; he saw them only at the last moment. He jerked the truck round in a sharp turn; Toribio gave a yell and was only saved from falling out by Taber's frantic grab at his collar. McKenna slammed on the hand-brake, threw the lever into bottom gear, then into neutral, and prayed fervently that the sequence would work. It did: the truck rolled to a stop, its motor wheezing but still ticking over.

The Indians were down on the ground at once, swarming all over the guard who had appeared at the small side gate beside the main gates. He must have just woken up or he was not very conscientious in his duty; he just stood still while Toribio and the others took his rifle from him and tied him up. They lifted him above their heads, flung him like a rolled-up carpet over a fence, then swung open the main gates.

McKenna winced as the guard was tossed over the fence. "I told them to be careful!"

"They were," said Taber. "They didn't cut his throat."

The two trucks drove into the big deserted marshalling yards. They bumped over the rails, past two ancient locomotives standing side by side like docile pachyderms: again Taber had the flashback image to East Africa. That had been a place where he had had no problems but his wife; after to-night he might be packing his suitcases again, but this time heading home for good. The Customs shed lay on the far side of the yards, a low adobe building with a corrugated iron roof. As the trucks approached it a guard, unslinging his rifle, stepped out from the corner of the shed.

McKenna went through the gears and hand-brake routine; the truck came to a halt and instantly there was a crash as Mamani ran into them for the second time. McKenna was torn between a hysterical urge to laugh and a frantic desire to turn and run: the raid had become farcical, it just couldn't succeed if it went on like this. Though he did not break into laughter, the hysterical laughter inside him made him too weak to run; and while he sat helpless Taber nudged Toribio and they both dropped down from the cabin. They were on the far side of the truck from the guard and in the moonless gloom the chances were he had not seen them.

"Stall him for a minute," Taber whispered.

"How?"

"Any bloody how!" Taber's low voice was hoarse with exasperation. "Call on some divine assistance or something. But for Christ's sake don't let him shoot off that gun or we're done!"

McKenna saw Taber and Toribio slide away into the tunnel of darkness between two railway cars; then, perplexed, he looked back at the guard who still stood by the corner of the shed, his rifle pointed at the trucks. Oh God, McKenna prayed, how about some inspiration? Then, whether divinely inspired or not, he turned his head and spoke through the glassless window in the back of the cabin.

"Agostino!"

"Yes, padre?"

"Stand up and ask the guard where the coal depot is."

"Why, padre? We have not come for coal."

Lord, hit him in the head with a little intelligence. "Just do what I say, Agostino. Quick!"

The Indian boy stood up, spoke over the top of the cabin. The guard, his rifle still covering the trucks, took a pace forward. "Why are you collecting coal at this time of night?"

Agostino bent down. "Why do we want to collect coal at this time of night, padre?"

Lord, I know you're trying to tell me I shouldn't have come on this raid; but I'm here now and I'm stuck. "Tell him it is freezing up on the altiplano."

Agostino was silent for a moment and McKenna knew the boy was going to ask another inane question. But just then Taber and Toribio emerged from the darkness behind the Customs shed. The guard must have heard them, for he spun round quickly; but he was too late. Taber hit him on the jaw and he went down as if he had been pole-axed. Toribio jumped on him at once, tied him up, slung him over his shoulder and disappeared back into the darkness. McKenna drove the truck forward to Taber.

"Round the end here!" Taber snapped. "We're in luck – you can't see the doors from the yards."

It took the Indians, with a crowbar, only two minutes to force open the doors to the shed. McKenna switched on the truck's headlamps and drove into the shed; Mamani's truck followed; then the doors were slammed shut. McKenna hesitated, then took the risk and switched off the motor; there might be difficulty in starting it again, but that was preferable to being asphyxiated by the gas being gasped out by the truck's exhaust. It took Taber only a minute or two to find the FAO consignment and at once the campesinos set to work to load it.

"How are we going for time?" Taber asked.

McKenna looked at his watch. "We're behind time. We've got to be up at the top of the road before the lights come on again, otherwise we could be picked up by the police up at the airport. They sometimes come out and patrol the road that runs past it."

The Indians were like schoolboys robbing an orchard on piece rates. They were scurrying between the trucks and the stacked boxes and drums, giggling with an enjoyment that made their usually sullen faces unrecognisable. They worked at a pace that would have exhausted Taber and McKenna in five minutes; Mamani went past carrying a drum on his back that would have reduced both the white men to their knees. They shouted to each other, making a game of their work; the shed rang with their merriment. Agostino went by and winked at McKenna, something he would not have dared to do up at the mission.

"They're making too much noise," said Taber.

"Let 'em go," said McKenna, glad once again that he had come on the raid. Out in the yards he had had a spasm of conscience when the guard had pointed the rifle at the truck; it was not a new discovery to find that one's moral sense could fluctuate in proportion to the pressure put on it; the rifle, even at 150 feet, had prodded his knowledge that he was doing something illegal. But the rifle now was propped in a corner of the shed and conscience, like a sympathy pain, had subsided till it could be felt no longer. "I've never seen them enjoying themselves so much. You and I have just been given the freedom of Altea."

"Well, don't let it go to your head." Taber had had no prick of conscience about the raid, only a practical attitude to not being caught. "We have to get back to Altea first. The freedom of Altea won't count for much if we're in prison in San Sebastian."

He went over to the doors of the shed, opened them slightly and peered out. Then he shut them abruptly, raced back to Toribio's truck and switched off the lights.

"There's something going on over in the station! Blokes rushing around with lamps and torches – "

McKenna suddenly hit his forehead with the palm of his hand. "Holy Pete! I forgot – to-night's the night the train comes in from Sucre! It's due in at ten-forty-five if it's on time."

"The way our luck has been running, it'll be on time all right." There was absolute darkness in the shed now, but Taber's voice had a sarcastic abrasiveness to it that was practically an illumination in itself. "How far did you get in your course on organisation in the seminary? Christ Almighty, by the time we've finished loading and drive out of here, those yards outside will be like Piccadilly Circus!"

"I'm sorry, Harry – "

"I should never have bloody listened to you! If there's anyone I hate it's a bloody amateur and I let myself be conned by an amateur bandit – and a priest at that!"

"Well, okay, save your bellyaching till we get out of here!" McKenna's voice took on its own abrasive note; he was as angry with himself as Taber was. The Indians stood invisible in the darkness listening to the two white men argue; if this thing goes wrong, McKenna thought, we'll have lost them forever and it will be all my fault. "Let's *do* something! You want to get out of here now, before the train comes in?"

Taber fumbled around in the cabin of the truck, found a flashlight, switched it on. "We haven't half the stuff yet. They still have to load the sulphur – that's what we need most up at Altea." He had clambered up on to the back of the truck, but now he dropped down again, waved the flashlight urgently at

Mamani and the other men. "Come on, for Christ's sake! Pronto, pronto, pronto!"

The Indians leapt back to the job with even greater speed than before; they had stopped laughing, but they were still enjoying themselves; they were still robbing the government. McKenna got his own flashlight from the cabin and stationed himself behind the truck. Taber moved down to where the boxes and drums were stacked; the Indians ran up and down the beams of the flashlights in a frantic parody of one of their own tribal dances. It took them another twenty minutes to finish loading the two trucks.

"The tarpaulins!" Taber yelled, and McKenna excused himself from the theft of those: conscience was being twisted into a pretzel knot to-night. The Indians grabbed a couple of large tarpaulins and flung them up into the back of one of the trucks. Now all they had to do was get out of town undetected.

As the doors of the shed were swung open there came the sound of a train's hoarse siren from up the tracks. Taber looked at his watch and said sourly, "On time."

"That must be the first time in years," McKenna said defensively. "If I believed in omens I think I'd get out now and walk back up to the mission."

"I thought you blokes subsisted on omens." Taber's tone was still acidic; he had never been in such a muck-up as to-night's caper. To-morrow, just in case, he had better start looking up other aid organisations that could use a soil scientist. "Righto, let's try our luck. If you get the bloody engine to start first time, maybe that'll be an omen. The first good one to-night."

The engine did not start at once. McKenna pressed three times on the starter: nothing. The train's siren sounded closer, a hoarse braying warning that sounded sardonic. Toribio jumped down with the starting handle, cranked furiously at the front of the truck; McKenna and Taber could hear him swearing at it as at a stubborn mule. The siren blew again: the train was now no more than two hundred yards up the track. Suddenly the truck's engine spluttered, coughed, then settled into an asthmatic rumble; McKenna let in the gears and they drove at speed out of the shed. And had to swing hard to the right as the train, a diesel locomotive and six carriages, came down the track immediately in front of the shed. The two convoys, the train and the two trucks, raced side by side down the yards to the small crowd waiting at the torch-lit station.

Taber flopped back in the seat and began to laugh. Beyond McKenna's silhouetted profile he could see the lighted windows of the train; faces were pressed against them, staring out in puzzlement at this escort of two trucks bumping its way down the ties of the neighbouring track. Up ahead several men, waving lanterns, had run out into the tracks. The diesel was blowing its siren, but Taber could hear only the mad laughter in his skull.

"Turn round!" he managed to gasp. "For Christ's sake, turn round!"

"I can't!" Now he saw that McKenna was laughing just as hysterically; they were both caught up in one huge joke that was going to write finish to them. "I can't turn the wheels over the tracks!"

The train was slowing, pulling into the long, ground-level platform, blotting out the waiting crowd. The two trucks rolled down the track, pulling in beside the neighbouring platform where three station employees were running up and down, waving their lanterns and shouting. A set of buffers, the end of the line, appeared ahead; Taber braced himself for the truck, brakeless, to run head-on into them. Then all of a sudden McKenna gunned the motor and yanked frantically on the steering wheel.

"Hang on!"

The truck lurched, its wheels skidding along the rails and bumping over the ties; then there was a series of bigger bumps and a moment later they were running on the smooth surface of the platform. McKenna drove straight ahead, blowing the horn; they drove right across the tessellated floor of the main hall, scattering latecomers for the arrival of the train. McKenna and Taber were still laughing; Toribio joined in, then the Indians in the back of the truck. They went right across the hall, out through the pillared portico and into the still-dark street on a gale of laughter. Toribio leaned out, looked back and shouted that Mamani's truck was following them.

"We've made it!" McKenna exclaimed; he hadn't had so

E

much fun since he had been in pantie raids at college. "Nothing more can happen now!"

Even Taber's optimism returned. The ancient trucks still had to accomplish the long twisting drive up to the altiplano, but it seemed that nothing could stop them now; they had had more than their share of mishaps for the night. "We've ten minutes before the lights come on. Step on it!"

They were slowing down for an intersection, McKenna again going through the gears and hand-brake routine, when they heard the fusillade of shots. The three men in the cabin instinctively ducked; but no bullets smacked into the truck. McKenna stepped hard on the accelerator, they shot across the intersection and a minute later they were on the road heading out of town.

They were only a quarter of the way up the long winding climb when the lights came on in the city beneath them. Twenty minutes later they passed the airport. Half a dozen cars were lined up at the entrance gates, blocked by two police cars. The occupants of the cars were standing in a line and four policemen, pistols in hand, were questioning them.

The two trucks sped on into the darkness of the altiplano. What happened in San Sebastian the rest of the night was no concern of McKenna, Taber and the campesinos. They had a night's work ahead of them up at Altea.

3

As soon as they arrived at Altea Taber took over the organising. "No reflection on the Church."

"Not much," said McKenna, but he was cheerfully unoffended.

"We'll spread the sulphur first, get it turned in. We'll hide what we can of the rest, including my share, in your mission – I'll take my share down in the Land-Rover to-morrow night. First light to-morrow we'll send as much as we can up to this mine of yours."

McKenna stood aside and watched Taber put the campesinos, men and women, to work. The Englishman had a talent for organising and handling people; he might not be tactful with those in authority but he knew how to get the best out of people who were working for themselves under his instruction. The fields above the village had been ploughed that day; since dusk the women, children and those men who had not gone on the raid had been clearing the ploughed area of rocks and stones. Everything was now ready for the spreading of the sulphur.

The moon had come up by the time the trucks had been unloaded and the sulphur distributed to the women. They moved out in a line, spreading themselves across the first field; the men moved in behind them with hoes and rakes. The still-rising moon, golden as an Incan amulet, softened the barrenness of the altiplano, turned the ploughed fields into acres of dark brown corduroy. There was only a slight wind, which lifted the loose dust into a golden mist all across the fields. The campesinos moved through it, following their shadows which rippled like shadows on water as the dust rose and fell with the wind. Arms swung out and back in unison; arcs of sulphur caught the moonlight and the women seemed to be wielding flashing golden blades. Behind them the men moved more slowly, turning over the dry crumbled earth, burying the fruits of to-night's raid that, they hoped, would bring forth fruit of its own in time. The moon rose higher, turning white, turning the altiplano into a reflection of its own vast lonely stretches. The Indians worked on, regardless of time and distance. McKenna, leaning against the iron fact of the truck, had the feeling he was watching some kind of magic, an image conjured out of the past by some alchemy of moonlight and inherited memory. Spanish troops, riding down this same road, must have witnessed something like this 400 years ago.

The country and the people wound their skeins round him again. I'm trapped here, he thought; though I'm diseased by loneliness, there's no cure for me anywhere else. Something had at last been started that might lift the villagers of Altea out of the misery of their poverty; he suddenly wished that it were he and Dolores, not he and Taber, who were responsible for the progress. But the Church would not have rival brides to herself. The men in Rome, solaced by comforts that compensated for their celibacy, did not understand the cancer of loneliness.

Taber, another lonely man, came across and sat on the

running board of the truck. "It gives you satisfaction, doesn't it? Seeing them doing something for themselves."

"Is it that apparent?"

Taber looked puzzled for a moment, then he nodded understandingly. "I was speaking rhetorically. But yes, you do look pleased. I guess I do, too."

"You do. Harry, have you ever been married?"

"Twice," said Taber flatly.

"Did your wives ever help you in your job?"

"Never." Just as flatly.

"Have you ever thought of giving up field work and going back to England?"

"There wouldn't be much work for me in England." Taber stared out across the fields, trying to remember England. But the fields of Buckinghamshire, where he had grown up, were now ugly council estates or had been cut up by speculative builders. In twenty years the England he had known had almost disappeared. "They took me back to Rome once, put me behind a desk. I didn't mind it for the first few weeks – Rome is a beautiful city and it has quite a lot of beautiful girls."

"What happened?"

"My arse got sore from sitting at the desk. My ears got boils on them, listening to some people there who are always looking the wrong way, not facing reality but a Technicoloured, Cinemascope home movie of their ideal. My disposition got worse than it normally is – "

"I'm glad I wasn't there." McKenna smiled.

" – and even the girls began to lose their attraction. Then one day I came across a quotation from Cato, who must have guessed that some day there'd be a lot of fellers sitting on their bums in Rome and doing nothing useful, for themselves or anyone else."

"What was the quotation?"

"It went something like: a man's life is like iron: use it and it gleams, don't use it and it rusts. I rusted in Rome. I'd do the same in England."

"I had a year at the Gregorian University in Rome."

"Like it?"

"For the year. But like you, I started to rust."

That was when the first doubts about being a priest had started. The theology had bored him; the bureaucracy of the Vatican had appalled him. He had found, to his distress, that he was not interested in God's work as a whole; it caused him no concern that churches were losing their congregations throughout the world. He had discovered, the longer he stayed in Rome, that the Church had come to look upon itself as an entity, that instead of being a means to the end that was the kingdom of God it saw itself as an end in itself: join the Church and you were set for the hereafter: it was an insurance company that guaranteed the bonus of Paradise. He had come to realise that he was really a social worker more than a priest. But when he had come to debate with himself whether he should leave the priesthood, he had recognised that he could not accomplish his chosen work outside its framework. The independent social worker, unless he had the prestige of a Schweitzer, stood little or no chance of success in the field; in every country in the world where there was need for a social worker there was also a bureaucrat determined to make his job more difficult. A missionary, religious or social, needed a powerful organisation behind him. And there was none more powerful than the Church.

"Perhaps you and I should get together, form our own organisation." It was a joking remark, but in his heart each man dreamed of the possibilities: to do your own thing, as it were, without regard to politics, bureaucracy or laws that were no longer viable. But even to dream was to joke: each knew he could never win. Taber stood up, looked at the old straw hat he held in his hand. "There are some fellers in Rome, on both sides of the Tiber, who should come out here and wear this hat for six months. Perhaps then they'd appreciate that people are more important than politics."

"Do you think that will ever happen?"

"No," said Taber sadly. "As soon as you get three men together there will always be politics."

At first light the bell in the church in the village began to peal. The sound came up on the wind, a centuries-old echo of command, but the campesinos, now in the far fields, did not look up from their work. Twenty minutes later McKenna, working a hoe beside Mamani, saw the fat little figure, like a trundled rock, appear over the edge of the path leading up from the village. Padre Luis stood looking around, then, soutane flapping in the wind, came stumbling across the fields towards Mamani. The little priest was ten yards away before he recognised the American priest in his sweater and jeans.

He nodded brusquely to McKenna, then looked at Mamani. "No one came to Mass this morning, Jesu."

"We are busy, padre." Mamani did not stop hoeing; only a few square yards of sulphur remained to be turned under. Traces of sulphur showed in the ploughed earth, but the wind would soon remove those or cover them with dust. "It is no sin to miss Mass on a weekday."

"Even the women did not come." Padre Luis did not look at McKenna, refusing to recognise the enemy. He had come up here fired with pious indignation, only to find that his authority was as loose as the dust that blew about the sandals he wore made out of old tyres. Already he knew that the American was to blame for his embarrassment, that somehow he had lost his flock to this intruder shepherd. He would have to complain to the Bishop again. "Why are you all working at this hour?"

Mamani looked at McKenna; he knew of the antagonism between the two priests. "Padre McKenna will tell you."

McKenna hesitated, wondering how much treachery there was under the flapping shabby soutane. But if Padre Luis squealed to the police, then he would have the campesinos to deal with later. Hating himself for the malicious glee he felt at the possibility, McKenna told the fat little priest what was going on. Then, taking pity on him, he added warningly, "But I should not say anything to anyone, padre. This means a great deal to Jesu and his friends." Then he added as a bribe, "It will mean more money in the village. You want a prosperous parish, don't you?"

Padre Luis looked at Mamani, who, taking over McKenna's implied threat, nodded emphatically. "It would be best if you knew nothing, padre. Or said you knew nothing. It would be no sin to tell such a lie."

The little priest recognised defeat too easily: all his life he had been familiar with it. But the look he gave McKenna was full of hatred. "Of course I shall say nothing, Jesu. Am I not a villager just like you? Those ones down in the city – " He spat his contempt for those he aspired to join. "If they come up here we shall tell them nothing. I shall go back and offer a Mass for us all."

"For me, too," McKenna could not resist saying; but Padre Luis was already walking away into the wind, trudging across the fields in the dawn light, a pathetic figure condemned forever by the meanness of his spirit. McKenna suddenly pitied him, wondering if the fat little man ever had doubts about *his* priesthood. He wanted to run after him, but he knew it would be useless. Padre Luis was so far gone in self-pity he would suspect even friendship. God, never let me get that far down!

Taber came across as the village priest disappeared over the edge of the path. "Where's he heading?"

"To say a Mass for us." McKenna turned back, grinned to raise his own low spirits. "I asked him to include you in it."

Taber snorted. "You fellers never give up trying, do you? Well, we'd better get the rest of the stuff up to your mission and the mine. Suarez could come up here any time now."

Half an hour later half a dozen boxes and drums were stacked in McKenna's bedroom at the mission, taking up most of the available space. Mamani, with four men, had already started for the mine, his truck loaded with the balance of the boxes and drums. McKenna and Taber, their work finished, sat in the living-room and looked at each other with the smug, juvenile satisfaction that the law-abiding get when they have succeeded in breaking the law. Successful larceny, McKenna was realising, could be as heady as strong wine; he would have to be more understanding in the confessional next time someone confessed to breaking the seventh commandment. Taber, more worldly, was debating what alibis they would use if Suarez came up poking around.

McKenna got up and threw back the curtain covering his larder beneath the altar. "Take your pick."

"Who's going to cook?"

"I am. But first I better wash my hands. I smell like someone who's just spent a week down a sulphur mine."

He picked up a pail, opened the door, then stopped. A Jeep

had pulled up in the yard and Suarez, his face dark with bristle and lack of sleep, was getting out of it. He came across, pulling off his gloves and putting out his hand. McKenna hesitated, then shook hands with him.

"Padre, it is a very early call. But I see you already have another visitor." His good eye flicked a glance at Taber's Land-Rover in the corner of the yard. "Has Senor Taber been with you all night?"

"All night," said Taber, coming out of the door behind McKenna. "Padre McKenna and I have started playing chess against each other. I stayed the night here."

"What's the trouble?" McKenna asked, amazed at his own poise. I'm a born crook, he thought. Or maybe I'll make a good papal envoy. "We've never had a visit from you before up here."

"There has never been any need for a visit, padre," said Suarez.

"Why now, then?"

Suarez's only good eye was fixed on Taber. "Thieves broke into the Customs shed last night. They stole all your consignment, Senor Taber."

"Oh?" said Taber, just as poised as McKenna. "That's too bad. I'll need a report from you, of course. For the insurance, I mean. And for my head office."

"This is the first you have heard of the theft?"

"Naturally," said Taber, and stirred up a little false indignation. "And I'm not very happy about it, I can tell you. If you are going to keep stuff in bond, you should see it's not easily stolen."

"The thieves would not have got away with it if there had not been a black-out in the city. For one whole hour, no lights. Everything was in darkness. It was a bad night for San Sebastian."

"Worse things have happened," said McKenna. "Senor Taber will just have to order a new consignment. It's a pity the campesinos will suffer, though. They were the ones who were going to be helped by it, isn't that right?"

"Yes," said Suarez, as if the campesinos were just a herd of wild llamas that had been driven off their feeding grounds by some natural disaster. He turned and looked back down towards

the village; the top of the church tower showed above the edge
of the ravine like a white cairn. The fields could be seen from
here and they were empty. "They must have been expecting
the fertiliser very soon. When I came up I saw all the newly
ploughed fields. Were you expecting the papers to arrive from
La Paz, Senor Taber?"

"Yes," said Taber. "I had sent off an urgent telegram."

"Well, the papers will be useless now. I am sorry you lost
your goods. Perhaps if our understanding had been better the
other day, you would not have lost it. You could have taken
delivery of it then and there."

"Yes," said Taber. "Except that I thought our understanding
was pretty well perfect."

Suarez's face stiffened and his good eye went as blank as his
blind one. He pulled on his left glove, then began to draw on
the right. Then he lifted that hand, the one that had shaken
McKenna's, and sniffed it. The action was deliberate, as arrogantly discourteous as he could make it. But he said nothing,
just stared at the two foreigners, then turned and went back and
got into his Jeep. He started up the motor, swung the Jeep
round, pulled up immediately in front of McKenna and Taber.

"If you have been up here all night, as you say, you will not
have heard the other news."

"What news is that?" asked Taber, not missing the inference
of Suarez's remark.

"Terrorists killed the mayor and wounded Senor Obermaier,
from the brewery, during the black-out. The police are questioning the night supervisor at the power station now. They
think he is in the pay of the terrorists. A bad night." He shook
his head. "Adios, senores. I shall send you your report, Senor
Taber."

Chapter 5

I

Fear and anger breed their own reaction; atmospherics brewed in the Ruiz household like an electrical storm. The killing of the mayor and the wounding of Karl Obermaier generated a dread in the servants that some day soon the terrorists might burst into the Ruiz house and kill anyone in their way; but the Indians' fear was only to be felt and not seen, an unease that was *there* but that their expressionless faces never confessed. Not so with Alejandro Ruiz's anger: it was as evident as the most threatening Andes thunderstorm.

"Execute them! Hang them by the neck in the main plaza or shoot them! Let their deaths be an example to any others who have their ideas – "

"You have to catch them first," said his wife placidly, pouring the morning coffee and handing a cup to Carmel. "Sugar, my dear? Calm yourself, Alejandro. Excitement is not going to bring back poor Carlos Limon, nor is it going to cure Senor Obermaier's wound – "

"The wound is nothing." Obermaier had his left arm in a sling and looked more proud than pained. Carmel recognised him as the sort of man in whom the boy was never quite dead: anything that set him apart from the crowd, the arm in the sling, the patch over a sore eye, a crutch for a stiff leg, any of these would be borne with pride rather than any sense of being inconvenienced. And of course, she thought, no good German was ever ashamed of his scars. There was a scar on his cheek and she wondered whether it was something he had suffered in a student duel or in the Nazi cause.

"But I think you are right, senora," Obermaier went on. "These men are not going to be easily caught. Not unless the army is properly mobilised, told to scour this part of the country with a fine toothcomb."

"La Paz will never agree to that," said Ruiz; he had the feudalist's contempt for government. "After the Guevara fiasco La Paz has convinced itself that the campesinos will never help any guerrillas or terrorists. They will just consider this a local outbreak, leave it to Colonel Gutierrez, who is a fool."

Romola smiled at Carmel. "You must not take my husband's outbursts too seriously. The army is inefficient and corrupt, but we need it and it does its job up to a point."

"It should not have dismissed its instructors," said Obermaier, meaning himself.

Ruiz had regained control of himself, realising again that his worst enemy was right here in the house: he would never defeat his wife, she was too good a guerrilla in domestic warfare. In a marriage like theirs one saw the merits of divorce; but his brother Jorge would only excommunicate him if he took such a course. "We must adopt our own course of action." Then added hastily as he saw his wife's sharp glance, "No, not a vigilante force. But we must see we do not leave ourselves open to attack. We have become careless and complacent since the army caught Guevara."

A week ago, Carmel thought, face hidden behind her coffee cup, I was in Paris wondering whether to go to Cortina or Klosters for the ski-ing this winter, trying to make up my mind whether to buy a maxi-coat or let the men continue to admire my legs beneath my mini-skirt. Both decisions seemed so important and now here I am sitting calmly (calmly? Well, almost) listening to three people discussing the best means of preventing themselves being assassinated. She looked up, blinking, as Romola said, "Does all this talk frighten you, Carmel?"

"I'm not sure. I – I can't quite believe it. I've been here less than a week and already I've seen – " But she did not go on to tell them what she had seen. There had been the dead policeman and the wounded bank clerk in the plaza; and there had been what had almost happened to her brother. She had guessed what the Indians had been about to do to Terry and she had had difficulty in not being sick in front of him; but she knew enough of men to respect their pride and their shame and she had not demanded to know more than he and Harry Taber had wanted to tell her. She was slowly coming to realise that she was in nightmare country, but she was not quite sure whether it was she or the others who were wide awake.

Then Francisco came into the room with his cousin Hernando. Both young men were in sober dark suits and looked like junior undertakers. Which was appropriate: "The funeral is to-morrow morning," said Francisco. "Senora Limon thanks you for taking charge of the arrangements, Father."

"The least we could do," said Alejandro Ruiz, somehow managing to suggest investment rather than charity. "Carlos Limon was a friend. We shall have to look for someone to succeed him."

"Why not Senor Obermaier?" said Hernando. Carmel saw the German look quickly at him, but it was difficult to tell whether Hernando was mocking Obermaier or not. He stood before the big fireplace, hands in the pockets of his jacket, his swarthy face lifted at just that angle she had seen in paintings of young men of the Medici period; the dark eyes were veiled and you could make a dozen guesses, and be wrong in every one, at what thoughts lay behind them. He and Francisco were much the same age, but he made his cousin look juvenile; he suggested that he already had as much experience as his uncle and more potential wisdom. Certainly he disguised his feelings and thoughts better than Alejandro Ruiz. "You are now a Bolivian citizen, Senor Obermaier. And you would like the job, would you not?"

Obermaier looked eagerly at his boss. "If Senor Ruiz felt I could divide my time between the brewery and the mayor's office – "

Ruiz shook his head. "No, Karl. It would be too obvious. There is already too much talk that we Ruiz run this city – " He looked candidly at Carmel. "It is not true, Senorita McKenna. But gossip needs little to feed on."

Obermaier did not move for a moment, then he nodded his head in agreement. His disappointment was as plain as the scar on his cheek; for a few seconds he had been the mayor.

"What is happening with the police now?" Ruiz asked.

"They are still questioning the night supervisor at the power station," said Francisco. "And they also have a man named Pereira, the cinema manager, with them. They want to

know if it was he who told the terrorists that Senor Limon and
Senor Obermaier were at the cinema."

"Pereira, the cinema manager?" said Ruiz. "Isn't he also the
agronomist? A talkative fool of a man. He put in a report to us
once at the Agrarian Reform Council. Pages and pages that
said nothing, as if he didn't want to offend anyone."

"That's the man," said Francisco, and turned away from
Carmel to face out the window, as if he had seen something of
sudden interest out in the garden. "He is working with Taber,
the Englishman."

There was a moment of silence in the room, then Alejandro
Ruiz shook his head. "That has no significance. Don't spread
that sort of talk."

Francisco flushed, but still did not look at Carmel. "I did
not mean to imply – " But his voice trailed off. He's just a
jealous schoolboy, Carmel thought; but wondered at the leap in
her breast when Taber's name had been mentioned. "But I
understand Captain Condoris will be questioning everyone."

"He even questioned us," said Hernando, amused. "Wanted
to know if we had seen anything when we were out last night."

"Where were you?" asked Romola.

"Out at the university. Some of the students there wanted to
ask Francisco about the Sorbonne." He took his hands out of
his pockets, pulled down his jacket. It was only a small movement but it suggested the demeanour of an older man, a judge
or a university chancellor adjusting his robes. He's wasted here,
Carmel thought. I wonder why he doesn't move up to La Paz?
"The funeral is at ten, Uncle. Uncle Jorge will say the Requiem
Mass. I took the liberty of saying you would read the eulogy
to Senor Limon. If you wish I'll write a draft for you and bring
it back this afternoon."

Ruiz nodded approvingly, but looked with disappointment at
his son, who had shown none of this sense of organisation. Two
years at the Sorbonne seemed to have taught him nothing, not
even how to handle an American girl who looked as if she was
used to being handled by all manner of men. "Don't make the
eulogy too flattering, Hernando. We don't want to make poor
Carlos unrecognisable to the mourners, especially his wife.
Only his indolence stopped him from being a fool."

"There are so many fools in San Sebastian," said Romola, innocence sitting on her face as incongruously as a child's mask. "It's a wonder we all survive. Hernando, Senorita McKenna is going to luncheon at Senorita Schiller's. Would you drop her off there?"

"I shall take her," said Francisco.

But there was no enthusiasm in his voice and his mother noticed it. Quick to relieve Carmel of any embarrassment she said, "No, I'm sure Hernando will be pleased to take her. I have things here for you to do."

Five minutes later Carmel, glad to escape from the house, was sitting beside Hernando in his battered and rusting Volkswagen. He had seen her raised eyebrows when she had got into the car and he said dryly, "Did you expect better of a Ruiz?"

"I'm not quite sure what I should expect of a Ruiz," she countered.

He started up the car, drove out of the courtyard, smiled as he looked in the driving-mirror and saw the big gates slammed shut almost against the car's tail. "I think my uncle's servants are more afraid than my uncle and aunt of the terrorists."

"Aren't you afraid of them?" asked Carmel, and suddenly felt afraid herself: she was riding with someone who could be a prime target for the bullets of any revolutionaries. She looked out at the streets through which they were passing, split like a surrealist painting into patterns of cold sunlight and cold shadows. Old men sat stiffly on park benches, like dark iron statues waiting to be carted away to some dump for monuments that had no further significance. A group of Indian women, their marketing finished, trotted along the roadway, shawl-wrapped babies bouncing on their backs like unsold goods. Two crippled beggars lay outside a church, like broken saints who had fallen from the empty niches in the walls above them. The only unusual note in the streets was the number of police and soldiers at every corner.

"Why should they try to kill me?" She was beginning to dislike his continual air of cool amusement, as if he got some smug satisfaction from the uneasiness of everyone else. "I am a very minor Ruiz. There are three or four of the family they would kill before they got to me. That is, if they intend to kill any

Ruiz at all." He patted the steering wheel, raised his voice above the noise of the engine. "In a country as poor as ours, I think it is a mistake to look rich. Uncle Alejandro thinks that a twenty-year-old Cadillac suggests that he is no more than one of the – what do the English call them? – distressed gentlefolk, that his best days ended with the revolution. I don't think that disguise is enough. Hence this old heap. I used it when I was at college in the United States and I brought it home with me."

"Where did you go to college?"

"Harvard. Where else would a Ruiz go? You forget I am a member of the Establishment." Again there was that cool smile that so annoyed her. "Here is Senorita Schiller's."

She did not get out of the car at once, but sat looking at him steadily. "Hernando, why do you stay here? You have nothing but contempt for this place."

The mocking eyes momentarily gleamed. "Better that than to be somewhere where people would only have contempt for me."

"What sort of answer is that?"

He got out of the car, came round and opened the door for her. "Carmel, go home. You are too naïve to be safe in a country like ours. Sooner or later you are going to ask the wrong questions of the wrong people. Americans are too curious for their own good."

"Are you anti-American?"

"In America, no. Down here, yes." He helped her out of the car, formally gallant; his manners, if not his manner, were faultless. "If I had met you when I was at Harvard, I'd have been one of your most devoted admirers. But down here, Carmel, you would just be a handicap to any man who courted you."

"Thank you," said Carmel, and managed a mocking tone of her own.

He drove off and she went in to the Schiller house. It was an old house, smaller than the Ruiz's, with a large iron-studded door opening right on to the street and two decorated farolas hanging over the pavement. The rooms were smaller than those in the Ruiz house and were more comfortably furnished; at least Carmel felt the whole house was much less museum-like.

Dolores, in pale blue slacks and a dark blue cashmere sweater, suggested an equally easy elegance. She smiled and looked at Carmel with an eagerness that surprised the American girl. "I'm so glad you came. I don't have enough girls of my own age come here. To tell you the truth, they bore me. All they talk about is marriage – either their own chances of it or someone else's. I hope you don't talk about it?" she said ruefully.

"Most of the people I know talk about divorce. That is an even more boring subject." Already Carmel was glad she had come; the atmosphere was so much easier with Dolores than with the Ruiz. She felt at ease enough to ask, "What do you and Terry talk about?"

"Not about marriage!" Dolores laughed, but Carmel wondered if she sounded a little embarrassed. Then she said soberly, "Your brother is a very lonely man."

"I know. Does he ever talk to you about it?"

Dolores didn't answer the question directly. "A woman can always sense loneliness in a man, even a priest."

Then an Indian manservant, thin and silent as a wraith, came in to say luncheon was served. They walked through to the back of the house, out on to an open balcony. Carmel was surprised to find that the ground dropped away beneath them; the house was on the edge of a deep narrow gorge that cut through the bowl of San Sebastian; in the distance through the gap the snow-capped cordillera lay humped like a range of cumulus cloud. In the gorge below a torrent tore at iron-coloured rocks in a white fury.

"The way I shall escape when the Indians come." Dolores waved a hand at the cataract far below them.

Carmel was shocked by the remark, but she made no comment. You did not ask a girl if she meant she intended committing suicide, not just as you were about to sit down to lunch with her. Instead she looked at her plate and said, "This looks good."

"It is seviche. This is trout, but you can do it with any fish. You scale and bone the fish, then leave it overnight in bitter orange juice. This morning my cook would have added salt, pepper, chopped onion and yellow peppers that she would have toasted and ground. The fish is raw, but as you can see, it looks cooked. What will you have with it? Potato salad or lettuce and tomato salad?"

"Lettuce and tomato. What would Bolivia do without the potato?"

"Starve," said Dolores. "At least most of us here on the altiplano."

"Us?" All at once Carmel felt she knew the other girl well enough to ask such a question.

Dolores looked down through the gorge towards the distant mountains. A shadow passed across her face and she bit her lip as if she were in pain. "*That* is what your brother and I talk about. I have no Indian blood at all, but I like to think that I belong to them. Bolivia is our country, theirs more than mine, but still *ours*. But I can never be sure that the Indians would want me to belong to them, nor any criollo, for that matter. And when they finally rise up – and they will some day, when they have found a leader of their own – I'll come out on to this balcony and wait to see how they come through that door there. If they come slowly, smiling, I'll know they are prepared to accept me. If they are running and shouting – " She looked down into the gorge, then back at Carmel. "Do I sound melodramatic?"

"No," said Carmel truthfully, conscious of a world opening up like a Pandora's box. Good God, she thought, how innocent you can be when you live in what is called the sophisticated society. "Terry told me the other day not to disbelieve anything I heard or saw in Bolivia."

"He would know," said Dolores; and Carmel wondered if he would tell her what the Indians had tried to do to him, another one who wanted to belong to them.

They were still out on the balcony, having coffee, when McKenna was announced. He came out on to the balcony, kissed Carmel on the cheek, then kissed Dolores's hand as she held it up to him. The old-fashioned gesture surprised and delighted Carmel, especially coming from an American and her brother; but she managed to show no expression. I'm becoming as inscrutable as the Indians, she thought; but knew that when real feeling had to be hidden she would always fail. That was why she had been vulnerable to so many men.

"I came to offer sympathy on your cousin's death," said McKenna; and then Carmel's face did open wide with surprise. "Didn't you know, Carmel? The mayor was Dolores's cousin."

"We were not close," said Dolores, who did not show much concern at what had happened to her cousin. "Perhaps that was why the Ruiz did not tell you – we were never invited to the house on the same occasions. It was at their house I once made the mistake of calling my cousin an arch-reactionary. It was rather like calling someone a Fascist in Franco's house."

"Have the police been to see you?" McKenna asked.

Dolores stiffened, with her cup half-way to her mouth. "No. Why should they?"

McKenna shrugged nervously, the gesture of a man for whom events had suddenly become too complicated. "I came in with Harry Taber – he stayed the night at the mission. The police were waiting for him at his house."

Again Carmel felt the leap in her breast. "Why didn't you stay with him? I heard them say at the Ruiz's house that the police were interrogating Harry's assistant, I forget his name. He also manages the movie house or something."

"Pereira." McKenna nodded glumly, his worst fears confirmed. "I wanted to stay with Harry, but the police said they wanted to see him alone. You don't argue with these fellers."

"Will he be all right?"

All at once McKenna noticed Carmel's concern and his face, awkward with his own worry, abruptly softened. "He'll be okay. Harry had nothing to do with last night's attack. I can swear that he was with me all last night."

"My servants told me that the Customs building was also raided last night," said Dolores. She too had become aware of McKenna's nervousness. She was not sure of her feelings for him, having trouble because of her upbringing in separating the man from the priest; but she knew that, whatever she saw him as, man or priest, she did not want anything to happen to him. "It was a raid by two truckloads of campesinos. That seemed a little strange, though the police probably aren't worrying about it just now. Not with the murder of Carlos on their minds."

"Why is it strange?" It was Carmel who asked the question

and Dolores noticed that McKenna, staring down the gorge, had given no reaction at all to her remark.

"The Indians don't have much talent for organisation, not something like a raid on a government building right in the heart of the city. They might attempt something like that at some remote place up on the altiplano, but not down here in San Sebastian. Not on their own." She looked hard at McKenna, forcing him by her will to turn back and face her. He is supposed to give comfort to others, she thought, but he is badly in need of it himself. But she did not know how to give it to him and instead said, "Were they campesinos from Altea, padre?"

He looked at her with pain in his eyes. Then the manservant came to the door of the balcony. "The police are here, senorita. They wish to see Padre McKenna."

2

Police headquarters were in the government palace on the main plaza across from the cathedral. The palace was seventy years younger than the cathedral; the first palace had been destroyed in an earthquake, but the cathedral had remained standing. The authorities, recognising God's bias and therefore left to their own ends, had built the present palace with walls thick enough to withstand the several major earthquakes that had occurred since. In the revolution of 1952 it had withstood the assaults of the campesinos for five days and its walls were still pockmarked with bullet and shrapnel holes.

Groups of Indians stood about in the main hall of the palace, looking bewildered, like children on their first day at school. The authorities were getting their revenge; the campesinos were being counter-assaulted by paperwork. Three men stood staring at a sheet of paper one of them was holding; their illiteracy turned their puzzlement into fear. A fat Indian woman leant against one wall weeping silently, now and again banging her bowler-hatted head against the wall with a loud thump; an Indian policeman was trying to comfort her, but her tears defeated him as much as the sheet of paper defeated the illiterates; he looked pleadingly at McKenna as the latter passed him, then suddenly realised that the priest was not on a mercy errand but in custody. The woman, catching sight of McKenna, wept louder and banged her head harder against the wall. McKenna, preoccupied with his own predicament, was half-way up the broad flight of stairs before he recognised the woman was Maria Mamani.

Condoris's office was on the second floor; McKenna guessed it was immediately below the office of the security police. Well, things could have been worse; God knew what would have happened to him if he had been taken another floor up. God knew what was going to happen to him now. He said a prayer, like a drowning man, as one of the policemen opened the door and gestured to him to go in.

The office was furnished in a style that suggested the occupant had no guarantee of permanency. There had been five chiefs of police since the revolution; two of them had died violently and two of them had made the mistake of backing the wrong presidential contender. Condoris was the fifth and so far he had survived because he had never gone out till the bullets had finished flying and because he had never been known to utter an opinion that could be remotely described as political. All the various factions, unsure of him, bemused by that rare South American species, an apolitical police chief, treated him warily but tolerantly. But Condoris, a wise man, did not antagonise any of them by making a show of permanence. The bleakness of his office had the effect of unsettling anyone who came into it. It seemed to offer comfort to no one, not even its occupant.

McKenna was no exception. He looked around him as he entered. This could have been the office of some monastery abbot; there was even a crucifix, Christ fly-blown and dusty, hanging on the wall. Condoris dismissed the two policemen, then looked up at the priest standing awkwardly in front of his desk.

"You may sit down, padre." He spoke in Spanish. He waited till McKenna sat down in the stiff-backed chair designed to discourage visitors from staying too long. Perhaps because he was apolitical, the police chief had never learned to waste words. He said at once, "Where were you last night, padre?"

"Up at the mission." McKenna's throat was dry, but he

managed to answer evenly. Apprehension scalded him, making him sweat; he was already far ahead of the police chief in the possible consequences of his being here in this office. Outside the window, down in the yard behind the palace, he could hear the tramp of feet as cadets marched back and forth in drill formation; they marched to the German step, their feet stomping down in a rhythm that to McKenna's ear suggested the sound effects of old movies he had seen on television. But he must not allow his mind to build up any images on *that* memory. "Why do you ask?"

"We have questioned the night supervisor at the power station. He says you came down to see him the day before yesterday, asked him to black out the city for an hour last night."

He sat primly in his chair, almost like a lawyer questioning some claimant to a small inheritance; there was no threatening air about him, his tone was conversational. McKenna had heard of the methods of police chiefs in other cities, of the security police upstairs, whose tortures, it was said, had all the beastliest refinements of both the Inquisition and the Incas; as far as he knew, nothing as terrible as those interrogations had ever occurred in this office. But McKenna knew of men who had been brought in for questioning and had never been heard of again, who were either dead or languishing in some prison in another part of the country. Condoris did not need to be threatening or bullying. In a land where the law was aimed to protect those in power, not the individual, an intelligent police chief did not need to step outside it to achieve his purpose. Here in his own office Condoris was not the little man he was occasionally when outside it, trying too hard to assume an air of authority. Here he did not have to try: the room had its own bleak suggestion of dominion.

"Before I answer any questions, captain, I think I should like to see the Bishop."

"This is not a Church matter, padre. You are not charged with heresy or anything like that."

"What am I charged with?" McKenna was regaining some control of himself. He was still afraid, but he was not going to help himself by being jelly-like. His request to see the Bishop had been no more than a time-waster while he sorted himself out; he did not really want to see the Bishop and was not sure he would be better off if he did. "Do you have a charge against me?"

"None so far. But I can find one if you want one, padre – " Condoris did not smile, but his sardonic humour was plainly apparent; it surprised McKenna, who had always thought the man incapable of any sort of humour at all. "You give benedictions, I hand out charges. Between us we must keep the soul in nice balance."

McKenna smiled, his guard let down. "I'll leave the charge to you, captain. I never let my parishioners choose their benediction."

"Perhaps it is just as well, otherwise you would have everyone asking for a saint's quota." Then without changing his tone he said, "Padre, why did you ask the supervisor to cut off the power for an hour last night?"

McKenna hesitated, then said, "Where is the supervisor now? Is he in custody?"

"Naturally," said Condoris blandly. He had a flat, slightly nasal voice, yet somehow it managed to suggest a dozen nuances without being raised or lowered even a half-tone. "He is there for his own protection at present. There is a great deal of feeling in certain parts of the city at what happened last night."

"You mean the murder of the mayor? He had nothing to do with that!" McKenna, suddenly fearful for Alfonso Olavero, could not keep his own voice down.

"Not directly, perhaps. But the coincidence is too great for us to ignore. The city is plunged into darkness, the mayor, having a night off at the cinema, is suddenly made aware of his civic responsibilities – " was there a note of amused irony in the flat voice? – "he comes out of the cinema into the dark street, four men are waiting there for him with guns – " Condoris put his hands together, steepling the fingers; he looked almost benign, an undernourished bishop. "Unless you can tell us something, padre?"

Us: the royal, ecclesiastical or political plural. It would be a relief, thought McKenna, to buck just an individual instead of an institution. He suddenly felt the weight of everything he faced and he slumped back against the hard straight back of his chair. He fenced again for time: "I saw one of the Altea villagers downstairs, a woman named Mamani. Why is she here?"

The steepled fingers stiffened; McKenna saw the knuckles whiten and knew that Condoris was losing his patience. But the voice was still flat and controlled: "That is another matter altogether, padre. We are looking for her husband. Unless you know something that connects the two?"

"Why do you want her husband?"

"Just for questioning. The Customs men think he may be able to help them recover some goods that were stolen last night from the railway yards. Would you know anything about that?"

McKenna looked carefully at the thin, composed figure on the other side of the desk. How did Condoris, a mestizo, feel towards Suarez, another mestizo? There had never been any organisation composed solely of mestizos; the dichotomy of blood seemed to militate against any common loyalty. He wondered if the police chief would know about the other man's corrupt attitude towards his job. He could not remember ever having heard a hint that Condoris himself was open to bribery; the man might be sometimes arrogantly authoritarian, but he was reputed to be honest. McKenna took a chance: "I understand you have also questioned Senor Taber?"

"Questioned him, yes. Unfortunately, Senor Taber did not give us any answers. The English still seem to think the world is their Empire."

That didn't sound like Taber; he must have had other reasons for not saying anything. "Then I'm afraid I can't answer any questions, either. Not till I have seen Senor Taber."

"Why, padre? Do you both have an alibi or something?" Condoris sat for a moment looking hard at McKenna; through the open window there came the sound of the marching feet, tirelessly, as if an army were passing below. Then abruptly he got up from his chair, came round the desk and crossed quickly to the door, jerking it open angrily. He said something in Quechua to the policeman outside, then came back and sat down. He sat up straight this time, his hands flat on the desk in front of him. "We do not like foreigners involving themselves in our affairs, padre. You Americans have a habit of doing that."

Here we go, thought McKenna. But all he said was, "I'll wait for Senor Taber."

Taber arrived, his very presence an encouragement to McKenna. Without saying anything, his air suggested that his abrasive personality had an even rougher edge to it this afternoon. He was still dressed in the dark sweater and jeans he had been wearing last night; but he had discarded his straw hat and had his checked cap pulled down on his red head. He took it off as he sat down on a chair beside McKenna, scratched his head and growled at the priest, "I think our game of chess was called off."

McKenna got the message at once: Taber was not insisting they persist with their alibi. "Captain Condoris says a friend of mine, Senor Olavero, is in trouble. He thinks maybe I could get him off the hook."

"Okay," said Taber, hooking one arm over the back of his chair, crossing his long legs. "They're holding Pereira, too. We have to get him off the hook."

Condoris looked from one to the other. "Do you gentlemen mind including me in the conversation?"

Taber glared at him, one ginger eyebrow quivering. "Captain, is everything we tell you in here going to go on the record?"

"That will depend on what you tell me."

Taber continued to glare at the police chief, then all at once he seemed to surrender. His face relaxed, he sighed and said, "Well, it started with Suarez – " He went on to describe his interview with the Customs chief. "I was being asked to pay graft for something intended to benefit your own countrymen, captain. I refused to do it."

It was Condoris's turn to sigh. "The habit is much too prevalent, but I am afraid it is as natural to our system as breathing. The English are addicted to snobbery, the South American to graft."

I shan't debate that one, thought Taber; he had met as much snobbery out here as one would meet in a whole continent of Cheltenhams or Bournemouths. "We needed that shipment, so we had to – er – break the law. That was where Padre McKenna came in."

McKenna then went on to describe his approach to Olavero and the subsequent raid on the Customs shed. Condoris sat listening with no expression at all on his face: the Indian in him had its uses in this job. " – and that's it," McKenna finished. "It was just a terrible coincidence that the terrorists should choose last night to murder the mayor and try to kill Senor Obermaier."

"Where is Jesu Mamani?"

McKenna hesitated. "He was just one of us, captain. Why are you so interested in him?"

"Five years ago he was arrested for political agitation."

"I didn't know that." McKenna looked at Taber: the water was getting deeper and muddier by the minute.

"He served six months in prison. He is still on probation." Condoris looked from one to the other. "Was he with you all last night?"

"All the time."

"Could he have told the terrorists there would be a black-out between ten and eleven o'clock?"

Down in the yard the marching had suddenly stopped; it seemed to McKenna that the whole police force was waiting on his answer. God, he thought, how have I involved all these people in this mess? Something that had begun almost on the level of a prank, an escapade in a good cause, had become a dangerous web. "I don't think so. He was with us all day yesterday. If you like, I'll bring him down to see you, captain."

"Can I trust you to do that, padre?"

Would he ask a Bolivian priest such a question, Padre Luis, for example? "You can trust me."

Condoris said nothing for almost two minutes; the cadets, as if they had got tired of waiting, had begun marching again. At last he said, "You are not in the clear, gentlemen. You will not be cleared till we find out who killed Senor Limon. So it will be in your own interests to help us. In the meantime we shall hold your passports." He held out his hand. "You must understand my position, gentlemen. A policeman who relied entirely on trust would soon be out of a job. I understand it is even that way in your countries."

McKenna and Taber passed over their passports, both

reluctantly but both knowing at this moment they had no argument. McKenna remembered the illiterate Indians downstairs and their piece of paper; that was all one's soul was these days in the eyes of government, a piece of paper; without it you were nothing, lost in limbo. He wondered how long before their respective embassies could rescue him and Taber from this limbo.

When the two men went downstairs, Carmel and Dolores were waiting for them. The women's faces lit up with relief when they saw the men were not escorted by policemen. But first McKenna went across to speak to Maria Mamani. She was no longer weeping or banging her head, but leaned against the wall, her face collapsed in misery and her eyes staring sightlessly at the four policemen lounging against the opposite wall.

"Maria."

She jerked her head as if she had been startled from sleep. "Padre? Oh, padre – " Then she stopped, looked at him from the corners of her eyes. "Did you tell the police?"

"Tell them what?"

"What – what Jesu and the men tried to do to you the other day."

All this is too complicated, thought McKenna, suddenly weary. All this suspicion and all this just cause for suspicion. Only a week ago he had been complaining about loneliness; now he was caught up in a cross-weave of relations such as he had never dreamed of. Maybe Condoris has been more trusting than he had given him credit for. He said patiently, "Maria, that is all forgotten. Jesu and I are friends again. But I have promised to bring him down to see the police chief."

"They will put him in prison!" She began to weep again. "They tortured him, padre. Beat the soles of his feet, made him walk on them. They put electric wires – I can't tell you where, padre – "

But McKenna knew. Electric wires applied to the testicles had become a standard twentieth century torture; technology had improved on the inventions of the Chinese and the Spanish. He looked up the stairs, saw Condoris standing at the top of them.

"I don't think Captain Condoris would allow that to happen –

he is not a cruel man. I'll guarantee they won't harm Jesu," he promised recklessly. Maria was weeping loudly now, banging her head against the wall again. There was no embarrassment felt by any of the onlookers, not even Taber, Carmel and Dolores: this big hall reeked of centuries of emotion. "My jeep is outside. Wait for me out there and I'll drive you back to Altea. And, Maria – " he tasted something sour on his tongue: doubt, a lie, he wasn't sure which – "you must trust me."

Maria dried her eyes with the sleeve of her blouse, straightened her hat: there was something comic about her movements, but McKenna was as empty of laughter as he was of confidence. "I trust you, padre," she said, and laid her husband's life on the priest's shoulders.

McKenna, heavy-footed, went back to join Taber and the two women. "Are you going to bring Mamani down here?" Taber asked.

"What else can I do?" Condoris still watched them from the top of the stairs. "Let's get out of here."

After the cool gloom of the palace hall the plaza was a volcano of light; the sun exploded from a glass-like sky. The four of them at once retreated behind their dark glasses; their faces at least now had a measure of composure. McKenna looked at his sister and said, "I think it would be a good idea if you went home, Carmie. Or anyway got out of Bolivia."

Carmel shook her head in puzzlement. "But why? Terry, if you're in trouble – " She shook her head again, this time determinedly. "No, I'm not going."

"Are you really in trouble?" Dolores asked Taber.

Taber took off his cap, scratched his head. In the glare he seemed to be running his hand through a fire of hair. He was not too worried that he and McKenna would finish up in prison, not so long as Condoris managed to remain in charge of the case. The trouble would come if and when the security police and the army moved in; then the very least that would happen to him and McKenna would be deportation. He did not like to dwell on what could be the worst to happen.

"I don't know," he said, and smiled a wry smile that none of the others understood. "But I'll pack my suitcases just in case."

3

McKenna, pale and haggard, went off in the Jeep with Maria Mamani. The Indian woman had stopped weeping, straightened her bowler hat again, and sat up in the front seat of the Jeep looking out at the other Indians with her face stiff with dignified superiority. Taber thought she looked like Queen Victoria.

Dolores, her concern showing despite her control of herself, looked after the departing vehicle. God, protect him, she prayed, he is out of his depth in what is going on here. Then, composing herself, she looked at Carmel. "Shall I drive you back to the Ruiz's?"

"Let me do that," said Taber. It had been a depressing day and he did not want to return immediately to the further depression of his empty house. Even an hour's postponement, if Carmel would give him that much of her time, would be a help.

The glance that passed between the two women was one that each understood: in your own loneliness you did not refuse the plea of a lonely man. Both women were more perceptive than Taber imagined; he thought he gave the impression of only being polite. Carmel got into the Land-Rover.

"I'd like to see where you live."

When they drew up outside the house Pereira, dressed in his best suit, his cinema manager's uniform, was standing on the front porch. His shirt collar was wilted and marked with finger stains, as if someone had grabbed him by it; there was a bruised swelling over his right eyebrow. His hands began fluttering at once, like birds tethered to his wrists. "Harry, I am greatly relieved to see you! I thought they had incarcerated you – " Then he broke off and smiled at Carmel. He brought his heels together and bowed, gallant as a gigolo. "Senorita, forgive me – I was too troubled for my good friend Senor Taber – "

Taber introduced Carmel. He had been upset by Pereira's being taken in by the police, but he did not want to listen to the garrulous agronomist's version of it, not right now. "Miguel, could you come back and see me this evening?"

"Of course, of course!" Pereira exclaimed, his smile stopping just short of a leer; he was not one to stand in the way of a little seduction or whatever it was Harry had in mind. He had not taken his eyes off Carmel, wondering how a priest could have a sister like this. Ah, how marvellous and varied the genes could be! "I shall come back later. To tell you of the indignities I have been through – you will not credit them! The police went crazy after the shooting – they arrested me, the cashier, even the poor projectionist! What would I know about assassination? All I am interested in is survival." He looked directly at Taber, his voice suddenly quavering. "Harry, what is there you haven't confided in me?"

Taber, feeling guilty, patted him on the shoulder. "Miguel, I'll tell you all about it to-night. But I promise you – you don't have to worry. You're in the clear."

Pereira went off only half-convinced. Taber let Carmel into the house, led her through into the living-room. She looked at the nondescript furniture, at the barren personality of the room. She felt that some comment was called for when a man took you for the first time to what he probably called home. But all she could manage was, "It looks comfortable."

"That's all I ask for," he grinned, noticing her restraint. He wondered for a moment what standard of luxury she was accustomed to, but he felt no embarrassment at whatever comparison she might have made with these surroundings. Possessions, as an environment, meant nothing to him. "Would you like a drink or some tea?"

"You look tired. Let me make you some tea."

He was not only tired, he was dirty, too; but he did not want to waste his time with her by going upstairs for a shower. He led her into the kitchen, where she looked around in surprise at the bottles and scales and test-tubes. "My laboratory," he explained. "There's more to come down from your brother's mission when the coast is clear, stuff we pinched last night from the Customs shed." He explained about the raid, laughing occasionally at the memory of the fiasco it had almost been. He was feeling more and more relaxed just being with her; even his tiredness began to disappear. He waved a hand round the kitchen. "This is where I really get wrapped up in my work."

"But where will you cook your meals?" She found an electric kettle and plugged it in.

"I'll eat out." He grinned, only half in mock self-pity. "Home cooked meals are few and far between."

"If I were a nice domestic type girl I'd volunteer to cook you a meal. They taught us Cordon Bleu cooking at the finishing school I went to in Switzerland – I got the lowest grade ever. My cheese soufflé looked like a piece of Kraft processed cheddar." She picked up the kettle, listened to it. "I can't even boil water."

"Water takes longer to boil at this altitude." He sat on the kitchen table, studied her candidly. "If ever you fell in love with a man, what would you have to offer him?"

She was surprised by the question; she was further surprised to find herself blushing. She turned away, busying herself finding cups and a teapot. "I don't know. Just myself, I guess. And my money, if that was what he was interested in."

"Are many of them interested in that?"

She was measuring tea carefully into the pot. "Too many of them, when they know how much I've got." She looked sideways at him from beneath an overhang of hair. "Would you marry a girl for her money?"

"If she was as lavish with the tea as you are, I think I'd have to. That's the tenth teaspoonful you're putting in there."

They both laughed, and she was glad of the interruption. Then the kettle boiled at last and that gave her more time to collect her thoughts. It was not that she was unused to such a conversation; her dialogues with men had run the full gamut of intimacy. But there was a prickly directness about Taber; even his banter seemed to have a purpose about it. She put the cups and teapot on a tray and led the way back into the living-room. She sat down in a chair and began to pour while he put his feet up and lay back on the couch. He slipped off his shoes and, being too long for the couch, hung his stockinged feet over its arm. She handed him his tea.

"This reminds me of when I was at the convent. The nuns taught us how to be young ladies, how to entertain our gentlemen friends in the living-room. We had one very old nun, from Boston, who always called it the drawing-room."

"Have you remembered everything the nuns taught you?"
He tasted the tea and managed with an effort to keep the curl
out of his lip: the nuns and the finishing school hadn't taught
her how to make a good cup of tea.

"I've done my best to forget them," she said. "But don't
mention that to Terry."

He wriggled his toes, staring over them at the window. Out
in the garden he could see a flamboyant tree, aflame in the
afternoon sun; there had been just such a tree in the garden of
the house in Kenya. There were certain things that he, too,
wanted to forget. He sipped the tea again, making an effort.

"What do you want to do with your life?" she said abruptly.

"What I'm doing now. Make things a bit better for the poor
bastards who could do with it."

She liked the quiet, flat way he stated that; there was no
attempt to sound like a crusader nor any mock embarrassment
as if trying to play it down. Too many of the men she had
known had been theatrical, even in bed, as if they had expected
her to be an applauding audience to their love-making. She
looked at him, wondering what he would be like in bed. It was
the first time she had looked at him in that way and she felt
weak from the current that ran through her.

He swung his legs off the arm of the couch, stood up. "I'm
going up to have a shower," he said, confident now that she
would stay as long as he wanted her to. "I stink like one of the
Indians. There's some airmail copies of *The Times*. Read who's
been having tea with the Queen."

He went upstairs and she went back into the kitchen and
washed up the cups and drained the teapot. She was not in the
least domestically-minded, no more than she was politically-
minded: God, she thought, I'm absolutely useless. Useless for
anything but bed. There was the feeling again, making her
weak.

She went back into the living-room, moved around straight-
ening the newspapers, shaking out cushions, being a wife. A
wife? She heard the shower go on in the bathroom, heard him
singing in a flat, tuneless voice: he was king of the road. Her legs
had a volition of their own. They carried her upstairs, past the
half-open door of the bathroom and into the main bedroom.

Her mind seemed to have stopped functioning, or if it was working at all it was through a brain that had turned to cotton-wool. She had no will, only desire.

She sat down on the bed, her knees primly together, just as the nuns had taught her. She heard the singing in the bathroom stop, then the shower was turned off. She looked about the bedroom with the cold, careless eye of a girl who had visited a score of bedrooms. The furniture was as uninspiring as that downstairs; no wonder romance had such a hard time staying alive in the suburbs; this was Grand Rapids at its worst. The clothes Taber had taken off were flung over the back of a chair; three suitcases were lined up in one corner. This room no more belonged to him than the rooms downstairs: she was in a stranger's house, waiting to be made love to in a stranger's bed. Suddenly her mind cleared and she stood up.

"Don't go." Taber stood in the doorway, a towel wrapped round his loins.

She shook her head, blinded by shame. "No, I made a mistake – "

He came to her, put one hand on her shoulder, with the other raised her chin. "No. I've been standing there under the shower *willing* you to come up here. It's an old African witch doctor's trick – " He grinned, then bent his head and kissed her gently on the lips; she tasted a sharp toothpaste, smelled the clean freshness of him. "I think I've been willing it ever since I first met you."

She recognised it as flirtatious flattery, but she didn't mind; he was doing it with the best of intentions, to make out that it was he, and not she, who had made the first approach. All she had to do was surrender, which she did at once. She put her arms round his neck and kissed him, nowhere near as gently as he had kissed her.

"How much are you affected by the altitude now?"

"Try me."

When it was all over each was as exhausted as the other. She lay in the crook of his long arm, her hand moving slowly over his body. He was bony, but he also carried a surprising amount of muscle. He was surprising in many ways. "I always thought only Negroes were as well-equipped as that."

"Out in Africa when the blacks saw it they used to call it the white man's burden."

"You're a very gentle lover, considering."

"Are you complaining?"

She could feel the calluses on his hand as he caressed her. "No. Men who come at you like a bull at a gate – " Then she stopped.

"What's the matter?"

"Nothing."

He put a finger on her cheek and turned her face towards him. "Look, I know there have been other blokes."

"I shouldn't talk about them. I don't want to hear about your wives."

He was silent for a while, then he said, "Have you ever been in love with any of these men?"

"Several times. Or I thought I was at the time." She rolled over on her back, stared up at the ceiling. "Why do you want to talk about them?"

"I don't particularly want to talk about *them*. I want to talk about you. But you haven't lived in a vacuum – "

"Maybe I have," she murmured, talking to herself. She knew that love was a mixture of pain and happiness, that love could never be an eternal euphoric drug; but so far all she had experienced was the pain and none of it had been the sweet, pitying kind that was the ache of true love. She said, not entirely truthfully but because it was how her mind was working at this moment, "I can't even remember their names."

"How did it all start? I mean, this gallivanting around – "

"I don't know. I was running away from my mother, I suppose. She's so damned holy – no, not holy. *Pious.* There's a difference. She goes to daily communion, won't have the word *communism* mentioned in the house, thinks the local archbishop is closer to God than the Pope. She turned me into what I am – " In her heart she knew this was not all the truth; but she knew enough not to substitute the love-bed for the analyst's couch. Taking your clothes off did not mean you had to strip yourself to the core. Only a masochistic man would want to know all the secrets of a woman and she did not think Taber was a masochist. "She wanted Terry to be a priest from the time he was

F   161

seven – as soon as he could pronounce the Latin words she had
him down to the church as an altar boy. She wanted me to be a
nun – a Carmelite. Get it? I started rebelling at twelve, I think
I was. I went *looking* for sin, can you imagine? Like a girl
collecting autographs or something. I had my first boy at thirteen." Now she had started the confession flooded out of her,
bitter as vinegar. "Does that shock you? And there have been
dozens since. But I've never fallen in love, now I come to think
of it. Not *really* in love. And you know why? Because basically
I'm a *good* girl. Does that make you laugh?"

She continued to stare up at the ceiling, her eyes stiff with
the strain of looking at the past. She had been seeing more than
she had told him: a vast emptiness with place names, New
York, London, Paris, Rome, that meant nothing. Her eyes
began to melt with self-pity; tears ran down her cheeks. She
turned away from him, her head still resting on his arm.

He felt her tears on his wrist. He said nothing, lying unmoving; he knew that a woman like her would not have limitless
tears. At last she turned back, her eyes puffed but no longer
weeping.

"Thanks."

"What for?"

"For not asking why."

He kissed her cheek, licking the salt there. "Sometimes I
wish I were capable of it. Having a good cry, I mean. You women
are the sensible ones."

She put her arms round his neck again. "Some day I may cry
over you. But not now. Right now I'm very, very happy with
you." She smiled, blinking to clear her eyes of the last of the
tears. "How's the altitude?"

"My altimeter's ready to find out."

The jokes are always juvenile in bed, she thought. But she
laughed, as much with happiness as with humour. It might not
last, but she was no longer lonely.

Chapter 6

I

McKenna sat in the sun outside the Mamani house in Altea. A woman and a boy went down the street, struggling with a barrow-load of potatoes that threatened to overturn in the rutted roadway. How would they survive without the potato? he wondered. He watched the barrow go by heaped high with the stone-like vegetable that came in a variety of colours from white through yellow and brown to grey and the almost black chuno, the frozen potato.

Agostino brought him a cup of chicha beer, offering it to him with a formal hospitality that made it more than just something to slake his thirst. He waited till the boy had gone back inside, then he took his handkerchief, dipped a corner of it in the beer and carefully wiped the rim of the cup: the beer was a good killer of germs. He looked over his shoulder to see if there were any bloodsucker nests in the adobe, then he leaned back against the wall and relaxed. Why the hell am I worried about germs and parasites? I'm in more trouble than they could cause me. What a pity the world can't be pasteurised of trouble, that a man can't be vaccinated against involvement with others. But even as the thought prickled his mind he knew he would not want it that way.

He finished his beer, got up and went into the main room of the house to put the cup on the table there. And wished he had remained where he had been. Maria, Agostino and two of the smaller Mamani children were in the kitchen brewing more chicha. They sat on the dirt floor round a yellow mound of maize flour, a large chipped bowl in front of them. Each of them put a handful of the flour into his mouth and chewed on it till it had turned to paste with his saliva. Then they dropped the small balls of paste into the bowl. McKenna knew that the bowl full of paste balls would then be put out in the sun for two days,

163

the sediment washed off, then that boiled for twenty-four hours and finally left to ferment. He knew the process and each time he drank chicha managed to put it out of his mind. But now, seeing the spittle-dribbling mouths working on the maize flour, still with the taste of the beer in his own mouth, was too much. He went quickly outside again before he was sick. He had a long long way to go before he would be one of these people.

He walked up to the end of the village street, to the end of the ravine where he could see out across the lake. Here his head was almost on a level with the surface of the lake; the water became an oblique mirror that foreshortened the landscape. Coming down the track past the end of the glacier he could see Mamani's truck, an ant crawling along the base of the mountain wall. A storm was building up above the far peaks, turning the snow on them to a purplish blue; snow and clouds merged and the peaks became part of the turbulent sky; the mirror of the lake pulled the whole scene together into one frightening fantasy. The sun was still shining above the village, but the clouds were racing to blot it out. He hoped the rain would not last too long. It had been a wet winter, the lake was well above its usual high-water mark, and a long spell of sunshine was needed to bring on the campesinos' crops. This mountain landscape never failed to awe him; it reminded him of the majesty and the wrath of God. He just wished that it and God would sometimes be kinder to the people who lived here.

The truck arrived with the first heavy drops of rain. McKenna had walked back down the street and stood waiting in the Mamanis' doorway. Jesu Mamani parked the truck in the narrow lane beside his house, waved to the men who had gone up to the mine with him, and came round to join McKenna. He ushered the priest into the house, half-closing the door against the rain that was now pelting down.

"It is done, padre. They will never find the stuff up at the mine." He was grinning broadly, hardly recognisable as the usually sullen Mamani. "It was a good night's work last night. I thank you for myself and the other men. Agostino, bring the padre a beer."

"No, thanks." Even if he had not seen it being made, McKenna knew he could not have drunk the beer. His throat had tightened with the strain of what he had to say: "Jesu, Captain Condoris, the chief of police, wants me to take you down to San Sebastian to see him."

The grin froze on Mamani's face like a grimace. Behind him the family crucifix hung on the wall: Christ looked over his shoulder with the same look of having been betrayed. "Padre, why did they send *you*?"

It was the only way I could go free myself. But he said, "It was the safest way, Jesu. Otherwise the security police or the army may come after you. Things went wrong last night, Jesu – the mayor was killed by terrorists."

"Padre, what has that to do with me?"

"Nothing. I shall be your witness, Jesu – " He heard himself continually using the other man's name; that was a habit people fell into when their argument was weak. "The police are going to do nothing about our raid on the Customs shed – " He hoped he was correct about that; Condoris had given the impression that what was missing from Customs was no business of his. "But they want to talk to you – "

Mamani shook his head. "No, padre. They will keep me there, not let me go. They took me in for questioning once before. Just routine, they said – " He was showing a sophistication that McKenna had never suspected in him; though he was still speaking in Quechua he was sounding much more educated than McKenna had ever heard him sound before. "They kept me for two months. They tortured me, padre – "

"Maria told me. Jesu, were you a political agitator?"

The Indian looked hard at the priest, as if debating how much he could trust him. Then he said, "I went to school down in San Sebastian, at the school run by the Franciscan fathers. I was a grown man, but I was not ashamed to go with boys of Agostino's age. Some of the criollo boys laughed at me, but I took no notice of them."

"Who got you into the school, kept you and your family while you were earning no money?"

"Senor Ruiz. He did not know me. He sent word up to Padre Luis to choose a man from Altea to go to the school. I was just propaganda," he said, and for the first time since he had stopped smiling his face showed some expression; sophistication was the crack in the inherited mask. "There was criticism in La Paz that the criollos were not doing enough in San Sebastian to help the campesinos. I had three years at the school, I was Senor Ruiz' answer to the criticism."

"Did you ever meet Senor Ruiz?"

"Never. He was not interested in me as a person. His nephew, Senor Hernando, brought me money each month for my family."

"Why did you come back here when you had finished school? With your education you could have done better than this – " McKenna gestured about him at the dim, dirt-floored room, the rough furniture, the scuffed and dirty llama rugs; the one bright note in the room was the garishly painted crucifix on the adobe wall. He knew he was making an insulting remark about the other man's home, but the issue was too important for mere politeness. "You could have gone to work for the government – "

"I was in a demonstration. The university students attacked the American information library. The school students joined in – I was one of them – "

"Why?"

"I was an Indian – I suppose I was trying to prove I was as good as they were – "

"What happened?"

"The security police broke up the demonstration. But they only arrested the mestizos and Indians, none of the criollos. They kept me for two months, then told me I was finished at the school. They said education was a dangerous thing for some people. I came back to Altea to be a campesino and nothing else." The bitterness turned his usually soft voice into a rasp.

Outside the rain was coming down steadily, turning the day a dull grey. Maria came into the room, tut-tutted at seeing the rain beating in on the dirt floor, shut the door and lit an oil lamp. In its yellow glow the Mamani family stood looking at McKenna; even the youngest child's face seemed full of suspicion of the priest. Oh God, he prayed, how do I help them?

"Jesu, how did you get enough education in the first place to go to high school? None of the other men in the village can read or write, not the ones your age."

"Don't you remember? Your mother taught us both to read and write when we were very small children."

A memory came back: his mother sitting between them reading nursery rhymes and a children's book of Bible stories. The web of involvement went back twenty-five years or more. "I had forgotten. But how did you go on from there? There was no school in the village till I came."

Mamani moved to a rough wooden chest in a corner of the room. He lifted the lid, revealed the chest packed with faded, dog-eared books. "I took them from your father's house when they closed down the mine. I taught myself from them."

He took out several of the volumes. His self-education had been catholic: *Tom Sawyer*, a Sears, Roebuck catalogue, *Gone With The Wind*, Sandburg's *Abe Lincoln Grows Up*; McKenna wondered how much of the books he had understood when he had first started to plough his way through them. But he would understand them now. McKenna recognised that this man standing with the books in his hands was not Jesu Mamani, campesino. He might still be infected with the superstitions of his ancestors, still be capable of their barbarities (McKenna felt the pain in his testicles, shuddered); but he was no longer entirely a man of darkness, an illiterate primitive. He had glimpsed another world but that of the altiplano. And he would not lightly put his trust in anyone, priest or police.

"Why didn't you tell me this before, Jesu?" Here was a man he could have talked to, who would have reduced his loneliness.

"How did I know I could trust you? As I grew up I came to understand what your father had done to my father and my brother and the other men from this village who died in the mine – "

"That is why I am here. I am doing my father's penance." But he could not be sure that Mamani would understand that. Nor, he doubted, would his own father.

There was a sudden banging on the door. Agostino opened it and two men, hats and ponchos dripping rain, stepped quickly inside. They ducked their heads to McKenna, sending a veil of rainwater down across their faces, then turned to Mamani. "The police are coming, Jesu! Their truck is coming up the road!"

Mamani's head swung sharply towards McKenna; the oil lamp, swinging in the draught from the open doorway, slashed his face with knives of yellow light. But McKenna got in first: "I didn't bring them, Jesu! The police chief promised me he would leave me to bring you down myself!" He went quickly to the door, looking down the street through the sweeping sheets of rain. The truck, sliding in the rutted mud of the road, was just entering the bottom of the village. "That's not a police truck! It's the army!"

He was flung aside as Mamani hurtled past him out the door. The Indian skidded in the mud, went down on one knee, then he was up on his feet again and had disappeared round the corner of the house. McKenna followed him, saw him desperately trying to start the engine of his ancient truck. Standing at the corner, McKenna looked back down the street, slitting his eyes against the rain. The army truck was less than a hundred yards away, the sound of its groaning engine in low gear coming clearly despite the rain.

Mamani, giving up trying to start his truck, jumped down. McKenna grabbed him, holding him tightly by the front of his poncho. "Jesu, don't run! They'll shoot you – !"

Mamani shook his head fiercely; water from his hat sprayed against McKenna's face. He grabbed the priest's wrists, forced him to let go of the poncho. "They'll shoot me anyway! All they want is someone to blame. Let me go, padre, let me go!"

He pushed McKenna away. The priest fell back against the wall, slipping in the mud, and sat down hard. Sitting there in a rivulet of water he saw Mamani go stumbling up between the houses. He reached the stone wall at the end of the lane, scrambled over it and went running off across the fields, disappearing into the swirling curtains of rain. McKenna got to his feet as the army truck drew up outside the house. Two men in civilian clothes and six soldiers in uniform tumbled out. One of the men in civilian clothes grabbed McKenna, forcing him up against the wall; the other man and the soldiers went running up the lane. Maria Mamani and Agostino had come to the corner of the house, the mother crying loudly, the boy blinking against the beat of the rain.

"Let me go!" McKenna struggled against the grip of the

man who held him; he knew that this was a security policeman, though the man had shown him no badge. "What the hell d'you think you're doing?"

For the first time the policeman seemed to recognise he was not holding an Indian. He dropped his hands, saw McKenna's Roman collar. "The American padre! What are you doing here?" There was no apology; his tone was as aggressive as his action had been. "Answer me!"

McKenna's temper was boiling; he forgot all about caution, the situation was too far gone for that. "Don't lean on me, buster!" He spoke in a mixture of Spanish and English, not caring whether the slang terms meant anything to the policeman; the tone of his voice was enough. "I'm one of the two priests of this village. Where do you think I should be when one of my parishioners is in trouble? I was trying to bring Mamani down to see Captain Condoris."

The policeman did not understand everything McKenna said, but he understood enough. He was a mestizo, a burly man with a brutal and brutalised face: he hated the world for whatever it had done to him before he had joined the security police. Rain ran off his broken nose, he glared at McKenna out of eyes almost hidden under brows swollen by scar tissue. "Mamani is our business, not Condoris's!"

McKenna glared back at him, but all at once he knew the fight was lost; the security police already had Mamani, one way or the other. The policeman pushed him back against the wall, banging his head against the adobe.

"Go home, padre! Go home to America, this is none of your business!"

Then he was running up the lane after the soldiers and the other policemen. McKenna wiped the rain from his face, saw Maria and Agostino standing in front of him. "Save Jesu, padre! They will shoot him!" Maria's face was a blur of tears and rain; her fingers clawed at McKenna's arm. "Save him, padre!"

McKenna wiped his face again, pulled his arm away from Maria's clutch, turned and ran up the lane. He had no hope that he would save Mamani, the soldiers would have shot him before he could get to him, but at least he would have made the effort, shown that he was on the villagers' side. He knew he was not acting out of pure charity; but he had never professed to be a completely selfless man. The need was to survive, to stay on side with the Indians in the hope that some day you could help them. There were more roads to Heaven than just the straight one.

He ran up out of the lane into the open fields, scrambling over the stone wall like a four-legged animal. The rain came sweeping down the altiplano in great dark gusts; it rode the wind in waves that lashed the face. McKenna was still dressed in his best clerical suit; he had put it on when he had gone down to see Dolores. He was wet through to the skin; the cloth was no protection against the elements; it probably wouldn't protect him against the security police either. He was frozen to the bone; he ran on legs that threatened to snap off like limbs of ice. For a minute or two he ran without direction, stumbling into the tumult of wind and rain; his mouth open gasping for air, he drowned his lungs as the rain gushed down his throat. Then sanity and exhaustion stopped him; he stood ankle deep in mud and looked about him. But the limit of his vision was twenty or thirty yards; the rain both threatened and taunted him. He opened his mouth against the lash of the storm and yelled, "Jesu!"; but the shout was swept away at once, was no more than a whisper ten yards from his strained throat. He trembled with cold, feeling that he was about to split apart; he stumbled on, as much to stay alive as to try and find Mamani. He began to pray, like a man in a fever, without any real hope. He had always been sceptical of miracles.

Then the figure, blurred, amorphous, appeared out of the swirling greyness. Headless, it plunged straight at McKenna; it saw him when it was only two or three yards away. The head came up out of the poncho; the nightmare shape turned into Mamani. He tried to evade McKenna, but the priest grabbed him.

"Jesu! They'll shoot you! Come back to the village with me, give yourself up!" He had to shout, forcing the words out against a gag of water. He struggled to hold the Indian, but his fingers were brittle with cold; he held him as much by will as by anything else. "Where can you go?"

Mamani just shook his head fiercely. He wrenched himself away from McKenna, went running on through the rain. The priest followed him, stumbling in the mud, still shouting, pleading with words that died against his teeth as the wind and water hurled them back at him. They came to a dip in the ground, neither of them aware of it till they felt the slope falling away beneath them. McKenna felt his feet go from under him, tried desperately to stay upright, but he had no strength left. He fell face forward, tumbling down the slippery earth; he hit a rock, bounced off and skidded down into the bottom of the shallow gully. He lay on his face, dimly conscious of water gushing over him. He tried to rise, to get his breath, but he was too weak. He lay there, too dazed even to pray, and waited to drown.

He felt the frantic hands turn him over on his back, pull him up out of the water cascading down the floor of the gully. He opened his eyes, looked up through the bullets of rain at the anxious face of Mamani peering down at him. Then he saw beyond the hunched-over figure the other figures coming down the slope of the gully, their rifles identifying them as plainly as if he were seeing them on a clear bright day.

2

McKenna came into the mission living-room wearing dry clothes and feeling a little more alive than when he had come back here ten minutes ago. He had gone first to the kitchen and started up the fire to heat water for a bath, but it would be at least half an hour before there would be enough hot water for a bath in which he could thoroughly soak the ice out of himself. In the meantime it warmed him to have Dolores here.

Still half-dazed from his fall, leaning heavily on Mamani, he had made his way back to the village. The security policemen and the soldiers had plodded along silently behind them, the soldiers, all Indians, showing no expression at all, the two mestizo policemen looking sullen, as if disappointed at being foiled at closing the case with a quick bullet. The silent little group had come down the lane, pushing its way through the crowd of villagers that now surrounded the army truck. The rain had ceased as abruptly as it had started, but low dark clouds still scudded overhead heavy with the threat of a further deluge.

McKenna slumped down on the bench outside the Mamani house. He was exhausted emotionally as well as physically. He had not saved Mamani after all; if Jesu had not stopped to help him, possibly the Indian would have got away. Shivering constantly, he leaned back against the dripping wall of the house and looked at Mamani.

"I am sorry, Jesu." Then he offered cold comfort: "At least you are still alive."

Only McKenna saw the wry smile in Mamani's eyes; the rest of the wet dark face was as wooden as ever. "Yes, padre. For a while, at least."

At that the brutal-faced security policeman grabbed him and pushed him towards the truck. The soldiers heaved Mamani up into the back of the truck and the policeman came back and stood in front of McKenna. "We shall write a report on you, padre."

"You do that," said McKenna, weary beyond caring. "Don't forget to mention that I tried to stop him running away. I'll explain why to your superiors when they send for me."

Sudden doubt messed up the man's face more than fists or knives ever had. "What do you mean by that?" The other policeman, a small silent man, had come to stand beside him. "This is none of your business, you know that."

"If it's none of my business, then your superiors won't want to see me when they read your report. If they do want to see me, I'll tell them I saved Mamani from being shot. I'm sure they wanted him alive, not dead."

The small policeman said, "You will not be mentioned in the report, padre. But in future concern yourself only with religion, not with politics." His companion was about to protest, but the little man silenced him with a jerk of the hand. "We are finished here. Let's go."

Maria Mamani tried to run after the truck as it went bumping down the street, but several of the Indian women held her back. McKenna, still sitting against the wall, still shivering, looked at Agostino standing in the doorway of the house, his arms resting on the shoulders of the younger children. "I'll do what I can, Agostino," he said, but even in his own ears the words sounded as hollow as a political pledge.

Agostino nodded, as shrewd as his father. He knew that he might already have taken his place, that Jesu Mamani had seen the village for the last time. His mother, sobs shaking her stout frame, came back to the house. She looked at McKenna, shook her head: he did not know whether in hopelessness or in dismissal of himself; then she went into the house, followed by Agostino, and the door was shut on further onslaughts against the family. At least for to-day, McKenna thought.

The Indians stood around him, staring at him but making no effort to help him as he sat shivering in his exhaustion. Then someone pushed through them: it was Dolores. He was past surprise; he just smiled at her as if it were the most natural thing in the world for her to be up here on the altiplano on a day like this. She took his arm, helped him to his feet, and walked with him across to his Jeep.

"Can you drive it?" she asked. "Or would you rather come in my car?"

"I'll be okay."

"I'll follow you."

He looked at her gratefully, got into the Jeep and drove it carefully, like a man conscious that he had had too many drinks, up the road to the mission. He pulled into the yard, got out on legs that were still unsteady and waited till Dolores had driven into the yard and got out of her own car. Then he said, "Did you see what happened?"

"I was there all the time. I followed the army truck up from San Sebastian."

"How did you know it was coming up here for Jesu?"

"I didn't. I thought they were coming for you."

"How did you know they were coming up here at all?"

"I have a contact in police headquarters. He rang me." She turned away from him, letting her back tell him that she wanted no more questions. "You'd better get out of those clothes before you catch pneumonia."

"I'll light the fire in the kitchen first."

He had also lit the fire in the living-room. Dolores sat in

front of it, staring into its flames. Now he stood for a moment in the doorway admiring her. She was a good-looking woman, he thought, but there was more to her than that. He had not been attracted to her solely by her looks; a priest who fell for a beautiful face and an attractive body had no business being in the priesthood. It had been her strength of character that had appealed to him, the suggestion that she was a woman on whom a man could depend when trouble hit him; it had been a bonus to find, as time passed, that she had the same social ideas as himself, that she did not believe in the criollo status quo. She had revealed herself only gradually to him; he was an American and a priest, and both species she had met in Bolivia had always been conservatives. Then their friendship had ripened and he had thanked the Lord for sending him someone in whom he could confide his hopes and plans. It was only in the last three months, as his aching loneliness had increased, that he had come to realise that he had fallen in love with her.

She became aware of him in the doorway. She did not straighten up in any fluster of embarrassment, but turned her head slowly and looked at him. He had gone into the bedroom dressed as a priest; now he stood in the doorway dressed an an ordinary man in jeans and sweater. She had occasionally seen him dressed this way before, but now somehow the transformation had an effect on her that disturbed her. He had the sort of open, manly face that she found attractive in contrast to the dark saturnine looks of the men of her own society; the sweater and the jeans showed the hard muscular frame of a man who had been an athlete and was still in good physical condition despite the ordeal he had just been through. She looked at Terry McKenna, man not priest, and was ashamed at the turmoil in her breast.

Keeping her voice steady, she said, "I've been saying prayers for Jesu Mamani."

"He needs them." He moved towards the front door. "I'll get some coffee."

"I've already put it on." She stood up quickly, beat him to the door; she wanted time to compose herself. "I'll get it, padre."

She went across to the kitchen, came back with the blackened

coffee pot. They drank the coffee and ate some of his English
biscuits; she smiled when he produced the tin from under the
altar. "I'm glad you don't try to live on an Indian diet. One can
take idealism too far. You'd be starving in a few months and no
use to them at all."

"I'm not much use to them now."

"Don't say that!" Then she blushed and smiled. "I'm sorry.
I shouldn't talk like that."

"You mean to a priest?" He looked down at his mug of
coffee. It was not good coffee, but with a house full of servants
what opportunities would she have had for learning how to
make it? He guessed Carmel would be just as bad. "Dolores,
on matters like this, can't we talk as man and woman? I'm not
concerned with religion right now, I'm not trying to save Jesu's
soul. I'm trying to save *him*."

She sipped her coffee, wrinkled her nose. "I don't make very
good coffee." He grinned at her, not being falsely polite, and
she smiled back at him. At once they felt easier with each other.
"All right, Terry. It's just – well, I was brought up to think of
priests as a race apart. I know you're not, but it is difficult to
throw off the habit of years." She smiled again. "Sorry. That
sounds a little like an old joke."

"I know it," he said. "Priests know all the jokes about priests.
We're like the Jews. We always tell the best jokes against ourselves."

"Why is that?"

"I don't know. Maybe because we're an oppressed people
too."

"Oppressed by whom?"

"Some of our bishops. And the Vatican."

"The nuns are more oppressed than the priests. Women are
second-class citizens in the Church. I think that fact works on
me subconsciously when I'm talking to a priest, even you."

He wanted to tell her that she was all wrong in her approach
to him, but the thought was awkward even in his mind; if he
tried to put it into words he was afraid that it would spoil the
mood between them. He got up and walked to the window,
opened it. His was the only house up here that had a glass
window; the houses in Altea either had no windows at all or

just openings covered by rough wooden shutters. He had
needed the light and view that the glass window allowed; in the
winter just gone he would have gone crazy cooped up in the
dark cavern of his house. The wind had dropped and the late
afternoon sun, breaking through the thinning clouds, warmed
him. He looked down at the lake flecked with silver as the sun
struck across it. A flight of coots curved away like a drawn bow,
then straightened into an arrow: they were aimed at the glacier
and disappeared into the shadows of the mountains. He could
see the water pouring down the gullies of the mountains, like
silver forks of lightning against dark clouds. The level of the
lake would be much higher by morning. He must remember to
go down and haul his boat up to a higher mooring.

Dolores came and stood beside him. He was sharply aware
of the physical presence of her, of her warmth and the feminine
smell of her. Her shoulder brushed against him and he shivered
as if he were still cold. This is damned ridiculous, he thought,
I'm like some high school kid on his first date. He was not a
virgin: in prep school he had had all the usual hungers, temptations and opportunities. It was only in his last year at college
that religion had really grasped him; he had been celibate now
for nine years. But he knew that if he put his hands on Dolores
their relationship would be destroyed. She would not allow
him to touch her till she had got the priest image of him
completely out of her mind. The Church left nothing to chance,
he thought bitterly: it brainwashed even the possible enemy.

"What do we do now?"

He started, surprised by her question; then he realised she
had an entirely different line of thought to his own. "You mean
about Jesu? I don't know. I'll try to see him if they throw him
in prison, but maybe they won't even let me near him. I'm not
a visiting prison chaplain – I don't have any privileges."

"Perhaps I could help you. I have some influence. My
mother's family name still has its advantages."

"They'll have started to work on him before I can get to him.
Torture him, I mean, trying to get some sort of confession out
of him."

She was not shocked: she knew the system. "I'll see my friend
as soon as I get back to San Sebastian."

"You seem convinced Jesu had nothing to do with the terrorists."

"Aren't you?"

"Yes. But I was with him all last night." He had removed any doubt from his mind that Mamani had been in contact with the terrorists about the blacking-out of the power station. "What has convinced you he doesn't know anything about last night's murder?"

"I went to see my cousin's wife this morning. The police told her that they had got a rough description of the men who killed my cousin. They were wearing hoods, just like those who held up the bank the other morning – they were probably the same men. The police were sure they were criollos or mestizos – they were too tall for Indians. Jesu could be in league with them, but I don't think so. I don't think the revolutionaries have yet made any contact with the Indians. Perhaps they have taken a lesson from what happened to Che – he failed because he learned too late that the Indians were not interested in backing him."

"Then why have the security police taken Jesu?"

"Don't the police in your country look for scapegoats when they can't find the real culprits? Whenever there is a demonstration, don't they grab anyone with long hair, who looks like a hippie, whether he had anything to do with the demonstration or not?"

"Jesu said they were looking for someone to blame."

"He was a scapegoat once before, when they arrested him because he was an Indian. If he'd been a criollo they'd have smacked him on the behind and let him go."

"How did you know he had been arrested before?"

"I found it out only to-day – from my friend." She smiled. "You are going to ask who is my friend. Don't. The less you know, the less you will be able to tell them if ever they get around to asking you."

"You think they might try to torture me too?"

"I hope not." She put her hand on his arm; her face clouded over. "But be careful. You should not have to suffer for our country's problems."

177

"I'm not concerned with politics, only with the people up here."

"You aren't so naïve as to believe that. You can't separate them, you know that."

She seemed to have been straightforward in everything she had said, but he was still troubled: something in her answers did not fit. "Dolores, do you know more about what's happening than you want to tell me?"

She looked directly at him, not trying to be evasive. "I'm not going to answer that. You will just have to trust me that I don't want you involved. We talked about what we could do for the campesinos – but that was before the shooting started. I don't belong to the movement, Terry – believe me when I tell you that. But if you get too deeply into this, you will finish up on the side of the revolutionaries, whether you know who they are or not. The security police will decide what side you are on, it won't be your decision. I don't want you shot or imprisoned."

He shook his head, bewildered by the terrible threats she had so simply stated. "I don't want to be that involved! But what about Jesu? I can't just forget him – I've got to do something for him – at least make an effort – "

"I'll see if I can get you visiting privileges to the prison. You might be able to go down with his wife, use her as a cover, tell them she needs your comfort and support."

"You sound such a professional," he said admiringly.

"A professional what?"

"I don't know. Professional agitator, I suppose the police would call you. Or revolutionary."

"I'm neither. I'm just someone who does not believe this is the best of all possible worlds. Not for ninety per cent of the people who live in it."

"I wish I had met you ten years ago."

She turned and looked out the window. Her voice softened, became slower, the voice of reminiscence. "I was only fifteen then. And I believed it *was* the best of all possible worlds. I believed that position and possessions were everything, and our family had both. You would not have liked me then, Terry."

"What happened to change you?"

"One grows up. When my parents were killed – " Her parents

had been in a plane that had crashed into the side of a mountain on a flight from San Sebastian to La Paz. Seeking contact with her in the early days of their friendship, he had looked upon it as some sort of bond that he had lost his own father in a plane crash; so it is that some men in love, who should not be in love, try to name sympathy as a disguise for their feelings. "The family rallied around, my mother's family. Only then did I come to realise that I belonged to a feudal system. I searched out some of my grandfather's books." This is an echo of Jesu, McKenna thought: books had changed the life of a criollo aristocrat and an Indian campesino, put them both on the same side. "It took time, but I changed. But you wouldn't have liked me ten years ago, I'm sure of that."

"Well, I like you now." He wanted to say *I love you*, but his tongue was incapable of the words: it was a foreign language.

She understood what he meant, but she gave him no encouragement: she, too, was in strange territory. She had glanced at him as she had finished the story of her conversion, but now she looked out the window again, avoiding his gaze. Then she said, glad of the interruption, "There is a car coming up from the village. It looks like one of the Ruiz's Cadillacs."

It would be, thought McKenna with an appreciation of irony. If anyone was going to see that a priest did not step out of line with one of the local criollo women, that the status quo was not upset by such a scandal, it would be a Ruiz. He just hoped it was not the Bishop.

It was not. The Cadillac pulled into the yard and Francisco and Hernando got out. The two young men, both in trench coats, picked their way fastidiously, like battery-bred cocks, through the mud and came to the front door.

"We were looking for your sister, padre," said Francisco, trying not to show his surprise that, instead, they had found Dolores. "She did not return after lunch – we were worried – "

McKenna looked at Dolores, suddenly worried for his sister. But Dolores put his mind at rest, if not Francisco's: the young man's brows came down in a jealous frown when she said, "Carmel went off somewhere with Senor Taber. I do not think you have to worry, Pancho – Senor Taber is a man capable of looking after himself and Carmel."

"We heard he had been questioned by the police." Francisco dropped Carmel from the conversation: if she was with Taber she was no longer his concern. What a jerk, McKenna thought. How the hell did Carmel ever get herself involved with a guy like this? But then was grateful for the ways in which God worked. If she had not met Francisco she would not be here in Bolivia and he and she might have gone on forever being strangers to each other instead of the brother and sister they had again become.

"I was questioned by them too," said McKenna, wishing he could set the young prig back on his butt in the mud. "Didn't you hear that?"

Hernando, seeing the way the conversation was going, took it out of his cousin's hands. "We'd heard it, padre. I gather the police acted with their usual crass efficiency."

McKenna had never liked Hernando Ruiz, never feeling he could get close to him. But it was difficult not to warm to a man who held the same opinion of the police as yourself; maybe that's my real vocation, McKenna thought, lawbreaking, thumbing my nose at cops. Except that in this country that would be too dangerous a vocation. He was sure that Hernando would never go that far.

"It was just routine," he said, wondering if the Ruiz had *their* contacts in the police department. He looked back at Francisco. "I'm sorry you've come up here on a wild goose chase. I'm sure my sister will be back at your home before it's dark. Senor Taber is probably just showing her the city."

Francisco nodded, keeping up the pretence that he was not really interested in Carmel: she could return to the Ruiz house if and when she liked. Then Hernando said, "We had a message for you, padre, from our uncle the Bishop. He asks would you come down to San Sebastian and help out for a few days? Two of the priests at the cathedral are ill."

McKenna hoped he hid the sudden suspicion he felt. He had said Mass at the cathedral, but he had never before been asked to come down there and take over regular duties as a locum. The Bishop had *asked* him to help out, but any bishop's request was also an order and obedience was expected. But why had the request come right now? Was he being called down to the cathedral so an eye could be kept on him? He felt a surge of rebellion, but it subsided almost at once: they injected you with obedience in the seminary and the bacillus never left you. "I'll come down at once."

Francisco and Hernando went back to the Cadillac. McKenna, leaving Dolores in the doorway, walked across to guide Francisco as he swung the big car round to drive it out of the yard. The young man was not a good driver; he made heavy going of the reversing and turning necessary to get the car's nose pointed at the gate. Hernando sat patiently beside him, looking out at McKenna with a slight smile on his face. At last the car was facing in the right direction.

Hernando put his hand on Francisco's arm as the latter prepared to move the car forward. He looked out at McKenna and said almost as an afterthought, "Coming up out of the city we saw an army truck going back. Had it been up here to Altea?"

McKenna nodded. "The security police came up to collect a man named Jesu Mamani. I believe you know him."

"Mamani? Not well. He was my uncle's protégé at the school, the one run by the Franciscans. Why did they want him?"

"For questioning, they said. I'm afraid they'll hold him just in case they don't catch the men who shot the mayor. Any sort of scapegoat will do. And Indians are the most expendable."

"You sound bitter, padre."

"Maybe you understand why," McKenna said, but wondered if Hernando would.

Hernando looked at him steadily, his face as expressionless as that of any Indian. Then he said, "Adios, padre," and tapped Francisco on the arm. It was almost the gesture of a master telling a servant it was time for them to leave. But Francisco did not seem to mind. He took the car out of the mission yard and down towards Altea. McKenna watched it go down the shining yellow mud of the road, its tyre marks reeling out from beneath it like long brown ropes.

"They should keep driving," said Dolores from the doorway. "Right on out of Bolivia and South America. They'll never amount to anything here. If they stay here they could be the last of the Ruiz. The family will end with Hernando's and Pancho's throats cut."

He felt a chill run through him at the matter-of-fact, almost callous way she spoke of tragedy. But he could not criticise her: she had lived in an ambience of violence such as he had never known. She might be protected from the immediate sight of it by the high walls of the criollo homes, by the brittle graciousness of the society through which she moved; but it was part of her heritage, part of the very air she breathed. It was a comment on her environment that, despite all the American economic intrusion into this country, he had never met an American life insurance salesman in Bolivia.

Dolores walked across and got into her car. She leaned an arm on the door and looked out at him. "Terry, be careful. It is much too easy to be a Don Quixote in South America. I should never get over it if they killed you."

She drove away before he could reply, skidding the Volkswagen in the mud as she slewed it on to the road. She drove fast, disappearing into the sun-shot distance as if she were afraid that he might chase after her. He stood in the mud of the yard, her last words ringing like blood in his ears. She feels the same as I do! he shouted in his mind; and in his violently excited eyes the mountains across the lake tumbled in a flood of avalanches. She loves me, God, he cried, and I love her! And what will the Church think of *that*? He went into the house, the mud feeling like crystal snow beneath his airborne feet. The agony would come later, but for now he could shut it out of his mind.

He sang as he packed a suitcase: love songs, not hymns. They were songs from his youth: his years of celibacy dated them: "Love Is A Many-Splendoured Thing", "Some Enchanted Evening". He rolled up his still-wet best suit, hoping it hadn't shrunk. He looked about the bedroom, saw his week's washing in one corner. He grinned, bundled it up and took it out to the Jeep; the cathedral could pay him for his services by doing his laundry for him; the Bishop was said to have twice as many servants as he had priests down there. He put out the fire under his bath-water; he would luxuriate to-night in a proper bath instead of in his tin tub. He fed the chickens, locked up the house, got into the Jeep and drove out of the yard still singing. He was going down to San Sebastian for possibly no more than a couple of days, but he felt as if he were starting out on a long leisurely journey to some paradise that had suddenly presented itself to him.

He was still singing as he drove down into Altea, waltzing the Jeep down the slippery road like a teenage drunk. He stopped outside the Mamani home, knocked on the closed door, and it was opened by Agostino.

"I am going down to the cathedral for a few days, Agostino. Will you go up and feed the chickens for me each day?"

"Will you try and save my father, padre?"

The singing had still been there in his head, love *was* a many-splendoured thing; but now abruptly it stopped. He was a priest, he had responsibilities he could not avoid. It is none of your business, the security police had told him, but they had been wrong. It was his whole philosophy, what had brought him here in the first place. To save people, not just their souls but the people themselves: that was what Christianity, his faith, was all about. He nodded, trapped as much by conscience as by the boy's cry for help.

"I'll try to save him, Agostino," he said, and the words sounded as hollow and false as the lyric of a popular song.

3

"We have to stop them, Jorge," said Alejandro Ruiz, his cheroot wobbling up and down in his big mouth. He took it out, looked at it as if he were surprised to find he had been smoking it, and dropped it into a large copper ashtray on his desk. He sat back, twisting the gold signet ring he wore. He was not given to wearing jewellery, but the ring had been handed down from generation to generation to each eldest son. The band itself had worn thin now, but the crest on the ring was still distinct. It was his badge of office, the family equivalent of the ruby ring that adorned his brother's finger. "We can't let them get away with all this. They will build up an atmosphere of terror – that's what they want, it's obvious – and when that happens, we shall find we can't rely on anyone. There is nothing like fear to make people neutral, Jorge. The Church used that method for years."

"Don't let your anti-clericalism show. You have used the Church as much as it might have used you or any other member of it. People like you always talk as if you think the Church should be run by divinely inspired saints. It's an institution of men, a community of human nature. Just like the United States Congress or the British Parliament or the Kremlin. We work in God's name, but unfortunately God allows us free will. That's where the damage is done."

"It's the hypocrisy of working in God's name that I can't stand!"

"Some day I may compile a list of the sins committed in the name of democracy. That is," the Bishop smiled, stubbed out his own cheroot, "if God would grant me enough years to complete the list."

They sat opposite each other in Alejandro Ruiz's study. It was a big room: three walls of it were lined with books from floor to ceiling, the fourth wall had a big barred window that looked out on to the garden. Beyond the garden was a high stone wall and beyond that a field, just turning green under a down of maize, sloped up to a stand of eucalypts. It was only five o'clock but the sun had already disappeared over the rim of the altiplano and a desk lamp had been switched on in the study. The two men sat in the wash of shadows thrown by the lamp, their faces only vaguely distinguishable to each other. Only three years separated the brothers in age and they had always been close, despite the time Jorge had spent away in the seminary and then in Rome. But their relationship had always had a certain grittiness to it, one that neither of them minded; it had never allowed them to lapse into a frame of mind where each took the other for granted. Alejandro knew that it was literally only an accident of birth that had kept him from being the one who should have gone into the Church: there had been a son before him who had died at birth. Though he was strong-willed now, he doubted if he would have had enough strength of will at seventeen to have defied their father, who had been even more autocratic than he himself had become. Jorge, for his part, knew he would never have made as good a head of the family as Alejandro; he had always been indolent and not even the Church's teachings had ever convinced him it was a cardinal sin. Nor, he told himself, even a bishop's sin. He had the authority of his own position and it amused him that at certain times and in certain situations Alejandro was answerable to him. Alejandro, in his turn, was aware that the Bishop had more actual power than he himself had. They had an unspoken, but understood, truce: neither attempted to impose his authority on the other.

Alejandro got up, switched on another lamp. His burly body bulged in a turtleneck sweater and a tweed jacket; he looks like a wrestler who has decided to be a gentleman, his brother thought. He began to pace up and down, not nervously but with his usual deliberate tread. "I've sent for Karl Obermaier."

"What on earth for?"

"He knows how to organise these things better than we do."

"What things? Look, you're not thinking of setting up some vigilante force, are you? Ruiz's private little army?"

"Only here at the house and on our properties. At the bank and the brewery and up at the farm."

"At the cathedral too? Perhaps we could form a cadet corps from the altar boys."

"Jorge, don't be so damned frivolous in your criticism! We are in the middle of a serious situation. We are in danger!"

"Don't you think you stand the chance of increasing our danger if you start teaching our servants and our workers how to operate as an organised armed force?"

"No, Jorge, we have to stick to the simplest solution to this problem. If they try to kill us, we shall try to kill them. And if I have to kill someone and I come to you in confession, don't refuse me absolution. It will be war, not murder."

A servant came to the door and announced Senor Obermaier. The German came striding into the room and, as always, the Bishop waited for the Nazi salute; but, as always, was disappointed. Obermaier suddenly relaxed, greeted the Ruiz brothers with a casualness that still managed to suggest a touch of deference, then sat down in the chair Alejandro indicated. He had this disconcerting habit of making an entrance with a stiffly formal gait, almost a military step, as if he had never quite left the parade ground; then there would be the abrupt transition, as if he had suddenly realised the old days had gone forever, and the starch would melt from him almost visibly. Well, almost, the Bishop thought: he will always have the starch of his arrogance in him.

"The rifles are available at once," said Obermaier without preliminaries. "Fifty of them. I took the liberty of ordering them."

Alejandro Ruiz nodded approvingly. "Where did you get them?"

Obermaier looked cautiously at the Bishop. The latter waved a hand in benediction. "Go ahead, Karl. I am, as it were, off duty."

Obermaier smiled, settled back in his chair, arranged his arm more comfortably in its sling. He liked the Bishop, who was a man who had an eye for the practicalities of life. When he had come here after fleeing Germany he had not been a practising Catholic; he had replaced his religion with another ideology that, in the thirties and in that country, had seemed to offer more for the future. But once in Bolivia, having made up his mind to settle here in San Sebastian, he had looked at the local practicalities and decided there were advantages to being a Catholic again.

"They are smuggled stuff, brought up from Paraguay. But brand new, very good Czech guns. With a thousand rounds of ammunition for each rifle and more available if we give them warning."

"I like the irony," said the Bishop, savouring the whisky his brother had just given him. "Communist guns being smuggled by capitalist criminals through a fascist dictator's country. What would you call us buyers?"

"Peaceful citizens," said Alejandro, trying to match his brother's humour. "With just a belief in staying alive."

Obermaier smiled, but only out of politeness. He was not without a sense of humour; he just did not think the present situation called for joking. He was not afraid; even the bullet in his arm last night had not frightened him. He regretted the death of the mayor; Carlos had not been too intelligent, but he had been a good drinking companion; he had been killed instantly, so had died as a good man should, without a whimper.

But in a way Obermaier had almost welcomed the terrorists' activities over the past week; the counter-measures called for a man of action and that was what he was. He was bored with his duties as the brewery manager; he felt a tingle of excitement at the prospect of drilling the workers he would choose as the guards. They all would have an elementary knowledge of how to use a rifle, but he would forge them into a proper military fighting unit. He might, he thought, allowing himself his own joke, call them the First Brewery Panzer Division.

"I don't think we should broadcast what we are doing," said Alejandro Ruiz. "The men at the brewery will talk, of course, and the word will soon get around. But that may take a few days. If the terrorists strike at the brewery in that time, before they learn what we have in store for them, we could give them a shock that might finish them off."

"They will know as soon as you hand out the first rifle," said the Bishop. "If you think they don't have a spy in the brewery, then you are under-estimating them. We aren't dealing with fools. These are intelligent men, educated mestizos or men like ourselves – they aren't stupid Indians gone crazy with the coca weed or on chicha. God forbid, but they may even be some of our own society here in the city."

"No, these are outsiders." Alejandro shook his head emphatically. "We have our misguided liberals here – Dolores, for instance – but not murderers."

Perhaps, thought the Bishop. But revolutionaries (they would not call themselves terrorists: everyone, in his own eyes, was on the side of the angels: even Karl sitting over there still thought the Nazis had been right) never thought of themselves as murderers. Che Guevara had never considered himself as such; the students of the world thought of him as a hero. What would I think if a man came to me in the confessional and told me he had killed a man for a political ideal? How many priests in this country have had to give absolution to political murderers?

There was further discussion on counter-measures against the terrorists, then the Bishop rose to leave. "I must get back to more peaceful duties. I am short two priests, so I have to take the benediction service this evening. You should come."

"If we came," asked his brother, "would you bless our venture?"

"I would never bless violence."

"Pius the Eleventh blessed the Italians before they went off to bomb Abyssinia."

"If you want a papal blessing, get in touch with Rome. I have enough troubles."

The three men went out into the entrance hall. As they did so, the butler opened the front door and Carmel came in. She pulled up short as she saw them and looked a little flustered. Strange, thought the Bishop: I should have thought that men would be the last creatures to have embarrassed her.

Then Romola Ruiz came through from the back of the house. She greeted her brother-in-law and Obermaier with a slight bow of her head, a gesture of formality that the Bishop recognised as being no more than that. There is the *real* revolutionary, he thought: she and other women like her will eventually conquer the whole of South America without any terrorist tactics at all. Machismo will be replaced by whatever is the female equivalent; but the latter will be more subtle and will probably last till Judgment Day. The statues of the Liberator and of San Martin will be pulled down and every plaza in the continent will have a statue of a woman like those dreadful ones the English put up of Queen Victoria. Thank God God was a man, or Heaven would be Hell. The Bishop all at once felt grateful for the security and comfort of the Church. He would be more than usually devout at benediction this evening.

"We were worried for you, Carmel," said Romola. "Francisco and Hernando have gone looking for you."

"Oh, I am sorry." Carmel explained the events of the afternoon, only paraphrasing her hours with Taber: "Then Senor Taber showed me some of the sights of the city."

"You are not afraid to move around our streets after what has happened since you arrived here?" Alejandro asked.

"I don't feel exactly – *easy*. But it would be a waste of time to come all this way and not see anything of San Sebastian." Carmel was composed now. Taber had dropped her at the front gate. During her drive through the streets in the Land-Rover she had been luxuriating in the memory of the last two hours. When she had entered the house it was almost as if she could still feel him in her; sexual pleasure had always been something that stayed with her long after the act had finished. When she had encountered the three men in the entrance hall she had been flustered because she had been sure they would have been able to read her thoughts in her face.

"You are right," said Romola. "These last few years I have seen too little of the city myself."

"She must be careful though," said her husband. "Things may get even more violent than they have been."

"What have you three been planning?" asked Romola shrewdly.

"Nothing," said the Bishop, hoping she was sufficiently devout not to think a bishop of the Church would lie; though he doubted that she was. "Politics, beer and religion do not mix." He kissed Romola's hand; he could not remember her having kissed the Episcopal ring on his own hand. God, he thought, how wise you were to teach us to treat them as second-class citizens in the Church. A female Pope! He shuddered at the thought; and almost sank his teeth into the fingers under his lips. "I'll say benediction this evening for your intentions."

"Thank you, Jorge," said Romola. "I'd like it to be said for more intelligence among our menfolk."

Then the door opened and Francisco and Hernando came in. In their identical trench coats Carmel thought they looked like a couple of movie private eyes; the effect was added to when Francisco said, "We have been looking for you."

Carmel smiled as graciously as she could, but she hated Francisco for the proprietary way he had spoken to her in front of the others. "It was thoughtful of you. But I was quite safe, thank you."

"We delivered your message to Padre McKenna," Hernando said to the Bishop. "He is coming down to the cathedral this evening."

The Bishop saw the look on Carmel's face. "Do not be disturbed, my dear. Your brother is just coming down to help us out for a few days. I already knew he had been questioned by the police. But if they have given him a clean bill, so shall I."

"Padre McKenna must not be drawn into our troubles."
Romola had noticed the silent clash between her son and
Carmel. The McKennas, it seemed, were being drawn too
deeply into the orbit of the Ruiz; and she felt sorry for them.
"Nor Senor Taber. Perhaps you should have a word with
Captain Condoris, Alejandro."

"The less I see of the police, the better," said Alejandro,
smiling to let his son and nephew see that he was only joking.

"Still, it might be an idea to have a word with Padre
McKenna," said Hernando. "The security police have taken in
Jesu Mamani, the Altea man you sponsored at the school.
Padre McKenna may feel he has to try and help Mamani."

"Can't he?" said Carmel.

"The security police do not like the Church interfering,"
said the Bishop. "Not even the home-grown members. Leave
him to me, Alejandro."

The group in the hall broke up as the Bishop and Obermaier
left. Carmel, avoiding Francisco's stern look in her direction,
went up to her room. She was not a girl who could cheat on a
man, even one to whom she had no commitment. Francisco
had introduced her to San Sebastian and to his friends as his
girl; he might not have used that exact term, but he had made
it clear that Carmel was here on his invitation. He was not
going to stand idly by while she continued to see another man.
And she knew she was going to go on seeing Harry Taber, every
day if possible.

She wondered if she should talk over her dilemma with
Terry. But then, she decided, he had more than enough troubles
of his own. Maybe – and she felt a sudden surge of excitement
at the possibility – he would turn to her for help. It would be
the first time in her life that anyone had ever done so.

Chapter 7

I

The funeral of the mayor, Carlos Limon Mijares y Sojo, brought every criollo in San Sebastian to the cathedral. It was as if a call had gone out to them to come and demonstrate their solidarity, to show the flag of their blood to the terrorists who were trying to depose them. Not all of them came bravely: they knew, though the thought appalled them, that the killers of the dead man might even be among the mourners. Many mestizos also came to the service, showing more courage than many of the criollos because they had had a choice of which blood they chose to show on that day. There were no Indians, not even among the altar boys.

Bishop Ruiz said the Requiem Mass. He was assisted by all the priests of the cathedral staff, including the temporary replacement, McKenna. The latter went through the motions of what was required of him, his attention distracted by those who thronged the cathedral. Soldiers and police, all mestizos, stood along the side aisles, not all of them to mourn: their gaze remained fixed on the congregation rather than on what went on up on the high altar. The old men from the parks had come to the Mass dressed in their sober best; some wore decorations on their breasts, as if this were a memorial service to some war dead. What war? McKenna wondered. There had been only one real war in the lifetime of these men, the Chaco War with Paraguay in the thirties; but of course these old men were always at war, with the present, with the inevitable tides of history. They occupied the front pews just behind the family mourners and the absolute aristocrats of the city such as the Ruiz: they knew their place on an occasion such as this and they were making sure that all those behind them knew theirs. They knelt, they stood, they sat with stiff backs and gravely arrogant faces that never changed expression: they resurrected the past and made it live again, flung out a silent challenge that could be heard as clearly as the requiem hymn *Dies Irae* that came from the giant organ at the back of the cathedral. Their spirit communicated itself to those who sat behind them. The vast chamber became a congregation of challenge. Carlos Limon became a stronger, more inspiring man in death than he had ever been in life.

The Mass finished and the crowd filed out. The proceedings had all the solemnity of a Spanish death; McKenna, following the Bishop down the aisle, contrasted it with a funeral service he had conducted up in Altea. Then firecrackers had been let off and a band had played: the dead Indian had gone to his Maker with a proper regard for occasion: after all, wasn't he supposed to be on his way to a better life?

The criollos came out into the bright white sunshine, flowed down over the wide steps of the cathedral, stood there in a thick unmoving mass; the white façade above them seemed to rise out of a base of black tar. A line of cars stretched right round the plaza, the tail coming back to meet the head; there was not one car in the *cortège* less than ten years old and there were several vintage cars from the twenties and thirties; the hearse was a Rolls-Royce that was forty years old. Taber's Land-Rover, parked at the very end of the line and therefore immediately in front of the hearse, was the newest vehicle in the plaza.

Taber had come to the service and stood at the back of the cathedral. He had no time for the mumbo-jumbo that had gone on up on the altar; but he had a practical appreciation of protocol and so he had put in an appearance. He was here to work for the good of the Indians, but he was here at the invitation of the criollos who governed the country. Yet as he stood in the shadows at the back of the huge church something of the atmosphere had pervaded him. He had not been won over by the religiosity of what he beheld; that was all just a manifestation of the superstition to which even intelligent men were subject. But he could not resist the power that ceremony had to sway one; he knew that it, too, in a way was superstition, but he was subject to it. He had seen the occasion that the peasants of Anatolia had made of a wedding, an extravagance that they could ill-afford but one that gave them a momentary release from the misery of their existence. Pagan celebrations among the up-country tribesmen of East Africa, Christian festivals among the poor of the favelas of Brazil: ceremony had its place in the heart and mind of man and he no longer denied it. He had been aware that the Mass this morning had had its effect on the Spanish-bloods who had attended it.

He stood now near his Land-Rover and looked about him, squinting against the glare. The pavements of the plaza were packed with Indians. They stood on three sides of the big square, their coloured ponchos making them look like a border of garden shrubs. The two sections of the city's citizens, the criollos and the Indians, stood and looked across at each other silently. For a moment Taber had the impression that he was looking at a huge picture: this whole scene was nothing but paint and canvas without the dimension of sound: the thin shining air was stretched tight with hate. Christ, Taber thought, is this what they call independence? Independent of whom? What had Simon Bolivar liberated the country from?

"You look sad, Mr Taber." Dr Partridge, dressed in a beauti-fully cut black suit, moved down from the crowd on the steps and stood beside Taber on the pavement. "I did not realise you knew Senor Limon well."

"I never met him," said Taber, testing his candour on this man who might well be as homeless as himself. "I was feeling sorry for Bolivia."

For a moment Partridge looked puzzled. But he was not un-perceptive: he looked around the plaza, then back at Taber. "I see your point, old chap. But one hopes for the best. One can't jolly well give in, y'know."

One jolly well can: here is one who jolly well might any day now. "No, I suppose not."

"I hear you had a spot of bother with the police yesterday. You want any help, old chap?" It was Taber's turn to look puzzled, and Partridge went on: "I'm the British vice-consul, y'know. Would be glad to help, y'know. One gets so frightfully little to do up here. Hello, old gel." Mrs Partridge, elegant and handsome in black, her blue-grey hair covered by black lace, had appeared beside him. "Been telling Mr Taber what little opportunity we get up here to help our countrymen."

G

193

"Does Mr Taber need help?" She gave Taber a cool smile, not quite sure of this Englishman who was not the sort of Englishman her husband would have been had he been fortunate enough to have been born in England. He did not have the right accent, though his voice was not unpleasant, nor did he have the ease of manner that one associated with the product of a good school. But she recognised that he was a formidable man and, after all, any Englishman was better than none at all. She would invite him to dinner one night and they could talk about Home.

"No, I don't need any help just now," said Taber, relieved to see the crowd moving down off the steps and spreading out towards the cars. "But if I do, I'll know where to come."

"Any time, old chap. Be a pleasure, y'know."

Taber moved towards his Land-Rover. He saw Carmel with the Ruiz family. He inclined his head and she returned the greeting with a small bow of her own; they were as formal as the criollos who surrounded them. He got into the Land-Rover, wondering if he would be expected to drive out to the cemetery. Then the passenger's door opened and McKenna, still dressed in his white surplice over his soutane, got in beside him.

"There isn't room for me in the Bishop's car. And this gives me a chance to dissociate myself from the ruling clique, just in case the terrorists are around somewhere taking notes."

"What if the coppers are taking notes about you and me being together?" He looked McKenna up and down. "You look pretty cute in that outfit."

"You should see me in my hair-shirt." McKenna had come to recognise that Taber's opposition to religion and its trappings was not bigotry; he just wished he could think up some reply about humanism, but what could you say facetiously about something which was part of your own overall belief? He stared out at the hearse as it drew out from behind the Land-Rover and moved slowly round the plaza, drawing the long line of cars behind it. "The terrorists have done one thing – they've made all the criollos forget their differences. That's the solidarity of the ruling class you're looking at there."

"Don't expect me to start cheering." Taber started up the Land-Rover; he might as well go all the way with this masquerade. He hated the hypocrisy of attending the funeral of someone you did not know; all over the world men were being lowered into their graves under the disinterested gaze of other men who were there only because political or business protocol demanded it. But he knew that some men's importance was only judged by the size of their funeral *cortège*; from what he had heard of Carlos Limon, the dead man had never commanded such an audience as he had now. But then Limon had never been called upon to carry the standard while he was alive. "But this may be their last rally."

The *cortège* snaked its way out of the plaza. The cars crawled past the watching Indians. The black-garbed occupants sat up straight, faces tight as drums, eyes fixed on the cars ahead; the Indians stared at them out of masks that were four hundred years old. The air was sinister with the bitter scent of history: this had all happened before. One of Pizarro's lieutenants had ridden across this ground when the city, under another name, had been no more than an Incan village. Simon Bolivar had ridden round this very plaza on a horse harnessed in solid gold, a gift from the criollos. On both occasions, Taber guessed, the Indians had watched with the same sullen stare as now.

There was no sound but the hum of the cars' engines; then the bells of the cathedral began to toll. Each note rolled out of the white towers and fell, dreamlike and heavy as the sound of doom, into the plaza. McKenna, waiting for the car ahead to move, suddenly found his gaze hurtingly acute, as if he were undergoing an attack of *petit mal* or was high on coca weed. The sunlight in the plaza became more brilliant, the shadows turned deep black, each note from the bells had its own sharp division of light and shade. He looked out on a nightmare that at any moment could turn into an even more horrible reality. He stared at the brown clay faces lining the pavements, knew that he and Taber, white skins, were included in the mass hatred.

"At last," said Taber, and rolled the Land-Rover forward and followed the *cortège* out of the plaza.

The Indians remained still till the last vehicle had disappeared. The centre of the plaza was empty; the golden condor atop the tall column in the gardens blazed like a firebird. Then the waves broke, spilled out in a flood, and the plaza was swamped. The Indians went about their business, waiting for

the day when . . . But it was not a day any criollo had ever heard
them mention. Time had stopped: it would be the morrow of
the day Atahualpa was murdered.

The cemetery lay five miles beyond the edge of the city. The
road was tarred, but was not wide; it had been built originally
for the convenience of the tin and silver baron who had paid
for it; it was known as El Camino de Plata, a grand name for a
highway that was now full of potholes. It ran absolutely straight
for three miles till it reached the gates of the estate of the tin
baron; coming home from parties his visitors, drunk on spirits
and the vision of what real riches could buy, would race their
carriages down the three-mile stretch. Beyond the gates the
road, no longer needed by the tin baron or his visitors, was just
a gravelled track that swung through a sharp S-curve.

As they approached the high wall that was the beginning of
the estate, McKenna could see the schoolboys working the
fields. It was now a school run by Franciscan monks; this was
where Jesu Mamani had gone. The tin baron, who had not
lived in Bolivia since 1921, had died in 1938; the estate had
known no one but caretakers for thirty years up till the revolution. Since then it had been a school, but it had never succeeded
in throwing off the ghost of the man who had built it. His statue
still stood in the neglected gardens: he had been a man who
built his own monuments to himself, knowing no one else would
honour him: he had raped his homeland and then gone abroad
to spend the proceeds. The main house, a huge villa brought
from Spain, the past bought and transplanted brick by brick,
was a museum; but only the criollos visited it, never the Indians.
The school itself was housed in the farm buildings of the estate,
in the cottages that had sheltered the peons, the great adobe
sheds that had stored the grain and the stables for the two
hundred horses that had been the tin baron's pride. Even in
death the old man had not been entirely conquered.

The funeral procession wound its way into the S-curve, disappearing into the cleft between the two brown hills that were
the beginning of the climb towards the altiplano from this end
of the city. Taber saw the cars up ahead move to the side of the
road, a sudden rippling movement running right down the long
line. Instinctively he moved the Land-Rover over to the verge,

knowing something was coming down the road from between the hills. Then the truck, swaying like a ship riding side on to a rough sea, came speeding out of the S-curve. It hurtled down the middle of the road, the Indian women high on its pile of freight swaying like giant dolls in a high wind. It swept by the Land-Rover, missing it by inches. Taber braked, looked in the mirror on the front mudguard. He saw the accident in concentrated miniature, but it was no less terrible for that. The truck left the road, already keeling over on its side before it was off the macadam; the women on top of it shot off like plump birds, their shawls flying behind them like useless wings. The truck hit the ditch beside the road, dust ballooning up in a giant cloud. Freight separated from the truck as if a bomb had gone off in it: tyres shot into the air, landed, bounced ridiculously and went rolling down the road; crates broke and chickens flew out like balls of exploding smoke; sacks split open and potatoes sprayed out like a barrage of rocks. Then the dust settled and the truck emerged as an unrecognisable wreck of steel and wood. But by then Taber had stopped the Land-Rover and he and McKenna were already running back to the accident.

The truck's engine was roaring, the back wheels still spinning furiously. Women were screaming and moaning, and somewhere beneath the truck an animal, a goat or an alpaca, was bellowing. Taber slid down the embankment, jumped the ditch, stumbled over a shoal of potatoes, fell up against the side of the truck. Four men were still in the cabin of the truck, two of them moaning, the other two instantly recognisable as dead. Taber, deafened by the thunderous roar of the engine, reached in and switched off the ignition. In the immediate comparative silence the screams and moans of the injured took on an added note of agony.

Several cars from the funeral procession had stopped and the men in them had come running back. Taber could see McKenna attending to several of the Indian women, his white surplice already bloodstained. Taber himself grabbed one of the men in the driving cabin and gently tried to ease him out; the man moaned in pain, but Taber tried to shut his ears against the sound. Two men came scrambling down from the roadway, took the injured man from him while he reached in again to

lift out the second injured Indian. But even as he took hold of
the man he knew it was too late. The agonised face that had been
turned towards him screwed up in one last fierce spasm, then
abruptly relaxed. Taber let go of the dead man, stepped back
and straightened up. The three dead men in the cabin were
huddled together, their faces turned towards him, staring at
him with the marble eyes of crumpled and discarded manikins.
Taber stared back at them, angry at the stupidity which had
caused their death: why did these Indians drive on these mountain roads in trucks that had no brakes? Then, as if his eyes had
been fogged, his gaze cleared and focused on the driver and the
man beside him. The driver was Toribio and this truck was the
truck that had been used by Taber and McKenna in the raid
on the Customs shed the night before last. And the man
slumped beside Toribio was not an Indian but a white man.

McKenna, bloodstained and dusty, came up beside him.
"Anything I can do?"

"They're all gone. You can do nothing for them now."

"That's where we differ." McKenna made the sign of the
Cross, murmured a quick prayer for the dead, raised his hand
again, then stopped. Then, puzzled, he looked at Taber. "It's
Toribio. But who's the other guy?"

As McKenna had begun his prayer Taber had moved away.
He stood at the back of the wrecked truck looking down at
two big packing cases that had burst open. "Come here,
Terry."

McKenna made the sign of the Cross again over the three
dead men, then joined Taber. The latter gestured at the packing
cases. "Where do you think Toribio was taking those?"

Each of the cases must have contained fifty rifles; a third,
smaller case had burst open and it was full of cartons of ammunition. Taber picked up one of the rifles. "It's brand new.
A Czech job."

Then there was the moan of a siren up on the road and he
dropped the rifle back into the case. The police car that had
been leading the procession had come back; Captain Condoris
got out, followed by two other officers. They spoke to some of
the men who were attending the injured Indian women, then
Condoris came and stood up on the roadway above Taber and

McKenna. His eyes missed nothing; he saw the burst packing cases and the rifles at once. But he said, "Are the men dead, padre?"

"Except for this man." McKenna nodded at the unconscious Indian Taber had dragged out of the driving cabin.

Condoris slid cautiously down the embankment, careful not to scuff his highly polished boots. As he did so another car came back down the road, drew up, and Francisco and Hernando got out. They crossed the road and stood up on top of the embankment as Condoris picked up the rifle Taber had dropped. The injured Indian women were still moaning and weeping; miraculously none of them had been killed. There were now half a dozen cars that had come back from the funeral; the criollo men and women, forgetting their feelings of twenty minutes ago, were proving that they were not without charity. The Partridges, careless of their clothes, were working as a team, doctor and nurse. But Taber and McKenna, Francisco and Hernando had eyes only for Condoris. The police chief examined the rifle professionally, nodded appreciatively to one of his aides, then dropped it back in the case. He told the aide to take charge of the rifles, then he looked at McKenna.

"Would you recognise any of these men, padre?"

McKenna wondered why he should be expected to know any of the men; but you did not ask a police chief how his mind worked, not even back home in the States. "The driver is – was a man named Toribio. He came from Altea – the truck was his. The others – " He shook his head. "I've never seen any of them before, not even the women. They could be from any village up on the altiplano."

Condoris had been peering in at the dead men, but he showed no surprise that one of them was a white man. The dead man was young, possibly no more than twenty; before the top of his head had been smashed in he might have been handsome. Condoris nodded to the second police officer with him and the latter reached in and attempted to search through the dead man's pockets. It was not easy, all three men were trapped beneath the crushed dashboard; McKenna hesitated, then moved forward to give the police officer a hand. They managed to extricate the bodies from the wreckage, not without Taber having to help them, and laid them side by side in the ditch. Condoris made no move to help, and Francisco and Hernando remained motionless up on the roadway. Taber looked up at them once, cursing silently, but he kept his mouth shut.

The police aide took a bloodstained wallet from the white man's pocket and handed it to Condoris. The latter took it fastidiously, examined the papers in it, then looked away from Taber and McKenna and up at Francisco. "It seems that he is not one of us, but a Frenchman. Would you know him, Senor Ruiz? You have just come back from France. His name is Jean Paul Perrier."

"I have never seen him before." Francisco's voice had an edge to it that McKenna had not heard before; it was no longer the voice of a petulant young fop. Standing up on the roadway, against the bright sky, the attitude of both Francisco and Hernando had an arrogance to it that belied their youth. They are Ruiz to the core, McKenna thought: they will take over from Alejandro and there will be no hint of a break in the line. Francisco looked down at Condoris and put the police chief in his place: "The only Frenchmen I know are in France. If any of them come here, I shall let you know, captain."

Condoris gave no reaction at all to the rebuff, did not even flush. It was bad enough having to keep on side with the fathers without having to toady to the sons too. He glanced at Hernando, asked without expecting any helpful answer, "You do not recognise him?"

Hernando shook his head, less offended than Francisco had been by the police captain's question. "No. But if I did know him, would you expect me to acknowledge him? Especially with those lying there – " He nodded at the rifles. "The man was probably a gun runner – he could have been supplying the terrorists – "

"I have thought of that." Condoris looked at Taber and McKenna. "Was this – Toribio? – in your little escapade the other night?"

"Which one was that, captain?" Taber kept his voice polite.

Condoris bit his lip but showed no other expression. "The one at the Customs shed."

"Yes," said McKenna, hoping the truth was going to be the

safest course. "Senor Taber and I used this truck. Toribio was
with us all the time."

"Did you know Toribio well, padre?"

I know none of the Indians well, McKenna thought; but
that was a confession of failure as well as a defence. "No better
than I know any of the others in Altea. His two children came
to my school."

Condoris nodded, but said nothing. He walked across to
where the injured women were laid out, spoke to Dr Partridge,
then climbed up to the roadway, stamped the dust from his
boots and went across to the police car. The two junior officers
looked at each other, then one of them looked at Taber and
McKenna.

"Help us put the rifles back in the case."

"Get stuffed," said Taber in English.

The police officer looked puzzled, then glanced at McKenna.
"I'm afraid that goes for me too," said McKenna in Spanish.

He followed the Englishman up the bank on to the roadway.
He walked along the side of the road till he stood above where
the Partridges were attending to a woman who appeared to
have a broken leg. "Is there anything more I can do, doctor?"

Partridge, on one knee in the dirt, looked up. "Don't think
so, old chap. The captain has radioed in for ambulances. Should
be here soon." His suit dusty, his hands and cuffs bloodied, he
had become his real self; even the clipped English voice could
not falsify him now. "They'll all survive, padre. No prayers will
be needed."

That's what you think, doctor. These poor devils will always
need prayers. "I'll come to the hospital this afternoon, just in
case."

He had to pass Francisco and Hernando to get back to the
Land-Rover. The two young men had not moved, still stood
above the two police officers who were now pushing the rifles
back into the cases and trying to hammer the timber slats of the
cases back into place with rocks. Students from the school had
come running across the fields and now the wreckage of the
truck was surrounded by a crowd of chattering youngsters.
None of the students, boys between thirteen and eighteen,
looked shocked or upset by what he saw; accidents like this

happened every week, death was part of their life. Their education had started long before they had come to the school across the fields.

Hernando said, "Did Jesu Mamani and Toribio ever work together, padre?"

McKenna, puzzled by the question, shook his head. "What do you mean by that? They had a sort of co-operative up at the village."

"I was just wondering," said Hernando, but his voice suggested that he had had a more definite line of thought than just casual conjecture.

McKenna's own mind suddenly sharpened. "Don't make suggestions like that to the police!"

"Suggestions like what, padre?" Hernando was still relaxed in his attitude, but beside him Francisco had stiffened.

"That Jesu might have had something to do with those." McKenna nodded at the packing cases. "He's already in prison for something he had nothing to do with."

"What are you, padre? His confessor or his advocate?"

"One could make me the other." McKenna could feel his anger rising, but it was cold anger: he knew he could control it.

"You mean if he told you the truth in confession you would – what do you Americans call it? – go to bat for him in the courts?"

"Jesu won't reach the courts," said McKenna, and knew he spoke a terrible truth. You had to be charged with something before you could expect justice; Mamani had been taken in only for "questioning". "Don't make things worse for him, Hernando. He's got enough trouble."

"I'm no friend of the captain's," said Hernando, glancing across to where Condoris still sat in the police car. A voice crackled out of the car's radio, flat and emotionless as the voice of a robot: two ambulances had been dispatched, the morgue had been told to expect three bodies, death and injury were routine, what else was new? God, McKenna thought, whatever happened to compassion and pity? "But let us hope he does not connect Jesu with Toribio. Those rifles are going to be a worry to everyone. It will be interesting to hear what that fourth man has to say when he regains consciousness."

McKenna looked back down at the unconscious Indian. He had been taken across and laid out beside the injured women; even as McKenna watched, one of the police officers moved across and stood beside the man. The police would know by this evening where the rifles had at least come from, even if they might not know where they had been bound.

"Whatever he has to say, it won't have anything to do with Jesu," said McKenna, but already he could detect the note of doubt in his own voice.

2

"The Indian gets enough carbohydrates," said Pereira, carefully scrubbing soil from beneath his nails in the kitchen sink, "and almost enough proteins. But he gets only twenty per cent of his calcium requirements. A small pinch of lime in every loaf of bread would solve the problem. But –" He shrugged, began to dry his hands. "I wrote a report, carefully composed in my very best prose – Henry James would have been proud, Harry, of some of the turns of phrase."

"What happened to it?" Taber closed his notebook, wondered how his own turns of phrase would sound when he got down to writing his report. In the past one or two of his reports had been noted for their angry sarcasm, till Verdoux had pointed out, with equal sarcasm, that he was employed as a soil scientist and not a Messiah.

"What happens to any reports?" There was no rancour in Pereira; he just shrugged again. "One just keeps writing them, Harry. We do our job – " He gestured at the jars and test tubes of soil in the racks on the kitchen bench. He and Taber had been working all afternoon in the makeshift laboratory and Taber had been surprised just how competent the garrulous Bolivian could be when he put his mind to work. He might hate field work, dislike intensely getting his hands dirty, but here in the laboratory he had demonstrated why he could hold his job. "Once your report is composed, Harry, then you stop being a scientist and have to become a politician. That is, if you want it adopted. Unfortunately I am not a politician. Or perhaps fortunately. My father – an interesting man you would have found him, Harry. Absolutely misguided in everything he did, went through life without even a compass bearing on his children – my father was a politician and he met a very sudden demise in the revolution. He was not living at home at the time – he had a mistress who had more ambition than my mother – and we only got the story second-hand, as you might say. One of the generals said to my father, 'Are you on our side?' and my father, being a politician and never lost for a word, said, 'Of course.' Whereupon the general's adjutant shot both the general and my father. *He* was on the revolutionaries' side."

He beamed as he finished the story, a joke from the family album. Taber laughed, though he could not remember ever having laughed at the death of another man's father. "Did Captain Condoris ask you whose side you were on?"

The smile died and Pereira shook his head, still bewildered by what had happened to him when the mayor had been shot down in the cinema lobby. He had always managed to remain clear of the police, and the twelve hours he had spent at police headquarters had been a traumatic experience. Compromise, he had come to realise, was no defence when the police were only interested in making the suspect convict himself. For once in his life he had managed to curb his tongue, though it had seemed to grow larger in his mouth the longer he had kept silent. He had wanted to burst out, to tell the police what he thought of their bullying, of their brutal intimidation aimed to make an innocent man plead guilty just so that they could chalk up an arrest; but the long dedication to survival at all costs had stood him in good stead, he had stuck doggedly and mono-syllabically to the truth and in the end it had been the police's and not his own patience that had given out. But he did not want to repeat the experience ever again.

"It was no laughing matter, Harry. If you had only taken me into your confidence, told me what you were going to do – "

"As it turned out, weren't you safer not knowing? How good a liar would you have been if you had known what we had done?" Taber still felt a certain guilt at how Pereira had been implicated in the events of the night before last. If there had not been a black-out, would the terrorists have assassinated the mayor at the cinema?

Pereira nodded glumly. "You are right, Harry. Ignorance was bliss – "

Taber made one of his rare gestures of affection; he patted Pereira on the shoulder. He wondered what the Bolivian had gained from the last revolution, what he would gain if there were another one. The middle classes were nearly always the losers in any revolution; they would continue to remain the middle classes but, whether the revolution was right or left wing, something was always chipped off the edges of them. In South America, unlike in Europe or the United States, the middle class still had no real power. He could not blame Pereira for putting so much faith in compromise.

"Well, we'll keep our noses clean from now on. Except – " He picked up his notebook, flipped it open, looked at the scrawl of notes in his untidy handwriting. He ran his hand through his hair, scratching it up straight on the crown of his head so that he seemed to be wearing a crown of red thorns. "I can't write a report that is going to finish up under a layer of dust on some bloody shelf!"

"Harry, what you want to suggest in your report would need more than a politician to have it adopted – I think only a tribunal like the Holy Trinity could get it up to La Paz. Do you think Senor Ruiz is going to allow his Agriculture Reform Council to – "

"It's not *his* Reform Council!"

Pereira shook his head at the naïvete of some Englishmen; how had they ever built an empire? "Harry, Senor Ruiz has been chairman of the council for seventeen years – no one has ever dared run against him, even La Paz has never suggested there should be another chairman."

"All right," Taber conceded. He leant back on the bench, like a boxer resting on the ropes between rounds: it was going to be a long fight. "What do you suggest?"

"Let me write the report. It will be so long no one will bother to read it. I shall spend hours composing convoluted sentences – "

"Nothing doing." Taber looked at his notebook again. McKenna would call it my missal, he thought irrelevantly; but he had no faith in it. There had been dozens like it, and how much dogma had emerged from any of them? Would Rome back him up if he said exactly what he wanted to say in his report? But then Rome would probably never see the report, at least unexpurgated, exactly as he wrote it. He had no direct line to Rome; he was just like McKenna. He had his own bishop: Verdoux, sitting down there in Santiago on his neutral bum, both eyes peeled for heresy. He swore obscenely, snapped the book shut again. "How do you think I'd go if I went and saw Ruiz first, told him what I intended to recommend?"

"Would you tell the Lord you intended to take over half of Paradise and give it to the devils?"

Taber grinned. "Nothing would please an atheist more. Anyhow, I think that's what I'll do. I'll ring Ruiz and see if I can go and see him now."

Pereira spread his hands. "You will forgive me if I do not accompany you, Harry. When you are recalled, I shall still have to go on living here – "

"Miguel, don't you, just occasionally, feel you'd like to thumb your nose at the Establishment? Walk up to them and tell them to get stuffed?"

"Every night, Harry. In bed, after the light is out."

Taber laughed, surrendered. "You win. What's on at the cinema to-night?"

"A film about the death of General Custer. We shall have a packed house to-night. All Indians."

"Don't the police think a film like that might give the Indians ideas?"

"Not until the Indians here find their own Sitting Bull or Geronimo. There are no leaders among the campesinos, Harry."

"One will come along some day."

"Then we shall show only films in which the white man always wins. If Hollywood no longer makes those sort of films, then we shall have to revive the Errol Flynn films. In the meantime all I have to think about is the box office."

"Speaking of the box office, have your cashier here tomorrow morning. I'll have some letters for her to type. Perhaps I'll even have my report – "

"Harry, Isabella cannot type – "

"Christ Almighty! She can't take dictation, she can't type – what the bloody hell did you employ her for?"

"Harry, she needs the money. At the cinema I can pay her only a mere pittance – F A O has *millions* – "

Taber gave up. He let Pereira out of the house, rang Alejandro Ruiz and was told he could see him immediately, went upstairs and showered, slicked his hair down, put on his best suit and set out for the Ruiz house. It was a twenty minutes' walk, through the criollo residential section of the city. The streets were deserted except for an occasional Indian street cleaner or messenger. The middle-class houses with their low, suburban garden walls (he could have been walking through a Spanish version of Wimbledon or Richmond; he passed a garden of rose bushes, saw a stone pixie grinning at him from behind a hawthorn hedge) gave way to the high-walled houses of the wealthy. A drink vendor came down the street on his tricycle, ringing his bell without any real hope of a sale; he passed Taber without looking at him, went on down the street, the bell still ringing mechanically, like a telephone that would never be answered. Taber came to the plaza in front of the Ruiz house, crossed it, nodded to the two policemen who sat slumped on a seat in the small garden square, their rifles resting beside them like walking-sticks. He banged the lower knocker on the big gate, wondering when last the horseman's knocker had been used, and a moment later the small inset gate was opened by the Ruiz's butler.

As soon as he stepped into the courtyard Taber saw the two armed men lounging in one corner. They were not policemen, but Indian workers, dressed in bright green overalls; on the back of each, stitched in yellow thread, was: *Inca Brewery*. Taber felt an urge to laugh, but nothing was funny, really; on the shoulder of each man was slung a brand new rifle. Even at a quick glance Taber recognised the rifles: he had seen dozens like them out at the wrecked truck on the road to the cemetery. Christ, he thought, how do you win? Ruiz seemed to own everything around here, even the police.

He followed the butler across to the steps leading up to the front door. A big bush of retama, Spanish broom, beside the steps caught the late afternoon sun: the yellow glare was like a spotlight on the face of any visitor. Taber squinted against the brightness of it, said to the butler, "It hurts the eyes."

"Yes, senor. But it is good for the heart." The butler tapped his breast.

Taber was about to ask how. But he had followed the butler into the entrance hall; and there was Carmel. He felt a catch in his breast and wondered if, as the novelists said, the heart did leap. Whatever the feeling was, it was good for the heart, better than a whole garden of retama. He smiled broadly, his craggy face breaking up to become almost youthful. He felt suddenly awkward, his big hands clasped together like mating crabs. Christ, he thought, I must be in love. But he had never felt this way about Beth or Sandra.

Carmel said, her own delight at seeing him plain in her face, "I was going to call you, then Senor Ruiz told me you were coming here. Dolores wants us to go to her house for dinner to-night."

"I'll pick you up," he said, still smiling; one of his hands found hers, squeezed it so hard that she winced. "Christ, I'm sorry – !"

"It's all right, Harry – "

"I'll learn to *kiss* your hand, be a bloody gentleman." He looked up, saw Romola Ruiz standing on the gallery that ran round the upper half of the entrance hall. He brought his heels together, bowed, showed what a bloody gentleman he could be: he made a better pretence of it than he knew. "Senora, I have come to see your husband."

"Not Carmel?" Romola came down the stairs, moving with the unhurried grace of a lady: she had to make no pretence to her breeding. "Senor Taber, I am disappointed in you."

Taber looked from one woman to the other, knew that if Romola Ruiz had not been told how he and Carmel felt about each other, she had made a pretty close guess. But she did not look displeased. "I was hoping to see Carmel too."

"You are welcome here any time," said Romola. She was looking at this tall awkward Englishman with new interest, now that she knew Carmel found him more interesting than her own son. She wondered what he would be like as a lover, and for a moment allowed the thought to show in her face. "We have so few new and interesting men come to San Sebastian."

In another city, Taber thought, I think I could try my luck with this woman; but kept his surprise well hidden. "It will depend on your husband, senora." Both their faces twitched; his words were at cross-purposes with their thoughts. He said hastily, aware that Carmel was now looking at him quizzically, "I have to see him on some business that he may not like. He may not want me here again."

"Let us worry about that when it happens," said Romola, and sounded as if it would be no worry at all to her. "We shall look forward to seeing you again, Senor Taber. Now you had better go in to see my husband – he does not like to be kept waiting." She smiled: keeping Alejandro waiting was one of her own favourite diversions. "Come, Carmel. Let us go out and have an inspection of the guard. I feel rather like the Queen of England."

She and Carmel moved towards the back of the house and Taber guessed there must be more armed guards stationed in the rear garden. When he was shown into Alejandro Ruiz's study he glanced quickly at the window and saw the two armed guards, in their brewery overalls, standing at sloppy attention as Romola and Carmel walked past them along a path. Romola looked them up and down, laughed and shook her head at Carmel, something the Queen of England would never have done.

Alejandro Ruiz had noticed Taber's glance towards the window. "Just a precaution, Senor Taber. One has to protect oneself. And one's womenfolk." He looked out the window at his wife and Carmel strolling in the garden, two beautiful women who did not seem to have a care in the world; beyond the closed window they threw back their heads and laughed silently. "Some of them don't appreciate the seriousness of the situation. Perhaps we men keep them *too* protected. Are the women in England molly-coddled?"

Taber could not remember any Englishman ever having been accused of *that*. "I don't think so. Dogs and cats and budgerigars, but not women."

Ruiz smiled expansively and waved Taber to a chair. Only

then did he acknowledge the presence of Francisco and Hernando, both of whom stood silently, hands clasped behind their backs, in front of the fireplace: Taber thought they looked a better pair of guards than the two armed men out in the garden. He wished he had been able to see Alejandro Ruiz alone.

"My son and my nephew will be interested in what you have to say. Eventually they will be running the family estate. A man does not live forever," he said a trifle bitterly, as if he resented his own mortality. "What did you want to discuss, Senor Taber?"

Taber, incapable of the diplomatic approach, plunged straight in. "Land reform, senor."

"Whose land?"

"Yours."

Ruiz glanced at his son and nephew, then back at Taber. "You don't mince words."

"Sometimes I wish I could," said Taber candidly. "But in the end I'd still have to say what I've just said."

"Why?"

"Senor Ruiz, your government in La Paz had me sent down here to see what could be done for the campesinos up on the altiplano. The FAO man who was here before me put in a report to your – " he only slightly emphasised the word " – Agriculture Reform Council. It never reached La Paz, but he left a copy in his files."

"We are still considering it."

"The report was put in six months ago."

"A copy went to the FAO regional director in Santiago. If he had thought it needed urgent attention, I'm sure we should have heard from him by now."

Not Verdoux: he wouldn't order a book of postage stamps without local approval. But Verdoux was too far away to be dragged into this. "I wouldn't know about that. All I can say is that I agree with the report – with a few additions of my own."

"The additions concerning land that belongs to our family?"

Taber nodded. "Your land up by the lake, properly cultivated and fertilised, could support three times the number of people there are now in Altea. And at a much higher standard of living."

Hernando spoke for the first time: "You seem to have a lot of faith in the Indians' ability to improve this land."

Alejandro Ruiz nodded approvingly at the point. Taber conceded it: "Not at first. It might mean someone staying here, me for instance, for a year or even two. But eventually they would be able to handle it themselves."

"I have less faith in them than you have," said Alejandro Ruiz. "Land *has* been given over to the Indians in other parts of the country and they have done very little, if anything, to improve it. Forgive me for saying so, but I think I know the Indians better than you. Our family has been dealing with them for four hundred years – I have inherited that knowledge and experience."

"You are English, Senor Taber," said Francisco; he made no attempt to disguise his dislike of the other man. "Have the English ever really understood the natives of their Empire?"

"We made our mistakes," Taber admitted. "But so did the Spanish."

"We are Bolivians," said Hernando. "We became independent of Spain a long time ago."

It was another point, but a fine one. The criollos were fiercely proud of their Spanish blood, but would not admit to Spain's mistakes. Taber knew that this dichotomy had existed in the American Spanish even before the wars of independence. But perhaps it was a condition that infected all ex-colonials: he knew that there were many North Americans who visited the graveyards and churches of Britain seeking their heritage, who paid as much homage to Runnymede as to Valley Forge. One could not argue with a man's blood.

"The Indians are not yet ready," said Alejandro Ruiz. "They took over the mines in 1952 and they still haven't learned how to manage them properly. The government broke up some of the estates and gave the land to them – but it produces no more than it did in the old days and is less of an economic proposition."

"Perhaps they needed more advice. That's why your government called on F A O."

"La Paz only understands La Paz. All capitals are the same. I have heard Americans say the same about Washington. I'm

211

sure a Scotsman has his own opinion of what Westminster decides."

I'm going to lose track of this argument if I don't watch out, Taber thought. He had experienced Spanish argument before, the sidetracking and shooting off at tangents that they had learned from the Moors. Doggedly he said, "Perhaps the Indians are changing and you haven't noticed it. I just can't believe a people can stand still for four hundred years."

Ruiz waved an impatient hand. "Now is not the time for experiment. Not with the terrorists so active."

"Perhaps this *is* the time for experiment," said Taber, trying not to sound political. "If you have the Indians on your side, whom will the terrorists have to lead?"

"He has a point, Father," said Francisco grudgingly. Taber, perversely, wished the concession had come from Hernando; he wanted nothing from the younger Ruiz. "What are you suggesting, Senor Taber?"

"Turn the land into a co-operative. If you like, you could retain a percentage of the return – you could be the supervisors, if you like to call yourselves that."

"You mean we'd run it under a form of communism?" asked Hernando.

Taber was not going to be trapped by that one. "I'd prefer to call it socialism, if you have to give it a label."

"Is there any real difference?" Alejandro asked; then waved a hand and made a concession of his own: "All right, there is a difference. But you can't have socialism in a country where there is a government of the élite. And that is what we still have in this country, despite the revolution. You are making the mistake of all outsiders, Senor Taber – you are trying to solve a problem according to your own standards."

"What solution do you have, Senor Ruiz?"

Ruiz's face went hard, but he did not rebuke the Englishman for his rude question. "Time, senor. And patience."

"I'm afraid I don't have enough of either." Taber knew he had lost; he had demonstrated no diplomacy at all, but now it did not matter. "What I'm even more afraid of is that neither have the terrorists. If they get the Indians on their side first, time and patience won't do you a damn' bit of good."

"I think our interview is ended, senor," said Alejandro Ruiz stiffly.

"Just a moment, Father." Francisco seemed to be taking on some of his father's air of authority; he still had a surface of brittle arrogance, but the man beneath it was no longer hollow and petty. He was back in his own domain and the Ruiz status had put iron into him that he had never found in Paris, where he had been just another student. "Senor Taber, what makes you think the terrorists have some support among the Indians?"

"That wasn't what I said. But you saw the rifles out at the accident this morning – it was an Indian truck that was carrying them."

"What made you think the rifles were meant for the terrorists?"

Taber shrugged, feeling that the conversation was becoming too political. But Alejandro Ruiz said, "They were meant for them, Senor Taber. Your guess was right."

Taber risked it: "But you managed to persuade Captain Condoris to let you have some of them?"

"Wrong, senor. Those rifles my men are carrying were delivered last night. It seems that the terrorists and ourselves had the same unscrupulous supplier."

"The Frenchman Perrier," Hernando explained. "Now dead."

"What about the Indian they took to the hospital? Was he able to tell the police anything?"

"Nothing," said Francisco. "Someone got to him in the hospital and cut his throat."

"So you see, Senor Taber," said Alejandro Ruiz, "now is not the time for any experimental reforms. It might be best if you persuaded La Paz to send you to another part of the country. If you wish, I shall write to your regional director in Santiago and recommend it."

Then the butler came to the door. "Excuse me, padrone. It is Padre McKenna. He wishes to see you urgently."

3

McKenna had never been inside the prison. It had once been a

Jesuit college, till the Order had been expelled from the Spanish colonies in 1767; when the Jesuits returned thirty-nine years later they found their cells had iron doors, their chapel was a workshop and the college was a prison. It had been that way ever since. The surrounding wall had been heightened, guard posts mounted on each corner, and a statue of Our Lady of Mercy hung over the main gate by a cynical governor who had never been known to demonstrate any hint of that virtue. There were far worse prisons in South America, but McKenna was nonetheless depressed by what he saw. No free man feels better for seeing another human being degraded.

"There are some vicious criminals in here," said Dolores, "but most of them are poor stupid people who did not even know they were breaking the law."

It was she who had finally got McKenna into the prison. Maria Mamani had been denied permission to visit her husband; so McKenna had lost his chance of accompanying her to see Jesu. Then Dolores had phoned him at the cathedral when she had returned from the mayor's funeral and told him that he could accompany her to the prison this afternoon.

"I belong to Catholic Action," she had said. "We go to the prison once a week, take them extra food to supplement their rations. They don't get much."

"Will you be alone or will there be other women from Catholic Action with you?" There had been another dream of Dolores last night, one from which he had woken sweating and burning with sex. But he did not want to accompany Dolores this afternoon if she was going to be in the company of other women. They, he felt sure, would read him like an open sex manual. The criollo women of San Sebastian, always looking inwards, could recognise every symptom at a glance.

"I think I'll be alone. Since the assassination of the mayor, most of the women won't go out without their menfolk."

"You're not afraid?"

There had been a moment of silence on the phone, then she said, "I think I am afraid. But I also believe in God's will. If something is going to happen to me, it will happen."

"That's fatalism."

"Is there any difference?"

He did not think he had that sort of courage, to accept the inevitable with equanimity. He would be fighting to stay alive even as the last breath went out of his body; he was not made of the stuff of heroes and saints. "I'll meet you outside the prison."

He had been unlucky enough to meet the Bishop as he had walked out of the priests' house and down the alley beside the cathedral. Bishop Ruiz, accompanied by his secretary and a workman, was inspecting the stonework of the cathedral.

"They tell me the foundations of our church are crumbling, padre. Do you think it has some symbolic significance?"

"Maybe, your grace." The secretary and the workman were smirking behind the Bishop; *they* knew what was wrong with the Church. "But there are so many new ideas to-day for holding things together."

The Bishop's eyes twinkled. "You are absolutely right. Do you think I should suggest the Curia lay in a stock of Nu-Glu? I see you are dressed in your best suit. Are you going visiting?"

"Yes, your grace," said McKenna reluctantly. "Over to the prison. One of my – Padre Luis's parishioners from Altea is in there."

"No serious offence, I hope?"

"No offence at all. He is there for – questioning, I think they call it."

"Yes, I believe that is what they do call it." The Bishop's eyes twinkled again; he seemed unconcerned at what might result from the questioning. A small bootblack came loping up the alley, his box like a hump on his back; the secretary shooed him away and the boy crept back again to the plaza. The Bishop did not even look at him: the secretary could have been brushing away a fly. "Well, offer him what comfort you can, padre. But be circumspect, don't get too involved in his cause, whatever it may be. The prison governor is an atheist, you know. He does not consider the prison part of my diocese." He nodded to McKenna, moved on, then stopped and looked back. "Oh, have you heard from your Superior on that little matter I wrote him about?"

"Not yet, your grace." But it would come, McKenna knew. His Superior up in La Paz had once been a liberal-minded cleric, but he was an old man now, ten to fifteen years older than the Bishop, thirty to thirty-five years older than McKenna, and hardening of the arteries and a troublesome prostate gland had left him with little patience for the weaknesses of those still young enough to feel the temptations of the flesh. The Pill, McKenna knew, would have the same rating as heroin.

He was depressed when he crossed the plaza to meet Dolores outside the prison. She commented on his quietness, but he put her off with the remark that prisons never made him happy. She took it as a comment upon her own mood, though she was anything but gay, and they entered the prison gate with a coolness between them. It was the first time there had ever been such constraint between them and it only increased his depression.

The prison itself did nothing to lift it. The prisoners, all male, all Indian or mestizo, ranging from teenagers to old men, were lined up against two walls of the prison yard. Indian or mestizo guards, armed with submachine guns, lounged near them, eyeing the rabble of men with the same cold indifferent eye with which they might have guarded a herd of llama or alpaca. Some of the long-term prisoners wore a kind of uniform, but most of the men were dressed in their tattered everyday clothes. The hardened criminals were the only ones who had any look of acceptance on their faces; some of them even looked happy, as if they had finally accepted prison as some sort of goal. But the majority of the prisoners looked bewildered, as if freedom was something they had not realised they had possessed till it was taken away from them.

Dolores had brought with her in her car the gifts of the Catholic Action women for this week: loaves of bread, bags of potatoes, tobacco, matches. It was all piled up on a cart which two of the prisoners trundled round the yard after Dolores and McKenna. Each man got half a loaf of bread, three potatoes, a twist of tobacco and a box of matches: it was not much, but anything that added to the prisoners' meagre rations was welcome. The prisoners grabbed at their shares as if they had been granted pardons.

McKenna was embarrassed by charity, both the giving and the accepting of it. All his life he had been accustomed to

money and the privileges it afforded, but he had never learned
how to share the privileges of it with other people. Charity was
not the easiest of virtues; in a way it was a demonstration of
power and not all men could handle that. He admired the cool
way Dolores handed out the gifts from the cart, somehow
managing to suggest the prisoners were entitled to what they
were getting and she was only there as their servant. When he
tried to help her, handing potatoes and bread and tobacco to a
wizened mestizo with a crooked leg, he felt awkwardly superior,
yet at the same time ashamed.

He was glad when the ordeal was over and he and Dolores
were able to escape down an alley between two of the prison
buildings. Dolores had asked when they had first entered the
prison that they be allowed to see Jesu Mamani and had been
told he was in solitary confinement; now a prison guard had
come to tell them the governor would allow them to see Mamani
and he was leading them down towards the cells. No sun came
here into the alley and McKenna shivered in the chill after the
bright sun of the yard. Dolores pulled up the collar of the
camelhair coat she wore.

Mamani's cell was a dark cave, the only light coming through
a barred window set high in one of the pitted walls. The iron
door screeched on its rusted hinges as the guard swung it open:
the sound was melodramatic, suggesting old historical movies:
the Count of Monte Cristo might well be in the next cell. The
cell's furniture was a wooden bed, covered with a straw mattress
and two blankets, and a vilely smelling bucket, with a wooden
lid, in one corner. A crucifix had once hung on one wall, but it
had been removed, possibly by the atheistic governor: there
was still the pale mark of the cross against the dark stain of the
wall. McKenna wondered which Jesuit had occupied this cell
in the old days, whether piety or punishment had condemned
him to this dark hole.

The guard stood outside the cell in the alley, leaned against
the wall and lit the cigarette McKenna gave him. McKenna
and Dolores went into the cell and Mamani stood up slowly and
with dignity.

McKenna said, "Are they treating you well, Jesu?"

The light from the doorway revealed all the ugliness of the

cell. Mamani looked at Dolores, then decided he could be ironic. He smiled and nodded around him. "They have given me my own room, padre."

All the months I've wasted, McKenna lamented to himself. I could have been talking to him, learning about him, getting rid of my own loneliness. Why did he keep me locked out? But knew in his heart the answer: he was an outsider, someone not to be trusted. "Were they rough? I mean, when they questioned you?"

Mamani shrugged, moved into the light from the doorway. There was a dark bruise on his cheek and a scab of dried blood over one brow. "No worse than last time."

Dolores had retreated to stand in the doorway, overcome by the smell from the bucket. "They have no right to treat you like this."

Mamani's tone was still ironic. "No, senorita. That was what I kept telling them."

"What did they want to know?" McKenna asked.

"What I knew about the men who shot the mayor. They will not believe that I know nothing."

McKenna hesitated, then said, "Things may get worse, Jesu. Toribio was killed this morning in a truck accident. He was carrying a load of rifles and ammunition for some gun-runner, a Frenchman."

Mamani blinked and frowned, but that was the only expression he showed at the news of the death of Toribio. "What has that to do with me, padre? The guns, I mean."

"I think – I'm not sure – they are starting to suspect we have something going up at Altea." He looked at Mamani for a reaction, but there was none. "Did Toribio ever tell you he was carrying guns for the smugglers?"

"No."

"Why would he do such a thing?"

"For money, padre. It is understandable, isn't it? Toribio had six children. And his wife is pregnant." The irony in his voice turned sharp.

Why did I come here? McKenna asked himself, suddenly resentful of Mamani, repelled by the whole atmosphere of the prison, feeling the remembered pain in his genitals again. He could smell the bucket, saw the graffiti on the walls: exhortations to the Virgin Mary, obscenities, men's names, a poignant *Adios!* He tried again, scouring himself for charity: "Jesu, I'll go to Captain Condoris, see if he can do anything for you."

"It will be useless, padre. I am the guest of the security police, not of Captain Condoris." Here in the stinking cell Mamani seemed to have grown in sophistication and intelligence; he was like a man who grows in stature in a president's office. He was unrecognisable as the man McKenna had known for nine months; the mask had been a total disguise. "I shall not be here long, padre."

"What do you mean?" But Mamani did not answer and McKenna went on, all at once perversely determined not to desert him. "Are they going to remove you to another prison?"

"Do not worry about me, padre. I shall be all right."

McKenna looked at Dolores for support, but she looked as helpless as himself. She shook her head, overcome by despair: help was not a gift one could hand out like a loaf of bread or a twist of tobacco, not when the man did not want it. "Senor Mamani, who else can help you if not us?"

There was a flicker of surprise in Mamani's eyes: he had never been called Senor before. But he still said stubbornly, "Do not worry about me, senorita. I shall be all right."

McKenna made a sudden stab in the dark: "Jesu, you're not thinking of breaking out of here?" Mamani's face went blank and stiff, the mask back in place, whipped on by a juggler's hand; and McKenna knew his wild shot had been right on target. "Jesu, for God's sake, don't you see what that will make you? You'll be an outlaw, a wanted man – where will you go? What about Maria and your children? You may not get out – they could kill you before – " He gestured at the guard leaning against the wall on the other side of the alley, the submachine gun hanging like a loose third arm from his shoulder. "They're all itching to use those guns." He looked at Dolores. "Has anyone ever escaped from here?"

"Only during the revolution. The guards opened the gates then." She added her plea to McKenna's: "Don't try to escape. Please let us help you."

Mamani shook his head. "It has all been arranged."

"Arranged?" McKenna's voice cracked with surprise. "Who by?"

But Mamani had said too much. "Please go, padre. Thank you for coming. And you too, senorita. But please go." He looked at them, dismissing them politely but firmly. "And do not worry about me."

He turned away from them, went back and sat down on the bed. McKenna looked at Dolores, but again she shook her head: Mamani had locked them out as completely as if he had closed the cell door in their faces. McKenna said, "Jesu, I'm going to see Senor Ruiz. He may be able to help you." But he might just as well not have spoken; Mamani continued to stare at the wall opposite him, all Indian again. McKenna wanted to curse him, but he held back the angry words; they would have no more effect on him than the graffiti at which he was staring. McKenna went out of the cell, almost roughly pushing Dolores ahead of him.

"What do we do?" she asked.

"I'm going to see Ruiz – now!" Anger and frustration made him determined.

"I'll come with you."

"No." His mood gentled; he pressed her arm. "No, stay out of this. If Jesu is mixed up in this business with the terrorists – "

"Do you think he is?" They had dropped their voices. They were speaking in English, but there was no guarantee that the guard, slouching along behind them, did not understand enough of it to report their conversation to the governor. It was un- likely, but after the way Mamani had revealed himself McKenna would not have been surprised if the guard spoke Latin or Urdu.

"I don't know. If he is – " McKenna felt totally dispirited; he shrugged helplessly. "But who *are* they? How have they got in touch with him in here?"

"A guard can be bribed," said Dolores. Behind them the submachine gun clicked; but it was only the metal hooks of the strap clicking as the guard shifted the gun on his shoulder. "A man like this one behind us earns only about eighty cents a day."

"I'll still go to Ruiz." McKenna now had a stubbornness of his own, but part of his mind could still look objectively at himself: he guessed that this was how the early fanatical missionaries had fought to save the Inca pagan who didn't want to be saved. But while a man was alive, so was his soul; though in this case Mamani's soul was in less danger than his life. Maybe, McKenna thought, he's more certain of Heaven than I am. "If we can get him released, he may just go back to Altea, settle down to being a campesino again – "

"Do you think he will? I don't think so, Terry. He's no longer a campesino – I think they beat that out of him when they questioned him."

McKenna nodded morosely, admiring her for her practical perception. "Whatever happens to him, he'll never be the same again."

The prison yard was empty when they crossed it. A guard up in his small tower on the wall turned his gun on them and watched them sullenly. The guard who was with them looked up and made a gesture: *Don't shoot, you might hit me.* Jesu will never make it out of here, McKenna thought. He'll be full of bullets before he gets as far as the wall; those guards are just itching to let off their guns. He missed a step, almost turning to go back and plead with the Indian not to throw his life away; but they had come to the door in the big gate, the guard threw it open and Dolores stepped through. McKenna followed her and the door was slammed shut behind them.

"I'll drive you to the Ruiz's," Dolores said.

"No. I'll walk – I want to think out what I want to say. Right now I wouldn't be much of an advocate for Jesu." He opened the door of her car, helped her in. "You have to go on living here, Dolores. It's better you don't get too mixed up in this."

"It's just because I have to go on living here that I should become mixed up in it, as you call it. Terry, one can't be un-involved – not if one is intelligent, if *one* cares – "

He looked at her, making no attempt to disguise the love that showed in his face. "You and I together could really have helped these people," he said, and turned quickly and walked away from her, tears scalding the corners of his eyes, his heart thumping as if trying to hammer its way out of the cage of his breast.

He walked blindly through the streets to the Ruiz house, his mind a belfry of ringing thoughts that had nothing to do with his arguments for the release of Mamani. He was outside the big iron-studded gate before he knew it, coming awake only when his hand had clanged the mailed fist that was the knocker. Maybe that was the argument that was best, the mailed fist. But all he had was words, and not a good selection of those.

The butler opened the gate, took him across the courtyard and into the house. He saw the two armed men in the corner of the courtyard, but did not take much notice of them. He had just come from a place where armed guards were part of the scene; he had not yet thrown off the atmosphere of the prison. As the heavy front door was closed behind him, he thought: this, too, is a prison. The Ruiz had built their own, condemned themselves to its narrow confinement with their refusal to give up the past.

The butler went away, came back, said, "Senor Ruiz will see you, padre."

McKenna sensed the tension in the study as soon as he walked through the door. Taber stood just inside the door, as if he had been on the point of leaving. Alejandro Ruiz sat behind his desk, looking, McKenna thought with a sinking heart, like some cardinal of the Inquisition who, in *his* turn, had been accused of heresy by the heretic before him: the red-headed heretic. Francisco and Hernando stood in front of the fireplace, the Ruiz household's own Swiss Guards.

"I'm sorry, Senor Ruiz. I didn't mean to interrupt – "

"Senor Taber is just leaving."

Well, now I'm here I might as well be hung for a sheep as for a lamb. "If you don't object, maybe he could stay." He glanced at Taber, seeking moral support. "Both of us are concerned with what I'm about to say."

"Are you a land reformer too, padre?" The blunt scythe of Ruiz's sarcasm was almost enough to drive McKenna back through the door. Why don't I choose my moments more carefully? But he had not been in a position to choose his time to call on Ruiz: the moment of Mamani's possible death was not going to wait on formality.

"In a way, yes." He could not betray Taber; the latter had stayed to help him. "But that's not why I'm here. I've come to ask you to do what you can to help Jesu Mamani."

"Mamani? The Indian from Altea?" Alejandro Ruiz looked at Hernando, then back at McKenna. "What concern is he of mine?"

"He was your protégé at the school."

"I have never seen the man."

Whose fault is that? McKenna wanted to ask. "I think if you met him, you would be impressed by him. Isn't that so, Hernando?"

But Hernando was not going to be conscripted on to the wrong side. "I don't know him as well as you do, padre."

Taber said, "I can recommend him, Senor Ruiz. If you allowed me to set up that co-operative I spoke of, he would be the man I'd name as the Indians' representative."

McKenna shot Taber a look of gratitude, then turned back to the stiff, unyielding man behind the big desk. The sun had dropped down below the rim of the altiplano and the room already had its own dusk. But none of the Ruiz made a move to turn on a lamp: this was an argument that needed no light shed on it.

"Senor Ruiz, Mamani is being held in the prison. There is no charge against him, but the security police have been ill-treating him. They've beaten him up while they've been questioning him."

"One doesn't interfere with the security police, padre."

"Not an outsider like me, no. But I thought you might have some influence."

"None." Then as if that was too much for his pride, he qualified it: "Not with the security police. Anyone else, yes. But not with them."

"He has to be released somehow!" McKenna tried to keep his voice down, but failed. "It's not just the man's life that's in danger. But if he is kept in prison – and they can keep him there as long as they like – forever, if they wish – "

"Why is his life in danger?" asked Francisco.

I've said too much. A little more restraint, McKenna, or you're going to walk out of here minus your head. "If they keep him in prison, he's not the sort of man who will take it lying down. He'll endanger his own life just by rebellion." He hoped he sounded convincing.

"You can't expect my father to interfere in security matters. Our own lives have been threatened this past week – "

"Mamani has had nothing to do with those activities!" McKenna drew a deep breath, trying to keep control of himself. "He is one of my parishioners – " This was no place to draw the line of distinction between himself and Padre Luis; but he knew that if Mamani had a rope round his neck and was as innocent as his youngest child, Padre Luis still wouldn't have come *here*. "I'm trying to do what I can for him, as his priest. The security police wouldn't listen to me – they've already told me to go home – "

"That might be a good idea, padre." Alejandro Ruiz switched on the lamp on his desk. "Go home to your mission and attend to what flock you have left – there is still enough of them."

The security police had meant the States as home; but he was not going to admit that here. "Then you won't help, Senor Ruiz?"

"I think we've come to the wrong man," said Taber. "We're wasting our time."

In the glow of the lamp Ruiz's fists rested like rocks on the desk in front of him; he raised one of them and brought it crashing down. "You have worn out your welcome, senores – in my house and in San Sebastian!" He nodded to Francisco, who pulled a bell cord beside the fireplace. "What we have here are our own problems – we do not want outsiders to solve them for us!"

"Your government would not have allowed us into the country if it had not thought we could help," said Taber.

"Governments can be as stupid as individuals. Collective stupidity just makes bigger mistakes." The butler knocked, opened the door; he must have been standing in the hall outside, guessing that he would be required to show one or both of the visitors to the door soon; he was part of the household, an

Indian on the Ruiz's side. "The padre and Senor Taber are leaving."

McKenna could feel himself trembling with anger at the curt way they were being dismissed; Ruiz's tone of voice had humiliated them even in front of the butler. He glanced at Taber, waiting for the Englishman to erupt; but Taber was half-smiling, had kept his dignity intact just by being sardonic. McKenna was not capable of mockery of other people, but he realised that Taber's was the best face to put on. He, too, managed a small smile, became an actor (who was it said the best actors were always the priests? Probably some atheist like Taber), even managed to put a little mockery into his stiff bow.

"Thank you for seeing us, Senor Ruiz," said Taber. "We shan't waste your time again." A slight pause, then: "Nor ours."

He stood aside, let McKenna go out of the door ahead of him. They went out of the room with a semblance of Spanish dignity: dismissed courtiers had left the presence of Charles V with less style. They walked side by side in silence down the long corridor, said nothing to each other till they were out in the small plaza and the gate had clanged to behind them. Only then did they look at each other and the truth of their defeat.

"Do we toss in the towel?" Taber said.

"I can't. Not yet," said McKenna, and told Taber what he had learned at the prison. "If someone is trying to spring him, it's someone who is going to use him. The Indians couldn't organise something like this. It must be the terrorists."

"Perhaps they're looking for a martyr. If he's killed, perhaps they're hoping they can rally the Indians round to avenge him. If he's not killed – "

"Yes?"

"If he's not killed, if he manages to get away, he could turn out to be the leader the Indians have been looking for."

McKenna shook his head. "If the terrorists are criollos or mestizos, as everyone says they are, they aren't going to let an Indian campesino take the revolution away from them. Revolutionaries are jealous of each other – the Bolivian Communists would have nothing to do with Che Guevara because he wanted

H 225

to run the show. No, these characters, whoever they are, will use Jesu, then dump him when he's served his purpose."

"So the poor bugger is doomed anyway?"

McKenna nodded, shivering as he felt the chill of evening. But he was colder inside at the thought of the man who, unwittingly sacrificing himself, was going to die for nothing.

Chapter 8

"It has come to our ears – "

The episcopal plural again, McKenna thought. What bit of gossip has Padre Luis brought down from Altea this time? "Yes, your grace?" he said as the Bishop paused.

Bishop Ruiz sat back in his chair, working the ring on his finger round and round like a loose knuckle. In the soft light from the bracket lamps on the walls of the study his jowls were dark and his eyes, under their heavy brows, almost black; he looked sensual, a Moorish caliph more than a prelate of the Church. A glass of Scotch on a silver coaster on the desk in front of him did nothing to suggest there was even a hint of the ascetic in him. He was a man of the world faced with a problem of the world.

Well, he thought, it is better to come straight to the point. Priests did not expect diplomacy from a bishop, not when they were on the receiving end; he had been a priest himself once, had been trodden on several times by a bishop who had delighted in humbling a Ruiz. "Padre, do you not think you are indiscreet in seeing so much of Senorita Schiller?"

Shocked by the unexpectedness of the question, McKenna played for time: "I don't quite follow – "

"If she were an old woman – like some of those who plague us – " The Bishop smiled, dispensing with rank for the moment: all men of the cloth had the same problem with demanding old women, those who thought that age was more entitled to religious comfort than youth. "But Senorita Schiller is not. She is young and very attractive."

Walking on eggshells, McKenna said, "Has someone been gossiping about us?"

"I'm afraid so, Terence." It was the first time the Bishop had called him by his first name: this was going to be a father to son talk, an explanation of the facts of life. "Would you care for a drink?"

McKenna was about to decline, then suddenly felt in need of some strength. He got up, poured himself a stiff Scotch from the decanter on the side table, then went back and sat down facing the Bishop across his desk again. He felt a little more confident as he sat down: you were never banished to outer darkness with a glass of the Bishop's Scotch in your hand. He had heard evening confessions in the cathedral, sitting there in the darkness of the confessional listening to the whispers on the other side of the grille and wondering, as he always did, at the ordinary penitent's inability to distinguish sin from short-coming: they confessed everything, as if human nature itself were a sin. The last penitent had been a woman, a real sinner yet one whom he could not condemn: a middle-aged woman, judging by her voice, out of love with her husband, sleeping with another man but never able to love him openly because divorce was out of the question. If only I could help you, he had thought; but the only help he could give her was absolution, a palliative that would only carry her through till she saw the other man again. He had come out of the confessional, depressed by his impotence to help the real sinners. The Bishop's secretary, bustling down the aisle like a fussy department store supervisor, told him that His Grace wanted to see him. Still absent-mindedly wearing his confessional stole, he had come straight to the Bishop's study, wondering if His Grace had had some word from McKenna's Superior up in La Paz. He had been totally unprepared for the subject the Bishop had in mind.

"Take the stole off," said the Bishop, sipping his drink. "I'm not seeking absolution."

McKenna removed the stole; then, imbued with Scotch daring, said, "Should I be seeking it, your grace? Absolution, I mean."

"I don't know. What have you done?"

"If we are still referring to Senorita Schiller – nothing." He looked down at his glass, uttered the cliché so usual with promiscuous film stars: "We are just good friends."

"Terence, I am not condemning friendship. I take your word for it that your relationship is entirely innocent. But – " He sipped his drink again, almost as if *he* needed courage. "Why did she visit you alone at your mission yesterday? Also, I saw you myself at the reception at my brother's house the other night – you were hand-in-hand. Is that the right sort of behaviour between a priest and a young attractive woman?"

McKenna shook his head, still staring down at his glass. "No. But it was all innocent – " But he could feel the flush of the lie in his face and was afraid to look up. "Senorita Schiller and I just happen to feel strongly about the same thing. Social reform."

"Was that why you were with her at the prison this afternoon?"

He has his sources of information *everywhere*. "Yes."

"My secretary tells me you have asked permission to go out to dinner to-night. Where are you going?"

McKenna had looked up. Through the study window behind the Bishop, beyond the palace garden, he could see the blue-green lamps, like ghostly skulls, in the plaza. People were strolling arm-in-arm in the pale aqueous glow of the lamps, seeming to float in slow motion as if they were walking under water. He guessed there was not one person out there who did not have a problem, some of them killing ones, but he envied them. At least they had a freedom to love, or anyway most of them did.

"To Senorita Schiller's. She is giving a small dinner party for my sister."

It was the Bishop's turn to look down at his glass. "I got a letter from your Superior this evening. He said he had written you."

"It was waiting for me when I came back."

"What did he say to you?"

"That he was leaving me to your discretion. He is not well enough to come down to San Sebastian immediately."

"How do you feel about being left to my discretion?"

McKenna felt hopeless, but you did not answer a bishop with a shrug. "I hope you will be understanding, your grace."

"I shall try to be, Terence." The Bishop sighed, took another sip of his drink. "I am conservative, but I like to think I am not reactionary. I am well aware that we have tremendous problems in the Church – the Church as a whole and ourselves as individuals. But I can't bring myself to believe that personal conscience will provide the answer to those problems. One could go out there," he waved a hand behind him towards the submarine strollers in the plaza: even a boy running through the garden square seemed to be running against an invisible tide, "and one would find as many different consciences as one would find different faces. What sort of answers would that give us?"

McKenna was not sure whether the question was rhetorical or wanted an answer. He said neutrally, "It might depend on the particular problem."

"The Church can't lay down a personal law for every individual."

"If we are talking about birth control, your grace – "

"We are. For the time being," the Bishop added ominously.

"I can't help thinking that God meant sex to be a personal thing. It is the most personal act there is between two human beings – even murder is not as personal. Murder can happen without any feeling at all on the part of the victim. The mayor, when he was killed the other night, was probably dead before he could even have had a thought towards the men who fired the shots. But even the woman who is raped is capable of deeper emotion than any other act against her could bring on." Then he added, "Except perhaps a mother losing her child. I understand that it is a traumatic experience for a mother to lose her child even before it is born, by miscarriage or abortion."

"One can never fully understand a woman's emotions – "

"That's just it, your grace!" McKenna leapt at the Bishop's slip. "But it is celibate men, Popes, who lay down the law for women. Ever since Gregory the Great in – when was it?"

"I have no head for dates. History, measured in dates, is one long blur to me." Even the history of the Ruiz, let alone the history of Popes, had never meant much to the Bishop. Mellowed by whisky, he sat back in his chair, content to listen for a while to this young rebel. "Go on."

"I think it was the end of the sixth century. Anyhow – " The whisky had loosened McKenna's tongue. "Anyhow, Pope Gregory laid down the law that sex even for the purpose of having children was a venial sin, because the man and the woman got excited in the act. Have you ever heard of anything so ridiculous?"

The Bishop did not appear to think the question was impertinent. He said nothing, and McKenna, half-way now between the tower and the water, plunged on in his high dive: "The Church since then has become a bit saner in its outlook, but it still treats sex as if it were sinful in itself. Have you ever asked a woman, your grace, what she thinks about the Holy Father's statement in his encylical when he condemns contraception as degrading the dignity of women?"

"Some women have put their opinions to me," said the Bishop, remembering the scathing comments of his sister-in-law. "But they don't alter the authority of the Holy Father."

"With all respect, your grace, I think their opinions should. Why should women be second-class citizens in the Church? What does a celibate old man – " I'm up for banishment here, McKenna thought, looking at the older man; but he plunged on " – know about the tensions and desires of a husband and wife who have to sleep together every night? Did God give man – and woman – the sex urge just to make life difficult for them?"

The Bishop, shrewdly seeing a target in the welter of the younger man's argument, fired a shot: "Does the celibacy law worry you, Terence?"

McKenna hesitated; but he had almost reached the end of his dive and there was no turning back. He said quietly, "Yes, it does, your grace."

"In regard to Senorita Schiller?"

"Believe me, your grace, nothing like that has ever risen between us." Then he blushed at his unfortunate choice of words; the Bishop raised his glass to his mouth, but it was impossible to tell whether he was hiding a smile or just playing for time. But McKenna, recovering, went on, "It is not the sex part that is my major worry. I am lonely," he confessed.

"You are warned of that before you take your final vows. We are supposed to find our comfort in God."

"I do find comfort in God. But, to be honest, He is not enough. Not in the vocation I have chosen."

"You mean as a missionary? Do you think marriage would be

the solution? A priest is supposed to belong to everyone, not just to one person."

The old platitudes, McKenna thought: he had begun to expect better of the Bishop. "Does that mean the father of a large family can't love his children as much as he loves his wife?"

"They are his flesh and blood – it is natural for him to respond to their demands. But the situation could arise where a married priest would have to choose between the demands oj his wife and family and those of his congregation. What happens then?"

"The same as happens now – it would depend on the priest's sense of duty. The Church in all its arguments talks as if all its priests were saints. We're not – you must know that better than I do, your grace. Priests neglect their duty, are capable of being uncharitable" – uncharitably he thought of Padre Luis, a priest who seemed to make a vocation of neglecting his duty – "just like ordinary men. If celibacy bred perfection in priests, I'd have no argument. Unfortunately it doesn't."

The Bishop reluctantly nodded. "True, true. Have you thought of leaving the Church?"

"No." There was no hesitation about McKenna's reply. "I want to go on serving God – I *need* to do that. But I think I can serve Him best by serving my fellow-men – particularly the Indians up on the altiplano. And I think I'd serve *them* best if I had someone to help me, who had the same aims as myself. That would be essential – I wouldn't want to marry just for the companionship alone."

"Does Senorita Schiller have those aims?"

"Yes."

"Have you spoken of marriage to her?"

"Not directly," McKenna replied honestly. "But I think she knows now what is in my mind." He put down his empty glass, but shook his head when the Bishop motioned towards the decanter. Suddenly in deep anguish he said, "Can't you help me?"

"How?" The Bishop put down his own glass and spread his hands. "For ten years now I've been watching the Church lose its priests – the exodus rate has been growing larger every year. But we – the bishops – have been able to do nothing to stop it.

We have sought guidance from Rome, but have never received any. I have a confession to make." He nodded at the confessional stole that hung on the arm of McKenna's chair; the young priest made a move to pick it up, then realised the older man was being satirical. "Sometimes I think Rome is not of this world. It still bases its authority on the *Lex Romana*, laws that often have no relation to conditions in the rest of the world. Pope John tried to open some windows, but he died too soon. I wonder at God's wisdom in taking him just when he was about to accomplish something."

"I have my own confession, your grace. I no longer have any respect for Rome and the old men who rule there. I saw some figures recently. In Holland, which Rome almost condemns as a heretical country because the hierarchy there is progressive, over sixty per cent of Catholics still practise their faith. In Italy, Rome's own parish, the figure is three per cent. It doesn't encourage you to have much faith in the old men of Rome, does it?"

The Bishop was not prepared for total agreement with this young rebel. He said cautiously, "We have no alternative at present."

"We could have if the bishops insisted on collegiality. The Vatican couldn't beat the combined strength of all the bishops."

"Ah, but that is the trouble – the bishops are not combined. There are still more conservatives than there are progressives – the Church has always tended to choose conservatives. It is just that the progressives make more noise – they always do in any field. We might do better if we had a non-Italian Pope." The Bishop sighed. "But the celibacy problem won't be solved overnight, even if we had a new Pope to-morrow."

We're back to it, McKenna thought; and felt the depression come down on him again. "I don't think any of us, in his heart, expects it to be solved overnight. You don't throw away a thousand years of law – or more than that, tradition – as if it's an old pair of pants. St Augustine still has too much influence on the conservatives. Since I've been faced with this problem I looked up what Augustine once said – 'I feel that nothing more turns the masculine mind from the heights than female blandishment and that contact of bodies without which a wife may not be had.' That put woman in her place forever as far as the Church was concerned. But I just can't believe that God created woman for the sole purpose of being a child-bearing machine. A lot of the Popes didn't think so – and I don't mean just the libertine ones. Adrian the Second was devoted to his wife – and there probably hasn't been a kinder or more charitable Pope than him." He looked up at the Bishop. "I don't know if a wife would make me a kinder and more charitable man, but I know there is going to be no improvement in me while I remain single. I need help and love, your grace – without it I don't think I can go on giving help and love to others. I'm shrivelling up with loneliness up there on the altiplano."

"Perhaps you should go back to the mother house in La Paz."

McKenna shook his head. "I don't want to work in the city – you're not much more than an ordinary parish priest up there. I could go down to Lima – we have a mission working in the slums down there, three or four priests together. But the Indians up on the altiplano are my real flock – "

"You want to pick and choose. How many of us can afford that?" The Bishop saw the look on McKenna's face and abruptly made the admission: "All right, I was able to choose. And influence can count in the Church just as in any other organisation. But in theory we are supposed to be humble, go wherever God's work calls us."

"It called me to Altea. You may not believe it, your grace, but I firmly believe I got a call to come back to this part of Bolivia and work among the altiplano Indians. I don't claim I had a vision on the road to Damascus, or even on the freeway to Pasadena, but I felt a *call*. I still feel it. But I just don't have enough strength to go on answering it. I need help."

"And you think Senorita Schiller would give you that help?"

"Yes."

"It is impossible, you realise that. The Holy Father has reiterated his stand on celibacy and unless he changes his mind – and I don't expect him to, he can be very stubborn on his decisions – I think the ruling will stand, at least till we have a new Pope. So your situation with Senorita Schiller is impossible and highly undesirable." The Bishop put down his glass, made his own decision. "I am sorry, Terence. But if you want to continue your work here, you will have to give up seeing Senorita Schiller. It is doing no good for you, for her or for the image of the Church."

"And if I refuse, your grace?"

The Bishop sighed. "Terence, don't you realise you can't win? A bishop's authority is too powerful. Priests all over the world are rebelling against the autocratic, feudal if you like, powers that we have. But so far they haven't got very far."

McKenna said with the daring of the hopeless, "Why don't you offer to give up some of your power, give the priests more say?"

"Do you think the Vatican would be influenced by some bishop from an obscure South American diocese?" The Bishop made a convincing show of humility, but he knew in his heart that laziness, satisfaction with the status quo, was the real reason he would never lead any reform campaign. He sympathised with the plight of this young priest, but he knew that any fight for reduction of the bishops' powers would be a long and frustrating one. The Ruiz had never had a tradition of being revolutionary, even that generation that had supported Bolivar had never been in the vanguard of the fight for independence, and he had inherited the family tendency to accept the order of things as they were. Just so long as the Ruiz were at the top. "I could relax certain rules, but on a major issue like celibacy I could not act on my own."

McKenna stood up. He had the feeling that his whole life had come to a full stop: a bleak altiplano stretched before him with no horizon but death. "You are condemning me, your grace," he said, with no wish to sound theatrical, but ashamed of the words as soon as he uttered them. So he said banally, "It's a big disappointment."

"We all have our disappointments," said the Bishop, equally banally. "But God will give you the grace and strength to overcome it."

"He hasn't so far."

"You must just keep praying," said the Bishop, who had never really believed in the efficacy of prayer; he prayed regularly, but it was more a conversation with God than a pleading. "God will not want to lose your services, Terence."

McKenna felt a sudden spasm of disgust at the platitude, as if God was on hand, an Instant Plumber, to repair any leak in the Church's efficiency. But all he said was, "May I go see Senorita Schiller this evening? I should like to explain why I shall be avoiding her in the future."

"You have my permission. It will not be easy, Terence, but I am sure that in time you will see it is for the best. You have a true vocation for the priesthood, haven't you?"

"For the priesthood – I don't know. For missionary work, yes. Or at least I like to think so."

"Well, then – " The Bishop spread his hands, as if a miracle were already under way: a little time, a little patience, and McKenna would soon have no worries at all. But the human man beneath the bishop's soutane knew it was not going to be as easy as all that for the other man in the priest's black cassock. He said, trying to sound convincing, "I'll pray for you, Terence."

"Thank you, your grace." McKenna went to the door, opened it, then looked back. "I'll have to come back to you, you know that."

"The door will always be open. And – " He spoke sincerely, man to man, not bishop to priest: "I am sorry, Terence. I wish there were some other answer."

McKenna nodded his thanks, closed the door behind him.

The Bishop looked up at the portrait of the Pope above the fireplace. "We are going to lose him, Father. And we can't afford to – not him nor the hundreds of others who are leaving us. For the sake of Christ, do something, Father!"

2

"What's the matter?" Taber asked. "You've been acting as if you've just been excommunicated."

"Almost as bad," said McKenna.

The two men sat in the living-room of Dolores's house. Dolores and Carmel had gone upstairs to do whatever it is that women do in the middle of an evening – visit the bathroom, repair their make-up, check their moral ammunition for the rest of the night: Taber had never bothered to inquire what made women disappear from the scene after a dinner like football players at half-time. The two men had been left with their coffee and brandy and McKenna's quiet mood that Taber had at last commented upon. Each of the women had remarked mildly on it during dinner, but McKenna had managed to put them off with a joking reply that had seemed to satisfy them. Taber, who had waited patiently to make his own comment, was not so easily put off.

"Trouble with the Bishop?" McKenna nodded, staring moodily into his brandy goblet, and Taber went on, "He could be a bastard, I think. He's not as bad as his brother, but he's tarred with the same brush. He'd enjoy his authority."

"I don't think he did this evening," said McKenna charitably. "Maybe he could do something more constructive to help me – I don't know what, but *something*. But at least he tried to understand."

"You want to talk about it?" Taber had got over the anger and disappointment of his meeting with Alejandro Ruiz this afternoon. He was genial from the good dinner and the last two hours of Carmel's company and he was in a sympathetic mood if McKenna cared to confide in him.

McKenna hesitated, not wanting to burden the other man with his troubles. But he did not know how he was going to broach the subject to Dolores, and perhaps while talking to Taber he might stumble on the right words to use later. So, like a man who practises how to fall before he attempts his first parachute jump, he began to tell Taber what the Bishop had forbidden him.

". . . I suppose you can't understand a man, in the first place, ever wanting to take a vow of chastity?"

"If you want me to put myself in your place, no, I just can't understand this doctrine of the Immaculate Erection. I'd finish up crazy and with a double hernia in a month. But when I take my own feelings out of it – well, yes, I can understand it, though it's bloody difficult. But I guess it's like the alcoholic – if he can stay out of sight of the grog, he can sometimes lick the problem. But once he gets a whiff of it, he's gone." Then he looked down at his brandy and said, "Sorry. That's not very complimentary to Dolores."

"The sex bit is only part of the problem. There's never even been a hint of that between her and me." He avoided his unfortunate choice of words with the Bishop; he was still treading carefully with Taber and he did not want the feeling between them spoiled by a vulgar joke. As Taber had said, it would not be very complimentary to Dolores. "What I want is the *companionship* of marriage."

"Christ, it's only an idiot who doesn't." The bitterness slipped out of Taber; he had not yet completely exorcised the spirits of his two wives. "I wouldn't want to marry without sex, but you can't spend all bloody day in bed. Look, mate – " The wine at dinner and now the brandy had had their effect on him; it was his turn to confide: "I don't know how your sister feels about me, but I'm keen on her. If I asked her to marry me, it wouldn't be only because she is one of the best-looking girls I've seen. It would be because I'd hope that on those days when I was feeling low and everyone else in the world was a bastard, she'd be able to convince me that I shouldn't cut my throat, that it would be worth while waiting till to-morrow when the bastards of the world might have improved. Like this evening. I met an arch-bastard this afternoon, that bugger Ruiz, and when I went to pick up Carmel I was all ready to write Rome and tell F A O to shove their job, sideways. But the last couple of hours with her – " He drank his brandy, half an embarrassed gesture, half a toast to Carmel. "I'm prepared to give to-morrow another go. And it's all due to her."

McKenna was surprised at what Taber had told him. He had been so preoccupied with his own relationship with Dolores that he had been heedless of what had been developing between his sister and Taber. I don't even make a good brother, let alone a priest, he thought. He looked at Taber with new interest, wondering if this was the sort of man Carmel could fall in love with. And realised he did not know if Carmel could fall in love with any man.

"Have you said anything to her?"

"I want to be sure this time. Both my other marriages were a

proper balls-up. Twice bitten, you become more than shy –
you're soured and bloody scared. I shouldn't want to make a
mess of things with Carmel."

McKenna wondered how his mother, who had made a mess
of her own marriage, would react to the news that both her
children were involved in relationships that could be equally
disastrous. There had been a letter this afternoon from Nell
McKenna saying that she would dearly love to come down to
Bolivia and visit him and Carmel – "all three of us together
once again, what I've prayed for day after day" – but her
doctor, God bless him, did not think her heart would stand up
to the altitude. McKenna had also blessed the doctor. The last
thing he and Carmel wanted right now was a visit from their
mother.

Upstairs Carmel sat in front of Dolores's dressing-table
repairing her make-up. The women had reached their own
intimacy of confidence, though they were more reticent with
each other than the men downstairs were. "Was Terry upset by
something at the prison this afternoon? He's been awfully quiet
this evening."

Dolores sat on the bed looking at her hands. She had broken
a nail this afternoon while fossicking in the cart for bread to
give to a prisoner; she had filed it down, but the short nail looked
out of place among the longer ones on her other fingers. Her
hands, beautifully proportioned and expressive, were her one
vanity; but a social worker with vanity, she told herself now,
was a contradiction in terms. She would file all her nails down
in the morning, file down her vanity too.

"He is worried about a man named Jesu Mamani, one of the
villagers from up at Altea. He loads himself with responsibility
too heavily, I'm afraid."

"Isn't that what a priest is supposed to do?" But Carmel did
not sound critical; even now she did not fully understand what
made a priest tick. She was only just coming to understand
Terry as a brother; it would take her much longer to comprehend
him as a priest. She had been given an overdose of religious
propaganda by the nuns and her mother, and the result had
been confusion and then, finally, a refusal to understand.

"I suppose so," said Dolores, who had seen too many failures among the local priests to have any illusions. "But he has more than the usual handicaps. He is a foreigner."

"Could you help him?" Carmel did not turn round but looked at Dolores in the mirror: the question itself was indirect, having another angle to it. She wanted to ask: Do you *want* to help him? Are you in love with him? But they were still strangers to each other when it came to questions like that.

Dolores remembered what McKenna had said to her this afternoon: *You and I together could really have helped these people*; and she remembered what had been in his face, the look behind the words as he had said them. She had come home and sat for two hours in this room, struggling with the ferment within her, the squalls of passion that she had so long held in check. She was not a virgin, there had been two men whom she had allowed to make love to her, one whom she had met when she was ski-ing at Portillo in Chile, the other in Rome; both affairs had occurred within a year of each other and she had thought she was in love with both men. But both lovers had had the same fault: ready to make love but not to fall in love. Since then there had been other men who had attracted her, but she had grown wary and none of the attractions had gone beyond a mild flirtation. She had known Terence McKenna for three months before she had admitted to herself that she was in love with him, truly and deeply in love. And had at once closed the door on the admission, knowing there was no more future for her in that direction than there had been with the two men she had loved in those other years.

"I don't think so. Perhaps in another country – " But she meant in other circumstances, if Terence were not a priest. She suddenly envied Carmel her freedom, all at once rebelling against her religion, her code of ethics, the pattern of the society in which she lived. Perhaps that was the only answer to real happiness: selfishness, irresponsibility, non-involvement with anyone but the man you loved.

Then Carmel said, "I envy you. You have permanence here, *roots* – " She looked about the big bedroom, at the huge four-poster bed, the chests and chairs dark with age and glistening with years of polishing, the portraits of the two beautiful women, Dolores's mother and grandmother, that faced each other across the room where the last of the Schiller women slept. "All right, I know you are afraid of an Indian revolution, but until then – and maybe even afterwards – you still have *this*. You have always had it."

"Roots are not enough. They are only the past." Dolores had recovered from her aberration of a moment ago; selfishness, everything for love, was not the answer and she knew it. She saw now that Carmel's way of life could be empty and un-rewarding. There was still hope for Carmel, but Dolores had met the addicts of that life in Portillo, in New York, in Europe: the so-called Jet Set, the only occasionally Beautiful People, social cannibals who lived off each other because they had closed their gem-encrusted, gold-hinged doors on the rest of the world. She herself could never go to that extreme, but there was more to life than even Utopian self-indulgence: even the hippies retreating to their isolated communes were guilty of a selfishness of which she would not be capable. The blood of her grandfather, the socialist from Hildesheim, was thick in her veins; the political blood of the San Juans, made sluggish by years of inaction, had been conquered. The ghost of the man who all his life had carried a boyhood memory of the funeral of Liebknecht, when a hundred thousand people had lined the streets to honour the Messiah of German socialism, would never allow her to turn her back on those worse off than herself. Charity, he had told her when she was young, was a pleasure for the rich; sacrifice was what guaranteed them their place in heaven. So far she had been called upon for little sacrifice, but she knew now that the day of reckoning would be soon.

"At least they are *something*." Carmel had the feeling that very soon she would be called upon for a decision of some sort: in regard to Harry Taber, to her mother, to her whole life in general. And she had come to realise that one needed a back-ground against which to make a decision. Yes or no meant nothing when one remained in limbo.

"Does Harry have roots?"

Carmel shook her head. "Even less than I have, I think. But maybe he doesn't need them. He has his work – that's enough for some men."

"Terence has his." Dolores took a tentative step out on to

thin ice; perhaps he has told his sister more than he had told her: "But sometimes I wonder if that is enough for him."

But Carmel couldn't help her: "I wouldn't know. Terry and I have never discussed vocations – ours couldn't have been more different. If hedonism *is* a vocation," she added apologetically. She looked ruefully at Dolores, suddenly candid. "I sometimes wonder what you think of me."

Dolores smiled, not to be trapped. "Perhaps I shall tell you when I know you better. But you have nothing to fear."

They had told each other nothing in words, but like women groping through a mist towards a light held by each other, they had grown a little closer. In the circumstance of her loneliness, each felt better for it. It was as if they had discovered in each other a new season of hope, though neither of them knew for what reason.

They went downstairs, faces and morale repaired, and found the two men, a drink or two away from being slightly drunk, laughing at a joke that both of them had forgotten as soon as it was told. Carmel, coming into the room, still not entirely at home either in Dolores's house or San Sabastian, and therefore still susceptible to atmosphere, was at once aware of a feeling of – despair? She was not sure what it was that possessed the two men, but she knew they had reached a frame of mind that bordered on the desperate. They looked like two men who expected the worst and were resigned to resorting to any methods to combat it. This, she guessed, was how men at war reacted.

Taber and McKenna stood up. Neither of them had had enough to drink to make them unsteady on their legs; they were only close to drunkenness in terms of all at once being careless of consequences. If it had been the Ruiz men who had walked into the room instead of Carmel and Dolores, Taber and McKenna would quite likely have invited them to put up their fists. They were only saved from belligerence by the fact that no enemies were present, only the women they loved.

Dolores offered them more brandy, but Taber shook his head. "No, I'm saving up for a real bender. I have the feeling that in a week or two I'll have to get drunk or shoot someone." He told the two women what had happened to himself and

McKenna this afternoon at their interview with Alejandro Ruiz. "Just before I came out this evening I got a phone call from my boss in Santiago – Senor Bloody Ruiz had already been on to him."

"You didn't tell me this." McKenna, who had flopped back in his chair now the women were seated, sat up in surprise.

"You have your own troubles, mate." Taber began to prowl about the room with that giraffe-like gait of his; Carmel marvelled that a man could look so ungainly and graceful at the same time. He paused for a moment in front of the blue-tongued fire in the big fireplace, then moved on, finding no images in the flames to comfort him. He was too restless and angry for contemplation. "The line was bad, but maybe that was all to the good – the boss probably thought my swearing was interference on the line. But I got his message all right, bad connection and all. I am to do nothing to upset the natives – particularly natives like Senor Ruiz and his Agriculture Reform Council." He came back from his patrol of the room, stood in front of them but addressed himself to Carmel: "I can be a terrible drunk if I have sufficient excuse."

Carmel made no answer because she felt that anything she said would be fatuous. She did not yet really understand Taber's problem nor his attitude of mind.

Dolores said, "We all need an escape valve of some sort."

A white coat appeared at the door, a butler ghost: his black trousers and brown face were lost in the shadows beyond the glow of the lamps. "Senorita, the padre is wanted on the telephone."

McKenna sat up, instantly cold sober. He looked at Taber: had something happened to Jesu Mamani? He stood up, surprised at how steady his legs felt, and followed the butler out into the hall and down to a small study. The voice on the phone, speaking in Spanish, was muffled and faint: "Is that Padre McKenna?"

"Yes? Where are you speaking from?" It could be a long-distance call; or the man could be speaking through a hand cupped over the mouthpiece. "Who is this?"

"I am in San Sebastian and it doesn't matter who I am. Or does having a name make a difference in the confessional?"

"We aren't in the confessional." Irritated, McKenna wanted to slam down the phone; but curiosity kept it glued to his ear. "What do you want?"

"I want you to hear my confession, padre."

"Now? Over the phone?"

"Can you do that?"

"If it is necessary – "

"No, padre, I prefer you to hear it in a confessional. What if this line should be tapped?"

"Don't be ridiculous – "

"Nothing is ridiculous in our country. You should know that. I shall be waiting for you in the confessional in the north-east corner of the cathedral, next to the statue of Saint Teresa."

"The cathedral is closed."

There was a muffled chuckle. "Any intelligent sinner can find his way into the church, padre." Or should that have been Church with a capital C? Intrigued, McKenna waited for more. "Fifteen minutes, padre. And come alone. Remember, I'm asking for the secrecy of the confessional."

There was a click: the caller had hung up. McKenna, alert and curious now, went back into the living-room. "I have to go to the cathedral. Someone wants me to hear his confession."

"Someone is dying?" Dolores asked.

"I don't think so. Unless – " McKenna shook his head.

"Unless what?" said Taber.

"I was going to say, unless he is expecting to be killed. But why would I think that? I've got violence on the mind."

"I don't think you should go," said Taber. "There's plenty of violence around. Someone could be laying for you."

"Why?" McKenna hadn't thought of any violence towards himself. "The people I've run up against aren't going to get rough to get rid of me. They don't need to – troublesome priests can always be shunted off somewhere."

"I think Harry is right," said Carmel; and Dolores nodded. "If someone was calling from their home at this time of night it would be different. But this seems too suspicious – "

"I *have* to go." McKenna tried not to sound stubborn. "I'm

a priest – I'm supposed to *trust* people, not question them – "

Taber, the drink still talking, said, "You're going against the grain, mate. I thought the Church never trusted anyone."

Put on edge by the others' concern for him, stung by Taber's cheap cynicism, McKenna snapped, "The day you humanists become an organisation you'll find you don't have a monopoly on the virtues. You said it yourself – get three people together and there'll always be politics. In the meantime some of us in the Church *do* trust people. If we didn't we wouldn't think it was our vocation!"

He went out of the room, forgetting to thank Dolores for having him as her guest. But she followed him, stood in the darkened hall just inside the front door. She opened the door for him, put her hand on his arm.

"I don't think Harry really meant what he said. He's worried for you – we all are. Be careful, Terence."

I'm supposed to be here to-night to say good-bye to you. But I can't; not now. "I'll be okay." He could feel her hand still on his arm; he moved his arm, took hold of her hand, felt the pressure of her fingers on his. He leaned forward and kissed her softly on the lips, the first time he had touched a woman's mouth with his own in ten years. He felt her fingers stiffen in his and at once he said, "I'm sorry. I thought – "

"Only be sorry that we can do no more," she said, and in the moonlight coming through the open door he saw the tears in her eyes.

3

When he got outside into the bright rain of moonlight he was shivering, not from the cold but from emotion. He turned up the collar of his overcoat against the wind that fell down from the altiplano; like a cold and invisible flood it swirled and eddied in the bowl of the city. Grit bit at his cheeks and once a sheet of paper, like the severed wing of a bird, wrapped itself round his head as he turned a corner. He pulled up sharply, tearing the paper from his face; when he had thrown it away he found himself trembling, sweat breaking in his palms. He hurried on towards the cathedral, praying now for control. He was going to be no fit person to hear another man's confession when his own emotions were in such turmoil.

The main plaza was deserted; the wind had driven everyone into the bars or their homes. Dust blew up around the golden condor, creating a curious effect: the giant bird looked poised to take off and McKenna would not have been surprised if it had come plummeting down to grab at him with its great talons. The usually greenish-blue lamps in the square had turned yellow in the dust; McKenna felt strange, as if he were in another, unfamiliar city. He looked around for someone he might recognise, but there was no one; even the bootblacks, the permanents of the square, had gone home to whatever homes they had. He went up the black alley beside the cathedral, pausing only a moment before he committed himself to its darkness. He had suddenly become afraid, as hopeless men do when they suddenly find they are possessed of something: Dolores with her expression of love, though it in itself might be hopeless, had all at once made him afraid for the man, not the priest, that was himself.

He went in through the back door of the cathedral from the priests' house: the tradesmen's entrance, he had heard it called in Rome among the iconoclasts at the Gregorian. The cathedral was lit only by the altar lamp; it hung in the blackness like a huge ruby. He did a quick genuflection in front of the tabernacle, then felt his way across the steps of the sanctuary to where he knew there was a box of candles beneath a statue of the Madonna. He fumbled for a candle, lit it and made his way down the long side aisle to the far confessional booth. His footsteps clacked hollowly on the stone floor and he almost dropped the candle when high in the roof an owl hooted. Get hold of yourself, McKenna: the house of God should not be haunted.

He came to the confessional. By the light of the candle he could see the man's legs sticking out from where he knelt on the penitent's stool. He had time to notice that the man's shoes were black and could be expensive; they were certainly not the sandals made from an old tyre that an Indian would wear; the man was not Jesu Mamani. McKenna did not know why he had suddenly thought the man might be Mamani; perhaps it had just been the hope that the fact of Mamani's being here meant he was safe, at least for the time being. But then the man's voice, if this was the same man, had been educated; even the muffling had not hidden the fact that Spanish was his mother tongue. Something told McKenna that he was going to hear more than the confession of another man's sins.

He blew out the candle and stepped into the confessional. He sat down, then discovered he had forgotten his stole. He felt around in the blackness: sometimes a priest left his stole hanging in the booth: but there was none. I'm still infected by conservatism, he thought: why are the trappings so necessary? He slid back the panel, heard the man's steady breathing on the other side of the grille. Whoever he is, McKenna thought, he is less nervous than I am.

"Padre, forgive me for I have sinned."

"How long is it since your last confession?"

"Six months, padre." In the absolute blackness of the booth McKenna could see absolutely nothing: he might have been blind. Yet he knew, as surely as if he were spotlighted, that the man was holding his hand or a handkerchief over his mouth. The voice was not recognisable as that of anyone he knew.

There was silence for almost a minute and at last McKenna, still nervous, said impatiently, "Confess your sins."

He could *feel* the man looking at him through the darkness. Then: "There are several minor sins, padre, venial ones. I have told lies, used the Lord's name in vain, slept with a woman – "

"A woman not your wife?"

"No, not my wife."

"You call fornication a venial sin?" But I could be guilty of it myself in other circumstances: he had already slept with Dolores in his mind. He felt the trembling again and tried to control it. He said, too sharply, "What are your standards?"

"Sins are comparative, padre."

"Leave me to judge that." Despite himself, McKenna could not keep the tartness out of his voice. I'm sounding just like an old Irish parish priest, he thought: Father knows best.

"As you wish, padre."

He sounds more patient and tolerant than I do, as if we should change places on either side of the grille. "Go on to the *major* sins."

247

"I have committed murder, padre." The hand must have come away from the mouth: the last words came out clear as a shout in the darkness. Then the voice was muffled again. "For political reasons."

"In the eyes of God murder is murder." McKenna felt no shock at what he had been told. No one had ever confessed murder to him before, yet now it had happened he accepted it, if not calmly, then at least without a feeling of horror. In the nine months he had been here in Bolivia he had learned how black the soul of man could be; he knew now that it had been only a matter of time before he heard a confession like this, that he had been subconsciously waiting for it. "God doesn't recognise politics."

"He should, padre. He burdened men with them."

"Politics are part of men's free will. Are you truly sorry for this act against your fellow-man?"

"Sorry in so far as a man lost his life. I should like to see a world in which no man's life was ever taken, either by another man or by the State. But this was necessary, padre."

"Are you one of the terrorists?"

The hand came away from the mouth again: the voice was sharp, proud. "I am one of the revolutionaries."

McKenna had cocked an ear, but the man had spoken too quickly; a note in the voice had sounded vaguely familiar, but it was not enough to identify its owner. It could have been a voice heard in a crowd, heard even here in the confessional: the man had said he had not been to confession for six months, but when McKenna had first arrived in San Sebastian he had heard confession three or four times in the cathedral before moving up to Altea. Science lately had proved that voices had their own distinguishing marks, like fingerprints, but McKenna's ear, still foreign to the Spanish tongue, was a long way from a scientific instrument. The man on the other side of the grille could be a complete stranger or someone he knew well.

"My apologies," said McKenna. "I guess it's which end of the gun you're at that determines what you're called."

"We have never threatened you, padre."

"No. But why should you?" There was no answer and McKenna went on, "I can't give you absolution unless you are truly sorry for what you have done. And you keep qualifying your repentance."

"I wish it were all clear-cut, padre. But it isn't. Does not injustice justify killing a man?"

McKenna leaned back, resting his head against the back of the booth. He closed his eyes, feeling suddenly exhausted. The owl hooted in the roof again, the sound of a lost soul. "How can you expect me to answer that when I don't know the circumstances? Who is to judge what is injustice? I presume you mean social injustice, not legal injustice?"

"I mean both. One dovetails into the other in this country."

"The confessional is not supposed to be a place for polemics." McKenna knew he was hedging; this was the old Roman trick. "All the argument is supposed to have gone on inside yourself before you came here."

"Why are you here then?"

"To give you absolution if I judge you truly sorry."

"You make it easy for yourself, don't you?"

Easy: the anguish of wanting to give absolution to people who are not truly contrite but whose sins are understandable, the difficulty of trying to separate hypocrisy from sincerity, the trying to find a simple word of sympathy that didn't sound like a platitude and yet knowing that the sinner on the other side of the grille would impatiently settle for anything that sounded like forgiveness. *Say for your penance three Hail Marys and three platitudes . . .*

"We are getting nowhere. Why did you send for me at this time of night if you only want to half-confess?"

"If I came to you in the middle of the day, confessed to murder, could you resist the temptation to look out of the confessional when I left, see who I am?"

It was McKenna's turn to be sharp and proud: "I honour the secrets of the confessional."

"I apologise, padre." The man sounded sincere. There was a sigh behind the hand or the handkerchief. "I suppose I really came to warn you."

"To warn me?" The owl hooted again.

"Padre, I fear there will be more killings before we are through. I may not pull another trigger, but I can't escape the responsibility. The death of some men is going to be necessary – " There seemed a genuine note of regret in the muffled voice. "It is the only way to justice."

"I can't condone it."

"The Church condones war, sometimes even wars of aggression. This is just war on a small scale." But as if sensing McKenna's agony of doubt, he went on, "I shan't press the point, padre. I think you are sympathetic to our cause – at least you are not against it."

"But why warn me? What against?"

"Padre, leave Jesu Mamani to us. We can do more for him than you can. Do not concern yourself with him."

"How do you know I intended doing anything for him?"

"We have our sources at the prison." Who are you? McKenna wondered. Could this be Condoris, the captain of police, on the other side of the grille? Could he have turned revolutionary because his powers had been usurped by the security police? "We can do more for him than you can, much more. You can do nothing for him, padre – you are an outsider, you always will be. But we can help him. Leave him to us."

You are an outsider, you always will be: the words hung in McKenna's ears like a death sentence. But he was not going to see another man doomed: "Is Jesu one of the men whose death is going to be necessary?"

There was a sharp intake of breath on the other side of the grille. Angrily the man said, "What makes you say that?"

"Wouldn't a martyr help your cause?"

"You're as cynical as all the rest!"

"You are wrong. I would be cynical if I didn't care what happened to Jesu Mamani so long as the larger cause was successful. I just happen to think one man's life is sufficient cause."

The man said nothing. The timber of the confessional creaked as he shifted on his knees; up in the roof the owl hooted again, a little doubtfully this time. In the silent darkness McKenna was now aware of the wind softly moaning under the big front doors of the cathedral, like sinners trying to get in. The booth creaked as the man shifted again. McKenna waited patiently, sure now that he had a good argument. The revolutionary might not agree that one man's life equalled the cause of justice for all, but one who did hold to that principle could not be accused of cynicism.

At last the man said, "I cannot guarantee that Mamani will not be hurt. All I can say is that it is not our intention to make a martyr of him. I tell you that as the truth, padre, here in the confessional."

"I believe you," said McKenna; but was still troubled for Mamani. "But I can't promise to leave him to you if ever he comes to me for help."

"We don't want his soul, padre."

"What *do* you want?"

But the man did not answer that. Instead he said, "Will you give me absolution?"

God, give me guidance. Do I condemn this man for using extreme methods for a cause I myself believe in? McKenna remembered the stories he had heard of the Franciscan friars in the Troubles in Ireland in the twenties, of how the Franciscans were still venerated because they had given absolution to the men of Sinn Fein who had killed the hated Black and Tans. "Have you actually killed a man yourself?"

"No, not if you mean have I fired a gun or thrown a grenade. But I concurred in men's names being put on a list for assassination."

"Was the mayor's name on that list?"

"No, padre. That was a mistake."

"It was Herr Obermaier you meant to kill?"

There was a moment's hesitation, then the man said, "Yes."

"Why him?"

"He is part of the system. He will never be a leader, but he and his boss, Senor Ruiz, are working for the return of a Fascist régime."

McKenna was still holding the candle in his hands; suddenly it snapped apart. "Is Senor Ruiz on your list? His son and his nephew too?"

"Padre, what sort of confession is this?" The mocking tone, that had been missing from the man's voice, came back. "I have already told you more than you could normally expect. I am here to confess my sins, not to betray my comrades."

McKenna leaned forward. "Say an Act of Contrition."

"You are going to give me absolution?"

"Yes," said McKenna, and asked for absolution for himself if what he was doing was wrong.

When McKenna had finished the man said, "You gave me no penance, padre?"

"I can't think of any," McKenna said simply. "Not to fit the sin of killing a man. Choose your own."

There was a shuffling of feet as the man got off his knees. "Thank you. And do not worry about Jesu Mamani. Leave him to us. Adios, padre."

McKenna heard the man's footsteps going down the aisle, then crossing the nave to go out of the side door of the cathedral into the alley. McKenna sat for a while, giving the man time to get away; his curiosity was suddenly dead, he no longer wanted to know who the man might be. It was better that he remained a stranger, no more than a muffled voice in the darkness.

Then he heard the footsteps returning. He tensed, feeling the blackness prickling at him as if it were tangible. He stood up, his legs weak and brittle; he flung open the gate of the confessional and almost fell out into the aisle. The footsteps had stopped: the man stood somewhere in the middle of the nave. McKenna still held the two pieces of candle in one hand; he felt for his matches, then decided against lighting the candle. He did not want to make a target of himself. Why had the man come back?

Then an only too recognisable voice said, "Terry, where the hell are you?"

McKenna sighed with relief, lit a piece of the candle and saw Taber standing in the main aisle. He leaned against one of the pews as the Englishman crossed to him. He could feel himself trembling again, but this time as reaction to the fear he had felt. Once again he cursed his lack of courage. I'm a weak man, Lord. Why did You choose me for this vocation?

"Are you all right?" Taber's voice was gruff with stifled emotion; he had come in here expecting the worst to have happened.

McKenna nodded, grinning like a death's head above the yellow glow of the candle. He was doubly glad to see Taber:

he was sorry now for his outburst just before he had left Dolores's house: wasn't he himself sometimes cynical about the lack of trust the Church showed? "I'm okay. The guy only wanted to confess his sins."

"A hell of a time to choose. Why couldn't he choose an hour when this place is open? He seems to have more time to spare than you or me."

McKenna heard himself ask, "Who?"

"Hernando Ruiz. I saw him coming out of the cathedral."

Chapter 9

I

The girl sat at the typewriter tentatively picking at the keys with one finger as if she expected them to detonate an explosion that would blow her, Taber and Pereira right out of the house. She was a pretty mestizo in whom the criollo had dominance; occasionally she would look up from the typewriter and flash Taber a smile that no Indian girl would ever have given him. There was a coquetry about her that was as obvious as the film posters that would surround her in her natural habitat, the cinema foyer. Her smile had gone through a thousand films on the faces of Elizabeth Taylor, Natalie Wood, Julie Christie; Taber had even seen it on old films on television on the faces of Ginger Rogers, Joan Crawford and Jean Harlow. This office in Taber's house was no place for Isabella and she was embarrassed by being here; she wanted to get back to the real world of the cinema foyer. For the first time Taber wondered if Pereira, in his efforts to survive, had talked the girl into taking the job so that he could get a kickback from her.

"Isabella – " Pereira was in the kitchen-laboratory working on soil samples; he would not hear what was said out here in the living-room-office. "How much a week are we paying you?"

"Twenty American dollars, senor. You are very generous."

"Yes, aren't we. Do you like working as a typist?"

"Very much, senor." Isabella smacked a key with one finger just to show her speed; the carriage reached the end of its run, the bell rang and she jumped. "It is very interesting."

"It gets more interesting as you learn all the keys. You have the whole alphabet ahead of you, plus numbers, punctuation marks, money symbols, margin spacers and one or two other keys. There is nothing so satisfying as learning and being paid for it."

"You have nothing more to learn in your job, senor?" He got the Shirley Temple smile, cute and innocent.

She's not so bloody dumb, after all: she wouldn't give a kickback to her crippled grandmother. Silently he apologised to the unwitting Pereira: he was beginning to suspect *every* Bolivian now. And that was not good; if he was to succeed in his job he had to trust *someone*. Pereira, for all his compromising, had proved loyal.

He went back to his report while Isabella went back to discovering the typewriter. Usually he could write his reports quickly; he had always had a facility for ordering his thoughts and finding the words to express them and his pen would fly over the paper. But to-day he wrote laboriously, having as much trouble finding a word as Isabella had finding a letter. A couple of illiterates, he thought, drawing money under false pretences.

Pereira came in from the kitchen, wiping his hands on a small towel. He saw the scribbled sheets on the table that served as Taber's desk and he shook his head. "You are wasting your time, Harry."

"Perhaps." Taber sat back, glad of the interruption. "But you never know. There could be a change of government overnight up in La Paz and, who knows, the new Minister for Agriculture might think my report was just what he wanted."

"He would never see it, Harry."

"He might if I delivered it to him in person."

"You could deliver it to the present Minister in person."

"But then my regional director, our bloody-minded Mr Verdoux, would have kicked me out for by-passing the local Reform Council. But if there were another coup I could plead that the situation was so unsettled – how would we know if Senor Ruiz would be reappointed by a new government? – that I had to deliver the report personally to La Paz."

"You are asking for a miracle, Harry."

"Since independence in 1825 there have been – what, a hundred and eighty, eighty-five? – changes of government. That's roughly one every nine months. By the law of averages there should be another one coming up pretty soon."

"You should be careful, Harry." Pereira shot a warning glance in the direction of Isabella, who sat with both her ears more alert than her hands, which were now folded in her lap. "Such talk could be mistaken that you hope for a revolution."

Taber accepted the warning. This was worse than Rome, where gossip flowed swifter than the Tiber in flood. He'd pay Isabella the twenty dollars, get rid of her this evening and to hell with her survival. He wasn't going to be reported to the police by a non-typing typist. "Miguel, you know that I only want for Bolivia what Bolivians want. I have no politics. No politics at all," he repeated for Isabella's benefit.

He excused himself from Pereira and Isabella and went upstairs to his bedroom.

His empty suitcases stood in one corner like faithful hounds. Should he start packing them now and accept the inevitable? He kicked off his shoes and lay down on the bed. Where would Rome send him if Verdoux recommended his removal from this region? His contract still had two years to run; it was hardly likely FAO would buy him out. They might call him back to Rome; he doubted if he could stand two years of that. But it might be the best way of starting a marriage with Carmel.

He had thought about that last night. When he and McKenna had come out of the cathedral he had turned down the side alley towards the plaza, expecting the priest to follow him. But McKenna had held back. "I won't come back with you, Harry. I've already said good night to Dolores."

"What's the matter?" In the darkness of the alley all he could see of McKenna was his silhouette against the pale glow of a lighted window in the priests' house beyond him. "You sound as if you've been kicked in the bum or something. You're not still upset by what I said back there at Dolores's? It was bloody stupid of me."

"I've forgotten it. No, it's just that I'm – tired."

"You're more than tired, mate. Is it something to do with Hernando?"

"If it were I wouldn't tell you. He's just trusted me in confession. But it isn't – " But McKenna's voice seemed forced.

"I don't believe you. But please yourself – if you want to carry this thing on your own, go ahead. But don't try to kid me that Hernando chose eleven o'clock at night to confess to you that he missed Mass on Sunday or he's put some girl in the family way."

"He has his problems, but I can't discuss them with you."

"Well, I hope he's showing a streak of conscience for his uncle's attitude. Or was the bastard threatening you in there?"

"He was confessing his sins, that was all."

"And loading you with something that's worrying the Christ out of you. Forget him, Terry. Do you have to carry every sinner in the Church on your back?"

But McKenna had then abruptly said good night and gone up the alley towards the priests' house. Taber had stood there in the darkness, not annoyed by McKenna's abruptness but worried by it; then he had walked back through the deserted streets to the Schiller house. The wind had dropped and a dead chill had replaced it; the cold drained the blood from him like invisible leeches. He walked faster to speed up his circulation, loping through the streets as if late for a particular appointment. But, of course, he had nowhere to go and time meant nothing.

He said as much to Dolores when, having arrived at her house, he and Carmel were saying good night to her. "Perhaps Terry and I should give up, subscribe to the *mañana* principle."

"Could you do that?" Dolores asked.

Taber looked at the two women in turn, asked for himself and McKenna, "Would you be disappointed in us if we did?"

Carmel pressed his hand. "I would."

Dolores said, "Things are bound to improve. If they don't, then our country will wither away and die. Johann Schiller, the poet, was my grandfather's great-uncle. He once wrote, 'Alas, there are no longer miracles'. But I think he was wrong and I pray for one every night. Don't give up, Harry. We need all the help we can get, even from outsiders. Bolivia has been a tragic country – it is time we had some happiness."

"Outsiders aren't going to bring you happiness. I'm a twelve-thousand-dollar-a-year Samaritan – but I'm not worth a penny to you if I can't persuade a criollo and an Indian that only co-operation will get this country up off its knees. Good night, Dolores." He kissed her hand. "Keep praying for your miracle, if you believe in prayer."

"It is all I have," she said.

Taber drove Carmel back to the Ruiz house in the Land-Rover. He pulled up outside the big gates and kept the engine running to keep the heater working. Two armed policemen, wrapped in overcoats and blankets, sat up in the plaza garden as the Land-Rover pulled up, then they lay back as they recognised the vehicle. Taber put his arm round Carmel and she nestled up against him.

"I've never had my arm round a mink coat before. It's a bit slippery, isn't it?"

"That's the idea of it. Once a girl has got a mink coat she should be harder to make than before she got it."

"Whose law is that?"

"I don't know. But I saw a lot of it with the crowd I used to mix with."

"You used the past tense there."

"Funny, that's the way I think of them now. Is your hand warm enough?" He had slid his hand inside the mink and was stroking her breast through her dress. She wore no brassière and she was glad of the gentle squeezing of his hand. There would be no love-making to-night, not here in the Land-Rover with the two prone policemen watching them like snipers. "Don't try too much, darling. I don't want to get too excited, not when we can't do anything about it."

She had called him *darling*; as she had yesterday afternoon when they had been in bed. But he was not really experienced in the nuances of endearment. He could not remember what his first wife had called him. His second wife had called him *sweetheart*, but she had also called their dog that; once he and the dog had arrived in her bed together in response to her call. Carmel's *darling* could be no more than the cheap call-sign of her crowd; but he hoped it was more. Taber was honest enough to admit that he had not yet called her *darling*, *sweetheart* or anything else.

He just let his hand remain on her breast; then she said, "What can we do about *anything*?"

"You and me?" Why am I so bloody hesitant? You love the girl; why don't you come out and say so?

"Who else? Oh, there's Terry. And Dolores. But they have

to work that out themselves – we can't help them." She twisted her head to look up at him. "You know they're in love?"

"Did she tell you that?"

"She didn't have to. God, it's dreadful for them, isn't it? At least we have this." She put her hand on his, squeezed it against her breast.

"Do you love me?" He whispered it, as if he were afraid.

"Isn't it obvious?" Suddenly she, too, was cautious; they whispered together while the police snipers watched them from the plaza garden. She said bitterly, "Don't tell me I've made another mistake."

She is as afraid as I am. He took his hand from her breast, put it under her chin, lifted her face and kissed her. "I couldn't answer that for you – you'll have to make your own judgment." Then for the first time in years he made his own confession, the one as difficult for him as those of some of the penitents who entered McKenna's confessional: "But I love you, if that's what you're asking me."

"Oh, I am!" She pulled his face down to hers, kissed him so savagely that he felt her teeth on his lips; she was weeping, he could taste the salt of her tears; she writhed in his arms in a spasm of painful ecstasy, and his arm slid off her mink-wrapped shoulders. "Hold me! Hold me tight!"

"I can't." Fumbling with the fur, he couldn't help himself: he began to laugh. "You're going to have to throw this bloody thing away."

"Anything – I'll throw away anything you want me to! Oh darling – "

He wiped away her tears with his finger, kissed her gently. "I was joking, you won't have to throw anything away. But that's going to be one of our troubles. You heard me say what I get – twelve thousand dollars a year. That's a lot of money to anyone where I come from. But for you – How much did this cost?" He grabbed a lump of the mink.

"I've forgotten. Four or five thousand dollars."

"You see? I once went off my nut, had a wild splurge and paid twelve quid for a pair of shoes. I've never forgotten the year – 1962. I'm still wearing them, got them on to-night."

"I never pay less than fifty dollars a pair for my shoes."

"Any wife of mine came home and told me that, I'd belt the daylights out of her."

"I think you would too, you brute. All right, I won't tell you, unless I'm in the mood for a bit of masochism." Then she sat back from him, leaning against the door of the Land-Rover, abruptly being serious. He had noticed this before: women all seemed to have to get *away* from a man when they wanted to talk seriously, as if they were afraid their mental processes wouldn't work properly if distracted by flesh. "Darling, don't let's talk about money. I think that's going to be the least of our problems."

"What's going to be our biggest?"

"Making sure you're happy in your job. I'm not blind, darling – I can see how much it means to you. I'll be honest – I don't know how I'm going to adapt, traipsing around the world after you, living in places like this – "

"Or worse."

She nodded. "I suppose there are worse. Anyhow, all I can promise is that I'll try, *really* try."

He reached for her, pulled her back into the crook of his arm. "It's only academic, but I haven't asked you to marry me yet."

"I accepted without you asking me. Oh darling!" She kissed him hungrily again. "Let's go back to your place!"

He shook his head, amazed at his own control. "No, we've been out here too long. Someone in the house must have heard the engine running. If I drove off now and you didn't put in an appearance in the house, we'd have Francisco or even Old Man Ruiz after us with his posse of armed guards."

"The Ruiz men don't have any responsibility for me."

"That's where you're wrong. No matter what sort of bastards I may think they are, I know they'll feel responsible for you so long as you're sleeping under their roof. You may find it annoying, but it's admirable. And in a way I find it comforting. I feel you're safer in there than in a hotel."

"I could come and live with you."

"This isn't St Tropez or wherever you're used to. If I had a mistress living with me – " He grinned, liking the idea; then shook his head. "Presidents and generals can have mistresses, but not visiting F A O men."

"I suppose I'd better get used to that idea – being an FAO wife, I mean. It's not going to be easy. I've never cared very much for what people thought of me."

"You're learning. You don't try so much now to sound like some messenger from the permissive society. You were pretty bloody hard to bear that first day."

"Don't ever stop flattering me," she said dryly.

He grinned, kissed her; then got out of the Land-Rover, went round and opened her door. "We'll talk to-morrow about finding you a place to stay – perhaps Dolores wouldn't mind having you. That is, if you still want to move out of here."

"The Ruiz will understand. Or at least Senora Ruiz will." She got out of the Land-Rover, wrapping the mink coat round her against the chill of the night. Across in the plaza garden the two policemen sat up again, snipers no longer but just simple *voyeurs*. Were the two gringoes going to make love outside the Ruiz's gates? Carmel looked across at them, then offered Taber her hand. "Good night, darling. Let's see how decorous an FAO man can be."

Taber, one eye on the policemen, clicked his heels, bowed and kissed her hand. Then he knocked on the gates and a moment later a sleepy armed guard, poncho wrapped round his overalls and hat pulled down over his ears, opened the small door and poked out his rifle. He blinked, then recognised Carmel and stood back to let her enter. She pressed Taber's hand, went in and the door closed behind her. Taber went back to the Land-Rover, got in and drove home through the moon-drenched streets of the city. He was only just beginning to realise what a decision he had made and though it worried him he did not regret it. Though he knew things would not be easy for them, that both of them were going to have to make concessions to each other, marriage to Carmel would be infinitely better than life without her. He could not be unlucky enough to have three marriages fail.

Now he lay on his bed this morning and knew there were other decisions to make. He could not stay here in San Sebastian if he was to be no more than a lackey adviser to Alejandro Ruiz and his Agriculture Reform Council. He could resign from FAO, but unemployment was the last thing an intending bridegroom wanted just now; he was not going to begin their marriage living on his wife's money. FAO might have lost patience with him and they just might ask for his resignation; there were certain officials in Rome who believed that politics were more important than production. It had been a mistake to set up FAO headquarters in Rome. The city was a natural breeding ground for politics; the miasma of compromise and intrigue hung over it as the foul air had once hung over the marshes that surrounded it. The Church had poisoned the atmosphere over the centuries and honesty and idealism died there now as the citizens had once died from malaria. But if he ever preached *that* doctrine in one of his reports he'd be out of a job quicker than a South American president.

There was a knock on the bedroom door. It was Pereira who opened it and came in. "Harry? A policeman brought back your passport, with Captain Condoris's compliments." He dropped the passport on the dressing-table, turned and looked back at Taber. "The policeman had some news. That man from Altea, Jesu Mamani, escaped from prison last night."

Taber stood up, pulled on his shoes. "Escaped? Without any trouble?"

"No, there was trouble. A guard was killed and another wounded. The terrorists engineered it. They will take over the city next. Harry, I'm worried." He wrung his hands, moved to the window, looked out at the flame tree in the garden. He dreamed of oaks, elms, beeches, the plump green trees he had seen in Technicolor films of England; the trees here in the Andes always looked so temporary, as if they had been imported only for a season. "How fortunate you are to be an Englishman, to live in a country that is so democratic and well organised."

"I haven't lived there for years."

"You English are never anything but English, no matter how long you have been away from your homeland. But we Bolivians, Spanish-bloods like myself – " Pereira turned back from the window. "Strange, though, I have never wanted to go to Spain. Do you think I should be happy in – where do you come from? – Slough?"

"I don't know, Miguel. I couldn't be." I've been lying up

here, he thought, feeling sorry for myself and here's a man who has much less future than I have. Pereira would be forever unhappy, ironically compromised by his blood, always afraid that his compatriots, of one side or another, might kill him because he accidentally voiced the wrong slogan. He made jokes about his father's death, but he was whistling in the dark. Taber made another of his rare gestures of sympathy, patted Pereira on the shoulder. "You might find it tough in England. There aren't too many openings for an agronomist, and from what I hear they are also closing down cinemas every week. What would you do?"

Pereira shrugged, smiled sheepishly. "I know, Harry. My wife is always berating me for my dreams. But what else does a man have in a country that has nothing else?"

Taber had no answer. He patted Pereira again on the shoulder, went out of the room and down to the phone in the living-room. Isabella, tired of the typewriter, was out in the kitchen making coffee. He flipped through the directory, found the number of the cathedral and dialled it.

"May I speak to Padre McKenna?"

"I am sorry, Padre McKenna is not here. Who is that?" The voice at the other end had a prim preciseness to it, the voice of someone who was conscious they had a position, if not of authority, at least in a house of authority; it reminded Taber of voices he had heard round the world, of junior assistant secretaries in government departments, in chanceries, at F A O in Rome. The sound of those who would never make it to the top.

"Just a friend. Where can I find him?"

"The padre went back to his mission on the altiplano this morning." The voice became primmer: Taber wasn't sure whether its owner was annoyed at him or at McKenna. "This is His Grace's secretary. I repeat, who are you?"

Taber hung up. He wasn't a member of His Grace's congregation, he did not have to answer to jumped-up altar boys. He turned round as Pereira came into the living-room. "I'm going up to Padre McKenna's mission."

"You will have to go through Altea. Perhaps in the circumstances I should come with you, Harry. If the police and the army are out looking for Mamani, it would be better if you had a native with you."

Taber was touched by the other's gesture; he knew that, though it had been made on the spur of the moment, it must have cost Pereira an effort. But all he said was, "I've never thought of you as a native, Miguel."

"I am not, of course," said Pereira. "That is the trouble."

2

At first McKenna thought the sound was that of firecrackers coming faintly on the wind up from the village. Preoccupied with the words he was chalking on the blackboard, his mind only half-aware of the distraction, he idly wondered what the villagers of Altea were celebrating. Then he heard the movement in the class and he turned round. The dozen children, all that he had been able to cull from parents reluctant to offend Padre Luis, were sitting tensed, faces staring at the open door.

"What's the matter?" McKenna had been writing Spanish words on the blackboard, but he asked his question in Quechua.

"Guns, padre."

Feeling suddenly sick, McKenna moved quickly to the door. The children tumbled off their benches and crowded round him, some of them pushing out into the yard. The sound now was distinct and recognisable. The sharp hard bursts of automatic gunfire hit the ear almost painfully; the children flinched as each burst came up on the wind. McKenna grabbed a couple of the children, tried to use them as a buffer to push the others back into the house.

"Wait here! I'll go down and see what's happening – it's probably just your fathers practising with their guns."

But he knew he hadn't fooled the children: their youthful eyes stared at him with fearful experience: they knew what the gunfire meant. He ran round to the back of the house, jumped into the Jeep; when he brought it round into the yard the children were waiting for him in a bunch at the gates. They jumped in, not a sound out of them, sitting all over each other without a word of complaint from those underneath. Afraid that some of them would fall out, McKenna drove carefully out of the yard and down the road towards Altea. He didn't pick up speed when he was out on the road, but still drove slowly, afraid for the children and afraid of what he was going to see when he reached the village.

There was no wind this morning and the lake stretched like a blue velvet carpet over to the rumpled white drapes of the glacier. Two puya trees, like armless men, stood by the shore; but there were no villagers round the shore nor fishermen out on the water. The Jeep passed a herd of llama, but there was no boy guarding them. Nor was anyone working in the fields above the village.

The firing was still going on when the Jeep reached the top of the village street. The Indians stood there in one large group; half a dozen armed soldiers stood guard on them. The men stared impassively down the street, but most of the women were weeping, those with children holding them close to their skirts. McKenna got out of the Jeep and the school children fell out after him. They rushed for the group and miraculously each found his own parents at once. McKenna was left alone beside the Jeep; no one came near him, neither the villagers nor the soldiers; he was the outsider, unimportant and unwanted. He looked down the street, sick and afraid at what he saw.

The two security policemen who had come up the other day to arrest Mamani were standing in the middle of the street. A dozen soldiers, working in two groups, were shooting up the houses on one side of the street. One group would go into a house and there would be several long bursts of gunfire; then they would come out and reload while the second group moved into the house next door. It was too methodical to seem savage; it was a cold-blooded exercise in revenge. But revenge for what? McKenna moved across to Padre Luis who, pale-faced and with his hands tearing at his rosary as if they were worry-beads, was standing in front of the crowd of villagers.

"What's going on? Why are they shooting up the houses?"

Padre Luis shot him a frightened glance, as if he did not want to be seen talking to the outsider. "Jesu Mamani escaped from prison last night. The security police think the villagers may be hiding him."

Despite the hollowness in his stomach as each burst of fire

came smacking up the street, McKenna felt a leap of relief. "Then Jesu got away unharmed from the prison?"

"Yes, yes," said Padre Luis impatiently. "Go back to your mission, padre. This is no business of yours."

"No," said McKenna, and looked back down the street. "But it's yours, padre. These people are your flock. Why don't you protest about their homes being destroyed?"

"What good would it do?" Then the fat little priest added bitterly: "It is easy for you to make suggestions. You've caused nothing but trouble ever since you arrived. We are the ones who have to live here – you can always go home to your comfortable America any time you wish. Go now, padre, go home now. We don't want you!"

The villagers standing immediately behind Padre Luis had heard what he had said; and so had the soldier who stood guard nearby. He brought his submachine gun round to point it at McKenna; he would shoot the gringo, even if he was a priest, if he caused trouble. Somehow McKenna found enough courage to ignore him. The hollowness in his stomach had begun to be replaced by a cold anger; he no longer heard the bursts of gunfire still coming up the street. He turned to the villagers, scanned the dark masks that stared back at him with an indifference that was worse than hatred. At least hatred was something you could fight.

"Is Jesu here in the village?" He shouted without realising it; the gunfire was an exclamation point behind his question. He looked from face to face seeking one that showed some reaction; then he saw Agostino trying to hide behind two men. "Agostino! Is your father here in Altea?"

The boy cowered back, but suddenly he was pushed forward. He stumbled out in front of McKenna, his mother behind him. "No, padre, Jesu is not here!" Maria Mamani glared round her, at the other villagers, at Padre Luis, at the armed soldier who made a hesitant step towards her, then changed his mind when he saw that the threat of his gun would have no effect on her fury. "The soldiers should not be destroying our houses! But what man here has protested? None of them! There is not one man here has balls enough to tell the soldiers to go to hell!"

The crude forthrightness of her language did not shock

McKenna; this was a peasant woman who knew only the fundamentals. Fundamentals not only of language but of existence: the right to defend one's home, one's children, the right to rebel against brutal use of authority. Her spirit, either by example or by shame, slowly communicated itself to the men. There was a shuffling of feet, a crowding together into a tight unit, as fingers turning into a fist. The soldiers raised their guns, but the Indians took no notice of them. All the soldiers were mestizos, men picked for this job for their blood; but it was their blood, that of their mothers, that now betrayed them. The Indians saw the indecision in the faces of the soldiers and they understood suddenly that they were not going to be fired upon, at least not by these men.

But the crowd still needed a leader; the men would never allow themselves to be led by a woman, not even by the indomitable Maria. Everyone looked towards Padre Luis, but the fat little priest, spirit shabby and worn as his cassock, could not help them. Dumbly he shook his head, his face awry with the pain of his helplessness: they were asking too much of him, his vocation wasn't martyrdom. Then suddenly Maria poked McKenna in the back.

"You, padre! You speak for us!"

McKenna had gone six paces down the street before he realised what he was doing. By then it was too late to turn back. Behind him was the crowd of villagers, men, women and children; like a slow landslide they moved down the street, pushing McKenna ahead of them. Oh God, he prayed, help me to help them! Turn aside the guns; don't answer my prayer with bullets! The crowd moved on, spreading out across the street as if no one wanted to shelter behind anyone else. McKenna, feeling the strength behind him, straightened up and strode on.

The firing had stopped. The two groups of soldiers had come out of the houses and stood in a line across the street, their submachine guns pointing up towards the approaching villagers. The two security policemen and the army sergeant, pistols drawn, stood about five yards in front of the soldiers. The air was still and there was no sound but the yelping and whimpering of a dog that had been shot in one of the houses.

"Stop!" It was the smaller of the two policemen who shouted; but there was a ragged edge to his voice and both the Indians and the soldiers behind him noticed it. The guns wavered a little and the villagers kept moving down the street, McKenna still a couple of paces in front of them. The policeman raised his pistol, fired it over the heads of the advancing crowd and shouted again, this time more convincingly. "Stop or I'll shoot the padre!"

That stopped everyone, including McKenna. He wondered what the Indians would do if the security policeman did shoot him; but he was not prepared to find out. Maybe the policemen knew the Indians better than himself; would they really throw themselves on the soldiers' guns just to avenge a dead outsider? McKenna looked back over his shoulder, but the faces there gave him no encouragement.

He looked back at the two policemen. The bigger of the two was glaring at the priest as he had the other day; he hated priests, and particularly busybody North American ones. But the smaller man was in charge and his face was as expressionless as that of the Indians. But his pistol was expressive enough. He pointed it at McKenna's chest.

"Take the people back up to the top of the street where we sent them."

"Only when you tell us why you are shooting up their houses." McKenna was surprised at the steadiness of his voice. A sense of fatalism had settled on him; the Indians had elected him their leader, at least for the moment, and had imbued him with their own stoic acceptance of what might happen. "What have they done to deserve this?"

"It is not what they have done but what they will not do." The policeman was an intelligent educated man, something his partner was not; he seemed to have accepted that he was not going to get rid of this troublesome gringo without some explanation.

"What won't they do?"

"They will not tell us where Mamani is hiding."

"They do not know." McKenna knew that if anyone in the crowd behind him did know where Mamani was hiding it would not show in his face; he took a risk, was glad now of their stone-like masks. "How could anyone be hidden up here on the altiplano? You could not hide a stolen chicken, let alone a man."

"They know where he is," said the policeman stubbornly, and beside him the big man nodded his head. "Get them to tell us, padre, or take them back up to the top of the street. We are going to finish the job if they do not tell us where Mamani is."

Oh God, what do I do now? Do I call his bluff and maybe see the Indians massacred? McKenna knew something like this had happened last year over the mountains in Peru. A crowd of Indian farmers had marched in protest against some new taxes, and an army officer, over-reacting, had given his troops the order to fire. Nobody knew how many Indians had died; the total had varied from the official report of fifteen to eyewitness's reports of over a hundred. Mob psychology was a double-edged sword: action bred reaction and reaction bred further reaction: soldiers often perpetrated massacres out of fear for their own lives. The twelve soldiers lined up behind the sergeant and the two policemen, and the other half a dozen now grouped to one side of the street, none of those looked as if they were intent only on enforcing authority. The guns in their hands were defensive weapons: they would shoot to kill to protect their own lives.

Then the two vehicles appeared at the bottom of the street, bumping their way up the rutted roadway. McKenna, alert for any sort of interruption, recognised them at once: Condoris's police car in front, followed by Taber's Land-Rover. The two policemen turned their heads as they heard the engines, but McKenna was looking at the soldiers. They had all glanced quickly over their shoulders, then turned back to face the villagers, their guns still held menacingly. But their faces were no longer tense, they looked almost relieved. There was going to be no massacre.

Condoris got out of the police car, leaving the driver behind the wheel. He did not look back as Taber and Pereira got out of the Land-Rover; almost leisurely he crossed the street in front of the church and came up to stand between McKenna and the two security men. Taber had been about to follow, but Pereira grabbed his arm; the two F A O men remained in front of the church. Padre Luis, who had disappeared when the Indians had begun their march down the street, now reappeared on the steps of the church, standing in the doorway as if ready to duck back inside in case of trouble.

"What is going on here?" Condoris addressed the two security policemen, but did not call them either by name or by rank. There was no tone at all in his voice and his manner was at best only coldly polite. He did not look at the army sergeant or the soldiers. "I heard firing as I came up the road."

"With all respect, captain, this is security business," said the small man, and again the big man beside him nodded emphatically.

"Law and order in this province is *my* business," said Condoris. "There was no communication from your headquarters that you were coming up here to – " he had been looking down the street at the splintered doors and shutters hanging drunkenly from their hinges; the wounded dog was still whimpering in one of the houses " – to destroy this village."

"We are not destroying it, just teaching them a lesson. They are hiding an escaped political prisoner."

"You have proof of that?"

"This is not a court, captain. We do not have to produce proof."

"The governor might ask you to."

For the first time the security policeman looked uncertain. McKenna suddenly recognised that the man had been acting beyond his authority, that he had no warrant to destroy the village as a reprisal against the Indians' refusal to co-operate. The security man glanced at his partner, who all at once looked equally uncertain, then turned back to Condoris.

"Captain, perhaps we could discuss this in private?"

Condoris nodded and led the way down the street and into an alley between two houses. He had not looked at McKenna or the villagers; he had prevented any further trouble for the moment and he had done it without appearing to take the Indians' side. He was a man who would keep all his options open and McKenna wondered now how he could have suspected last night that Condoris might have been in league with the terrorists.

McKenna nodded reassuringly to the villagers, then he crossed the street to Taber and Pereira. He shot a look of contempt at Padre Luis, standing on the church steps behind the F A O men; he knew it should have been a look of pity, but right now he was incapable of charity towards the fat little priest. Padre Luis, standing there on the steps of his rundown church, was too representative of the Church as a whole, the force for good that too often was too slow in leading the people in protest against their social conditions. McKenna turned his back on him and spoke to Taber and Pereira.

"Maybe you could have picked a better time to come up here."

"I'm noted for always being in the wrong place at the wrong time." Taber grinned; then he looked soberly at the houses that had been shot up. "They've buggered up the roofs. How long will it take them to re-thatch all those with holes in them?"

"Several weeks," said Pereira. "They have to cut the totoras, then wait for them to dry. They usually keep some in reserve for patching their roofs, but not enough for that job there."

"In the meantime the rain comes in and buggers everything they own. Jesus Christ!" Taber spat savagely, glared across at the soldiers as if he might rush across and attack them on his own. "Why the bloody hell – !"

"Steady, Harry." Pereira was nervous, but he had got out of the Land-Rover and allied himself with Taber and he was not going to retreat. But he looked towards the Land-Rover, as if wishing he had remained in it, posing as no more than its neutral driver. "Did not the British shoot up houses in Palestine when they were looking for Jewish terrorists? Are not the Israelis doing the same thing now, looking for Arab terrorists? It is a pattern, Harry. I don't condone what the soldiers have done, but don't ask why they did it."

"You and your bloody logic!" But then Taber abruptly grinned when he saw the hurt look on Pereira's face. "I'm sorry, Miguel. You're right."

"Of course he's right," said McKenna. "But that doesn't make us happy about it."

"Who said I was happy, padre?"

But McKenna did not have an answer for Pereira, and he was

glad of the interruption when Condoris and the two security policemen came back up the street. Leaving Taber and Pereira, he walked back to meet the three police officers. The Indians had remained in the middle of the street, silent and motionless as a dying garden, the sun occasionally highlighting a faded red or green poncho like flowers or leaves ready to fall. McKenna could not tell now how the villagers felt: the sullen faces showed no hope nor defiance nor despair. But he was no longer afraid. He had gone so far out on a limb there was no retreat and once having committed himself he was surprised to find he no longer had any fear. He had put his trust in God and God was helping him. But he was going to need a lot more help before this thing was through.

Condoris still did not look at McKenna but faced the villagers. "The soldiers will leave Altea now. But you will have to produce Jesu Mamani by – " He looked up at the clock on the church tower, but it had stopped at 8.25 on some morning or evening thirty, forty or fifty years ago; he looked back at the Indians, probably none of whom owned a watch or clock. "You will produce Jesu Mamani here outside the church by the time the sun is two hands above the peak beyond the glacier."

The Indians said nothing, but all their heads turned towards McKenna. He was still their spokesman, they still had hope in him if in nothing else. Oh God, don't desert me now! "The villagers do not know where Jesu is. That is the truth, captain."

The two security policemen were behind Condoris; they could not see his face. He stared at McKenna, allowed the priest to see the anguish in his eyes. He is on our side, McKenna thought with a leap of excitement; but knew at once that Condoris would not, could not, make any commitment. "Padre, I came up to return your passport. But I am afraid I shall now have to keep it."

"Why?"

"Because you have announced yourself as spokesman for these people. You will have to find Mamani and bring him here by noon to-morrow."

"And if they can't, captain?"

Condoris's eyes were dull with pain, but his voice was steady. "The whole village, every house and shed, will be

destroyed. The security police will have the proper authority
by then."

3

"The governor is waiting on instructions from La Paz," said
Alejandro Ruiz. "He wants martial law declared so that he can
hand over control to the army."

"Something has to be done," said Francisco. "It was just
too easy the way the terrorists broke into the prison last night
and took that Indian."

"We had army law here once before," said Romola; then
corrected himself: "No, half a dozen times I suppose it has
been. It only means replacing one body of incompetents with
another, except that the army is more inclined to shoot people."
Then she looked quickly at Hernando. "I am sorry, Hernando.
That was stupid of me."

Hernando bowed his head, agreeing silently that it was. There
had always been a tacit agreement that the way his parents had
met their death would never be discussed.

"I think you should try and persuade the governor to do
without martial law," said the Bishop. "I'd hate to think that
our lives were in the hands of trigger-happy idiots."

"The governor won't listen to me!" Alejandro jerked savagely
at his moustache, swelled in his jacket till it seemed the seams
would split. "He is as frightened as most of the other lily-
livered people in this city. Once La Paz takes over it may be
months before we can run our own affairs again."

"You'll have to disband your little private army." The malice
glinted in Romola's smile. "Just as I was learning how to salute
you."

"It is no joke, Mother!" It was the first time Francisco had
spoken sharply to his mother since his return home.

Romola looked mildly at her son, wondering at her disappointment in him. He was handsome, he was intelligent, he
was attractive to women; but he belonged to the past, he was as
reactionary and blind to the future as his father. She had no
aims to lead a social revolution; she felt sorry for the Indians
when she thought about them at all, but she felt no devotion

to their cause. All she wanted was for her husband and son to bow to the inevitable before it was too late, to close up the house here in San Sebastian and the one up in La Paz, to make a gesture, just in case they ever wanted to come back here for a visit, and hand over the brewery and the estates to the workers, and go to Europe to live. The Ruiz account in the bank in Zurich, when the statement arrived yesterday, showed a balance of just over two million dollars. At eight per cent, a rate she had been told was easily available in Europe, that would yield an income on which they could live very comfortably and much more safely than here in Bolivia: so far there were no terrorists in London or Paris or Rome. But Alejandro and Francisco, damn them, were diseased with the Ruiz tradition. She had married history and now she was sick and tired of it.

"Nothing in this house is a joke," she said, stood up and moved sedately to the door. "Except us and our damned pretensions!"

Hernando, silent and careful, watched his two uncles and his cousin as his aunt disappeared. Aunt Romola was a selfish bitch, but he had to admire her; she had more fire and courage than a dozen other San Sebastian women put together; it was a pity she was on the wrong side. His Uncle Alejandro, he knew, was split between hating her and being unable to do without her; he would strangle her with jealousy if ever she went off with another man. Francisco, as selfish as his mother, was afraid of both her and his father, yet needed them; he tried for a show of self-sufficiency, but he would crumble like an ant-hill if he lost them. Uncle Jorge *was* self-sufficient, there was no doubt about that: he was a Ruiz, he was a bishop of the Church, and only heaven could offer more. How am I going to save them all when the revolution comes? he wondered.

"Damned woman!" Muttering to himself, Alejandro went across to a sideboard and poured himself a drink.

"While you are there," said the Bishop and held up his hand.

Alejandro brought a Scotch to his brother, leaving Francisco to fix drinks for himself and Hernando. "The Church is right, you know, to treat women as second-class citizens. It would be the end of organised religion if ever they were any better."

"Don't be too hard on her," said the Bishop, trying to be

charitable. He looked at his drink. "It is a little early for this. The sun, as the English say, is not yet over the yardarm. But I fear that a lot of us in the coming weeks won't be drinking by the sun or the clock. What is the feeling among the young people, Hernando?"

What young people? Should I tell him the truth that there are some young people like myself who feel that the old order is finished, that the future for our country lies only in a new society? Should I tell him that he and Alejandro and Francisco are on a list of those to be assassinated if our aims are not achieved according to schedule? "I'm afraid a lot of the young people are apathetic. If their fathers would give them the money I think they would leave the country and go elsewhere."

"At least they are not a lot of wild-haired, bearded hippies like those they have in the United States," said Alejandro.

"No." Hernando had little time for the North American rebels he saw in copies of *Time* and *Newsweek*, who were as conformist in their scruffiness and long hair as the older generation was with its neatness and weekly haircuts. Rebellion in looks and dress had always struck him as childish; the new society was not going to be better for being born in bed-bugs and lice. The revolutionaries he worked with, when they took over, would be indistinguishable from the old order; only their deeds and their plans for the future would be different. "But they still don't care."

"I don't think they are like that at all," said Francisco.

Hernando shrugged; he wouldn't miss Francisco very much if he were shot. "I suppose it depends on whom you talk to."

"Whom did you talk to?" asked Alejandro.

Hernando sipped his drink, smiled. "You can't expect me to betray confidences, Uncle. You wouldn't expect Uncle Jorge to tell us what he hears in the confessional."

"Have you been holding confessionals, Hernando?" The Bishop smiled at his nephew. He had always liked the boy, but he had never managed to get close to him; he doubted if anyone had, though Alejandro seemed to have tried hard enough, letting him run so much of the family business. He was the only child of the youngest of the three Ruiz brothers, but he had been an orphan since his last year at school. His parents had been shot by troops during one of the previous periods of martial law in San Sebastian. Accidentally delayed when returning home after the curfew hour, they had been slow in halting their car when challenged. Alejandro had seen that the corporal in charge of the soldiers had been tried and shot, but it had done nothing to repair Hernando's loss. He had loved his parents and they had loved him. He had borne his grief stoically and, come to think of it now, the Bishop could not remember his ever having discussed his parents' death even once.

Hernando returned his uncle's smile. The Bishop might once have had potential for good, but he had become trapped in the worst department of the Establishment, the Church, and there was no hope for him now. There had been some argument in the revolutionary group when the Bishop's name had come up for discussion, but in the end there had not been enough in his favour to save him from being put on the list for assassination. Hernando sometimes despaired at the waste of human life that was going to be necessary to achieve their ends, but eventually he always convinced himself that the waste would never be as great as that that had gone on for so long under the system that had always considered the Indians as less than human.

"Who hasn't been this past week?" he countered.

"This isn't the time for confessions," said Alejandro. "It is the time for action!"

"What action?" asked the Bishop.

"That's it, damn it! How can you fight shadows? These terrorists are so well organised – I hate to say it, but they are not some crude rabble. Whoever is running them has a genius for organisation. He must have had a long course of instruction at some Communist school, in Cuba or Moscow or – God help us – China."

No, thought Hernando, I had only two weeks in Cuba, enough to know that the people there could teach me nothing I did not know about organisation. The Ruiz had always had a talent for it; it was now just being applied to the other side. Hernando sometimes thought that Che Guevara might still be alive if he had come to see him first.

"The prison attack last night was a model of organisation," he said, trying to sound grudgingly admiring and not smugly satisfied; he did not know how good an actor he was and he was taking a risk making any comment at all. "It was all over in less than five minutes."

"But why go to all that trouble just to rescue that Indian, Mamani?" asked Francisco.

Hernando let someone else answer that. It was Alejandro, who was no fool like his son: "They want either a martyr or a puppet leader. He is not worth anything to them as anything else."

"We could make a gesture to counteract them," said the Bishop, looking up from his glass as if he had found inspiration there in the whisky.

"Such as?"

"What have the terrorists been able to give so far? Nothing but promises and some blood-letting gestures. Let us give a constructive one. Turn over the land up near the lake to the villagers of Altea. They have been asking for it – give it to them."

"It could be valuable land," argued Alejandro. "It only needs development. I told you what that fellow Taber said."

"It has been in the family for God knows how long. Have we missed it by not developing it all these years? If we give it to the Indians we can at least harvest some propaganda out of it. Why should we allow these terrorists to make all the running? Am I not right, Hernando?"

You are right, Uncle, but you are too late. "I think it is worth considering." He would have to stall them for a day or two, get Mamani to lead the Indians in taking over the land before it could be offered to them. Some of the Indians, possibly even Mamani himself, could be killed, but that could not be helped. He looked at Alejandro. "Would you like to leave it in my hands?"

Alejandro hesitated, looked at his son for support. But Francisco was a boy eager for action, any action: he would never stop long enough for second thoughts. "Let's do it, Father. It's something they won't expect – they'll be expecting us just to hole up and await events – "

"I am in a minority, I can see that." But now that *he* had had second thoughts, he could see that the suggestion had merit.

Sometimes you had to lose a little to win a lot; and what was to be won was the guarantee of their continued existence here in San Sebastian. Romola was always arguing for abandoning everything and going to live in Europe; she never seemed to realise that the bank account in Switzerland had not been designed for that particular end, but was no more than a safeguard if ever the worst did happen here. She also never seemed to realise, or deliberately ignored, that his life, and the continuing history of all the Ruiz, would be over if they abandoned Bolivia and settled in Europe. There was a lot still to be won so perhaps he should be prepared to lose a little. "All right, we'll give the villagers the land. You arrange it, Hernando, then I'll make the announcement. We might even arrange a ceremony. You could bless the land, Jorge."

"Why not?" said the Bishop, draining his glass. "The Lord will always forgive hypocrisy if it is in a good cause."

Hernando stood up. "It will take me a day or two to arrange the necessary deeds, but I'll do it as quickly as I can."

"Don't forget to invite Padre McKenna and Senor Taber to the ceremony." Now that he had accepted the suggestion, Alejandro saw all its possibilities. "It will be an opportunity to put them in their place."

4

McKenna sat in the Jeep in the street that led out of the plaza that fronted the Ruiz house. He had driven down from Altea to Hernando Ruiz's house, only to be told by a servant that the young master was at his uncle's house. So now he had been waiting half an hour for Hernando to emerge from Alejandro Ruiz's home and he knew exactly what he was going to say.

As if it had needed a flood of disasters to flush it out, his mind had begun to function more clearly and decisively than at any time since his arrival in Bolivia. There had been the ultimatum from the Bishop last night in regard to Dolores; later there had been the discovery that Hernando was one of the leaders, if not *the* leader, of the revolutionaries; this morning early there had been the refusal of the Bishop to allow him to see Dolores again and ordering him to return to his mission at once; and then later, just as shattering as all the other shocks, had been the threat to totally destroy Altea to-morrow morning if Jesu Mamani was not produced. He was here to see that Hernando did produce Jesu.

The Bishop had sent for him after early Mass. He had lain awake most of the night trying to accept the fact that Hernando was one of the revolutionaries. True, he had never really known the younger man, but to all outward appearances Hernando had seemed the logical successor to his uncle as the real, if not titular, head of the Ruiz family: Francisco, as the only son of the eldest son, would hold the title of head of the family but he would never be more than a figurehead. McKenna knew there were other instances of scions of aristocratic families turning out to be revolutionaries; even in the United States these days the way-out radicals seemed to come from families well on their way to being part of the Establishment. Hernando had sounded cool and pragmatic last night in the confessional, as sardonic and controlled as he always was, but the fact remained that he was a leader of a group dedicated to the uses of terror to achieve their aims.

McKenna had said Mass automatically, going through the motions half-asleep. His mind had still not been functioning properly when the Bishop had sent for him.

"Did you speak to Senorita Schiller, Terence?" The Bishop was spreading English marmalade on his toast. He offered McKenna some coffee, but the latter shook his head.

"I didn't have the chance to, your grace."

"Why not?" The Bishop this morning was sharper-toned than he had been last night. He, too, had lain awake and had decided he had been lenient enough with the young American. He knew that priests in his diocese were discussing the celibacy problem, but none of them had yet dared approach him. If the word got around that he had been discussing it with the American, had proved sympathetic even if unable to help, then in no time he would have every young priest, and even some of the middle-aged ones, on his doorstep wanting open discussion and some action. He was not prepared for that, not now and perhaps never, and he had decided to call a halt to any further encouragement of McKenna in his dilemma.

"It was difficult, your grace. My sister and Mr Taber were also at the house."

"Could you not have waited till they had gone?"

"I had to leave early." But he held back from telling the Bishop that he had been called back to the cathedral to hear a confession. He was supposed to report all out-of-hours calls and though the Bishop would never ask what the man had wanted to confess in the cathedral at that time of night, he would certainly wonder why McKenna had responded to such a call. Confused as he was about Hernando, McKenna felt it was better that he did not mention last night's encounter at all. "I – I was not feeling well, your grace."

"You don't look your best this morning, I must say. But I think you were just evading the issue, Terence. I am not evading it myself, but I have had further thoughts on it." The Bishop poured himself a second cup of coffee, stirred it thoughtfully. He did not like doing this to this young priest and he knew he *was* evading the issue; but with the political trouble that was now brewing in San Sebastian he did not want himself distracted with other problems. Priests had been celibate for a thousand years; they could wait a little longer. Which, he told himself, was probably what other bishops had been telling themselves for far too long. He looked up, burying his self-disgust with a tone of voice that was much too sharp for the occasion: "You will return to your mission at once – this morning! – and you will write Senorita Schiller and explain what has passed between us. I shall take further steps if I feel they are needed, but for the time being I shall trust to your sense of duty as a priest. God be with you, my son."

When he had left the cathedral McKenna had almost succumbed to the temptation to disobey the Bishop and go and see Dolores and explain what had happened. Then he had thought about the effect on her, guessed that it might be more distressing for her than he himself could bear, and had decided to go straight up to the mission. He would write her to-night when he had sorted out his thoughts and send the letter down to-morrow by messenger. What happened after that would depend on her reaction to the letter. And that was something he dared not think about.

Then had come the incident at Altea this morning. When Condoris and the security policemen and the soldiers had left, he had already made up his mind what he was going to do. He had turned to the villagers and asked them to trust him. "I know none of you knows where Jesu is. Neither do I, but I think I can find him. I shall try and get in touch with him and tell him what the police plan to do to your homes."

"We do not want him to sacrifice himself for us, padre." One of the men standing close to Maria Mamani had spoken up and Maria had glanced gratefully at him.

McKenna hesitated, then nodded. "All right, I'll let him decide. But I think he has to know what the police have promised to do to your homes."

"God will take care of us," said Maria; and McKenna wished that he had her simple faith. "We shall pray for you, padre."

He had left them then and walked across to Taber and Pereira. "I've promised to find Mamani for them."

"Where do you start looking?" Taber asked. "If those revolutionaries have got him, mate, you're asking for trouble."

"I'll be okay." He wanted to add *God will take care of me*, but he was not sure he could make it sound convincing enough in the face of Taber's cynicism. He had come to learn that faith, to sound positive, too often needed to be heard by another believer.

"Do you want me to come with you?"

McKenna shook his head. "One neck at a time. You can shove yours out if I don't get anywhere."

"How?" Taber looked around him. "What the hell can I do now?"

"Be neutral, Harry," said Pereira. "Take the long view."

"One of these days, Miguel, perhaps pretty soon, I'm going to knock your bloody head right off your shoulders," said Taber. "Just because I know you're going to be right."

"I admire you, Harry. You are a fine person. And you, too, padre. It is a pity neither of you have learned to compromise."

And now, sitting in the Jeep waiting for Hernando to come out of the Ruiz house, McKenna thought how right Pereira was. If he compromised, took the long view, perhaps all that he dreamed of for the Indians would be granted. Perhaps the Church might even relax its law on celibacy and he would be able to marry Dolores. But in the meantime Indians would die too young after having lived too degradingly, and he and Dolores would grow old and dry before the Church changed its mind. Compromise was fine for those who already had something to comfort them.

The gates to the Ruiz courtyard swung open and Hernando drove out in his shabby Volkswagen. He passed McKenna and the latter, feeling like a television private eye, started up the Jeep and followed him. The Volkswagen drove out of the residential section, across the main plaza past the prison, round in front of the cathedral and then up the main boulevard leading out of town. Where's he going? McKenna wondered; and hoped Hernando was not on his way to a meeting with some of the other terrorists. He did not want to meet them as a group, not till he had talked to Hernando.

The Volkswagen began to climb up the twisting road that led to the altiplano, threading its way through the mule and llama traffic carrying unsold goods back up from the market. Indian women, hump-backed with their shawl-wrapped babies, baskets balanced on their heads, hurried up the steep hill. Hernando went by them, blowing his horn and missing them by inches, looking for all the world like a criollo who did not care a damn about them; McKenna gave them a wider berth, going within inches of traffic coming the other way and getting angry horns blown at him. Then abruptly the Volkswagen swung off the main road and went down a narrow track towards a stand of eucalypts high above the railway yards. McKenna, cutting across in front of a horn-tooting bus, followed him.

The Volkswagen drew in among the tall pale trunks of the eucalypts and pulled up. Hernando got out, leaned against the car and lit a small cigar. He glanced towards McKenna as the latter stopped the Jeep and got out, but he made no attempt to approach the priest. He waited, and after a moment's hesitation McKenna went across to him.

"Are you expecting anyone, Hernando?"

"Only you, padre. You're not a very good – what do they call it in American movies? – a tail."

"I wasn't tailing you. Not if you mean I was trying to spy on you. I wanted to talk to you."

"What about?" Hernando was still sitting on the car's mud-guard, arms folded, cigar in mouth, a man looking completely relaxed. But McKenna, sensitive now to nuances as he had never been before, could feel that beneath the cool exterior Hernando was tense and nervous.

"About Jesu Mamani. I want him, Hernando." McKenna too was calm; but inside, he knew, he was more relaxed than Hernando. In the past hour or so he had begun to shed doubts like a man getting rid of old habits; he was not yet completely confident, but he felt almost as fatalistic as the Indians. Or Dolores. Whatever happened to him now did not matter; he had started something and he would see it through; even if he himself failed the movement itself would not fail. Once it had started it must gather momentum. But it would need Jesu Mamani to lead it. "I want him no later than noon to-morrow up in Altea."

"I don't know anything about Mamani, except that he escaped from prison last night."

"Hernando, I recognised you last night in the confessional." It was a lie, but one he knew the Lord would forgive.

Hernando stood up straight, threw away his cigar. High in the trees the breeze whetted the edges of the hard leaves, hissed warningly; a shredded length of pale bark fell slowly through the air like stripped skin. Up on the road there was the scream of brakes and the hoarse blast of a horn; both men glanced up towards the road waiting for the crash, but none came. Hernando looked back at McKenna.

"Padre, if my friends knew you had recognised me, I would not put much value on both our lives. They don't know I came to see you last night."

"Is Francisco one of your friends?"

Hernando smiled, more just a baring of his teeth than an expression of humour. "Don't ask me who my friends are. But Pancho isn't one of them. He is very much his father's son, if you know what I mean."

"Why did you come to see me last night?"

Hernando sighed, as if he might be wondering himself why

he had taken such a risk. "I am still a Catholic – I still have a conscience. But my friends aren't. They were once, but not any longer. The Church has lost them, padre – I don't think they'll ever come back to it. Not unless the Church changes its attitude."

"Some of us are trying to do that."

"You are only priests, padre. You can do nothing until the bishops and the cardinals and the Pope change theirs. You have some bishops on your side here in South America, but not enough, padre, not enough. And my friends are tired of waiting."

"Why did you join them?"

Hernando relaxed again, sat back on the mudguard. "Desperation. I've waited eight years, ever since my parents were murdered in the name of law and order, for some sort of democracy to come to our country. But it hasn't and finally I got tired of waiting for miracles."

"How long ago did you join them?"

"After Che Guevara was killed. I knew then that a new approach was needed and I thought I could provide it. They believe I can."

"So you're their leader?"

Hernando shook his head. "*One* of the leaders. We're a committee – I am just responsible for organising certain projects."

"Like getting Jesu out of prison last night?"

Hernando sighed again. "All right, padre. We got him out and we have him now. But you don't expect us to turn him over to you just because you ask for him?"

"You better let me have him. If I can't produce him to the security police by noon to-morrow, they are going to destroy Altea."

"They'll kill him if we hand him back to you."

"I'm hoping they won't. We'll blame his escape on you, say he wanted no part of it and that he has come back to give himself up."

"It won't work."

"We'll try it. It's the only hope we have."

Hernando swore under his breath, but then he looked at McKenna and said, "And if we don't let you have him?"

McKenna took a deep breath. "I'll tell the police who's holding him. It's a question of you or a whole village. And I'm on the side of the Indians." Hernando said nothing and McKenna went on, "All I can do is appeal to your conscience. And your trust in me. You deliver Jesu to me and I vow to you, as solemnly as any vow I've ever taken as a priest, that I'll say nothing to anyone about who you are."

"You guessed my identity in the confessional. What about your vow of secrecy there?"

"To save a man's life I'll break that vow. I want Jesu!" For the first time McKenna raised his voice.

Hernando turned away. He looked down through the trees to the railway yards, saw the long train pulling out of the station. It was the once-weekly train that went all the way down to Rio de Janeiro, through the passes of the eastern cordillera of the Andes, down the long slopes into the jungle country, across the Matto Grosso . . . All he had to do was drive fifty miles up the line to the train's first stop, buy a one-way ticket, get aboard and never come back. Uncle Alejandro was not the only one with money in a bank in Switzerland; even idealistic revolutionaries had to be practical; only a fool never left himself somewhere to flee to. But he had not waited all these years just to take the easy way out. He watched the train, still pulling hard against the grade, slowly disappear round a bend in the tracks. Then he looked back at McKenna.

"As I told you, I am only one of a committee. It won't be my decision, but I'll do what I can. But I'll have to tell them why I have to hand over Mamani to you." He straightened up again. "And that will put you on their list for sure, padre. You open your mouth to anyone, anyone at all, and you're a dead man."

Chapter 10

I

Romola Ruiz normally did not come down for breakfast but remained in her room almost till noon. But Carmel, impatient and nervous, could not wait that long; besides, she wanted to see Romola alone and the latter's bedroom would ensure them privacy. She did not want to be interrupted by servants or, worse, by Alejandro or Francisco. When she learned from Romola's maid that the senora was awake and had had her breakfast, she sent up a message asking if she could see Romola at once.

"It must be terribly important," Romola said as Carmel came into the big bedroom. The bed was a huge fourposter affair covered with a rich silk canopy; Romola sat propped up in the middle of it in a foam of white sheets and blankets. Alejandro had his own bedroom and this room, unlike the rest of the house, had no concessions to masculine taste. "I hope you haven't been waiting hours to talk to me. I slept, as the English so ungraciously put it, like a log." She looked carefully at Carmel. "You don't look as if you slept too well."

"I didn't," Carmel admitted. She looked around for a chair in which to sit, but Romola waved her to sit on the end of the bed. It was a simple gesture, but Carmel appreciated it; it made the atmosphere between them more intimate, put her a little more at ease. "This is like a mother and daughter talk."

"I never had a daughter to talk to," said Romola, and there was just a faint tinge of sadness in her voice. "I had such a bad time having Francisco, I couldn't have any more children. I had a hysterectomy – that was over twenty years ago and you have no idea the amount of discussion it caused in those days. One would have thought I was preparing myself for whoredom. Try not to settle down in a man's society, especially one where the Church is so strong."

"I'll try." The small revelation by Romola had increased the intimacy between them; Carmel felt she could make her own admission: "I was never able to talk to my mother. Not the usual girl stuff. I was never able to go to her with any of my problems. I knew that all I'd ever get would be the advice to get down on my knees and pray to God for guidance. I could never bring myself to believe that God was interested in a schoolgirl's crushes."

"Do you have a problem now?" Romola had taken some tissues and was wiping the night cream from her face. She looked her age this morning, but she did not seem to mind exposing her true face to Carmel. They *could* have been mother and daughter, and Carmel knew now there was going to be no difficulty in talking to her. "A crush on Senor Taber, perhaps?"

"It's more than a crush. I'm in love with him. He wants to marry me."

"Do you want to marry him?"

"Yes." There was no hesitation at all about Carmel's reply: she had lain awake a long time last night and thought everything out. Their marriage might be a gamble, but what marriage wasn't? "When you married your husband, were you absolutely sure he was the man you wanted to be with for the rest of your life?"

Romola, having accepted the role of surrogate mother, did not feel she could be offended by the remark. She was flattered and pleased by the fact that Carmel had chosen to confide in her; it was not often that anyone in this house ever came to her for advice or comfort. "As sure as any young girl of twenty can be. Unlike a lot of marriages in our sort of society, I actually did love my husband." She smiled. "Of course it did not harm things to know he was the son of the richest and most powerful man in San Sebastian."

It was Carmel's turn to smile. "I don't think Harry is the richest and most powerful man in F A O. He keeps bringing up the question of *my* money."

"Well, at least he's not a fortune hunter," said Romola. She hoped that when Francisco married he would be intelligent enough to choose a girl who was not a fortune hunter. She finished with the tissues, picked up a silver-backed hand-mirror and looked at herself. "Middle age is a terrible time for a woman. You are still young enough to desire a man, but you wonder if you are still young enough for him to desire you. At least when you are old you no longer have the wonder and doubt."

"You are still beautiful. I saw a look in Harry's eye the other morning that said he thought you weren't too old."

Both women laughed, allied for a moment against all men, even husbands and lovers. "Still, stay young for him as long as you can. When are you going to marry him?"

"As soon as possible. That's why I wanted to see you. I think I had better find somewhere else to stay. I know how Senor Ruiz feels about Harry – "

Romola nodded sympathetically. "I understand. Where will you go?" She picked up a silver-backed brush that matched the mirror, began to brush her hair. "Our hotels here in San Sebastian are not exactly first class. They seem to be designed mainly for travelling government officials whose daily allowance doesn't amount to much."

"Senorita Schiller has invited me to stay with her. But she wanted your approval first. She did not want to offend you."

"Carmel, I should not want to spoil your chances of happiness just because of protocol. Love has enough difficulties without that stupid hindrance."

Carmel impulsively leaned forward, put her hand on Romola's. "I wish my mother were as understanding as you."

Romola shook her head. "I don't know your mother, so I can't say whether she is right or wrong. But perhaps she is to be pitied. If she had a daughter to talk to and missed the opportunity – " She went back to brushing her hair, her face hidden beneath the thick fall of it. "Do you want me to explain to my husband what has happened?"

"Would you? I mean, prepare the way – "

"Of course." Romola looked up. Whatever had happened while her face had been hidden, it was composed again. "I shall see that he understands."

Carmel went back to her room to finish her packing, her mood considerably lighter than it had been an hour ago. She had had an unpleasant night, but now everything looked so much better. Except, of course, for poor Terry.

Late yesterday afternoon she and Taber had driven up to the mission. Taber had come back to the city, phoned her and told her what had happened up at Altea that morning. "Terry has shoved his neck out and promised to deliver this bloke Mamani to the police by noon to-morrow."

"Do you think he can?"

"I wouldn't bet on it, unless one of your Catholic miracles turns up. Perhaps you could talk him into going a bit more carefully."

"I'll try," she said, but had no confidence that she could: the years of separation were still not entirely eradicated.

They had driven up through Altea, not stopping as they passed through the village. "Take a look," said Taber, "but don't look too curious. I'm still not sure how these people are reacting to what happened this morning. Right now they could be hating all gringoes, especially inquisitive ones."

The village looked calm enough. Women were going about their chores, bringing in washing, grinding corn. One woman was hanging a small white flag outside her door to say she had newly brewed chicha for sale: perhaps to-night some of the men would want to get drunk to forget what might happen to-morrow. Men were up on roofs repairing the thatch against the possibility of to-night's rain, and others were trying to hang doors back on broken hinges. Some youths kicked an old football around amongst themselves, only stopping to stare sullenly at the Land-Rover as it passed them. Padre Luis watched the vehicle from the steps of his church, then turned and scurried back out of sight as it drew opposite him.

"He's the bugger should be shoving his neck out," said Taber. "He's the only one in the village who could be their leader."

But McKenna denied that when Taber repeated the remark later. "Jesu is their leader, make no mistake about that."

"Are you going to be able to produce him?" Taber asked.

"I don't know."

"Did you make contact with the fellers who are holding him?"

"Yes."

McKenna offered no further enlightenment and Taber did not press the question. Carmel was watching the two men closely, gradually becoming aware that a bond existed between them but was not yet complete enough to allow absolute frankness. McKenna had been out on the lake when she and Taber had arrived at the mission and now he was cleaning some fish for their supper. He worked expertly, gutting the fish like a professional fisherman, and she marvelled at the skill he had acquired as he had learned to look after himself. She looked at Taber and said, "I hope you won't expect me to do things like that?"

"Naturally. *And* milk cows *and* gut a sheep." Taber grinned. "We're never likely to be anywhere near a bloody supermarket, unless they send me back to Rome."

McKenna looked up. "What's going on?"

"We're engaged," said Carmel. "You can read the banns next Sunday at Mass." Then she looked at Taber. "That's one thing we didn't discuss. Where we'll be married."

Holding his fish-stinking hands high, McKenna advanced on Carmel, took hold of her with his elbows and kissed her. "You look so damned happy, I couldn't be anything else but happy for you. You look pretty happy too," he said to Taber. "Congratulations."

Taber nodded, grinning delightedly: he looked twenty years younger, a man young enough not to have been married before. He took off his cap and scratched his head. "I might even stretch a point and let you marry us."

McKenna knew Taber had not made the concession lightly. "Whenever, wherever you like." He looked at Carmel. "Mother will want to be there."

Carmel hesitated, but Taber said, "I'd like her to be. She should have a chance to look over what's marrying into the family."

Carmel kissed him on the cheek. "I never realised what a diplomat you can be when you really try."

They had dinner of grilled trout, cooked by McKenna, tinned English plum pudding, as a mark of respect for Taber, a bottle of Chilean white wine, and finished off with coffee and some Benedictine.

"Those old monks knew a thing or two," said Taber, sipping the liqueur. "Five Hail Marys and a drop of this and what more could the soul want? Perhaps that's what you should do. Tread water – or rather tread grapes for a while, invent your own liqueur and get the campesinos working with you in a co-operative. Forget politics."

"Don't you think I'd like to forget them?" McKenna knew Taber was only trying to lighten the mood of the evening, but he was beyond response to-night. "If I could get those slopes out there to grow grapes or any damn' thing at all – " Then he shrugged, sipped his own liqueur. "Maybe. We'll see how things go to-morrow."

"I'll come up first thing."

"You don't have to," said McKenna, but he sounded grateful.

"I'll come too," said Carmel.

McKenna shook his head, looked at Taber for support. "I think she should stay down in San Sebastian."

"That's the first order I'm going to give her," said Taber, and reached out a large hand to cover one of Carmel's. "It won't help, your being up here. Terry and I aren't going to be in any danger, the police won't touch us. But they might get a bit rough on the spectators and that won't be pretty to watch."

So Carmel had agreed not to go up to Altea. But when she had been saying good night to her brother she had held his hand tightly and said, "I hope things work out to-morrow the way you want them."

She had wanted to weep at the sadness in his voice. "I hope so too. Otherwise – " They were out in the yard, standing beside the Land-Rover. A full white moon had turned the snow-capped peaks and the lake to silver; the altiplano stretched away like a vast exposure of the earth's bone. McKenna looked down to where the white tower of Altea's church showed above the level of the ravine. "Those people turned their back on Padre Luis this morning and became my flock. It's what I've been working for ever since I came here – I don't mean to kick Padre Luis out, but to have the Indians accept me, let me help him to help them. They accepted me and now I don't know if I really can help them."

"I'll pray for you," she said, and last night had done so, the rusty words coming back to her tongue with more ease than she had expected.

Now this morning she finished her packing after she had left Romola, had a servant take her suitcases down into the entrance hall, then went along and knocked on the door of Alejandro Ruiz's study. Alejandro rose as she entered, but, with his back to the light of the window, it was impossible to tell at first what his mood towards her was going to be.

"I have come to say good-bye, Senor Ruiz, and to thank you for your hospitality."

Ruiz said nothing for a moment, still standing with his back to the window. Out in the garden one of the armed guards strolled around, rifle slung over his shoulder and a transistor radio strapped to his ear like an ear-muff. At last Ruiz motioned Carmel to a chair, came round the desk and sat down opposite her, the light now on his face. He did not look angry, but he did look sober.

"My wife has told me of your engagement to Senor Taber. I hope you will be happy." His voice sounded so formal it was difficult to tell whether his wishes were sincere. There was a long silence that Carmel found awkward, but that did not seem to discompose Ruiz in the least. At last he said, "Is your father alive, senorita?"

"He died when I was a child," said Carmel, but did not explain the circumstances of her father's death.

"A pity. Perhaps he could have offered you some advice at this time. Was he a wealthy man, a member of what is called the Establishment?" He uttered the last word as if he thought it were an obscenity.

Carmel was not sure what label could have been hung on her father. "Yes, he was wealthy, though I don't quite see your point in asking such a question." But Ruiz did not apologise, and she went on: "I don't know if you would have called him a member of the Establishment – I suppose he was. He was very conservative in lots of ways – " Though not in his love life; but she did not mention that. What a man did in bed was not related to his politics when out of it; Establishmentarianism in bed had never been accurately defined, as far as she knew. "He voted for President Eisenhower and I believe he thought all Communists, whatever their nationality, should be sent to Russia, preferably Siberia."

"I believe the same." Ruiz had been sitting stiffly in his chair, but now he sat back, relaxing. "I wonder what he would have thought of your marrying Senor Taber. A radical."

"I am not marrying Mr Taber because of his politics," Carmel said spiritedly; all at once she no longer felt uncomfortable with this arrogant, interfering man.

"Perhaps not. But you will find that you can't ignore them, not when the first bloom has worn off your marriage."

"I think you are being terribly impertinent, Senor Ruiz – "

Ruiz smiled. He had been called many things, mostly behind his back, but he guessed he had never been called impertinent before. "Senorita, I do not mean to be – impertinent. I am just trying to point out to you a few things that your father, being the man you have described, might have tried to make you see. The world is changing, senorita, much too fast for its own good, and it is the duty of some of us to try and resist that change."

My God, he thinks I am one of them! A member of what I suppose he would call the Ruling Class. It was incredible to her that someone as archaic as this still existed. She had moved amongst a lot of wealth in the last few years, but none of the people she had known had ever been the sort to talk about class or politics or the changing world. They had lived in their own plastic-enclosed world where those things were never allowed to intrude. "Senor Ruiz, I have never thought that my money gave me privileges – "

"Not privileges," said Ruiz almost primly. "I do not advocate that. But responsibilities. It is people like us who should be the bastions of stability."

He *is* incredible, she thought. She wanted to laugh at the image of herself as a bastion of stability, whatever that might mean. But she said, "Are you trying to imply that my fiancé – " the word tasted strange on her tongue " – is unstable?"

"Not Senor Taber personally. Just his politics. Dreams are no substitute for experience and that's all Senor Taber and his kind have – dreams and nothing else. I am only trying to help you. You are taking a big step into a way of life that is completely foreign to you."

"If I had come to tell you that Francisco and I were engaged, how would you have felt? I'd have been stepping into a way of life that is just as foreign."

Ruiz shook his head. "Only superficially. You would be marrying into your own class."

I've been waiting for him to say that word, she thought. Though she was still as politically ignorant as she had been when she had first arrived in San Sebastian, she had at least begun to look sensibly at a condition of man's existence that she had once deliberately dismissed as no concern of hers. A month ago, even a week ago, she could not have imagined herself saying, "I think you are living in the past, Senor Ruiz. You accuse Mr Taber of being a dreamer, but only dreamers, people who dream of the past, still think they must marry into their own class. Whatever that is, because I've never been sure. I don't consider myself any better or worse than anyone else – I mean, taking into consideration the defects we all have in our characters. I do have more money than most people, but I don't think that makes me a better person than – well, Mr Taber. I'm not being a traitor to my class, if that's what you are trying to tell me, Senor Ruiz. Who knows, I may even be improving it by marrying Mr Taber. Only time will tell, but I'm willing to take the gamble. To tell you the truth, I couldn't care less whether Mr Taber improves my class or does it tremendous harm. I'm marrying him because I love him. Which, I gather from talking to Senora Ruiz, is why most intelligent women marry. She married you for love, senor. You should count yourself lucky."

She left on that note. Angry at Alejandro Ruiz's attempted interference in her private life, she did not trust herself to the reaction of Francisco and was relieved, when she got out into the hall, to be told by Romola that he had gone out on business.

"I trust my husband gave you his best wishes." Then Romola looked more closely at the younger woman. "He gave you more than that, didn't he?"

Carmel was learning how to be as composed as Romola herself: "We had a small talk, senora. I think we understood each other."

Romola was an expert at reading between the breaths in a

voice, but all she said was, "I'm glad you understand him, Carmel. The circle of people who do understand him is growing smaller and smaller. But," she said sadly, forgiving her husband everything else for the moment and loving him as much as she had as a young girl, "he does not seem to realise it."

She had placed one of the Cadillacs and a driver at Carmel's disposal. She followed Carmel out into the courtyard. "Will you be married in San Sebastian? If you are, may I expect an invitation?"

"Would it be diplomatic?" Carmel glanced back towards the house.

Romola smiled. "My husband may not come, but there's no reason why I shouldn't. I am trying very much to live in the present. Perhaps not on Senor Taber's side of the street, but at least in his world. Please give him my congratulations. And I am happy for you, my dear."

The car drove out of the courtyard and the big gates closed on Romola standing on the steps of the old house. She was wearing a white dress and in the bright glare from the surrounding white walls she looked insubstantial, a ghost who, despite herself, was claimed by the house she despised.

Ten minutes later Carmel was being met at the door of the Schiller house by Dolores. She got out of the car smiling happily, but at once the smile died when she saw the strained look on Dolores's face.

"Harry just called. He's gone up to Altea. The security police are going to arrest Terry whether he produces Jesu Mamani or not. They suspect him of knowing who the revolutionaries are and they want to question him. Their methods of questioning are pretty horrible."

"What do we do?"

"I think we should go up there at once. Try and get Terry to leave. Go up to La Paz or down to Lima. Anywhere. But he must get away at once!"

2

Hernando's servant brought the message early in the morning before the sun had come up above the eastern cordillera.

McKenna, who had slept only fitfully, was already up and out in the yard feeding his chickens and collecting the few tiny eggs they had laid. The cow was bellowing to be milked and McKenna was turning to go back into the kitchen to get the tin pail when he saw the battered Volkswagen coming up the road from Altea. He stood in the yard feeling a sense of excitement: he had only half-expected Hernando to produce Jesu Mamani, but now here he was and six hours early. But before the Volkswagen had reached the gates he saw there was only one man in it and he was neither Hernando nor Mamani.

The Indian got out of the car, muttered a greeting and handed McKenna a sealed envelope. He had not switched off the engine and he at once got back into the car.

"Aren't you going to wait for an answer?"

"Senor Ruiz said there would be no answer, padre." The Indian swung the car round, went out through the gates and back down the road, driving much faster now than when he had been coming up it.

McKenna opened the envelope. The note was typed and un-signed: *It is impossible for me to speak to my friends. Your man is being held up at the old McKenna mine. Please burn this note.* Leaving the cow still bellowing, McKenna went into the kitchen and dropped the note in the fire. Then he went across to the living hut and into his bedroom. He slipped on his anorak and a pair of gloves, knelt down in front of a crucifix and prayed for help, then went out of the hut, locking the door behind him, and round to the Jeep. As he drove down the road and began to skirt the lake he saw the first Indians pushing their boats out into the water. They stopped and watched him, but he took no notice of them, just drove on at gathering speed.

It was a clear bright morning, everything sharply defined and seemingly so close that distance had no meaning. Ice still sparkled on clumps of puna grass; the sweep of land round to the glacier, Ruiz land, was covered in what looked like discarded gem-encrusted turbans. Twenty or thirty barefaced doves burst out of the wild crown of a puya tree as the Jeep roared past, billowing up like a small cloud of smoke. Other birds were rising from the lake: a pink mist of flamingos; grebes and teals whirling like lengths of dark rope above the ice-blue water. On

other mornings McKenna had stood awed by the sight of the
lake and the altiplano coming alive to the new day, but this
morning he saw nothing but the winding track ahead of him
that led up to the McKenna mine. Nothing that might happen
this day would have any beauty about it.

As he drove up the last part of the track to the mine he could
not see any sign of life. The place looked as desolate as some
forgotten Inca ruin; the broken winches stood out like totem
beasts. He pulled the Jeep round to face down the track, got out
and looked about him. He could see no one, but he had the
feeling that he was being watched. The sun had not yet reached
the small mine plateau and the cold here pressed in on him like
heavy metal. His heart was thumping, from fear and the altitude
and the cold, and his unprotected face seemed to have frozen
into bone. There was a sharp crack somewhere high above him,
like a rifle shot, and he jumped; then he heard the rumbling
and knew it was only an avalanche, ice breaking off some steep
slope as the sun reached it. Tense, sure that he was covered by
rifles every step he took, he walked along towards the shell of
the main house. He stopped when he saw the dirt- and ice-
covered heap of books; several of the books had recently been
turned over, as if someone had been looking for something to
read. He looked up towards the mine shafts, put his courage
in his mouth.

"Jesu! I want to talk to you!"

The shout echoed and re-echoed back from the slopes and
the cliffs; there was another sharp crack and another avalanche
started, set off by the ricocheting yell. Then Mamani and two
men with rifles came out of one of the mine shafts and looked
down at McKenna. He stared up at them for a moment, then
started up towards them, his hands held above his head to show
he had no weapons. By the time he reached them he was
gasping for breath. But none of the others spoke, all three
waiting for him to speak first.

"Jesu – " He spoke directly to Mamani after a glance, that
he hoped they interpreted as friendly, at the other two men.
They were both mestizos, young not-very-bright-looking men,
the sort who in any revolutionary enterprise would always draw
the job they had now: guarding prisoners. "Jesu, you have to

come back to the village. If you are not there by noon to-day, the security police are going to destroy it."

"How did you know he was up here, padre?"

The mestizo who spoke was a boy of about twenty whose intelligence would never equal his fanaticism; he was calm enough now, but McKenna could imagine the zealous way he would go about an ambush or an assassination. He wondered if these two had been among those who had killed the mayor, but then quickly put the thought out of his mind. His only concern must be Jesu.

"Jesu and I used to live up here as children." He saw the look of surprise on the faces of both the mestizos; that meant they were strangers to this part of the altiplano. "I guessed that if Jesu wanted somewhere to hide, this was where he'd come."

"Padre," said Mamani, "are they going to hurt my family?"

"To be honest, I don't know. I think Captain Condoris will do all he can to prevent any harm coming to them. Or to the other villagers. But it is up to you, Jesu. All I was asked to do was find you and bring you the message. If you are not down at Altea by noon, they will completely destroy the village. The houses, the sheds, everything."

"Did my people ask you to come and get me?"

It was no more than a shade of tone in the words *my people*, but McKenna caught it: Mamani had used the words the way a leader would. "They said you were not to sacrifice yourself for them. But, Jesu – they will be sacrificing themselves and their homes for *you*."

"He cannot leave here," said the second mestizo, a hawk-nosed man of about thirty with prematurely grey hair. There were scars on his cheeks and McKenna wondered if they were burn-marks, the result of torture; there had been men in the prison the day before yesterday with the same sort of scars, only fresher. "It is unfortunate, but the people of Altea will have to look after themselves."

McKenna looked at Mamani. "Is that the way you want it, Jesu? Are you going to let these men use you for their own ends while your people have their homes destroyed, are perhaps thrown into prison? Is that what you want? Do you want to be a real leader or just a figurehead?"

Mamani said nothing, his face blank; but the two mestizos brought their rifles up, shoved them at McKenna. "Get out of here!" the younger man snarled. "Go back where you came from, you religious parasite!"

But the grey-haired man, though he was angry, was still clear-thinking. "We can't let him go! He'd bring the police up here!"

They were both looking at McKenna, had taken their eyes off Mamani for the moment. Even McKenna did not see exactly what the Indian did, his movement was so quick. But the younger man went down with a groan, Mamani had his rifle and had turned it on the grey-haired man. The single shot came back at once in a barrage of echoes; the grey-haired man folded over, clutching his rifle to his stomach; it, too, went off, but the sound was lost in the echoes and the gathering thunder of avalanches. McKenna looked up and around him wildly. Ice and rock were peeling off the cliffs and slopes like the grey bark had peeled off the trees in the eucalyptus grove yesterday afternoon. The mountains were crumbling, dark apparitions gradually becoming lost in the grey fog of dust billowing up out of the ravines: these mountains, he thought, had been born in this same agony of thunder and dust. Then gradually the tumult died down, the thunder gave way to a decreasing rumbling and the sun came over the tops of the peaks and turned the ravines to cauldrons of red dust.

McKenna looked back at Mamani. The Indian was just lifting the smoking barrel of the rifle from the chest of the younger man. A dark stain was appearing on the man's shirt: the sound of the third shot had been lost in the reverberations of the avalanches. "Good God, Jesu!"

"It had to be done, padre. They would have killed you. And I haven't forgotten that you saved me from the lake. These men don't value any lives but their own – especially not mine and yours. I found that out yesterday when they brought me up here. You were right, padre. I should have listened to you when you came to visit me in prison. Wait here!"

Still carrying the rifle he ran back into the mine shaft behind him. McKenna, standing with the two dead revolutionaries at his feet, made the sign of the Cross over them; he felt weak and sick, but he knew that Mamani had been wise to kill the men. They would have shown him no mercy and he might already be dead. The Church condoned war, Hernando had said last night; and he had also said the revolutionaries were in a small war. So Hernando had to expect and accept killing on both sides. But the logic did not make McKenna feel any better.

When Mamani came back he was carrying a box of dynamite on one shoulder.

"Where did you get that?"

"I stole it the night we raided the Customs shed. I saw it there and knew we could use it. Forgive me, padre, for I have sinned – " Mamani's grin was sardonic yet friendly. He put down the box and looked down and around at the ruins of the mining camp. "Remember when we played Spaniards and Incas?"

"Oh God, Jesu – " McKenna could not help the thickness in his throat. Jesus Christ, he thought, the time and the opportunities we have wasted! "Why didn't we talk about this before?"

"I wasn't sure, padre, who you still were – Pizarro or Atahualpa."

"I'm neither," said McKenna sadly, and looked down at the skeleton of their childhood.

Mamani picked up the second rifle and divested the dead men of their bandoliers. Then he hoisted the box of dynamite back on his shoulder and they went down to the Jeep. They put the box in the back, tied it down, then got in and drove carefully down the track away from the mine. There were several sections where the track was covered by rubble that had slid down from the slopes above it, but McKenna, with some skilful driving, managed to negotiate them. Now that he was on his way back to Altea, Mamani had fallen silent. He still carried the two rifles on his lap and one hand kept sliding the bolt of one of the rifles up and down.

"Do you have to do that?" McKenna at last said.

Mamani was puzzled; then looked down at his hand as he realised what it was doing. "Sorry, padre. I am still wondering what answer I am going to give the security police."

"One of those rifles isn't going to be any sort of answer. They'll shoot you down as soon as you step out into the street with it."

"Can I trust them not to shoot me if I meet them unarmed? I think I would trust Captain Condoris. But not those other pigs!" The bolt clicked sharply. He looked at McKenna. "I have just killed two revolutionaries. That should put me on the side of law and order. But do you think they will see it that way?"

But McKenna could not give him an honest answer. Mamani was no longer a simple campesino who could be fobbed off with a few words of comfort and the advice to trust in God. But if he was not so simple why – "Jesu, why did you try to castrate me that day? Would you really have done it?"

Mamani hesitated, then nodded. "I think so, padre. Though I was glad later that Senor Taber stopped us. It was the chicha, I suppose. And – " he looked sideways at McKenna, not sure he should be revealing so much of himself to the priest " – it was my first test as the leader of my people. It was not my suggestion to do that to you. But once it had been suggested, I had to lead them in it."

"How would you have felt if you had gone through with it?" Then McKenna shook his head, laughed to relieve the other man of the weight of an answer. "No, that's not fair. The real question is, how would I have felt?"

Mamani did not respond at once. He still looked carefully at McKenna, then he seemed to accept that the priest's humour was genuine, that if there had been any ill-will it had all gone. Slowly a smile spread across his face and he leaned back and began to laugh. They were both laughing, all the years of separation and the months of distrust swept away, when the Jeep bumped down the track beside the glacier, swung round the hip of a hill and came out on the smoother road running round the lake. Far ahead of them, just coming up in a long line from below the level of the moraine, tiny figures silhouetted against the far sky, were the villagers of Altea.

The Indians had halted by the time the Jeep reached them. They closed up into a loose group: men, women and children, all their possessions packed into mule-drawn carts or on the backs of llama, the herds of alpaca and goats milling about: the whole community waiting on their leader to lead them God knew where. McKenna knew now that the fishermen who had watched him drive round the lake earlier had guessed where he was going and at once had gone back to the villagers and organised them for this journey that so far had no destination.

Mamani jumped from the Jeep and was hugged by his wife and children. Then he turned to the villagers. "You cannot leave your homes because of me. You must go back!"

There was a murmur that grew into a shout: "No! We stay together, Jesu!"

McKenna could see the emotion flickering like pain across Mamani's face. The Indians no longer wore masks: oblivious of him, the outsider, they were all caught up in an agitation such as he had only seen grip them in religious ceremonies. It was as if after four hundred years they had climbed up out of an open grave, had found a leader. McKenna looked at Mamani, knew now who was to play Atahualpa.

The same realisation hit Mamani. He jumped up on to the bonnet of the Jeep, threw up his arms.

"We'll find a new home!" he shouted, and the Indians yelled their agreement. "We'll build a new Altea!"

3

Taber drove the Land-Rover up through the deserted village. He had sensed the emptiness of the place before he had reached the bottom of the main street. All the doors of the houses were open and there was no sign of even a dog or a chicken. Chicha-sale flags hung limply outside a few doors, but they could have been cemetery flags, hung out to farewell the departed spirits. Then he saw the donkey come out of the alley beside the church, its legs almost buckling under the weight of Padre Luis.

Taber swung the Land-Rover over towards him. "Where is everybody, padre?"

The look the fat little priest gave him was one of hate: Padre Luis had just had his world walk out on him. "They have deserted me! They have gone up there – " He waved a hand behind him, up towards the lake. "All my life I have worked for them – "

But Taber couldn't find it in himself to be sorry for the petulant scruffy little man. "Where are you going now?"

"Down to San Sebastian."

"Not to see the police, I hope?"

"To see the Bishop." For a moment a touch of pride turned the suet of Padre Luis to bone and muscle. "I am not a police informer, senor!"

He kicked the donkey savagely, went trotting on down the street, looking neither to right nor left. Taber stared after him for a moment, then started up the Land-Rover again and drove on up towards the lake. He came to the junction where the road turned off to skirt round the lake. He slowed, looked across and saw the dark crowd of people and animals surrounding McKenna's Jeep on the road just above the moraine.

When he reached them there was an argument going on between McKenna and Mamani, but even before he could make out what was being said Taber could see that McKenna's heart was not in what he was saying. He looked like a man in whom emotion and sentiment had won out over intelligence.

"I can understand what you want to do, Jesu – " He turned as Taber got out of the Land-Rover and came up. "You see? I found him – "

"You have any trouble?"

"Some." But McKenna told him no more, just turned back to Mamani. "Jesu, it's crazy, giving up everything to try for a new life up there in the mountains!"

"We shan't be the first people who have looked for a new home," said Mamani. "You taught us that in the Bible, padre, you and Padre Luis. Didn't Moses lead his people to the Promised Land?" There was a swelling murmur of agreement from those villagers close enough to hear the argument. "They taught me history down at the school – our ancestors fled into the mountains from the Spanish. They told me about Machu Pichu – for almost four hundred years no one knew about that – "

"Times have changed, Jesu." Taber joined in the argument when McKenna looked at him for support; but he knew he was not going to change the mind of the Indian. This was the first time he had seen the new Mamani. McKenna had been right: this man *was* a leader. "They have planes now, helicopters. Machu Pichu was lost for so long because there were no planes to fly over the mountains – " He had seen the ruins of Machu Pichu in the Peruvian Andes and at first had marvelled that such a large fortress-town could have remained lost for so long; but then one had only to look around at the peaks that surrounded it, look back down the narrow tortuous gorges that led to it, remember that in 1912, the year Hiram Bingham had discovered it, all explorers were still earthbound. "They would find you in no time now – "

"If we get away, Senor Taber, will they bother to follow us? Is a village of poor Indians really that important?" Mamani's mouth twisted with the bitterness of his words. "We'll find a valley where we can live."

It's possible, Taber thought. Somewhere in this chain of the greatest mountain range in the world there were valleys inhabited only by vicuna and guemal deer and guanaco, the ancestor of the llama, where men of purpose could carve out a life for themselves. He looked up towards the distant peaks, to the great cordillera lying like a barricade of defensive rock and ice against the invasion of men. But if any men could conquer it, they would be these Indians, the last of the Incas.

There was suddenly a shout and a movement at the rear of the crowd. Taber, a giant among the stocky figures, looked over their heads and down towards where several of the men were pointing. Far down beyond Altea a convoy of four trucks was coming up the road from San Sebastian, dust trailing behind it like a moving explosion, sun glinting on the windscreens of the trucks like the flash of gunfire. The convoy was not moving fast but steadily, as if its commander knew there was no need to hurry, that the purpose of the expedition would be achieved as surely as if it were no more than a routine exercise to give the troops something to do.

"That's why I came up here early – " He spun round to McKenna. "Miguel got the word this morning from one of his mates – those buggers down there are going to doublecross you." He spoke in English, but went back to Quechua as he brought Mamani into the conversation: "The police are going to take in Padre McKenna whether he brings you in or not. They say he is an accomplice of the revolutionaries."

McKenna said nothing, looking bewildered by the news of the treachery. But Mamani, an old victim of it, said, "Come with us, padre. Be one of us – we'll need a priest – "

The Indians near him nodded their heads, ready to accept the American, the outsider, as one of themselves. Taber, feeling more helpless than he had ever felt in his life before, unable to offer McKenna any advice that he felt the priest would accept, looked back down past Altea. The convoy was about half a mile from the village, still coming on at the same steady pace: the very immensity of the altiplano, the distortion of distance, seemed to make its progress look inexorable.

Suddenly there was a stir behind him. Mamani had run back to the Jeep, was dragging out of it a box that Taber instantly recognised as a case of dynamite. The Indians were looking at him in puzzlement and McKenna was yelling, "What the hell are you going to do now?"

Mamani came back, pushing his way through the crowd and down towards the jumble of rocks and earth and clay that was the moraine. He dumped the case, began to pull out sticks of dynamite. He ignored McKenna and Taber, looked up and around at the Indians who stood in a semi-circle on the slope just above him. Some of them had already guessed what he had in mind and Taber could see the apprehension and doubt in their faces.

"We'll flood the village, wipe out our homes and the soldiers too!" Taber felt a curious detachment, was able to remark Mamani's shrewd use of "we", the leader who adopted the principle of collective responsibility, who tried to carry the people with him instead of being away ahead and having to look back for them all the time. He had seen the latter kind in Africa, the ones who finished up lonely and arrogant and were eventually thrown out. But that wouldn't happen to Mamani: "We'll wipe out the past and start a new life!"

There was a doubting murmur from the crowd, then someone shouted, "But what about our lake? It is sacred – "

Answer that one, Taber thought; and remembered the fear on the faces of the Indians when Mamani had been rescued from the lake.

But Mamani did not hesitate: "The gods will understand! Did not the lake let me be saved – did it not give me back my life so it could be used for some purpose? And this was the purpose – to lead you to a new life! The Almighty God, the Great One, will help us – " Taber looked across at McKenna. You've got him, mate. Whether you meant to or not, you've taught him how to play one religion against another. "The lake is our weapon! It will guarantee our new life!"

The Indians remained silent and still for a long moment, trying to break out of the fear and superstition that had encased them all their lives. Then abruptly the men started forward, yelling excitedly. They descended on Mamani and, his face alight with the power he had all at once discovered within himself, he began to hand out the dynamite, shouting at the men where to place it. The women and children moved back up on to the road, ready to commit themselves now that their men had made their decision. The men scurried over the moraine, looking for the weakest spots in the great natural wall. The convoy had reached the village and there was no time to be lost in blowing the moraine.

Taber moved across to McKenna. "They don't need us any more. Unless you're thinking of going with them – ?"

McKenna looked haggard, almost aged. "They're committing suicide – they'll never find another place – "

"Balls!" said Taber, but without conviction; he was afraid that the priest could be right, but he had to shake him out of his morbid depression. "Christ, haven't they survived here for bloody centuries? What can they find worse than this? If they can get over those passes up there, there are greener valleys on the eastern slopes – "

"But how will they get over the passes?" McKenna looked back over the lake and up at the peaks beyond the glacier. "With the women and kids and all those animals? If the army wants to, it can track 'em down by plane – "

"Do you think you can talk logic to them now?"

The Indians were caught up in a frenzy of excitement such

as he had never seen before. They were running up and down
the rocks of the moraine like alpaca that had run amok; three
weak spots had been found in the wall and groups of men were
scurrying from one to another. Up on the slope some boys had
produced devil masks from the packs on the llama, had donned
them and were dancing back and forth towards the moraine.
Others were beating drums and playing quena pipes, while in
the background the women swayed and chanted. The whole
scene had become barbaric, a ceremony to sacrifice the lake for
the good of all; but it was also religious, as family crucifixes
were taken out and paraded up and down. The sun blazed on
the green, yellow and red masks, huge demon faces that to a
civilised eye could only presage disaster, but somehow, on the
prancing, dancing youths became a mass expression of triumph.
Dark red, green and brown ponchos swirled like wings and the
dust rose in a mist about the stamping feet. A dozen Christs on
their crosses swayed drunkenly above the heads of the crowd,
while the drum-beating and the pipe music and the chanting
got louder and louder. The Indians, men, women and children,
were crazed with their vision of the future and their revenge
on the past.

"We don't stand a chance," said Taber. "The best thing we
can do is get to hell out of here, find another road back to San
Sebastian. That one down there is going to be washed right off
the map in a few minutes – " Then he stopped. He was looking
down towards the village, to the convoy now just entering the
bottom of the main street. But beyond it, coming up the road,
he could see the small yellow car that he knew was Dolores's
Volkswagen. "Oh Christ, no!"

McKenna had seen it at the same time. He raced down
towards Mamani, grabbed him and yelled at him, pointing
down towards the village. But the Indian angrily shook him off.
Taber, already running down towards the Land-Rover, heard
none of the argument. He jumped into the Land-Rover, swung
it round as McKenna came running down over the rocks of the
moraine and leapt in beside him.

"He'll hold the dynamiting if the soldiers don't come up
beyond the village, give us time to get Dolores out of it! Come
on, for God's sake speed it up! Faster!"

307

The Land-Rover tore down the road, bouncing over ruts, swaying dangerously as Taber swung it up the slight rise towards the road junction, then down towards the village. Ahead of them he could see the four army trucks halted in the main street outside the church. He sped down the street, holding desperately to the wheel as the ruts in the roadway threatened to wrench it from his grasp.

The two security policemen and an army lieutenant jumped down from the trucks as Taber skidded the Land-Rover to a halt. "Go back!" he shouted. "The Indians are going to blow up the lake wall! Go back or you'll all be drowned!"

Then he put the Land-Rover into gear again and drove on down the street; he could see the Volkswagen coming up the last straight stretch a hundred yards below the village. "What's happening?" he yelled to McKenna.

The latter was hanging out of the vehicle, looking back up the street. "The stupid sons-of-bitches are going on up to the lake!"

Taber braked hard, almost throwing both of them through the windscreen. He leaned out, twisted round and looked back up the long street. The trucks were moving again, heading in convoy up the rise towards the top of the street, going faster now but still not fast enough. Taber swung back into the Land-Rover, but the Volkswagen, picking up speed, had almost reached them. Only then did Taber see Carmel in the front seat beside Dolores. He went cold inside, felt all his limbs freeze for a moment. Then, as McKenna jumped out the door on the other side, he tumbled out and raced across to the Volkswagen. He grabbed the door handle on Carmel's side, slammed the door back so hard he felt it grate on its hinges, reached in and pulled Carmel into his arms.

"Don't ask questions! Over to the Land-Rover – quick!"

But even as he said it he heard the series of dull explosions. He still had Carmel in his arms; on the other side of the car McKenna was holding Dolores. All four turned and looked up towards the lake. A dark cloud of dust and flying rocks rose up and something that looked like a wave of brown mud rolled out from under it, like something obscene and loathsome exposed for the first time. It appeared to move in slow motion, spreading

down over what remained of the moraine, its top edge becoming
streaked with green and yellow and white. Then spray began to
rise up from it and at once it gathered speed.

"Quick!"

But even as the four of them made the Land-Rover and Taber
put it into gear again, they all knew they were going to be too
late. The flood, carrying rocks and earth with it, poured down
from the lake, a yellow and white wall pushed by millions of
tons of darker water behind it. It hit the four army trucks as
they crested the rise at the end of the street. Each truck rose
nose first like a boat being launched into a rough surf, men
spilling out of the back like so much loose gear; then all four
swung side on, rolled over and were instantly lost to view as the
water crashed on down the slopes and into the village. Houses
crumbled like children's sand-castles; a thatched roof flew high
into the air. The church somehow remained standing, the white
tower now becoming a blind lighthouse in the boiling surf
hurtling past it. The flood came on, a battering ram of water
fifteen feet high and a hundred yards wide, turning the ravine
in which the village of Altea had once stood into a raging
torrent.

It hit the Land-Rover at the bottom of the village street.
Taber felt the water come in under them and lift them; out of
the corner of his eye he saw the terrified girls clinging to each
other and to McKenna. The Land-Rover rode the surf for a few
moments, driving straight down the road, the going now
suddenly and ridiculously smoother as they were lifted above
the ruts; for one wild, crazed moment Taber wondered if they
would ride the flood till it petered out. Then abruptly the
water built up behind it, came in the back and over the sides,
and then Taber knew that was the end. He let go of the wheel
and clutched Carmel to him, hoping they would die quickly.

The Land-Rover suddenly tilted on its nose and turned over.
Taber went out the door as it swung open, still holding tightly
to Carmel, flinging himself backwards into the yellow flood that
now filled the entire world. He almost passed out as the freezing
cold of the water drove straight into him. He could see nothing,
could feel the terrible pain in his chest as his lungs threatened
to burst, felt the crash of rocks or timber or perhaps even the

Land-Rover against his hip and legs; but he never let go of Carmel, held her to him while he kicked desperately for the surface, knowing they were both doomed but unable, while he was still alive, to give up living and hoping. He did not pray nor shriek in his mind for God to help him, but some spark in his consciousness told him this was not his time to die, that somehow he and Carmel would survive.

As the Land-Rover turned over McKenna had grabbed Dolores and pulled her out after him. Something hit him and he felt a numbing pain in his arm a moment before the cold killed all feeling in him. He kicked hard, still holding on to Dolores; he had let out one silent prayer for help as the water had hit them, but from then on he was acting only on an animal instinct for survival. The dark yellow world that enveloped them both was like liquid ice; everything in him froze: flesh, bone and mind. Dolores was tearing at him, but it was as if he were in the middle of some terrible dream in which he knew her hands were clawing at him but he could neither see nor feel them. Then suddenly she was gone from him. He did not feel her go, but all at once he knew he was alone in the darkening world of the flood. His eyes already blind, his mind blackening, he wept a greater flood than that that engulfed him. Oh God, he cried, mouth open as the water choked the life out of him, why choose Jesu to kill me? Why did You waste what I offered? He went out of life into the mystery even darker than the flood, the mystery that had sustained him all the time he had lived, went out not understanding the God Who had called him.

Five yards, but an ocean, away, Taber and Carmel were swept by him. They came to the surface, Carmel unconscious but Taber still struggling to stay alive. He saw the shoulder of the hill coming up in front of him and somehow he managed to swing round so that at the moment of impact his legs could take the shock. He felt no pain as his feet struck the rock; the block of ice that was his body, Carmel frozen within his arms, was flung up on to a ledge. The water wedged them into a crevice, then tore at them as if it regretted what it had done; but the cracked rock of the hill held them fast, denied the water its victims. The flood tore on, ranks of waves sweeping after it, some of them rising to slam at the two people crouched on the ledge; but always the cracked rock held them, like protective arms, and gradually it dawned on Taber that they were safe. The water still poured over their legs, but slowly some feeling came back to his torso and arms, slowly his mind began to function again. He lifted a cold skeleton of a hand, turned Carmel's skull-like face towards him; he slapped her once, then again and again. Her eyelids fluttered but did not open, and her lips moved in a whimper that he could not hear for the roar of the water. But he dropped his mouth on hers and wept for joy.

He had no idea whether it was moments or minutes that passed, but all at once he was aware that the water was no longer tearing at his legs. The flood level had dropped, only a foot or so, but enough to leave the ledge clear above the still plunging torrent. Painfully, carefully, he pulled Carmel up into a sitting position, then stood up on legs that threatened to snap at any moment. He leaned back against the rock that had saved them, wiped the water and mud from his face and looked back up towards Altea. Nothing remained of the village but the white tower of the church. Beyond it the lake was still pouring through the broken wall of the moraine, a white cataract now that might flow for hours till the level of the lake had fallen to that of what remained of the moraine. On the road above the broken wall the last of the Indians were turning away: silhouetted against the far white peaks they moved away in single file, the sunlight striking across them, fading away like figures gradually being washed by time out of a historical frieze. Then they were gone from his sight and he could see nothing but the white-capped timeless peaks and the stark, uncaring sky.

Then he turned his head and saw Dolores on the jumble of rocks thirty yards upstream from them. She raised her head and looked sightlessly at him, then fell back in a limp heap. He looked around, down the whole length of the torrent from the moraine to where it spread out below the ravine on to the altiplano, but there was no sign of McKenna. Then he wept again, this time in grief.

Chapter 11

The Bishop himself said the Requiem Mass for McKenna, the two security policemen and the forty-four soldiers who had died in the flooding of Altea. He spoke of men dying in the course of duty, but even the most insensitive ear could not miss the fact that he spoke with more feeling of the death of McKenna than he did of the other men. He did not dismiss those deaths lightly; after all a Cabinet Minister and a general, down from La Paz, sat in the front pew right beneath his pulpit. But he spoke over the heads of the government officials and the élite of San Sebastian when he spoke of McKenna. He addressed himself to the Indians who crowded the back of the cathedral, and when he had finished his eulogy to McKenna those Indians who understood Spanish replied with a loud "Amen!" Some of the officials and most of the San Sebastian criollos could not understand why the Bishop should speak so well of an American priest who was suspected of having contacts with the terrorists, who had always taken the campesinos' side against themselves. They would never know that the Bishop spoke out of his conscience, a privilege he had once denied McKenna.

When the Mass was over Taber escorted Carmel and Dolores out into the grey overcast morning. He had listened with only half an ear to the eulogies for the dead policemen and soldiers. He had felt some sympathy for the soldiers, poor bastards who had only been doing what they had been ordered to, who may even have been driven up towards the dam without knowing what threatened them; but had felt nothing for the two security policemen, had felt himself seething with anger as the Bishop had sprinkled them with all the old stale platitudes. But when the Bishop had finished speaking of McKenna he had found himself echoing the "Amen!" of the Indians. Carmel had squeezed his hand and Dolores had turned her head and nodded gratefully. No one else in the criollos' pews gave any response at all.

Dr and Senora Partridge were waiting for them as they came out. "We understand you are going home to-morrow, Senorita McKenna," said Partridge. "I hope you will not leave thinking too harshly of our country. There are some of us, y'know, who feel your brother was trying to help us."

Then why didn't you speak up in church? Taber wondered; but recognised another man who, like Pereira, would survive by compromise.

"Thank you," said Carmel. There was a calm dignity to her that she had not had a week ago; tragedy had stripped her of all frivolous pretence; grief, Taber knew, could break some people but it seemed to have strengthened her. He had no doubts now that he would be marrying the right girl. "My mother will be pleased to hear Terence's work was appreciated. She wanted to come down for the funeral, but her doctor wouldn't allow her. She had a slight heart attack when she got word of my brother's death."

"She should be a proud woman," said Senora Partridge.

"Thank you," said Carmel again, and wondered if her mother's pride would tarnish the image of Terry by trying to make a martyr of him. He had not died for Christ but for love of Dolores; but her mother would never understand that that had not made him less of a priest.

She, Taber and Dolores moved on down to one of the Ruiz's Cadillacs that had been lent to them for the funeral. There were forty-two coffins on the open army trucks at the head of the *cortège*; the bodies of five soldiers had still not been found. Taber, the day after disaster, while Carmel and Dolores were still in hospital recovering from their ordeal, had gone back up to the altiplano with Captain Condoris. The flood had subsided somewhat, spreading out into arroyos across the altiplano. What remained of Altea had emerged above the level of the water that still flooded the ravine: the mud-stained church, one wall shattered by the onslaught of boulders washed down from the moraine; adobe houses that had melted into great heaps of chocolate-coloured mud; and clumps of dark scrub that had once been thatched roofs. Army skiffs moved among the ruins of the village, occasionally stopping as a body was found and hauled aboard. McKenna's body was among the last to be found, and after he had identified it Taber rejoined Condoris in the police car.

Condoris drove up the road to the mission. "Is there anything Senorita McKenna will want to take away of her brother's?"

"I'll ask her." The Jeep still stood on the road above the broken moraine and he nodded across the lake towards it. "I think she would probably like the Jeep to be sent up to Padre McKenna's missionary order up in La Paz."

"It shall be done," said Condoris, and Taber knew he would be a man of his word. He had come to have a grudging admiration for the police captain, realising that, in its own way, the man's job was as difficult as his own, that he had just as many interfering bosses.

"What's going to happen to Mamani and the campesinos?"

Condoris shrugged. "A plane flew over the mountains this morning and saw them going up one of the passes. They could bomb them, but why kill women and children for what one man did? Personally, I don't think Mamani had anything to do with the terrorists – at least he did not belong to them nor ever will. Though perhaps I'm wrong about the latter – he and the men from Altea could join the terrorists and become guerrillas. You were the last man to see them. Do you think they will?"

"Not a chance," said Taber, and tried to sound emphatic rather than just hopeful.

Condoris nodded. "There is an election early next year. The government will not want to antagonise the campesinos by massacring several hundreds of them. The government is slow, but it is sympathetic to the problems of the Indians. No, I think Mamani and the people of Altea will be safe so long as they don't cause any more trouble. I hope so." He looked across the lake towards the distant peaks, then he looked back at Taber and smiled. "But do not quote me."

"As Padre McKenna would say, we're in the confessional. Your secret is safe."

"What are you going to do now?"

It was Taber's turn to shrug. "My regional boss phoned me

this morning from Santiago when he heard what happened. I am to meet him in La Paz the end of this week. One of the cardinals from Rome is coming out on a South American tour."

"A cardinal?"

"A joke. We call anyone over a certain level at FAO headquarters a cardinal."

"What are you?"

They were driving back now and ahead of them was an army truck, its freight of dead bloated humanity covered with a tarpaulin. He's under that tarpaulin, Taber thought, poor defeated bugger. "Just someone like Padre McKenna. A missionary priest."

And now on this grey morning that other missionary priest was on his way to be buried. Taber helped Carmel and Dolores into the Cadillac, then turned as Alejandro Ruiz came down the steps of the cathedral.

"We understand you are leaving immediately after the funeral," said Ruiz.

"Senorita McKenna and I are catching the afternoon plane for La Paz."

Ruiz put out his hand. "Good luck, Senor Taber."

"I could be back," Taber warned.

"I do not think so," said Ruiz. "The Reform Council has recommended a postponement of all agricultural development till the flood damage has been assessed and repaired. That could take months."

"Yes," said Taber dryly. "I guess it could."

He got in between Carmel and Dolores and a moment later the funeral procession started. They rode in silence till they were out of the main plaza, then Carmel leaned against Taber and began to weep. He put his arm about her and looked at Dolores.

"Go ahead."

"I have no tears left. I wish I did – I think it helps. But I have nothing left now – no tears, prayers, nothing."

Carmel dried her eyes. "What would you have done if Terry had lived? I tell myself his death was a dreadful waste – "

"It was," said Taber. "Any good man's death is a waste. It's the bastards we can do without."

"I know you're right, darling. But – " She looked across him at Dolores. "Am I being cruel in asking what sort of future you and Terry could have had?" She and Dolores had shared a room at the hospital and they no longer had any secrets from each other.

Dolores stared ahead of her, then at last nodded. "That's partly the reason I have nothing left inside me. Most of it had already died before he – " She looked ahead at the army trucks with their sombre loads. "Perhaps it was for the best. But what woman ever wants to believe such a thing?"

In their car farther back in the *cortège* Alejandro, Romola and Francisco rode in the back seat and Hernando sat beside the driver. None of them spoke till they were out of the city on the road going past the estate of the dead tin baron. Then Alejandro looked out at the wreck of Toribio's truck, already stripped to a skeleton by plunderers looking for spare parts for their own ancient vehicles, and said, "Have the police still got those rifles impounded?"

"Yes," said Francisco.

"Perhaps we should buy them. They are no good to the police or the army – they aren't the same make as the general government issue."

"What will you do with them?" asked Romola. "Raise another of Senor Obermaier's amateur panzer divisions?"

"Women's wit is like cheap wine," said her husband. "Always a little vinegary."

"You're improving," said Romola. "You're starting to sound original. But you still haven't answered my question."

"We'll buy them and lock them away in a safe place. Perhaps even destroy them. But we'll just make sure the terrorists do not get their hands on them. One can't trust the police to be careful enough when it comes to safeguarding anything. They'd be fools enough to lock the rifles and ammunition in a tin shed and leave one stupid Indian to guard it."

Hernando turned round in his seat. "Shall I try and arrange the purchase? And I think I know a good place where they can be stored out of harm's way."

"Where?"

"The old McKenna mine up in the mountains. No one ever goes up there."

"How do you know about it?" asked Romola.

"I went up there once with Padre McKenna," Hernando lied. "The rifles will be safe there till they are needed."

"Do you think they will ever be needed?" said Francisco.

"Who knows?" Hernando looked back at the three people behind him. Two of them would be dead within a month if the assassination list was kept to schedule. And Romola would be making this funeral journey once again, but with only herself for company. "All we can do is trust in God."

"You sound like your Uncle Jorge," said Alejandro. "One bishop in the family is enough. Did you get that transfer of the land to the campesinos under way?"

"No," said Hernando. "There is no need for such a gesture now, is there?"

"Good boy," said Alejandro, and just wished his son beside him had as much wit and acumen.

Then the funeral procession was turning into the cemetery. Half an hour later the last coffin, McKenna's, was lowered into the last grave. Taber stood silent while a murmur of prayer rose towards the cold grey sky. A wind blew down from the altiplano and dirt drifted off the heap beside the grave and fell in on the coffin. Rifles had been fired above the graves of the soldiers and the policemen, but the rifle squad of a dozen men was already marching towards the cemetery gates as the Bishop said the last words above McKenna's grave. Most of the mourners had drifted away, driven home by grief or boredom, and there was only a small group around the final grave.

" – dust to dust," said the Bishop, and thought: What a pity the body should end in such indignity. He looked down at the coffin and wondered if he had shown as much charity as he might have towards a man who had needed it. But the Church itself rationed charity and he was trapped in the creaking laws of it.

Taber looked across the grave and nodded at Miguel Pereira. The latter nodded back, then blessed himself and dropped his head as McKenna was lowered into the patient earth that waited for him and everyone else here in the windswept

cemetery. Taber had told him yesterday of his call to La Paz
and the plump, nervous man had shrugged philosophically.
Resigned and dedicated to compromise, he was always ready
for the worst.

"I shall miss you, Harry. Perhaps we could have done
miracles if we'd had the chance – "

"I don't believe in miracles, Miguel. I'd have settled for
just some co-operation and an ounce or two of luck."

"But no compromise?"

"No," said Taber. "Never compromise."

"You'll never win, Harry."

"Perhaps," said Taber. "But it will take them all my bloody
life to beat me."

The gravediggers, both Indians, began to toss earth in on the
coffin. One of them looked up and caught Taber's eye. The
man's face was the same mask Taber had been seeing ever since
he had arrived in Bolivia, but there was something in the dark
eyes that hinted at a message in the cocaine-dulled mind behind
them. Taber tried desperately to read it, but it was too vague,
like an echo of a whisper in a long-forgotten tongue, to catch
and translate. It could have been a message of hate or pity or
just plain careless indifference. Then it struck him that since
the time of Pizarro it would have been the Indians who would
have been digging the graves and tossing the earth in on the
Spaniards, the criollos, the Americans, the British, the Germans,
on all outsiders. For a people for whom time had stood still for
centuries, whose patience rivalled that of the earth itself,
perhaps that was revenge enough.

Samaritan, he thought, and turned away, *go home*.